Crescent Veil

Judith Sanders
399-6646
1115 Willow Pond Lane

PUBLISHERS NOTE

This is a work of fiction. Names, characters, places, and incidents either are the product of the author's imagination or are used fictitiously, and any resemblance to actual persons, living or dead, business establishments, events or locales is entiirely coincidental.

ISBN: 1-4196-1880-6

Cover design by George Foster

Library of Congress Control Number: 2005909860

To order additional copies, please contact us.
BookSurge, LLC
www.booksurge.com
1-866-308-6235
orders@booksurge.com

Crescent Veil

Judith Sanders
with Dr. Frank J. Malinoski

2006

Crescent Veil

Acknowledgments

I am deeply grateful for the support, wisdom and competence of my friend Lonnie whose editing has made all the difference. Most of all I would like to thank my husband for his unflinching encouragement. You have given me more than I could ever put to words.

Prologue

1991

They were flown to a remote village in an unmarked military transport. Dr. Miryam Stollar, leader of the team, never learned the exact location or the name of the place. As they approached their landing site, foul smelling, sticky smoke drifted through the cargo plane. All conversation ceased.

The magnitude of the crisis had been overwhelming. And it was obvious there could be only one solution. The entire village would simply have to disappear. It would be as if three hundred and thirty two men, women, and children never existed. Many of Miryam's team members agonized over the decision, but to stop the infection from becoming rampant-and to cover-up the accident—that was all they could do. While the South Africans were very knowledgeable, they did not have the resources to contain a biological accident of this magnitude by themselves.

All the employees, approximately fifty people, at a state-owned technical institute for pesticide production had been infected with combinations of various genetically engineered viral agents. The tragedy had been further complicated when the employees carried the infection home from work and it spread into the nearby village.

The small village was quarantined, and slowly every inhabitant of the village succumbed to the infection. Miryam would always remember the face of one young woman who had tried to escape the quarantined area with her small infant. When she saw Miryam, she held the baby out to her and cried for mercy. Without hesitation the guards shot both of them. Miryam had understood that the shooting was necessary to control the spread of the infection, but it still tore at her heart. Later, as the contagion spread, she thought back to that woman and baby and was thankful their deaths had been quick.

Miryam's team members were experts in clean-up and decontamination. She was a physician, a healer, but she had no comfort or cures to offer those who were suffering. It ate at her that science could be so distorted to cause so much pain. For two weeks she and her team watched and prepared as death ran its course. When everyone who had been infected was either dead or too ill to attack them, her team entered the quarantined area in biohazard suits to start the clean-up process. It was immediately evident that no one had died an easy death. Masses of flesh lay in every state of decay in the streets and in the buildings. It had been a nightmare moving before her eyes. Blood, black and contaminated with the hemorrhagic agents, lay clotted in dirty clumps, like filthy snowballs on cold winter ground. The floors and walls in every home were decorated with macabre smears of blood and other stagnant body fluids.

The intense African heat hastened the decomposition process and the native army had to shoot and burn the many animals that had been attracted by the scent of death. Thankfully, her team's biohazard suits masked some of the smells given off by the dying and the dead. But to everyone's horror, the suits had not filtered out the sounds of those still dying. Their pain and agony surrounded Miryam. Like a thick inescapable coating, it clung to the inside of her suit. She imagined its weight pressing against her. The sounds of so many people at different stages of dying: gasping, retching. Worst of all had been the sobbing, wailing, and crying which would echo in her brain for the rest of her life.

The attitude of the scientists who had been on site was appalling. Amid this useless disaster, some of the South African scientists still studied the progress of the infection and took notes in this, their human laboratory. They would not allow a quick death even to colleagues suffering at their feet.

As the last of the villagers died, the words of one of the scientists gave Miryam an unforgettable insight into how easily men propagate evil under the guise of science. "We're fortunate. It's not every day we get to see firsthand the effects of our viruses on humans. And now we have an abundance of specimens that will enhance our virus inventory until such time as the market for those viruses emerges in third-world countries." He actually said that the whole hideous affair would be very profitable. The same scientist had then given orders to remove and store the organs and tissues from the dead, obviously to be used to grow more of the viruses. Using the dead as if they were merely incubators had been devastating to the South African soldiers as well as to Miryam and members of her team. It was inhuman to think of a child's heart being used to make a biological weapon.

When Miryam had returned home, she and her team had been vigorously de-briefed. The Israeli military's keen interest in the South African biological weapons capability seemed out of proportion for a government that had supposedly stopped its offensive program thirty years earlier and destroyed all chemical and biological weapons agents under a presidential decree. Yet everything about the mission was top secret and labeled a forbidden subject. Ordering her to keep quiet was possible, but forgetting was impossible. The government made it perfectly clear that if she breathed one word about South Africa's active biological weapons program she would be branded a liar and arrested as a traitor. This event, like many others that the government insisted remain hidden, was what had turned her waking life into a nightmare. She was determined to do something to bring world attention to the problem—even at the cost of her life.

Chapter 1

Assyria, 811 B.C. – Duty and Honor

Ninyas entered, wearing full battle armor and the short linen tunic that many of the young beardless soldiers preferred. His long white wool cloak billowed out behind him as he walked with broad deliberate strides toward the throne. The two daggers in his sash and the short sword in his hand confirmed that he had come on important business. He knelt before Queen Semiramis, but he did not bow his head.

His disrespect has always mirrored his feelings, thought the queen. "It is our custom to also bow one's head as a sign of respect. I see you still have much to learn, my son."

Ninyas did not reply or comply. Instead, he fixed his gaze on his mother and met her look eye to eye. Then he stood, breaking away from those eyes and the queen's all-knowing gaze behind them. It was a game they played, a test of wills and he always lost.

She was a mighty queen. Her very presence had overshadowed him all his life and he hated her. He longed to be free of her eyes.

Semiramis wondered: *will I ever be satisfied with what I find when I look at him?* Today she saw what Ninyas always showed her and that was that Ninyas paid homage to no one but Ninyas. But what else should she expect when he was so impatient to have the throne and possibly her death? Sadly, it was the path of succession that the ruthless Assyrian kings had followed for generations.

Queen Semiramis was a legend, and the only woman to ever rule in the Middle East. In fact, the ancient Assyrian code stated that the sons of Ashur could not be ruled by a woman. It was the law. And so, after King Shamshi-Adad V's death, the people looked upon her as the guardian of the young Prince Ninyas. But they soon came to admire, respect, and depend on their queen. She was as comfortable on the throne as in the saddle; and with a man's strength of body, she could drive a chariot while remaining womanly and graceful. She carried herself with a dignity that exuded wisdom and power. The army was completely loyal to her and often referred to her as their "beautiful king."

As Ninyas grew to maturity, his mother saw something lacking in his character and continually delayed his ascendance to the throne. In subtle ways, many of the court officials and army generals told her they would not yet pledge their allegiance to Ninyas and the rumbles from the populace that they disliked the cruel, unpredictable prince verified the queen's own disappointment that her son would not be a competent and just ruler. And so the years passed, and the crown remained upon her head and the waiting prince's resentment deepened. He knew he couldn't move against his mother without first winning over the army and they stood behind the queen. At least until today.

Suddenly, heavy black clouds rolled in from the west and everyone in the throne room gasped. This darkening, along with Ninyas' unannounced armed appearance was seen as an evil omen. The generals, grumbling, gathered around the queen. Captain Hazael, the head of the queen's personal bodyguard and truest friend, walked forward and whispered to the queen. "Perhaps this discussion should be in private?"

For a moment, when she felt Hazael's hot breath on her

ear and glanced up into his brooding eyes, she hesitated. She nodded approval and watched as he walked away. *Is there something unsaid behind Hazael's eyes that always watch me? Perhaps love... huh... an emotion I have never experienced.* She dismissed the fantasy. *No, he would never disrespect me with such feelings. To you, my handsome Captain, I am just a warrior.*

Queen Semiramis walked around behind her throne and out onto a broad open veranda. She looked into the distance where horses grazed peacefully on the lush green grasses that grew along the Tigris River. Beneath the veranda her soldiers paced the ramparts of the city's fortified walls, bantering with their comrades. The hum of the thriving capital of the Assyrian empire, Calah, drifted pleasantly up to her ears. There was much of which she could be proud.

Although Assyrian kings were said to be savage conquerors, they planted the first seeds of civilization. Cuneiform script paved the way to the formation of a legal system, the arts, and the vast libraries throughout Calah.

The city sat at the junction of the Tigris and the upper Zab Rivers. To the west, grassy plains stretched out as far as the queen could see and majestic mountains sheltered the east at the back of the city. Babylon and the swampland flourished in the far south, providing much of the barley harvest so vital to Assyria. The land to the north contained the riches of the Anatolia, or Fertile Crescent, and was a chronic battleground. Repelling the neighboring Urartu who raided this area in an attempt to gain a foothold in Assyria was a major irritation and always a threat to peace.

The queen interrupted her daydream when Ninyas and Hazael walked out on to the veranda. Her counselors joined them and drew in around Ninyas. Now with her sixteen-year-old son so close and at eye level she saw a curious flare of color on his normally pale smooth cheeks. *What could have affected him so?*

Her eyes hardened when she spoke. "What you have to say had better be worthy of your flamboyant attire and your insolent attitude." In that soft voice which often signaled danger she hissed: "Speak."

Ninyas' lips quivered as he reported. He told her that he had just come from the slave pens where the captives from the Egyptian conquest were being kept. Many of them were sick, and some of the captives had already been sold to a caravan heading south to Babylonia. "Many of the Egyptian scum are dead! The Asu has tried all his poultices, salves, potions and enemas, but to no avail. The Ashipu used all his spells, incantations, and amulets and called upon the spirit of Gula to stop these demons. They have begun to spread into the city. If these demons infect the Anatolia and the workers in the lower province, I fear that when the rains come and the great Euphrates and Tigris swell, the barley crops will be lost without men to tend the waterways," Ninyas ranted, his volume rising. "We cannot lose the lower kingdom. It took years to conquer them." Spit dribbled from his lips with his fervent words. "In your thirst for conquest, you have brought evil into my kingdom." His face turned scarlet with emotion.

Semiramis did not move or show any emotion for she had always been a master of drama. She waited, letting Ninyas' insulting tone evaporate from the air before she spoke. Impatient, he began to speak again, but the queen silenced him with a dismissive wave of her hand.

"Do not speak to me of conquest. I was at your father's side when we vanquished the Babylonians. We crucified thousands that day. It was glorious!" A smile of triumph fluttered over her lips. In her mind she savored the battle once more. She knew that all Ninyas thought of were the riches the barley crop would bring him. "You are greedy beyond hope. The barley production allows us to balance the economy and control the people. Have you learned nothing?" Her next words she would regret long after her death. "Your personal glory on the battlefield is still waiting to be proven, young fool."

One of the older battle-scarred generals made an unsuccessful attempt to stifle his laughter. Ninyas' head jerked around and his knuckles turned white as he gripped the hilt of his sword more tightly, fighting for self-control. The young prince had a reputation for being a coward and now his mother publicly acknowledged the rumor.

Her public rebuke without respect for his princely title was a wound that would never heal and it infuriated Ninyas. But, he had learned how to play her game, so with great effort he regained control of his voice. His tone was conciliatory when he told her that it was her duty to find a way to deliver Assyria from the demons. It was his duty as her loyal subject to notify her of the illness.

Semiramis looked into his eyes and at the dark curls that fell over his brow. She was reminded of the little boy who had once adored his warrior mother, but that had been a long time ago and the rift between them was beyond repair. Nevertheless, she was pleased with his respectful tone and asked him to explain in what way the demons revealed themselves.

Ninyas' strong youthful body became rigid as he described what he had seen. "These demons are like none we have seen. At first, the slaves are overwhelmed with a sickness in their temples. Later, their foreheads looked bruised and the inside of their throats looked skinned and bloody.

I examined one of them myself to verify this. Both red and black blood leaked from their eyes, nose, ears, and bowels. The high priest said the bleeding is caused by demons tearing apart the insides of their victims. When the court physicians sliced into several of the dead slaves to examine their entrails and divine the nature of the demons, all they found were large clots of black blood in all their organs."

The queen's counselors gasped.

"No one has survived an attack by these demons," Ninyas continued, "the priests say it is the hand of Marduk." It was a desperate pronouncement. With an uncharacteristic display of courage, Ninyas turned away from his mother, showing her his back.

Hazael jumped forward to grab the insolent prince, but the queen stopped him. "Let him go," she said. "We have more important things to worry about. If this infection escapes into the city, every bandit in the area will think Assyria weak and ripe for the picking. If we fail, not only will we lose the workers, we will have a much broader problem." The queen rose slowly while she watched Ninyas depart through the audience chamber.

When Ninyas reached the outer door he stopped and half turned. "You have brought this death from Memphis to Assyria and it is up to you to find a cure," he called out over his shoulder to his mother. He pointed a shaking finger at her. "I will not support you and bring the wrath of the gods down on me. The responsibility is yours. Live or die by what you do today, Mother."

She should have known that he was an actor on a stage, sowing the seeds of mistrust into the minds of her supporters with this public display suggesting the gods were against her.

The physicians and priests said there was only one way

for her to destroy the demons and that was to kill them where they lived. And so the days of slaughter began. She beseeched the gods to care for those she sacrificed and to understand her heart. Her army surrounded the slave pens. Archers were posted on the rooftops. When the army entered the slave pens, once again the queen marched at the head of her army. The sick were easily dispatched, but those who had not yet fallen ill fought back. Many of her soldiers were wounded, bitten, and scratched by the women and children they slaughtered.

Semiramis and her men become exhausted from the killing. The queen stayed with her army throughout the night and long into the next days. She killed as they killed. She spurred them on in their bloody mission for she feared they would grow tired of the slaughter and let some of the slaves escape.

When they completed their unholy task, the ground was thick with bodies and blood. The dead formed a bridge between the slave pens and the gate and they had to wade through them to exit. They killed over two thousand men, women, and children. Killing in wartime was an easy decision, their life or hers, but this slaughter had been a total waste of life and sickened the queen.

Then the priests and physicians took over. The bodies were stacked like bricks, ready for the furnace. On the fifth day after Ninyas' announcement, when the first pile of "bricks" were lit, the queen knew she and Assyria were doomed. The funeral fires were higher than the tallest building in Calah. The bodies sizzled and smoked like mutton fat on an open flame. The night sky was turned to day by the light from the fires. The yellow twisted flames, the black smoke that made the air sour and difficult to breathe, further roused the frightened people in the town.

The queen sent out a patrol of healthy men to keep order but it was too late. The physicians had asked the queen to put to death any of her men who had been wounded during the killing frenzy, but she could not.

Ninyas and his cohorts were already on the hunt. They incited the people to rebel against their queen by telling them the land had been cursed because a woman sat on the throne. And she knew it was just a matter of time before the priests and Ninyas would try to kill her using the pretext that her death would appease the gods.

A few of her personal bodyguards—the qura'du, or strong ones—along with Hazael, remained healthy and loyal to their queen. They waited outside the Temple of Ekur as their queen sought insight from the gods.

"Justice!" The word hissed from her cracked dry lips. "Justice is what I seek." Smoke from a human bonfire stung her bloodshot eyes.

The dirty queen of Assyria lay prostrate and exhausted on the earthen floor in front of her patron, the goddess Ishtar. The queen had been at the temple for hours, pleading for her beloved Assyria. Queen Semiramis swayed back and forth. Her weary voice swelled as she fell into that singsong chant, which, as a child, she had been taught to adopt when communing with the gods. "Ishtar, great goddess of love and death, hear my appeal for rebirth. I pray to thee, O lady of ladies, goddess of goddesses. O gleaming one, Ishtar, assembler of the host. Where thou dost look, one who is dead lives, one who is sick rises up, the erring one who sees thy face goes aright. I have cried to thee, suffering, wearied, and distressed, as thy servant. Pity!'" [1]

In the distance, the queen heard shouting and crying, but she felt protected in her surroundings. The temple stood within the fortified walls of the palace grounds on a raised mound overlooking her vast and once beautiful city.

"Calah, the jewel of my vast empire." There was cynicism in her voice as she spoke to the idols surrounding her. She looked up at the center of the dome ceiling supported by huge cedar beams, where it was open to the air. Her eyes followed the path of the black smoke as it rose into the sky. "The evil blots out even the stars."

For the first time in her life she felt the hopelessness of defeat. And for the first time in her reign she could not overcome Assyria's enemy. Her warrior skills were no match for the raging demons burning a path of death across her land. All hope now lay in the hands of the gods.

Half-mad, Queen Semiramis screamed again. "Revenge! Great EnLiL, who presides over the assembly of the gods and has ordained my destiny, I pledge my life and future lives to you. Anu, most high father of the gods, who has embodied me with your daughter Ishtar's power and cunning, show me the way to save Assyria from the demons that threaten her very existence. I am insignificant. Holding the empire together is everything."

The penitent queen was surrounded by animal sacrifices that she had brought to pacify the gods. Earlier, the high priest had disemboweled the animals in an attempt to divine the god's wishes from the entrails. But the frightened high priest had abandoned the dead goats and sheep. The decaying carcasses lay unattended on the altars. She imagined their decaying stench clinging to her skin.

It had been hours, but she continued to wait and to pray. Her steel breastplate intensified the feeling of cold and the silver spiral bracelets she wore on her upper arms grated with every movement against the hard-packed earthen floor. She heard the crazed populace prowling outside the citadel. Unconsciously, she reached out for the short sword with the lion's head hilt that lay at her side.

Lying in the dirt she appeared ragged and beaten, more like a defeated slave than a queen. Under her armor she wore a long linen tunic. It had once been a light shade of purple but now a deep crimson stained most of the shredded skirt as well as her exposed flesh. The tears she had shed for her people and herself had dried, leaving her face streaked with lines of dirt and blood.

The lush curls of her long black hair were matted and rank. Her gold tiara, a sign that she was royalty, was buried beneath her knotted tresses and the weight of royal responsibility bore so heavily upon her mind she imagined that the tiara was tearing into her forehead. The tops of her knee-high boots were stained scarlet from the blood oozing from her knees after her long hours of kneeling at the feet of Ishtar, and her sandals were caked with the bloody carnage she had waded through in the preceding days.

She forced her stiff limbs to bend as she sat back on her heels. Her body weaved back and forth as if she was in a trance. The queen wished she could correct her mistakes and live another life. She thought about all she had done. *Will the gods forgive me? Does their silence mean they never will?*

The queen twisted to one side, crept a little closer to her protector, Ishtar, the goddess of fertility and battles. She looked up and saw the bow and quiver slung over Ishtar's shoulder, not unlike that which the queen carried with her now. Sheaves of weapons sprang from Ishtar's shoulders. There was a certain mystical power and beauty surrounding the goddess. She was radiant: a lion at her feet, a serpent in her hand, and doves, representing love, encircled her head like a crown. Semiramis' own crown and necklace carried the design of the dove.

"Ishtar, do not abandon me." Semiramis was a compelling replica of the goddess.

Overwhelmed by the torment within her, Semiramis again screamed, "Mother! Ishtar, the only mother I have ever known, come to me now. I will not give into the demons that take the lives of your people. Do not take your countenance from me. You have taught me to be a patient hunter. I will follow your teachings and wait until the time is right to reap revenge. I know I have lost today's battle. Give me tomorrow. I will honor you with my deeds." Drained of all strength, she collapsed on the cold floor of the temple. Within seconds, she fell into a deep sleep filled with wondrous dreams.

She was being held in strong, soft arms. Warmth spread over her. Not just warmth but a filling of her soul. Something had entered her body. A future filled with righteous purpose. She would endure! She would prevail! Ishtar had shown her the way.

Chapter 2

Israel Today — The Price of Service

Dr. Miryam Stollar arrived at her small rundown apartment exhausted. She threw her medical bag on the kitchen table and jumped when a cold wet nose rubbed against her leg. Then she relaxed and scratched behind Strider's ears. She was tense and angry and the dog sensed her apprehension.

Her mind was still on the events of the day. The scientific review board had denied her request for funds to defend the country against chemical and biological weapons. This was her final attempt to bring some attention to what she knew was a threat that still existed. *Those unqualified idiots on that board laughed at me.* The sting of their mocking voices still hurt and her face winced at the memory. She regretted that she had responded with heat, accusing them of a self-serving decision. The angry words she hurled at them reverberated in her mind. *You would rather take a chance and pay a human price than increase your precious budgets and risk not being re-elected. You are jeopardizing our people's very existence.* She had lost control. That rare event caused her to be thrown out of the meeting and out of the science center. She was losing her credibility. Her colleagues ridiculed her and she had received strong warnings from her superiors to forget about defense against a chemical and biological weapons threat that didn't exist. But she could not stop herself.

The dog, sitting at her side in the dimly lit kitchen, nudged her.

"Good boy, Strider." The huge white German shepherd was her single comfort and friend; a gift from Wayne, a love from her past. That love was part of another life, a happier time, before her life became so devious and complicated.

Strider went to the door and sat waiting. "Yes, you're right, I've neglected you. Ready for a walk?" The dog's tail wagged in anticipation of an outing with his mistress. "I probably couldn't sleep anyway. Today was a miserable day. First the board's decision," she said while walking to the window and peeking out, "and now someone is watching me." She didn't see anyone lingering outside her nearly abandoned apartment building, but she felt uneasy. She licked her lips. Quickly, she changed into sweatpants and a T-shirt, then she secured her long black hair at the nape of her neck with a clasp. She picked up Strider's leash and clipped it to his collar as she continued to think out loud. "Then there is Rijah's confusing message."

She picked up her key and locked the apartment door behind them. Their footsteps echoed in the narrow space as they descended the two flights of stairs to the street.

The beautiful dog was protective of his mistress and even more so in the dark. He stayed close to her, his eyes and ears sharp to the sounds and sights of the after-midnight hour.

As they walked, the dog tensed and growled. He was facing the alley next to her building. Miryam halted and listened. She heard nothing except the scurrying of the rats on their nightly feasting in the garbage cans. As Miryam and Strider resumed their walk, she let out a long cleansing sigh, wondering why she had been holding her breath. But Rijah's message would not let her mind rest. The note said it was urgent. *She needed to meet with me as soon as possible.* She thought about it. *My network hasn't picked up anything. What could have happened?*

Feeling a trifle silly for being melodramatic, she picked up her pace to a jog and hurried around the corner toward the park. *Still, who would be interested in an unimportant person like me? I've been on the Mossad's inactive list since my return from Iraq. Do they think I can't be trusted to keep their secrets?* She smiled to herself. *If so, they were right.*

Strider was excited and his whole body waggled as they entered the park. In the half-light of the park she gave him a hand signal and he sat down next to her. She leaned over and detached his leash. Then she gave him another silent signal and he ran off to play in the wooded area nearby.

Miryam sat down on the park bench and her rigid posture sagged as she finally relaxed. She enjoyed the park in the sleepy hours just before dawn. The air was cool and restful. Gentle breezes brushed against her creamy skin and massaged her face. She sank into the peaceful surroundings. *Sometimes my purpose blurs. When this began, my mission was clear, but now...* Her thoughts began to wander and her eyes closed. *Who am I helping: Israel, Iraq, mankind or myself? The things I've done and plan to do get people killed.*

She rubbed her temples in an attempt to lift the fog in her mind. *Rijah is an invaluable informant but she's been in Iraq too long. It's time to find a way to get her out. She only got into this because of her brother, but I must encourage her to get out, even if she has to leave him behind.*

Again Miryam tried to relax. She stretched her long slender legs out in front of her willowy frame and looked at the trees outlining the park and the canopy of sky overhead. A faint hint of morning began to lighten the horizon, outlining the shadowy trees with a dark blue hue. The leaves swayed as the wind trickled through the branches. The only sound was Strider scrounging in the brush to her left. The scene was hypnotic and finally her mind became silent. She began to drift with the breeze into a twilight sleep.

From her half-sleep, Miryam sensed the presence of a lone man sitting on a bench not far from her. She opened her eyes just enough to glance in his direction. His posture was casual, yet her mind tingled. She was well trained and could take care of herself and then, of course, there was Strider.

Soon, a second man joined the first on the bench. They carried what looked like lunch bags. A car drove up and they walked over to it, got in, and drove away. *They must work one of the early shifts at the factory and ride together*. She checked her watch. *It will be dawn soon. Sorry, Strider, but I must get a few hours sleep before my day begins.*

She whistled and the dog was there in an instant, licking her hand. As Miryam leaned forward to put on Strider's leash, he tensed. A second later she heard the dull thud of a bullet exploding into the bench where she had been sitting. Splinters of wood flew through the air as Miryam vaulted off the bench, ran across the path, then rolled into the darkness of the nearby underbrush. Strider crouched close to his mistress, waiting for her command. She pulled her weapon from her waistband just as another bullet buried itself in a tree, barely missing her head. She laid a calming hand on the dog. They both remained silent and still in the shadows. In her mind she evaluated her position. *Looks like one of those men on the bench didn't get in the car. That second shot was a guess, and an attempt to ferret us out*. She whispered and stroked the dog. "Now, Strider, let's see if we can figure out where our assassin is hiding." Miryam smiled at the dog and whispered in his ear, "Take little bites, I need him alive." Strider's long tongue licked his muzzle as if he understood Miryam's joke.

She didn't panic or feel animosity toward her assailant. She decided the street side was her attacker's closest escape route. When his job was finished, he would signal his friends to come back and pick him up. *So he will favor that side of the park, plus he has the bushes and trees to conceal him.*

Strider followed Miryam's lead and crawled behind his mistress as she made her way to the edge of the woods where she could see the street. The assassin could always go through the park and out the other side, but that would be a long run with Strider on his heels. Then a faint rustling of clothes against tree bark, undetectable by a human ear, caused Strider to jerk around and fix his gaze on the area directly behind where he and his mistress lay hidden.

Miryam came up to a crouching position and pivoted on one foot to follow the dog's stare. *He's trying to circle around behind us for another shot. The fool should have worn night vision glasses and he'd have had us. So, he's stupid as well as inexperienced.* Thinking it made her smile.

She gave Strider a hand signal that instructed him to circle around behind the trees. He loped off, without a sound, to obey. Miryam kept low to the ground, hoping the uneven terrain of the shallow ditch would hide her movements as she approached her assailant from the opposite direction. Together they would have him between them. She placed her .38 revolver back in its holster. *Too noisy.* Instead, she pulled the six inch, needle-sharp metal clasp from her hair. She turned it over in her hand several times to become accustomed to its weight. Her hair tumbled down her back and fell around her shoulders, cloaking her face. She came up to a crouching position behind a tree.

A sharp cry of pain shattered the stillness of the night. It was quickly followed by Strider's growling. The man broke from the woods and made a run for a car that came screeching around the corner. Miryam recognized it as the car she'd seen earlier. "Damn. I'll never catch him." She sprinted toward the fleeing assassin. Strider hung fiercely onto the man's gun arm, fighting him every step of the way, the dog's weight slowing the man's retreat.

As the car got closer, Miryam saw the window come down. One of the men inside unleashed a torrent of bullets. She threw herself to the ground and pulled out her weapon. But to her surprise they were not shooting at her: the gunman was shooting at her assassin. She blew her dog whistle, signaling Strider to return to her. He was unharmed.

It was all over in a matter of seconds. The car sped into the darkness, leaving the assassin behind.

Miryam walked over to the dying man. "Let me help you," she said. He shook his head, declining her offer.

It was the veteran soldier in her, not the physician, who jerked the man closer to her face and spoke to him again in a harsher tone. "Die if you like. That is your decision. But before you die, tell me who sent you to kill me!"

He was getting weaker and he whispered in Arabic, "You were supposed to be an easy kill."

She answered in his native tongue. "I'm happy to disappoint you." She nodded in the direction the car fled then repeated her question. "Who sent you to kill me?"

He forced out his response between bloody lips. "No."

Miryam searched the man as she spoke. "Your own people have killed you and yet you protect them? I promise to give you a proper burial in the Muslim way, but first tell me who sent you."

He smiled, whispered, "No," and then in Arabic said, "the hatchet man is worse than this. Death is what I expected." And then he died.

Miryam looked at the man's empty face and wondered: *Who is this hatchet man that he is feared more than death.*

Glaring lights and blaring sirens reflected off the nearby buildings, alerting Miryam that the police were just a few blocks away. She could not afford to get involved with the police. She and Strider sprinted across the street, down an alley and into her apartment building.

"We made it, boy!" She reached down and hugged the dog.

Later, Miryam nibbled on some cheese. "Someone is worried," she said to the dog as she washed the blood from her clothing. "But that's good." He looked up at her, then returned to gnawing on a bone.

As light filtered in through the edges of the drawn blind Miryam yawned and burrowed down between the crisp sheets. She fell into an unnatural sleep. In no time she was seeing through the eyes of Queen Semiramis. Miryam saw the majestic mountains far to the north of Calah and was transported back to Assyria. She twisted in her bed trying to reject the scene that played inside her mind. She choked from the smoke she imagined filled the air around her. In this altered sleep, Miryam whispered to the night in the ancient Assyrian language called Akkadian. Although the language had been extinct for three thousand years, she articulated the words perfectly.

"Calah, the capital of my empire."

Chapter 3

Assyria 811 BC — Escape from Calah

The queen's plan to travel to the mountains was accelerated when masked mercenaries, sent by Ninyas, stormed the palace.

Thinking back, she should have known her son's anger and humiliation would not wait to be avenged. The intent of Ninyas' secretive raid was to capture her and take control of the palace. After her untimely disappearance, he would assume the throne and take control of the army. The army and the people would have no choice but to obey the law and accept him as their king.

But, honorable Hazael and the queen's personal guard fought with her and together they held off the assassins her son had sent to do his dirty work of matricide. They were outnumbered three to one, but their skill against the thieves and robbers made the difference.

The fight began in the throne room. The song of their swords clashing thundered off the high ornate ceiling. Alas, their numbers pressed the queen and her guard and they had to retreat. As they drew back, down the hall to the queen's bedchamber, she looked upon the scene. The tile floor was a grisly mosaic of bodies of the brave and the treacherous. The waste of life, in the face of the empire's desperate situation, angered the queen beyond words and hardened her heart against her son.

Ninyas' assassins followed, breaking through the doors. The queen and her few remaining guards were forced to retreat to the veranda to make their last stand. The narrow confines of the terrace slowed the assassins, for they had to come at them in pairs. In hand-to-hand combat they struggled. The queen's men stood as a wall protecting her. As one man fell, another from behind stepped forward and took the fallen man's place. In the end, Hazael and Semiramis were all that remained. Triumphantly, they killed the last of their attackers. With deep sighs of relief, Hazael and the queen walked among their fallen soldiers, checking to see if any had injuries that needed attending. To their surprise, all were dead. The throats of the wounded had been cut. Ninyas' message was clear: anyone who supported Semiramis could expect the same treatment.

Hazael knelt over the corpse of one of the assassins and pulled away his mask. The queen was shocked when she saw the tribal scars on his face. The dead man was from the land of the Urartu. This was a surprisingly bold move for the marauding would-be-king. Queen Semiramis had never expected that her son was capable of making such a despicable alliance.

A bloody Hazael threw the assassin aside and stumbled to the veranda to check the courtyard and then looked beyond, toward the city, searching for a safe way for his queen to escape. When he sighted a dust cloud traveling toward the palace gates, he called to the queen and pointed. Semiramis strained to see through the tan haze. As the dust cloud moved closer, she made out Ninyas at the head of the column, driving his chariot like a madman. He whipped his horses viciously, urging them and his little make-believe army to the palace.

Among Ninyas and his mercenaries rode several rebellious priests. Their black robes fluttered out around them, making them look like bats on a blood hunt. As Ninyas reached the palace gates, Semiramis laughed. "At last, the cowardly prince has arrived. Excellent! It is time he learned the cost of betrayal."

Hazael grabbed his queen's arm in a powerful grip. Semiramis was stunned by this extraordinary action, for this was the first time any man had dared touch her. With the exception of accidental contact during combat, there had been no physical contact between her and any man, other than her husband. In fact, the jealous king had decreed that any man laying a hand on his wife would be flayed alive. Yet this man, whose name meant "the son of nobody," was holding her arm. His strong rough hands instantly warmed her skin. She did not pull away but looked up into his enigmatic eyes.

He too savored this unexpected first contact with the woman he had loved from a distance for many years.

The intimate moment evaporated as the echo of approaching footsteps and loud voices reached their ears.

Hazael broke the silence. "My queen, only you can hold the empire together. Save yourself and you save us all." Hazael loosened his grip on her arm, but Semiramis did not retreat.

In her heart she knew he was right. Once again she was torn away from the dictates of her emotions toward the demands of her monarchy.

Hazael removed Semiramis' sword from the baldrick, a scabbard that hung from her waist, and placed the blade in her hand. She remembered the feel of his hand and how it had lingered over hers.

"There is little time," he whispered as he drew his long sword. "I will give you as much time as possible. Your chariot remains ready at the outer wall." Then he pulled out his short sword and, with a weapon in each of his calloused hands, nodded for her to go.

Semiramis lingered a little too long and the mercenaries burst into the room with Ninyas at their center. The potential for violence hung in the air as mother and son stared at each other. Brandishing his sword, Ninyas began to taunt his mother. "Now who is the fool? Stupid woman..." Without thinking, she lunged past Hazael to get to Ninyas.

The sudden attack caught Ninyas off guard. His mother's blade slashed at his pretty, beardless face. He screeched in pain and fell to the floor, trying to staunch the rivulet of blood pouring down his smooth cheek.

Hazael was quick to push past the intruders to get to his queen. With one arm, he propelled Semiramis into her bathing chamber and bolted the door between them and their attackers.

The multitude pressed forward at Ninyas' enraged command.

"Go!" Hazael shouted. He pushed his queen toward the tapestried wall with its secret exit. Before the material dropped, she looked at Hazael and saw him salute her with his sword over his heart. As the door splintered, Hazael readied himself. When Ninyas' mercenaries broke through, Hazael flung himself into the throng that poured through the door. His battle cry echoed throughout the palace.

As Semiramis exited the hidden passage outside the east wall, she knew that although she had escaped the palace grounds, the battle was not over. There would be more blood to shed, and this battle would be like no other. There would be no army at her back and, most devastating, no Hazael at her side. She glanced at the forty unmanned towers built to defend the city. All her planning and these defenses had been useless against the demons and this new treachery. The broad upper walls where the queen had once driven her chariot directing the defense of the city lay empty. Like a city already dead, the ghosts of past glories was all that remained.

Stepping into her chariot and picking up the reins, the queen jerked around and smiled as she again heard Hazael's battle cry ring out across the palace grounds. He was still alive. She whipped her horses into a gallop and rode wildly into the wind.

As the queen drove her chariot through the gates, she looked back, half expecting, and wishing, to see Hazael running to catch her. Instead she saw her detestable son standing on the verandah, shaking his fists at her. Then Ninyas threw Hazael's body over the side.

Ninyas gathered his men and rode into the mountains in pursuit of his mother. The dust cloud of his troop was like a bloodthirsty devil always at her back. Somehow he knew his mother's last friend and refuge would be the mountains.

He was right. At the end of the sixth day, as night dropped its veil of darkness, it was in the mountains that the queen of Assyria's journey came to a halt.

The queen's eyes burned from driving her chariot hard into the turbulent wind. Sand and dirt collected in the corners of her eyes and mingled with tears of frustration and anger. Her tired vision blurred and could not penetrate the approaching night, nor discern landmarks she knew so well, as she streaked through the flatlands and began ascending the mountains northwest of Calah.

At the base of the mountains, she slowed her chariot and her lathered horses snorted, their hot moist breath streamed from their nostrils forming misty phantoms that danced in the cool mountain air. The rocky steps would be difficult to maneuver at night when the formidable mountains added their own craggy shadows across the trail. But she would not and could not rest. She pulled on the reins and brought the chariot to a halt in a cloud of dust. She stepped down into the rocky ground and gazed at the stars, hoping to get her bearings, but the stars were obscured by the cloud-choked sky.

Although she hated what Ninyas had become, she was still aware of the law. She had raised her sword against the king's son. Her death would be nothing compared to the retribution the gods and the dead king's spirit would extort in her afterlife. She rubbed at the sticky blood that covered her armor. Some of that blood was her son's. A cruel smile lifted the corners of her mouth. *The gods will have to wait to take their revenge on me and that scar on your pretty face will remind you, Ninyas, who is the master of the sword and who is still a pupil.*

Restless, her horses stomped their feet. Semiramis reached out and stroked and comforted each animal.

She lifted her slender muscular arms up to the heavens and spoke into the night, praying to her gods. "Direct my footsteps and guide my revenge. The young and the old lay in piles at the doors of the temples pleading for help, waiting for me to intercede with the gods and save them. Is Assyria's future gone with the dead?" She paused and then screamed into the wind: "Hear me, Ninyas. Hurry! Join me and Anunnaki, god of the underworld. I will show you the way."

She was shaken back to reality by the distant rumble of chariot wheels spitting out rocks. She slowed her breathing and listened, bending down to put her ear to the rocky earth. *My son is moving more slowly*. She recognized the cautious sounds and vibrations of chariot wheels creaking as the assassins traversed the rocky terrain. The direction of the sound was distorted by the mountains but she knew the route Ninyas used and she was still safe from discovery, for the moment: her son was on the other side of the mountain. When he reached the hard uneven earth of the canyons, he would be forced to progress on foot to search the many ravines. She hoped the rocky earth and the moonless night might help conceal the tracks of her own chariot.

As she rested, the queen's sharp tactical mind went over the past days and she wondered how Ninyas was able to take advantage of the arrival of the plague.

She pulled her wool cloak from the floor of her chariot and wrapped it tightly around her shoulders. The frosty mountain air penetrated to her bones. Her trembling hand grasped her talisman. Her knuckles turned white as she squeezed the necklace. She cleared her head and asked Ishtar to whisper the answers in her mind. "Ishtar, reveal yourself as you have done so many times in the past."

One word echoed in her mind. She said the name out loud: "Byblas." Ignoring the impatient stamping of her horses, she tried to recall every detail. Byblas was a minor province, one of many like Tyre, Sidon, and Armad strung out along the Mediterranean coast. On the way to attack Memphis, these were the first to fall in a series of small raids that let the world know Assyria was the greatest power of the age.

She remembered: *Byblas is only important because of its location on the sea coast, not far from Damascus. We used it as a supply outpost during our campaign. My armies did not even enter the city: supplies were brought to us at our camp in the Rift Valley.*

Semiramis stared into space with a searching expression as a mist in her mind lifted and a vision formed. "Yes, I see Ninyas and his troops in Byblas getting ready to fill the water bags at the well. Wait, who is that he is talking to? It's the governor of the city. He is angry. No: frightened."

She frowned in concentration and leaned forward as if to enter the vision. The town had been abandoned. The governor was yelling at Ninyas' men to stop what they were doing but they continued to fill the water skins.

The queen's probing eyes strayed to a sign outside a merchant's store. She read the cuneiform symbols, then drew back in fear. The sign forbade anyone from entering the town on pain of death. *Such a warning would be given if...if they feared demons or plague.*

She gasped as, in her mind's eye, she watched Ninyas walk over to the governor of Byblas and casually slit the man's throat. It took little courage for him to kill the unarmed old man.

Then bandits poured from the empty buildings and killed all of Ninyas' men. They put on Assyrian army uniforms. The vision fell away. These bandits must have been some of the same Urartu scum he had with him today.

In her mind she relived the campaign. *We had marched into Memphis and laid siege to the city. On the twenty-fifth day, the sappers collapsed the wall by the main gate. The Egyptians had been ill-prepared for our attack. We thought we had surprised them and that the gods had smiled upon Assyria and given us an easy victory. When the gates were down and we entered, we found that many of the townspeople had already fled by ship. The Egyptians had even abandoned much of their personal property, including their slaves, a commodity worth their weight in barley. Our enemies had known it was our practice to separate the captives and spread them throughout Assyria to demoralize and weaken the slaves' capacity for rebellion.*

The rest was easy to figure out. Ninyas' counterfeit soldiers returned to camp with the contaminated water and gave it to the slaves. Ninyas, her only son, was responsible for bringing this obscenity back to Assyria.

The truth chilled her soul and pierced her heart. Queen Semiramis trembled. Knowing the truth and accepting it were two different processes. But neither could be denied, and the magnitude of her son's betrayal seeped into her body against her wishes. One question remained for Semiramis: what could be done to stop this evil now that it had been unleashed? More importantly, would Assyria survive?

She knew the sun would rise in a few hours and she would not have the night to hide her. Even now she heard Ninyas' scouts searching on foot in a wadi nearby. She had to find shelter and a defensible position. To help her people, she must survive. An image formed in her mind of the limestone caves that honeycombed the hills. There she would find protection from immediate discovery.

Israel Today

When Miryam woke, she felt refreshed and confident. She thought about the dreams that dominated every moment of her sleep. As she showered and dressed, she reminded herself that—like this warrior queen—her roots were in Assyria.

Her mother had been a nomad and her father a farmer

in northern Iraq. Her mother had believed in an ancient religion and her father was Jewish. When Saddam's persecutions of the Jews started, the family was always on the move, hiding in caves in the mountains. Miryam's memories of her childhood were dominated by the need to run and hide. Her hand automatically went to her neck to caress the gold necklace that always hung there. It was gone. She searched the apartment but could not find it. The necklace had two doves, an arrow design in blue lapis. It was the only thing she owned that had once been her mother's. Later, after work, she would retrace her steps in hopes of finding the precious necklace. To Miryam it was a talisman and she felt strangely vulnerable without it.

And also like the queen, Miryam had to make life and death decisions. She wished she could block out all the death that saturated so much of her life. Even more, she wished she could tell the world about these terrible things. But if she did, she knew the government would make her disappear permanently.

The events she had witnessed in South Africa were so bizarre as to be quite unbelievable. But the proof was coming, and then the world would have to listen. *Tomorrow I leave for Australia and perhaps I will find out what happened to Rijah from one of the Iraqi scientists.*

These weapons of mass destruction are uncontrollable. How could anyone think he could harness such a storm of infection? Those organisms are a part of nature and totally unpredictable. We can no more easily control them than we can control a hurricane or a flood. The term "black biology" fits all too well since the result of the flood of such infections is masses of humanity lined up in black body bags.

Chapter 4

Australia – Dove of Death

Hundreds of scientists from around the world attended the annual Emerging Pathogens Infectious Disease Conference. Many of the participants had much in common, but one among them had an agenda like no other.

Through a small gap in the heavy window drapes, the sun pushed a streak of warm light across a shapely bronzed leg sticking out from under the bed sheets. The sleeping woman roused and began to rise from the luxury of her soft bed, but fell back onto the pillow. Her head felt heavy. She had slept deeply. Her mind easily turned off her other world and other identities.

Last night, when she had returned to her hotel, the moment her head had touched the down pillow she had slept the sleep of an innocent child. Slowly, her thick dark lashes parted and with one hand she attempted to wipe the sleep from her amber eyes. Jet lag and the previous night's socializing were taking their toll. She realized that she felt the effects more than she would have in the past. Of course, not to participate in the macho drinking challenges of the pub crowd would have raised suspicions. The thin, cultured veneer of a conference participant was cast off when her job demanded it. And fitting in with the rowdy Australian pub crowd last night was necessary. In her profession, she had to be many people.

But today was a new day and, like the day, she would assume a new identity. She focused on the final touches. She shook her head in an effort to clear the remnants of sleep from her mind. A small ray of sunshine danced on strands of her dark hair. The hint of red hidden among her dark curls made it look as if someone had sprinkled glitter in her hair.

She glanced at the chair next to her bed. The wrinkled and dirty airport maintenance uniform still lay where she had thrown it the night before when she had returned from what she amusedly called her "date." Her full lips parted in a sly smile as she inspected the uniform thinking. *Huh, blood splatter. Looks like dirt. No one will notice. What was his name? It doesn't matter. I must focus on the game of life and death I play once more today.*

The face of the young dead man materialized in her mind. Again she shook her head, but this time in an attempt to dispel the image. "Stop!" At the sound of her voice in the empty room the ghost withered away. "Today of all days I cannot afford to develop a conscience." Then she remembered. *Bobby, that was it, the airport maintenance man. After a few drinks in that sleazy bar, it was easy to convince him to take that fatal stroll. Like so many others, he thought we would be "close."*

Sex was not part of her game plan. She didn't need to give them sex. They had always come to her willingly. Their fantasies pulled them along. All she had to do was give a little tug, as if to a dog on a leash, and her victims would follow, waiting for their promised treat. For Bobby it was the quick knife. The authorities would never find his body. Now it was time to finish this.

She pulled back the covers and slid her sensuous body to the side of the bed. She sat there a moment and enjoyed the feel of the luxurious softness under her feet. Her toes scrunched into the thick, peach-colored carpet for a few seconds before she stood. She was taller than most of the women in her country and her slim frame made her look even taller. Standing in front of the window, she opened the drapes and pulled back the gauzy curtains to a clear view of Sydney below. The bright sunlight bounced between the high-rises onto her naked, muscled body. The sun felt wonderful, but its kiss on her flesh always made her a little homesick. She stretched and caressed her body. She did not think of modesty, for no one could see in her room on the 37th floor.

Still nude, she settled into the chair at the desk and opened her briefcase. She removed a sheaf of papers to check the conference agenda for the day. She had to admit that Sydney was a beautiful city and mingling with so many old associates and making new friends would be very useful. She picked up a tourist brochure and glanced at it as she walked back to the window. People were beginning to fill the streets and piers below. Perhaps she would indulge in some personal time to explore the city. She moved back to the desk and checked for the third time on the day's meetings. Fortunately, the schedule was light. The organizers of these international conferences always provided attendees a little free time to spend their money at the local shops. She wished she had more time in Sydney, but she must leave the following day, so she promised herself she would make the most of this one.

As usual, she had every detail planned. Her delivery would take place during the lunch break, between sessions. It was the perfect time. After she had a cursory lunch with the Brits, she could leave and no one would miss her. *I'll be back in time for the last meeting and make it for the bus tour of the city.*

Her smile was hard, humorless. Her military training served her well. It made her feel at ease in any situation and her dazzling smile melted away many obstacles and masked her true nature. No fear, no self doubts for this soldier. She could not remember when she had not been at war or preparing for battle. Her future had been decided for her by the government when she was just a child, and nothing would cause her to deviate from that ingrained path. Today was just another battle. The difference was the battlefield.

Satisfied that she had planned for every contingency, she put her notes down on the desk and went into the bathroom. She heard the alarm on the clock radio click on. As the sweet sound of jazz filled the room, she turned on the shower. She reacted to the music with silken movements, gliding into the stream of shimmering warm water, barely disturbing the flow. The cleansing water running down her body carried the final remnants of Bobby and other ghosts from her thoughts. She was ready and excited. *Let the performance begin!*

Right after lunch she took a taxi to a busy shopping district and strolled around a little before jumping into Bobby's truck. As she pulled away from the curb, she glanced at the airport security decal in the window. That and Bobby's ID badge would easily get her through security and out onto the tarmac. She laughed at the fact that it was now easier to change her own appearance than to try and change the photo on the badge. She remembered her favorite motto that the people at Langley always quoted: *When you make the rules you can only win.*

❧

In another part of the airport, Dr. Matthew Rogers guided his mother through the concourse traffic and security checkpoints. "Mother, are you sure you have everything?" he asked as they neared her gate.

"Yes, Matthew, stop fussing over me. I may be eighty-nine-years-old but I am still alive and functioning, in case you haven't noticed. And stop holding onto my arm. People will think you're blind."

Martha Rogers giggled and straightened the skirt of her pale gray suit. Her snowy hair was drawn up on top of her head into a bun, which made her feel and look elegant. Small pearl earrings and a matching brooch at the neck of her white lace blouse completed her traveling ensemble.

"Here's your gate," Matthew said to his mother. "I have your luggage checked through to Heathrow. Now don't forget, Olivia will meet you at the gate in London. So don't go wandering off."

"Yes, Matthew. Yes. Yes. Maybe, I should get one of those little dolls all the Americans have in the back of their automobiles."

Matt looked puzzled. "What are you talking about?" he asked in his stiffest British accent. "It's almost two-fifteen, time for you to board your plane."

"You know: those dolls that bob their head up and down. Then I wouldn't have to nod all the time. It's not good for me with this arthritis in my neck, Matthew." Like many doting mothers, Martha always called her son by his proper name.

Matt smiled down at the tough, petite lady on his arm. He relaxed and smiled, but the physician in him pushed on. "Have you been taking your arthritis medicine?"

"Yes, Matthew, yes. I take all my pills: the one for my knees, the one for my blood pressure, and the one for my thyroid. Will you ever stop worrying?"

Her son changed the subject. "I have a surprise for you. I had you upgraded to first class. They will take good care of you and you'll have a nice comfortable flight."

"Oh, you didn't have to do that. I appreciate it, but I don't need very much room." Mrs. Rogers laughed, "I'll feel like the queen, you wouldn't want me to get used to that." Martha peeked out the window in the gate. "Is that big one my plane?"

"Yes, Mother. That's a Boeing 767. It's very reliable." Matt knew that, for all her bravado, his mother was nervous about flying.

In the cabin of the 767, Victor, the head steward, was making a last-minute check of the cabin when he noticed a maintenance man in the economy area. He approached the man who was working on an overhead compartment.

"Excuse me. Is something wrong?" he asked while wishing that the maintenance service would provide clean uniforms daily for their employees. The overalls the maintenance person was wearing were filthy. *Look at those disgusting stains. Yuck! I'll have to report this. Just plain sloppy!*

"Nothing is wrong, sir, I was asked to check the locking mechanism on this overhead compartment. I'm almost finished, three seconds more."

"Good, we're ready to start boarding passengers. By the way, when was the last time you put on a clean uniform? Your appearance is disgusting, you'll give the airline a bad image. Give me your ID badge. I'm going to report you."

Without turning around, the maintenance man's gloved hand appeared, passing his badge to the inquisitive steward as he continued to work. Victor jerked the badge away and walked to the front of the plane to find his clipboard.

The maintenance man paid no attention to Victor. "He" had other things on "his" mind. *Just one last check to be sure the packet sticks to the door of the overhead. It'll take months for CDC, USAMRIID (United States Army Medical Research Institute of Infectious Disease) or the center in Porton Down to figure out this one ... if, that is, the Brits share their little problem with the rest of the world.*

Turning, head bent, the maintenance man called to Victor who was walking back as he wrote on a clipboard. "Sir, everything is ready. Sorry about the uniform. I'm pulling a double shift."

"Really?" Victor tossed the ID badge back to the maintenance worker and ripped the report from his pad, tearing it into pieces. "I know how that is. Don't worry, I won't turn you in."

"Thanks," said the maintenance man.

Victor watched the worker leave the plane through the back galley exit. *That's odd; he should have gone out up here in the front, past me. I guess after what I said, he was too embarrassed.*

The maintenance man concealed a sly smile. "Damn, my face itches like hell." The Dove walked away from the plane, scratching her chin. She wondered if she was growing allergic to the face mold glue she was wearing.

Matt helped his mother rise from her seat in the waiting area. "You can board now, Mother, they just called for you."

"Yes, yes, I heard what they said, Matthew. 'All those needing assistance can board now.' Do I look like I need assistance? There you go again. Trying to make everyone think I'm old."

"Mother, you are old. But, they also said all first class passengers can board. That's you."

Martha placed her arm in her son's and patted the strong hand that supported her. "Oh yes, you're right. I forgot: I'm queen for today," she giggled.

They walked up to the boarding agent together. "Excuse me, miss," Matt said to the clerk at the gate. "This is my mother, Mrs. Rogers. Would you help her board?"

"I would be happy to help her," the clerk replied in a South London accent as she eyed the old woman's handsome escort while scanning the boarding pass.

As the clerk turned her attention to Martha, her warm expression was quickly replaced with a wooden smile, one reserved for senior citizens. She turned her speaking volume up two notches and greeted Mrs. Rogers.

Martha winced. "I heard that: don't think everything you hear about older people is true," she raised her own voice, "We are not all deaf!" Martha donned her sweetest smile as several of the other passengers turned and looked her way. As she turned toward the boarding ramp a sudden chill caused Martha to tremble and rub her arms.

"Are you all right? Do you feel ill?" asked Matt.

Standing on tiptoe, Martha Rogers gave her son a hug, then, smiling up at his rich brown eyes, she kissed him on the cheek. "I'm fine. See you in two weeks. Say hello to Wayne for me."

"You know, I'm very glad you took me up on my offer

to visit Aunt Nettie in New Zealand. This scientific conference was the perfect opportunity for me to escort you. You've wanted to come for so long." Matt patted his mother's hand, then returned her to the waiting clerk, who was becoming impatient. "Well, right enough, Mother, you're off."

Matt gave her one more hug as she started for the door. "Flying isn't so bad, is it? Don't have such a gloomy look on your pretty face, Mother. You had a nice visit and you'll have a comfortable trip home."

Doing her very best to be brave, Martha mustered her most maternal tone. "Matthew, you worry too much. Go to your gate or you will miss your own plane."

Matt laughed. "Mother, I have plenty of time. I'm not leaving this spot until your plane takes off."

With a pained expression on her face, the clerk took Mrs. Roger's arm.

The clerk's pace, which a turtle would find too slow, gave Martha plenty of time to boast, as they started down the boarding ramp. "Young lady, do you know who my son is?"

"No, Ma'am," replied the irritated attendant.

"He's a very successful doctor. Don't you think he's handsome? He graduated from medical school with honors," Martha smiled. "We celebrated his fortieth birthday at my sister's just this week."

The attendant turned and took a long look at the lean man standing at the exit door, thinking. *Not bad. Light brown hair and sexy brown eyes.* "Is he married?" she asked.

"Oh, yes. He has a wonderful wife, Olivia. They've been married for going on fifteen years. Those two are always together, except of course when he's traveling all over the world for the government. Sometimes he is gone months at a time but Olivia keeps the home fires burning."

Losing interest in the old woman's son, the clerk walked a little faster.

Before Martha was out of sight, Matt waved once more and called out, "Safe journey."

She's a wonder, still going strong. He marveled how she still enjoyed getting out and making new friends. She had told him often that young friends were more invigorating than old people who only talked about their illnesses and all their medications. Her attitude was simple. "When the highlight of my day is getting her blood pressure taken," she often said, "call the undertaker." She had such a glowing spirit, one that the people she met truly enjoyed, even if she was two or three times their age.

The day before, at lunch, Matt had introduced his mother to some of his associates and a longtime friend from UNSCOM (United Nations Special Commission) days. She had made the error of treating his mother like a senior citizen. Big mistake. Matt's mother had then maneuvered the conversation around to her occupation, in her usual subtle way.

"No one has asked about my professional goals," she said.

Matt had prepared himself: *Oh no, here it comes.*

Sure enough, she looked around the lunch table, ensuring her audience. "Now that I have mastered law," she'd said, "I have applied to the United Kingdom's astronaut program. I hope to be the first really mature woman in outer space." Mouths fell open.

Matt's mother then stood and excused herself. "I am on

a special diet in preparation for my upcoming physical fitness test," she told them.

She had kissed her son on the cheek and whispered in his ear. "You have such stuffy friends, dear," then left. It was at least thirty seconds before anyone at the table could speak. It had been the highlight of Matt's day.

Now at the airport, Matt stood at the concourse window, watching his mother's plane.

The gate attendant deposited Mrs. Rogers with Victor and hurried back up the ramp thinking it was too bad the old woman's handsome son was married.

The first class cabin where Martha sat had seats for twenty passengers. Right behind the partition that divided the section was business class that held fifty people. The economy class had a capacity for one hundred and seventy-five. The flight was filling to capacity.

Martha grew restless in the twenty minutes before take-off. She was prone to leg cramps and decided to get up and exercise before the long flight home. She'd always been a people watcher so she paced in the galley, out of the way of those boarding but close enough to satisfy her curiosity.

"I'll watch the passengers board and get a little exercise," she explained when a flight attendant asked if she could help with anything. Martha moved to the middle of the business class section where passengers were now boarding.

The last of the economy class passengers were filing past Martha when a young woman boarded. She was pregnant and carrying a sleepy boy of about two with blond curly hair. *Curls like Matthew had when he was a baby,* thought Martha.

"Pardon me," Martha stopped the mother. "Do you

mind?" Martha stroked the child's hair. "What a beautiful child. Are you traveling alone?"

"Yes. We're meeting my husband in London. His company has relocated him."

"Hmm, I think you're going to the wrong seat," said Martha. Victor, who had been keeping an eye on Martha, was at full attention. "You will both be much more comfortable in the first class cabin." Martha exchanged tickets with the surprised young woman.

The woman was clearly taken aback. "But I couldn't let you..."

"It's quite acceptable," Victor told the expectant mother as he helped the exhausted women to the first class seat Martha had offered.

Victor returned with Martha's carry-on bag and guided her to what had been the young woman's place in the economy section, seat 21B. After storing Martha's bag in the overhead and closing the compartment, Victor gave her a peck on the cheek. "You are beautiful, Martha," he said warmly.

A few curious passengers glanced at Martha and Victor. One, seated across the isle from Martha, asked if he was her grandson.

"No, my fiancé," giggled Martha.

Victor could only roll his eyes and smile.

Dr. Matt Rogers watched the plane roll away from the gate then headed for his plane to Los Angeles, where he'd catch a connection to Albuquerque, New Mexico.

Boy, do I need this down time, said Matt to himself. He was en route to visit Wayne Swift, an M.D., Ph.D. who was also his closest friend. Wayne, who had literally created the specialty of biocriminology, was still the world's sole practitioner in this incredibly complex and demanding field. *And,*

Matt thought, *knowing Wayne, this holiday will be totally different from any other.*

It was a beautiful and pleased face that smiled and watched as Martha's plane rose off the runway.

Up, up and away. Fly into history, my lovely silver bird.

The spy, known as the Dove, had now added terrorism to her resume of crimes.

Chapter 5

New Mexico – Escape to Death

Matt awoke to the sound of a harsh, unfamiliar voice. He unzipped his sleeping bag, swung his legs over the side of his cot, and slipped his stocking feet into his waiting hiking boots. He shivered, feeling the chill of the cool New Mexico spring morning. The strange voice sounded coarse; the words were clipped and in a deep baritone tenor.

Matt picked up his fishing knife, perhaps a reflex action from past exploits with Wayne or his own days in the Royal Navy. Not that his friend couldn't take care of himself: Wayne had proved that many times. He pushed back the tent flap a few inches, taking in the situation. Wayne was busy building up the fire and talking to a stocky man who looked to Matt like an ad for a Wild West show. The visitor was dressed in bib overalls, a bent and soiled brown cowboy hat, dirty boots, and a long-sleeved faded flannel shirt. Mr. Bib Overalls stared back at Matt and his clear, piercing black eyes confirmed Matt's idea that the man could handle himself. Wayne did not seem worried. He motioned for Matt to join them.

Relaxing a little, Matt stepped out and the man in the overalls unfolded himself from his sitting position and came to his full height of six feet seven inches. Matt stopped in his tracks. The man was not just tall, he was also broad and muscular: a cross between a Brahma bull and the Terminator. Even at six foot four himself, Matt quite suddenly felt like Jack at his first meeting with the giant. He couldn't control his curiosity as his eyes tracked the man's outline from his boots to his face. The high cheekbones and straight line of the nose told Matt he was about to meet his first Native American.

Captivated, Matt's feet felt like they were frozen to the ground and his fishing knife puny. He watched as the unsmiling man tossed an ax end-over-end into the air. The man was not looking at the ax, but caught it perfectly in his right hand every time. As the two men stared at each other for long seconds, sizing each other up, the big man tossed the ax into a nearby tree. Matt wasn't sure if it was his imagination, but he could swear the whole tree vibrated from the impact of the blade.

Smiling, Wayne interrupted the silence and introduced the visitor. "This is my neighbor. He came up the mountain to bring my mail and help me entertain my friend from Britain. Sorry if we woke you but it's about time for us to get going anyway."

Matt shook his head to refocus his attention. "Go where? It's still dark. I'm happy right here. My back to nature holiday is working. I feel great! Eating, fishing, and the solitude are enough for me."

"Have you eaten any fish yet?" Wayne smirked as his friend, "We've been fishing for over a week and you haven't caught anything that would make a meal. By the way, has anyone ever told you that you're a lousy fisherman?"

"It doesn't make any difference if I catch anything. I love the relaxed pace and the seclusion," Matt replied.

"No real fisherman ever said that. It *does* matter," said an emphatic Wayne. "Never mind. If it's seclusion you want, then what I have in mind is right up your alley." Matt looked puzzled and Wayne continued. "Let's just say you're going to have my version of a Huck Finn adventure!"

The visitor smiled. He moved close to the fire and started to kick the logs around.

"Get ready for a walk," Wayne said to Matt then extended a hand toward their visitor. "Hal Cavemouse, Dr. Matthew Rogers."

They shook hands but to Matt it seemed like a contest to see who would blink first.

"Hal will be coming with us," explained Wayne, handing Matt a cup of coffee. He sat down on a tree stump to finish his own. "I told him we used to work together when I was in the Army. Hal was a Seal in both Gulf Wars. He's not much of a talker."

Matt looked from Wayne to Hal and then back to Wayne. "You are making me think too much, old boy."

"Just get your hiking gear, we leave in fifteen."

Now Matt was curious and a little worried. Wayne was wearing that cocky smile that spelled trouble. "It had better not be anything like our last adventure," Matt said. That had taken place the night before their inspection team had been scheduled to leave Iraq. One last night with Saddam's spies, then out of Iraq and off for a fine seafood dinner at the famed Al-Safina restaurant back in Bahrain before they would fly back home.

They had been younger and cockier then, and their UN team—part of the special commission on weapons of mass destruction—had been the third such group into Iraq after Desert Storm. The atmosphere in Baghdad had been tense. Wayne, the group leader, had OK'd a farewell get-together given by their lovely translators, three young beauties. They wound up on a sandy dune at midnight. As usual, Wayne was prepared. He had an ample supply of his favorite Polish vodka, Zubrowka, and Russian caviar. The girls thought they had struck it rich. It was the first time Matt had ever seen Wayne get drunk.

They had all become more than a little rowdy and reckless, something strictly forbidden as representatives of the United Nations in a foreign country.

Matt chuckled. After he dressed and grabbed his gear, he sat by the dying campfire to gulp a second cup of coffee and some bread and cheese. He thought about how, in spite of all the trouble Wayne got him into and out of, he was damn lucky to have him as a friend.

In fact, Wayne was not just Matt's friend, the friendship extended to Matt's whole family. Wayne had helped Matt and Olivia mend their marriage when, on subsequent trips to Iraq, Matt had gone astray with the temptress Ghariba. There were numerous other times when Wayne had helped Matt. Twice he had saved Matt's life. In return, Matt had given Wayne the one thing that seemed beyond his reach, a feeling of family. Matt's wife and children, even his mother, looked on Wayne as a family member.

Matt mused about his friend as he sipped his coffee. *Wayne Swift, only you and I and a few others know how close this planet came to self-destruction. That knowledge has bound us.*

He watched as Wayne placed his treasured New York Yankees baseball cap over his graying brown hair. The brim of the cap shaded Wayne's deep-set, sometimes brooding, eyes. Matt knew the first time he met Wayne that he would like him just by the way he described the color of his eyes on his security clearance paper work during a visit to Britain. "Dirt brown" was all he had written. Matt laughed, remembering the rest of Wayne's self description. His friend seemed taller than his five-feet eleven inches. His hands were calloused and broad, not soft like the hands of other medical doctors. Matt could see the signs of arthritis seeping into the joints of Wayne's fingers, a residual effect from inoculating himself with trial vaccines during his microbiology days with the Army

Wayne called out as he picked up his backpack. "What's the matter, Matt? Don't you trust me?"

Matt shouldered his gear and followed Wayne. "No, I do not! Aren't you going to tell me what you're talking about? Remember, I'm a happily married man. No playing in the sand, if you get my meaning."

"Relax," said Wayne. "Don't worry. Did you pack those PVC overalls I gave you the other day?"

Matt's anxiety increased exponentially.

They left the campsite just before sunrise, setting off single file with Hal leading and Wayne bringing up the rear. Hal set a brisk pace along a narrow and worn footpath that angled up the side of a rugged mountain. He appeared to be in a hurry to get somewhere.

They had been hiking for a good twenty minutes when they rounded a sharp bend and came out from under the protection of the dark morning shadows of the pine trees. All three of the men stopped.

"This is why I live here," Wayne said.

Cliffs dropped away to deep purple ravines on three sides. The rising sun was cresting over the Guadalupe Mountains to the east and the blackness of the night was receding; a sliver of the moon was still visible in the west. The cactus-laden Chihuahua Desert could be seen in the distance. Wayne's ranch was a dim outline in the shadows of the rugged foothills below them.

Matt's mouth fell open. The air was alive with color. Gold light from the rising sun reflected off the desert sands. Reds, oranges, and pinks blended and mingled in the sky like a watercolor painting. As the sun kissed the tributaries of the Pecos River that ran south into Texas, the water sparkled like tinsel threads. After a considerable silence, the trance was broken by the coo-coo, coo-coo of a mourning dove echoing behind them. They resumed their climb without uttering a word.

As they hiked higher up the side of the mountain the winds intensified. Traces of the winter's snow still lay in patches on the ground. "Late spring is the end of the windy season," Wayne explained in a voice loud enough to be heard over the wind. "Sometimes the winds reach hurricane force, but this is nothing. Hal checked the forecast on the radio before he came up to our camp this morning and the locals say the winds are diminishing."

"Yeah," said Hal, "some of the old timers say they put their wives out in these winds and they come back in the house without a wrinkle on their faces."

Matt laughed, surprised that Hal had finally said something.

Forty minutes later, they stopped on the side of a hill. Matt sat down to rest and sip from his canteen.

"We're here. Go easy on that water. You might need it later," cautioned Wayne.

"Here? Where is here?" asked Matt.

"Matt, look at the landscape... I thought you were an amateur archeologist? Don't you know anything about geology?"

"Give me a minute. Does this place have some American historical meaning?" Matt joked. "Some president carved into a mountain somewhere?"

"My friend, you disappoint me," said Wayne. "When we were in Iraq... come on, in the mountains?"

"Ah. I see it now, karstic terrain." Matt took in the geological formations surrounding him. Wayne waited, giving his friend a chance to discover what was special about this spot.

"All right. I'm looking for a sink hole..." Under his breath he said, "I wish I wasn't," then louder, "a disappearing stream, underground drainage?" Matt walked the ground. "There she is," he said, whirling around. "A cave."

Wayne was delighted. "Not just any cave. It's an unexplored cave. Hal and I were up here one evening, right over there." He pointed to a rock ledge. "It was just before sunset. First we heard the drumming of their wings. Then all of a sudden a black cloud came out of the earth. It looked as if a genie had been released. It was like nothing I'd ever heard or seen. You could actually feel a hypnotic pulsation flowing through the air."

Matt followed Wayne's gaze into the blue sky.

Wayne pounded Matt on the shoulder, "Too bad you missed it."

"I'll take your word for it. I'm not that fond of bats. I always thought they were dirty beasts. You always had the strangest choices for pets, like poisonous snakes and lizards."

Hal gave a noncommittal grunt and swung his backpack down off his shoulder. Moving to a flat area, he began to unpack his equipment.

"Wayne, are you sure you and Hal know what you're doing?"

"Yeah, sure. Don't worry," replied Wayne with a slight shrug. "Hal's done a lot of caving all over the world. He's been dragging me along and teaching me the ropes for the last two years." Wayne rubbed his hands together excitedly. "Okay, let's get our gear together."

Matt moved over to the edge of the cave opening for

the first time and peered down. That old, here-we-go-again feeling came over him.

"Wayne, how far down is it to the cave floor? I've never seen so much ...black. In Iraq we drove Humvees into the caves." Matt craned his neck, trying to see into the impenetrable darkness.

"It's damn dark." Wayne laughed. "OK, seriously," he said, leaning into Matt's shoulder while his hands framed an imaginary television screen. "Imagine this. Zero light. You're crawling around feeling your way along the walls, all of a sudden, the floor or the ceiling drops or rises several feet, plus you're tripping over boulders that litter the floor of the cave. And don't forget the drop-offs. After a few hours of total darkness, your mind starts playing tricks and you have auditory and visual hallucinations. While your mind is trying to compensate for the lack of visual sensory input, you're lost." He dropped his hands and slapped Matt on the back, "Fun, right?"

"Great. Thanks. I feel better now that you told me more than I ever wanted to know about caving."

"No fear, my friend. We always have three light sources and back-up batteries and plumber's candles. Just like the Boy Scouts: we're prepared. Come on, I'll help you get ready. I brought extra gear for you."

Wayne and Matt laid out the equipment from their backpacks: Leather gloves with gauntlets, knee pads, pocket knives, canteens, water purification tablets, and three large plastic garbage bags each.

"What? Did the cavemen leave a mess down there?" Matt dangled his garbage bags at Wayne.

"Just hope we don't need them." Wayne continued to check his supplies.

Matt snapped on his helmet with attached light. "This

gear looks more like what we used for rock climbing, not caving."

"Still remember the old training? Good. Caving requires a little rock-climbing talent too. All right, let's get this show on the road."

Matt stepped closer to the edge of the mouth of the cave. "Wait a minute, old chap. What's really down there?"

"I'd like to keep a few surprises for later," said Wayne. "But I'll give you a little hint: Hal and I've been down a few times exploring and mapping. We spotted a side tunnel the last time we were down but didn't have time to explore it, so that's our destination today. We think this cave 'goes.' It might even have a connection to the Lechuguilla labyrinth."

"Matt, check around the perimeter of our descent for breakdown. That's loose rocks or any area that might break away," Hal said.

"Got it." Matt gave a half salute and began to stomp the ground and kick away loose rocks.

Hal worked on the wrap-around rigging. He took three wraps around a large boulder to make sure that the rope going into the pit came off the top wrap high up on the rock. He secured the other end of the rope with a bowline and added two keeper knots securely against the knot itself and clipped the loop with a carabiner onto the main line. Next he tied a rope pad to the rock at a lower level than the wrap, with a separate cord to protect their rappelling rope. Matt watched Hal's large but nimble fingers fashion the knots and secure the lines.

"Did you get that, doc?" said Hal over his shoulder. "Didn't they teach you this stuff in Her Majesty's Navy?" Hal motioned for Matt to stand near the cave opening. Wayne and Hal checked Matt's gear and secured him to the seat harness through the carabiner that was attached at waist level.

Wayne hovered over his friend. "Matt, you've rappelled before so you know the drill. The thing to remember is that a cave is a very fragile environment, so be careful where you walk down there. Ready? You're the first one down and I'll be right behind you. It's about a hundred feet to the cave floor." He spread his arms in an expansive gesture. "Gentlemen, let the adventure begin." Wayne switched on Matt's light and tapped him on the head. "Down you go! Ready on belay."

"Belay is on," Matt responded and stepped back. "Rappelling," he shouted.

Matt's descent into the darkness was abrupt. The daylight receded above him. His light blinked off and on once or twice when his head bumped the sides of the narrow opening and he felt his adrenaline pumping and his pulse rate increasing. *Why did I let Wayne talk me into this? Like I had a choice once he gets an idea?* Matt felt panic rising in his throat. His foot slipped off a wet rock outcropping and he swung into the wall behind him, banging his head hard against the limestone. "That didn't feel like it was too damn fragile."

"Are you all right, Matt?"

"I'm getting to know this bloody cave up front and personal," Matt muttered. "My lamp went out," he yelled up.

"After you touch down, wait for me there and we'll fix it," Wayne called down.

Matt's light did not come back on even after he banged it several times with his free hand, so he continued down in total darkness. He wondered how cavemen had ever gotten up enough nerve to enter these black holes. His feet hit solid ground with a jolt. "Off rope," he called up. His voice reverberated. To himself he added. "Thank God."

The absolute darkness was a desolate place. Matt had no idea what was around him and the slight bend in the tunnel he had descended cut off even the dot of light that had comforted him as he rappelled down from the surface. *I hate to admit it but it kind of feels good, the adrenaline pumping like old times. I didn't think of work all the way down. I was too damn scared.*

Wayne was next to rappel down. Waiting his turn he felt like a child waiting to open his birthday presents. He couldn't get enough of caving. He'd never experienced anything like it. He felt a different excitement every time he descended. It electrified him, and he could almost taste it. He slipped down the rope thinking how wonderful it was to be the first man in a thousand years to put your foot down on a rock formed millions of years ago. *Now that's something. A man can be an explorer here, a Christopher Columbus.* He looked up at the entrance, now a shrinking pinpoint of light, and breathed in the dank smell that surrounded him. His acute hearing caught the sounds of minute rustling bats and water dripping. When Matt's hands grabbed his ankles and he touched down, Wayne was a little disappointed the ride was over.

Hal was last. He melted down the rope in effortless, fluid movement, never stopping to check his footing. It was extraordinary that this giant of a man could move without making the slightest noise. The first thing Hal did was walk over to Matt and smack him on the back of the head. Like magic, Matt's light blinked on.

Matt shook his head to clear it. "Thanks!"

"OK: we've done the easy part, now let's get started. I'll lead off. Matt, you're next and Hal will bring up the rear.

Let's go single file, so we make one track in the cave. Take easy steady strides. Try not to kick up the guano dust and, if you want to look at something, stop. Don't try walking and looking at the same time, you might end up in a bad place. The air temperature is nice, but the spring rains mixed with the melting snow running down from the mountaintop will make any water crossings chilly and you can lose body heat fast, so remember to play it safe. No hypothermia."

As they started off, Matt looked up. His headlamp illuminated hundreds of furry bats clinging from various recesses in the jagged cave ceiling. He was immediately besieged by the disgusting taste of guano dust billowing up and around him. Every step he took caused more and more of the disgusting dust to become airborne. Hal tapped him on the shoulder and pantomimed that he should pick up his feet. Matt got both messages. The first was don't talk, because the taste of bat shit almost made him vomit. The second was to duplicate Hal and Wayne's walk, which didn't make guano clouds billow up in your face.

Soon the cave widened and showed its hidden beauty. Matt's short frequent gasps of amazement dotted the silence.

"Matt, you might want to be careful there," Wayne called out as Matt reached out to a dolomite formation. "Those worm-like fossils will tear your skin and clothes. Cavers call them Velcro because of the way they catch onto you. It can be painful."

They passed a small pool of water and Wayne pointed out the cave pearls at the bottom, glowing as if each had an inner light. Gypsum crystals had rubbed off onto their gloves and shirtsleeves and, as the disks of light from their helmets swept around like a light show at a rock concert, their arms and hands glistened.

"Here's the side tunnel we want to explore. Matt, take off your cave pack," Wayne said.

"What tunnel," asked Matt. "Where?"

"Right there in front of you." It looked to Matt as if Wayne was pointing at a solid stone wall. Then Matt saw a small split in the rock.

"Are you joking?" Matt removed his pack, still doubting anyone could fit through the crack.

"Hal and I have fit into openings smaller than that," said Wayne. "That opening is at least fourteen inches wide, and I think it widens out about six feet in. Let's go." Wayne removed his pack.

"Wait a minute. You think? What if it doesn't widen?" asked Matt.

"We just back out the way we came," Wayne smiled. "Matt, when it's your turn to go through, keep your cave pack ahead of you, and push off with your toes. Remember I told you there's a little climbing, walking, and crawling to caving. This is the crawling part."

Wayne entered the black hole first. His body looked as though it was boneless, he seemed almost to pour himself through the small opening.

Matt was next. Pushing himself into the small crevice in the rock face was exhausting, and Matt was soon drenched in sweat even though he was progressing only by inches. The tiniest creases in his clothes snagged on the "Velcro" protruding from the sides of the tunnel. Coupled with the fact that the tunnel floor was slimy and his toes kept slipping, the wonder Matt experienced earlier evaporated. He felt very much alone in the narrow space. He couldn't see Wayne or Hal, but it was comforting to hear their ragged breathing. The energy it took to crawl along like this astounded him.

Just when Matt thought he couldn't crawl anymore, the tunnel opened up and they could duck-walk, which relieved the spent muscles in their toes. But it wasn't long before Matt's thigh muscles began to tighten up. The passage gradually slanted down and, as the incline became steeper, they had a harder time keeping their footing. They secured a rope to an outcropping and went back to crawling, feet first this time, hoping the rope would help them control the speed of their descent. The deeper they went, the damper the tunnel became. Now a slimy gray sludge covered the tunnel floor.

Wayne didn't say anything, but he was worried. He had not expected the passage to be so long. They had traversed about sixty feet and there was no sign that it was opening up. All of a sudden, the passage dropped away. Wayne maneuvered himself around so he could take a look and saw a pool of impenetrable black water about five feet below him. It was difficult to tell how deep the water was. He and Hal consulted and decided Wayne would go down first using the rope.

"Refreshing," Wayne called out when his legs were in the icy water. "OK, Hal, I'm set. I can stand, it's only waist deep. You're really going to appreciate your PVC overalls," he said, to prepare them for the big chill.

The others dropped down one by one into the pool. All three men were glad to be standing upright and stretching their stiffened muscles as they waded across the small lake. They shivered. The water was freezing. Even Hal couldn't stifle his reaction to the frigid water.

"This is great, just the kind of place you see in old horror movies. When you're almost safe on the other side, a monster pops out and grabs you," chuckled Wayne. "Matt, hold your cave pack above your head, we don't want to contaminate the water more than we already have. If we'd had enough room in that crawl space we should have stripped before crossing, but we had no choice."

"You mean drop into this freezing water naked?" Matt's eyes widened.

"Yes, what are you worried about?"

They all laughed, remembering the old shrinkage jokes.

When they reached the other side, twenty feet away, they stopped to look around. Wayne was thrilled at finding this new large cavern. The domed ceiling was covered with glittering stalactites of varying lengths, pointing down at them, the intruders. Stalagmites littered the floor. Many of them were huge, stretching up to reach their mates protruding from the ceiling. It was as if they had traveled back in time the moment they entered the cavern. Flowstone covered the floor and made walking difficult.

"Can you imagine the ocean that once flowed through here?" Wayne asked. He rubbed the polished surface on the grotto floor and pointed out the ripples.

Sweat dripped off Matt's chin and hair. His PVC overalls had kept his lower half dry when they crossed the pool but everything he had on was drenched with sweat. To add to his discomfort he was thoroughly chilled. He was more than ready for a break. "Why aren't you sweating?" he asked Hal.

Wayne answered for him. "He told me he becomes one with the cave. I know it sounds weird but he does just that. Hal has an uncanny instinct for finding passages. And he's saved us from some tight spots when we were caving. All I know is he seems to be at home in the darkness of a cave. Caving is easy for him."

Matt rubbed his chin and his brow furrowed, not understanding Wayne's explanation.

"Time for a break," Wayne said. They removed their backpacks. Wayne broke out the snacks and drinks and they settled back to rest. "We'll take a thirty minute break. Matt, turn off your light; conserve fuel."

They relaxed into the darkness. Matt was so bushed he didn't mind the lack of light. Wayne rested against the rocks, his eyes shut. His thoughts turned to Iraq and Miryam; she never left his mind. Had Matt seen Miryam at the meeting in Australia? If so, he hadn't mentioned it. "Matt, you didn't say much about the EPID conference. How did it go?" Wayne felt more comfortable talking about personal things in the dark.

Matt was ready for Wayne's real question. "Yes, I saw Miryam at the meeting and she looked great. I never understood what happened between you two. The Israeli government stationed her in the north, a remote location for someone with her talents and background. But I didn't pry. She asked if I'd seen you. I told her you kind of dropped off the earth for a while but I was seeing you on my way home."

Wayne remained silent, within himself. He shifted his head on the hard rock and wished he was back in Iraq with Miryam, at their beach, in those magic moments before sunset.

Their lagoon was a thumb-shaped projection of large Shari Lake, eighteen miles south of Baghdad, along Route 9. Most of the people looking for a good time preferred the hustle and bustle of the resort area at the other side of the big lake. But the upscale restaurants, fast boats and general party atmosphere had not been for Wayne and Miryam. The soft sand and azure pool that was screened by tight clusters of reeds created an unblemished space. The bombings had not touched this private Garden of Eden; and they had been thankful for that touch of heaven in their troubled world.

He wanted to hold her again and keep her in his arms. He wanted to feel her warmth when she snuggled and feel her touch on his arm. The last time he'd seen her had been the night he was going to propose. His plans had been shattered when Miryam's beeper buzzed. She had prepared to ignore it but then noticed the code: extreme emergency. She had hugged Wayne and said she had to get back. He understood that. But he didn't understand that it would be the last time he would see her.

Wayne frowned and wiped the sweat from his face with the back of his hand. She was still so much a part of him.

Matt's voice penetrated Wayne's daydreams and he reluctantly pulled back from this rare moment of self-indulgence. He stared into the shadows of the cave, glad his companions couldn't see the pain on his face. The same questions he had asked himself then resurfaced now. What changed Miryam's life and her love for him that she no longer wanted to be with him?

"Wayne, did you hear me? I asked what happened between you and Miryam," said Matt. Wayne remained silent and Matt pressed on. "Maybe you should try again."

"I tried, Matt. We almost made it but then she changed. She's focused on her career. She told me not to try to contact her. No explanation, thanks for the dog and then nothing. Two sentences, that's it. Beats me what was going on. Can we please change the subject?"

"OK. Ghariba was at the conference. She was doing her friendly hands-across-the-ocean thing by hosting evening wine and cheese get-togethers and translating for some of the Kurdish diplomats."

"Anything happen?"

"No, of course not. Olivia and I are closer than ever. But it was fun to see Ghariba and put old ghosts to bed, figuratively speaking. Anyway, she's in love with someone new. Wouldn't say who but swears it's true love. Our affair meant nothing to her. I'm the one who was messed up for a while."

"Yeah, well, I'd never trust her. Nobody changes sides that easily. Apparently she works now as a go-between for the Iraqi government and the Kurds. She sure gets around."

"Give the kid a break, Wayne. There's a lot you don't know about her. She had a hard life in Saddam's youth camp. She never said what happened there, just that it was the worst time in her life. I think she was mentally and physically abused."

"I heard all the stories about those camps. Miryam spent time in one, too. But once Ghariba was free, she chose to support Saddam. Have you forgotten why she went after you in the first place? There's no doubt in my mind that, if she'd found out about our covert operations during our first trip over after Desert Storm, she'd have had you thrown in prison. Then Saddam would have had another excuse to kick the inspectors out of Iraq. When I went back to help destroy Hussein's biological weapons factories after Operation Iraqi Freedom, we crossed paths and she was less than friendly." Wayne sipped from his water bottle.

Matt sat up. "What are you trying to say?"

"I wouldn't count on her sincerity if I were her lover. She's a driven woman with her own plan." Wayne checked the luminous dial of his watch. "On your feet, gentlemen, let's continue the adventure. We've only got about three hours of cave time left, we need to pick up the pace."

"Next time you plan an adventure, my friend, give me a

bit of warning. Or should I assume if you're talking about a back-to-nature excursion you mean to look under Mother Nature's skirts?" joked Matt.

Hal was ready. He moved so silently that Matt hadn't heard him packing and was startled when he turned around and came nose-to-neck with the big man. Hal moved like a cat. It was creepy. Plus, Hal had not said more than ten words since they first met. But Matt could tell that Hal was the experienced man of the trio, so he held back from asking too many questions. He didn't want to chance getting the big guy mad and end up a scalping victim in a foreign country. Matt walked behind Hal, chuckling at the thought that clearly he'd watched too many Westerns as a kid.

They fell into line with Hal in the lead and Wayne bringing up the rear this time. As they walked toward an extremely small slit in the rock wall at the far end of the grotto, Wayne paused. He looked back over his shoulder, half-expecting the tall columns that looked like soldiers standing guard to warn him if there was trouble ahead. He gave them a half salute. The limestone gnomes mutely watched the small group leave.

Matt noticed a slight squishy sound under his feet as he stepped on the soft limestone at the entrance to the tunnel leading down, away from the grotto.

"This is more a crawl space than a tunnel," Matt said. "Why is it squishy underfoot?" He didn't get an answer. The space was so narrow they were unable to face forward. Their movements were restricted and their shoulders rubbed against the rock walls. The scraping sound grated on Matt's nerves. He would never have admitted it, but the confined space was making him feel anxious.

About forty feet in, Hal called back to Wayne, saying that a shallow stream intersected their path and ran along the passage for a few yards, then flowed into a narrow hole.

Matt's frustration level was rising as they turned and squeezed sideways, inching along the twists of the tunnel.

"Suck in your gut," suggested Wayne to a mildly irate Matt.

"Very amusing. Wait till you've had a desk job for a couple of years, you'll look like me."

A strong wave of claustrophobia swept over Matt as he tried to compress himself and push through the crevice. This was the tightest spot he'd ever been in. Matt watched Hal slide through yet another tight spot. "Damn, the man's a magician."

Imitating Hal, Matt put one arm in front so that his shoulders angled sideways and squeezed though. They came out into a tunnel wide enough for them to walk with their shoulders facing forward instead of sideways. But it was only a momentary relief for Matt. As if the cave resisted the alien intrusion, the ceiling in the curving passage lowered to a height of five feet. Stoop-walking, Matt's back scraped the cave ceiling. At least he wasn't getting cut by the sharp edges, but the situation was grating on his nerves. The adventure and fun of the excursion were rapidly diminishing.

The stream had disappeared somewhere below the tunnel floor, but the slime reminded them they were deep in the mountain. Underfoot, the passage felt like spongy cushions and the walls oozed droplets of water. The humidity in this part of the cave was high, but the temperature remained constant.

"Most likely we're below the level of the river we saw up on the surface," said Wayne.

Matt was praying the passage would end soon and reward them with a surprise like the limestone grotto they had left some distance behind, but the tunnel rolled on. Wayne could hear Matt's ragged breathing. He knew his friend was fatigued and that his muscles didn't have the benefit of being conditioned from regular caving expeditions like his and Hal's. He started to consider other plans when their advance was halted. They bunched up behind Hal in the narrow space, listening.

At first it was just a slight change in the air movement.

"Did you feel that?" Wayne asked Hal.

"Yes. Listen," Hal whispered with a finger to his lips.

A low rumble vibrated under them. They heard rushing water nearby. Matt inched up behind Hal, who put a large muscular arm out so Matt could go no further. "Be careful," Hal said. The beam of Hal's light revealed a gaping black hole directly in front of them. Matt eased forward and shone his light into the abyss. Peering around Hal as best he could, he saw frothing water rapidly filling a pit a good three feet below where they were standing. The hole was at least eight feet wide, which made jumping across chancy.

"It looks as if someone plugged up the drain and the water's backing up into the tub," joked Matt. At first he was fascinated by the turbulent water, but when it started to spill over into the passage where they stood, he recognized the danger.

Wayne's tone was serious. "There must be a spring thunderstorm going on outside. This is probably the runoff path for that creek we crossed near the cave entrance. We're not going any further."

"Are you saying we're standing in an underground river?" asked Matt.

"I guess the weather report was wrong again. Hal, we've got a sump here. Let's move back to the grotto, fast!"

Wayne yelled over the increasing sound of rushing water. "Go! Now!"

They scrambled to turn and make it back before the grotto filled and cut them off from their escape route. Wayne and Hal knew what to do. Matt was caught in the middle. He didn't have room enough to turn his body around in the narrow passage and, as he felt the level of the water creeping up his legs, so did his anxiety reach new heights. The freezing water was already knee high. He tried walking backwards.

"What the hell do you think you're doing?" Hal sounded irritated.

"Every time I try to turn around I can't because my knees and shoulders hit the sides of this blasted tunnel. I can't stand up straight." Panicky sweat covered Matt's face and ran down his back in icy drops as he thrashed around.

Wayne realized that Matt was panicking. "Matt, lie down on your back under the water, then roll over to your stomach, pull your knees up under yourself. *Now*. We're getting out of here!" Wayne had to shout to be heard over the noise of the surging water that was filling the narrow passage. The urgency in Wayne's voice spurred Matt on, even though being submerged in the frothing water was one of the most frightening things he'd ever experienced. He did what Wayne had suggested and came up facing the right direction.

"Hal, watch him," said Wayne.

Wayne didn't have to tell them time was of the essence: the water was up to their chests. Soon they'd have to tilt their faces up to the roof of the passage to breathe.

Wayne and Hal had been in deep water before but it had been calm, still water, a world of difference. This was an aggressive, surging body filling the tunnel and exerting tremendous pressure on their bodies. They were in danger of losing their footing and being smashed into the rock walls as the water swirled and rushed by. The confinement of the space helped to a certain extent because they could brace their hands against the ceiling or on the sides of the tunnel and control their progress and stabilize their bodies against the current. They felt the stings of the sharp rocks as their bodies were propelled forward by the surge of water.

Wayne was exhilarated and frightened at the same time. He knew the other two felt the same excitement. "Come on, let's keep moving," he yelled.

The first stages of hypothermia were setting in and the uncomfortable tingling in Wayne's feet was spreading up his legs. He knew that Matt's fluid loss from the physical effort would be greater than his or Hal's because their bodies were conditioned. The air, cooled by the icy grotto water, increased the risk of hypothermia. Wayne's worries were justified.

Matt's body temperature was dropping at a precipitous rate. Matt's light disappeared and Hal lost sight of him. Then a blur of light emerged from the water about ten feet in front of Wayne, bouncing wildly off the walls.

"Matt, you still there, buddy?" Wayne didn't stop to look back, Hal was behind Matt and Wayne had confidence in him.

"I lost my helmet," Matt slurred through numb lips. He was so close behind Wayne that he could see the back of Wayne's head in the light from Hal's helmet.

The water was creeping up their necks. Matt had never been so scared but he was smiling. *I must be nuts*. He laughed out loud and heard Wayne and Hal laughing, too. Their hysterical laughter bounced around the tunnel as if dozens of people were enjoying this wild water ride with them.

They heard the rumbling sound of rock tearing loose and then an increase of water pressure swept Matt off his feet. Hal grabbed him by the collar and hauled him up. A sharp rock narrowly missed Matt's head and he gurgled his thanks as he found his footing and waded forward again. The water was up to their chin now and the only way to breathe was through their noses.

Matt's legs and arms felt like someone was poking him all over with sharp needles; the frigid water was getting the better of him. His PVC overalls were heavy, full of icy water and he couldn't stop shaking. He knew the signs of hypothermia and he had them all, but it was senseless to worry about it. Drowning seemed the worst of the two evils and the one he would most like to prevent. He concentrated on the back of Wayne's head, telling himself he could do this—and if he did he would never enter a cave again. Certainly not one with running water.

Suddenly, Wayne disappeared. Matt felt around under the water, but there was only water and rock. He panicked. Had Wayne been swept away through some underground passage? He had to help his best friend. His fear was subdued by his courage. Holding his breath, he submerged himself in the icy water, feeling frantically for Wayne or a passage. *Maybe I took a wrong turn? Where's Wayne?* Confusion and disorientation engulfed him. *Which way did he go?* Matt surfaced and saw only darkness. *What did Wayne say—I'd never be able to find my way out without a light? Where's my cave pack?* Matt fumbled behind him and found the cave pack still secure on his shoulder. By now he was shivering uncontrollably. Then a strong hand tugged at him.

"Matt, stand-up, get your head out of the water and tilt it back! You've got to squeeze through that narrow opening like Wayne did. Remember how you did it when we came in?" A gurgling Hal shook Matt.

The crevice was impeding the water's natural path and acting like a dam so that water was building up behind them. The pressure was incredible, like someone pounding on their backs.

"Matt!" Wayne's voice floated across the watery divide. "Exhale and squeeze through. I'll help you as soon as I can reach you. Push him in, Hal."

"I'm pushing. He's out of his mind. The hypothermia's got him," Hal said.

"Hal, I can't reach him," Wayne yelled back.

"Wait... he's caught on something." Hal fumbled in the dark water.

"Cut off his PVCs—anything," shouted Wayne. "Get him through or you'll both drown!"

Hal worked as fast as he could, but he too was feeling the cold and had the shakes. The numbness made his large hands clumsy and slow. Hal pulled out his pocketknife. "Hope I don't circumcise you, buddy," he said.

He cut, ripped, and tore at the waterlogged PVC overalls. Soon he had Matt stripped to his long johns and boots and guided him into the crevice, feeling the tugs on Matt as Wayne pulled from the other side of the opening. Submerged in the water, Matt's limp body was maneuvered through the crevice.

Hal gulped in air, held his breath, and propelled himself through, right behind Matt.

Wayne was waiting on the other side. Once he and Hal had Matt in the grotto, they dragged him to the higher, dry side of the grotto, thankful that the large space wouldn't fill for a while so they'd have the chance to catch their breath and work on Matt. Fortunately, their escape route sloped upward from the grotto, but they knew it was only a temporary reprieve.

Matt's hiking boots were soggy and shreds of his old pants hung down around his feet. Hal cut the remains of Matt's pants away and Wayne pulled off his boots. Hal got his extra set of dry wool underwear out of his waterproof cave pack while Wayne stripped the wet clothes off Matt. He'd almost finished putting the dry ones on him by the time Hal had found a dry flannel shirt in his pack.

"Hold on, buddy," Wayne vigorously rubbed Matt's arms and legs and spoke to him soothingly in an effort to calm the other man's babbling. "You'll be warm before you know it." The extra-large Long Johns hung down over Matt's feet, but Wayne didn't crack a smile or a joke, concentrating on rubbing Matt's freezing feet through the red wool. Hal vigorously rubbed Matt's arms and legs. Matt tried to form words through his blue lips but his speech was slurred and he couldn't control his shivering so they couldn't understand what he was trying to say.

Wayne and Hal knew that needed to raise the other man's core temperature. Wayne got out the lightweight garbage bags, which would act as an emergency heat tent. They propped Matt up, pulling his head through the hole Wayne tore in the bottom of the bag, bending his knees into his chest so the bag could slide down to cover Matt's shoulders and legs. He took off his helmet and placed it under Matt's knees, knowing that the carbide lamp's modest light would provide a source of heat.

That was all Wayne and Hal could do right then, so they took care of their own wet, chilling bodies, discarding the sodden PVCs in relief, appreciating the warmth of dry clothing against their bodies. It didn't take long for Matt to come around. His voice quavered with the cold when he spoke. "What, no fluffy bath towels at this club? Hal, thanks. I could hear you but I couldn't make myself do anything."

"We Americans are used to getting you Brits out of trouble," was Hal's wordy response.

Wayne knew the inner strength Matt possessed and hoped it would see him through the next couple of hours. They still had some strenuous caving ahead of them in order to reach the exit and then they had to climb out of the cave. Matt would have to pull his own weight. Fortunately, they'd been able to halt the hypothermia before it progressed too far.

"Matt, if you can crawl under your own power, it's time to get moving," said Wayne.

With a sigh of regret, Matt pulled his makeshift warming tent over his head. He stood, picked up Wayne's helmet, and handed it to him. "I've been ready. I was just letting you blokes rest a bit. Love the plastic bag sauna and that trick with the carbide lamp is a neat way to help thaw out." He stretched, flexing, wincing at the cramps in his lanky legs. "By the way, you don't have to come up with any more adventures."

Wayne and Hal glanced up from arranging their cave packs and began to laugh.

"What? What is it?" Matt asked, slightly irritated that he was not in on the joke.

Wayne and Hal tried to stifle their laughter but couldn't.

"What the hell's going on?" Incensed, Matt stood with his hands on his hips, waiting for an answer, turning to see if something was happening behind him. But, all he could see was the widening lake as water streamed down the wall from the crevice where they escaped the flooded passage. "What's so bloody funny?" Matt asked again.

"You, my friend," said Wayne. "Your hair is standing straight up, and the red wool long johns are so large that if there were a wind, you'd be a sailboat. But, the piece de résistance is that, in all the time I've been caving, I've never seen the moon shine so bright this far below ground."

Matt stared blankly at Wayne.

"Your back door's open. The trap door of your Long Johns," Wayne spun Matt around and tugged on the dangling flap.

Matt was embarrassed at first, then he joined in the laughter. "Ah, I understand. It's difficult being in the shadow of my indomitable light." He reached around and buttoned the offending flap.

They had almost finished packing when a grinding noise rocked the grotto. "I hope that's not what I think it is," said Wayne.

"What else could possibly happen?" Matt laughed nervously.

Before Wayne could speak, the rocks around the flooded tunnel entrance exploded and debris hurtled toward the explorers. They scrambled out of the way as loose rocks and dirt filled the air. Boulders rumbled down the incline of the flowstone, heading straight for Wayne who barely managed to roll out of the way.

Matt jumped up to help Wayne.

"I'm OK. Change of plans, gents, we leave now," said a breathless Wayne as Matt hauled him to his feet.

Water was gushing into the grotto through the gaping hole like the flow from a fireman's hose opened at full pressure. It shot from the fissure with tremendous force, creating a majestic plume that spouted high in the air before falling into the once tranquil grotto.

"Lucky you rolled the right way, buddy," Hal said, pointing to the spot where Wayne had been before the boulders came crashing through. Wayne's helmet lay in the debris, crushed. Hal grabbed the mutilated headgear and handed it to Wayne. "A souvenir."

Wet again, they waded in water that rose to chest height as they traversed the lake. On the other side, one at a time, they shimmed up the rope they'd left dangling so they could easily exit where they had entered. As Wayne waited his turn, he stripped off his wet shirt and wrapped it around his head a couple of times and suggested to Matt that he do the same. "It'll protect your head from the rocks."

Hal took the lead, Wayne brought up the rear. Water was just beginning to enter the low end of the tunnel when Wayne crawled in and pulled the rope up behind him.

Hal was the only one who still had a headlamp and helmet. Wayne and Matt had back-up flashlights which helped, but if it hadn't been for Hal's clear view of the winding passage, the going would have been slow and treacherous. The small hand-held lights made crawling on their bellies difficult for Wayne and Matt, so they put the lights in their mouths. Once their hands were free, they made better time pulling themselves up the tunnel's incline. Crawling was a taxing process and it was pure adrenaline that kept them moving.

They'd gone about forty feet into the passage when Hal called back, "It's got to be duck walking from here on. Pick up the pace."

"Good idea," Wayne said, "but I think we're making headway against the water or else the tunnel has sprung a leak. It's not filling as fast as it was and the level's staying pretty constant."

He was right. A fissure at the side of the tunnel was acting as a natural drain, so they could relax and slow their grueling pace. When the tunnel narrowed again, Hal knew they were close to the main corridor. This time, Matt made it through the narrow opening without assistance. From there it was an easy walk back to their ropes and then up, emerging from the cave exhausted and relieved.

They took it slow hiking back to camp, grateful when the rain stopped. The air was cool but they were tingling from the constant exertion and felt warm despite soggy clothing. It was twilight by the time Hal nodded goodbye and turned off, leaving Wayne and Matt to continue on to their campsite.

Later, as they sat by a roaring fire, dry and comfortable at last, Matt suggested a drink.

"Sir, I have a nice little domestic beer that will go well with these beans and franks," Wayne said, putting a towel over his arm like a waiter.

"No, thank you. I've something even better. I've been saving it." He went into his tent and reemerged holding a bottle of clear liquid that had a piece of grass reed in the bottom. He presented it to Wayne.

"I haven't had any Zubrowka since Iraq. Where did you get it? I can't find it anymore." Wayne wasted no time pouring them each a generous drink.

"That will remain my secret. Cheers," said Matt, and they emptied their paper cups and savored the heat of the vodka as it spread through them.

Wayne stirred the pot of beans, threw in the hot dogs, and put the rack over the fire. The alcohol was helping them relax and come down from the high of the day's adventures.

Matt was ravenous. He ate his food and got up from the log for more, refilling both plates.

"I never thought..." Matt stopped in mid-thought.

Wayne filled their paper cups for the third time and finished Matt's sentence. "You never thought you'd like caving?"

"No," laughed Matt. "I never thought I'd like American beans and bangers, I mean frankfurters, as you say."

They laughed, ate, and drank without talking until Wayne broke the sleepy mood. "I've finally grown up, my friend. No more stunts like what happened in Iraq for me. I like my peaceful life."

"Oh, really? What do you call today?"

"I said no more stunts. Adventure is another matter."

"I'm glad to hear it. A life without some surprises would be a bore." Matt switched gears. "Hey, did I tell you my mother was with me in Australia? We took a side trip to visit her sister in New Zealand and went to this subterranean lake in the Waitomo Caves. It was a tourist attraction thing. They took us in a boat out into the middle of the lake then turned out all the lights. The whole cave ceiling lit up with hundreds—no, thousands—of glowworms on it, like stars in the night sky. My mother loved it."

"'Her eyes the glowworms, lend thee,' I'm too drunk to remember the rest," Wayne's voice was slurred.

"I remember this game. Herrick right? Robert Herrick," said Matt after a lengthy pause.

Wayne lifted his paper cup to salute Matt. "Yeah, you were always my best competition."

"You always throw one liners at me at the most inopportune times. Here's another one, 'Glories, like glowworms, afar off shine bright,' a famous English writer," bragged Matt proudly.

Wayne frowned in concentration. "'But, look to near, have neither heat nor light,' from *The Duchess of Malfi* by John Webster."

By now they were sprawled out, sipping their vodka. They were dozing when Hal entered the circle of light from the campfire.

"What brings you up the mountain so late, Hal?" Wayne asked, quickly coming fully awake.

"I've a message from your wife, Matt." Hal's somber expression brought Matt to his feet.

"Is something wrong with one of my boys?"

"No," said Hal. "I'm sorry, it's your mother. She's been taken to the hospital. She's in critical condition. They said to come home as soon as possible. I have my car down below. As soon as you're ready I'll drive you to the airport. My wife is checking on flights now. She'll have you booked on the next flight out by the time we get down the mountain."

Matt's heart raced with the shock of Hal's news.

Wayne slapped Matt on the back. "Let's get our things." Matt frowned at Wayne. "I'm going to London with you."

Chapter 6

The Farm—Today

It was noon when former Major General Tariq Saeed arrived home from his private meeting with the Dove. He lived with his wife and son on what he jokingly called a farm in the small village of Aski Kalak, a suburb of the bustling city of Mosul in northern Iraq.

Tariq hated every moment he was forced to spend in what he called, "this backward territory." Outwardly, he maintained the facade of an Iraqi loyal to the new order after Operation Iraqi Freedom, but his heart ached for the power he had become accustomed to during Saddam Hussein's reign. In the past, war had been one of the most profitable enterprises in Iraq and Tariq had been very successful. But that was in the past and almost all the wealth he had accumulated during that fruitful time was spent. The Americans had taken it all away. But, he thought, *I will make them pay. I will enjoy watching CNN when their blood runs foul and black down the golden streets of America.*

If Tariq had to describe his farm he would say it was barely adequate, even though he lived in comfort and with far more than the average Iraqi family. Neither Aski Kalak nor nearby Mosul provided the luxuries he had grown so fond of when he was part of Saddam's inner circle and lived in the fashionable section of Baghdad on Felastin Street. How he hungered to dine once again at the expensive dinner clubs in Jadriyab or go to the racetrack in the Mansour district. Instead of fine wine and gourmet food, Tariq drank arak, the local brew, and ate a poor substitute for the rich Tigris River fish he liked so much. He closed his eyes and inhaled, trying to remember the spicy scent of the fish drenched in herbs and roasting over an open flame, but the memory did not come. The only flavor he detected was the bitter taste of Saddam's betrayal when the Americans invaded and he did not respond with biological weapons. He enjoyed his painful memories, it kept his hate alive and his spirit determined. Tariq then licked his lips and savored the flavor of his impending revenge against the Americans.

Tariq's resentment toward Hussein had threatened to overwhelm him until he realized a way to profit from Saddam's mistakes and weakness. He had enlisted his Dove to expand her network. Although she still worked as a spy she was, in the end, devoted to Tariq. Her present assignment allowed her to move around in the world more easily than most people. He thought of people as tools. His job was finding the right tool for the job and the Dove was a powerful tool. He'd been able to exploit her fanaticism for a United Arab Republic. She hated America and Israel and was disillusioned by the new Iraqi government's weakening position in the Arab world. He thought of how pleasing their arrangement was. Her background and experience during Desert Storm and his connections in the military had helped them plan their revenge. And now the culmination of years of planning was drawing near.

He walked to his closet, eyeing his old uniform hanging there. He fingered the shoulder boards, still proud to have been a General. *And so I will be again*, thought Tariq, *but this time I will have four stars*. The crossed sabers below the gold eagle glinted in the light. He mused about the fact that a golden eagle had also been the emblem of the conquering Romans. Tariq would be the next conquering golden eagle and his prize would be Iraq. And perhaps many other countries?

His daydreams were interrupted by the sound of a jeep pulling up outside his home. His driver knocked on the door, ready to take him to his office at the farm.

The upper, public level of the farm appeared to be the same as that of any other. Tariq had been very successful with developing and producing genetically engineered hydroponic crops. His farming expertise contributed much to the hungry people of Iraq. The fact that the UN subsidized the facility as part of the rebuilding of the republic was fortunate, and an ideal cover. But, beneath this façade, four levels below ground, he directed his real business.

As he exited the elevator on sub-level three, the men came to attention. He had handpicked every man in this, his elite personal guard. For three years he had pampered and protected them, giving each the taste of a privileged life. He had discovered their strengths and weaknesses and cultivated them as easily as he spread fertilizer on his crops. Some had become drug addicts. With others, he fed their appetites for violence. Still others were tied to him by a variety of lusts: money, power, and women. He had even subverted a few into thinking their mission would make them honored patriots and heroes throughout the Arab world.

It was a small group, but each man was battle-hardened. He watched them practice hand-to-hand combat and applauded their skills. Prudence dictated that Tariq keep a low profile and limit the number of troops to 100.

The vast hydra-like complex of the lower levels of the farm contained barracks and laboratories and was modeled after one of Saddam's secret storage facilities that had been destroyed. Tariq longed for the day in the near future when the fourth level would be filled with the chemical and biological weapons he hunted and required to destroy Israel and America.

As a child growing up and going to school in Hussein's Iraq, Tariq had been taught—like all Arab children—to hate Israel first and America second. The Arabs' defeat at the hands of the Israelis in 1967 was a festering wound every loyal Arab suffered and nurtured. These truths permeated every aspect of life in Iraq and every facet of life had something to do with these politics.

Tariq, like Hussein, believed that terror, corruption and an unrestrained secret police was the best and only way to control the populace. Tariq's team of international terrorists numbered forty. But that would grow once he could rely on his fellow countrymen to support him. For now, he had to be careful because, thanks to the rewards offered by the Americans, there were spying eyes everywhere.

Violence had always been an intricate part of Tariq's life. At the age of two, he was the victim of his father's alternating violence and generosity. At first he hated his father and then, when he was old enough, he adopted the same behavior himself. He enjoyed the power he had discovered in violence. At thirteen, he was expelled from school for beating a teacher. As a favor to his father, Saddam had Tariq placed in a youth camp. It was there that Tariq learned the value of discipline and education. And it was there that Tariq practiced the lessons he learned. The first was that power and money were strong aphrodisiacs. He was one of the rich kids at the camp. If he couldn't intimidate the other children with his physical strength, the dinars in his pockets could buy them. The second lesson was that violence was contagious. To survive in the camp, Tariq recruited a small band whose capacity for brutality was equal to his own. And it was in the camp that he had met his Dove when she was just eleven. He had lost no time making her part of his ruthless band.

Almost all the young men he had associated with in the youth camp had entered the military and he had built his innermost circle of trusted officers at the farm from this old gang.

Moving to the second sub-level, Tariq walked through a lavish foyer and down the plush carpeting of the hall to his office. His assistant lowered her head and stood to one side after opening the door to his sanctum. No one knew how much of the money from his secret supporters he had spent on his office and its antiques. Included in the cost were the hidden surveillance devices, silent alarms and many other gadgets he had insisted on for his personal protection. He was as paranoid as Hussein had been.

"Rijah, have Abu al-Tubar—I mean, Colonel Abbas—come to my office," Tariq sneered, pausing to enjoy the fear that the Colonel's nickname provoked.

Indeed, Rijah shivered at hearing the name. Abu al-Tubar meant hatchet man. It was meant literally, for it was this butcher's favorite weapon and he liked the title almost as much as he liked Rijah. She placed the call and shuddered, trying not to think of the reason the hatchet man had been summoned.

As Tariq waited for Colonel Abbas, he thought about how it was impossible to compete against Israel or the United States with conventional weapons, but a large army meant nothing in a biological war. What was it he'd heard biologics called? The poor man's nuclear weapon? In his capacity as an aide to Brigadier General Mahmoud Bilal, Tariq had been in charge of the filling and deployment of the biological and chemical weapons. He was also privy to vital information. Once, he had overheard General Bilal and Dr. Hamid Jasim, one of the creators of the bomb, discussing where to hide the filled bombs and virus stocks. Inspectors were returning to Iraq after Desert Storm and they had to move quickly to hide their arsenal and falsify their documents. Tariq had heard them say something about the mountains in the north, but the area was too large for him to search thoroughly without being noticed. This information was useless without the exact location, for now that area was patrolled from the sky by American planes and satellites and by the Kurds on the ground.

Then fate smiled on Tariq. One of Hussein's aides approached him with a proposition. The man described the pearl ring Saddam always wore and quoted Hussein: "It is my most precious possession."

Saddam had never let the ring out of his sight. He took the large cumbersome piece of jewelry off when he had sex and even then he kept it within his reach. In the final days of Hussein's reign, one of his women had stolen the ring to buy her way out of Iraq. Tariq had sent al-Tubar to France where the ring was made. He had tracked down the jeweler who'd made the ring and discovered it contained a secret compartment. Tariq had seen Brigadier Mahmoud Bilal transfer information onto microchips for Saddam many times. He had surmised that the ring's compartment was the perfect hiding place for information about the location of Hussein's most precious possession, his chemical and biological weapons stockpiles.

But, time was running out. Tariq had to act quickly. He had let loose the Dove and she would not be contained now. He must have the biological weapons in order to maintain momentum and, if necessary, make good his threats. Retrieving that ring was the key to finding the storage sites. *If the site had just half of what I know still exists, my plan cannot fail*, thought Tariq.

His secretary tapped on the door. "General, Colonel Abbas is here."

Rijah feared Tariq, which was just what he wanted. That she also hated him with uncommon passion was something he did not consider. At times, the latter emotion was so intense that it was a struggle for her to come into the office and face him without betraying her loathing. But he held the fate of her misguided brother in his hands and so she locked her hate away and bided her time.

Colonel Abbas stepped into Tariq's office and saluted. "Relax, old friend," Tariq signaled for the Colonel to sit down. "Aquid, I am happy to see you. Please give me some good news," said Tariq congenially.

The Colonel was one of the few people who was not afraid of Tariq and he refused the seat. They had been together a long time, since the youth camp, and Tariq encouraged and indulged Abbas' bizarre, sadistic desires.

"My General, I have made discreet inquires and spent a lot of your money, but I believe the information I have is valid. I'll have the ring within the week." When the hatchet man smiled he looked even more repulsive.

"Excellent," Tariq rubbed his hands together as he spoke. He was thrilled. "But don't underestimate the need for secrecy."

"Everyone in the line of information has been silenced," Al-Tubar assured him.

Tariq got up and paced excitedly around the room and then returned to sit behind his desk and check security devices once again. "If my initial information was correct, only caves in the mountains to the north could accommodate storage of such a large volume of supplies." Tariq clenched his fist with enthusiasm. "We are very close. I can feel it."

"I have asked the little flower, Rijah, to track down military movement in the north around the dates you said the supplies were transferred," al-Tubar continued. "She came up with bombings of a Kurd stronghold two days before the inspectors entered Iraq. Knowing Hussein, the bombings were the usual distraction to give his military a chance to hide the supplies in that region."

"That is good, very good, but there are hundreds of places to hide in the mountains: caves, dam excavations and bombed-out villages. We have to be in and out before anyone is the wiser. The eyes in the sky will have to be diverted," Tariq said, pointing up. "As soon as you have the location, take my son and two or three other men—a small inconspicuous party—to secure the site. Remember, time is of the essence. I must have those weapons under my control within the month." Tariq walked around the desk and patted al-Tubar on the back. "You have exceeded my expectations, old friend. Now rest. With an unusual burst of affection, Tariq embraced the standing Abbas. "My dear friend, you are my treasured right arm."

Abbas saluted, then turned to open the door when his General spoke once more. "Oh, I almost forgot. I have a gift for you. I think you know who I'm talking about. You've shown some interest in this 'flower.' She meddles in my business too much. Find out the extent of her betrayal. Names, I need names. After that you may do whatever you wish with her. I will send her to you." The General dismissed his boyhood friend with a wave of his hand.

"Thank you, my General," The hatchet man flushed with excitement.

Tariq returned the Colonel's salute and dismissed him.

Colonel Abbas was delighted. He had always had a secret desire for the beautiful Rijah. Now his dreams would become a reality. This was an unexpected reward. He smiled to himself. He had amassed a fortune working on this project. Perhaps his little flower could be persuaded to share it with him. Soon he would have enough money to disappear, if necessary, and she would make a fitting companion. One thing the youth camp had taught Abbas was that his first loyalty was to himself.

Back in his office, Tariq was considering how close he was to having it all. He admired himself in the mirror and smoothed his black shiny hair with his hands. *I will tread where other men fear to go. My footsteps will be heard all over the world.*

"Glory and Victory!" He addressed his image in the mirror. "Soon, my Arab brothers, we will have Glory and Victory!" It was the old Ba'thist slogan.

Chapter 7

Assyria, 811 B.C.—Blood Betrayal

Cautiously, Queen Semiramis coaxed her horses deep into the narrow ravine. Her instinct guided her down this path and, when it became more difficult to navigate in the darkness, she stepped down from her chariot and gripped the reins, leading the horses forward.

As she walked, Semiramis wiped the white foam from the lathered bodies of her horses, Sin and Shamash, named after the moon and sun gods. Her touch comforted the animals and their warmth comforted her.

From what she could make out in the darkness, the path ended at the entrance to a cave. She released her grip on the reins and drew her short sword as she entered. She inspected the area as best she could without lighting a torch that might disclose her location to Ninyas.

Deeming the cave her only safe haven, she returned to the chariot and attempted to lead the horses into the cave. They recoiled, snorting as if they smelled danger inside the black hole. Patiently, she coaxed the wild-eyed animals to enter, even though she knew—as the horses did—that mountain lions and other wild animals made these caves their home. The war chariot groaned, as if it objected to being taken into a space so confined it would be useless. She tightened her grip on the reins as her beauties flared their nostrils.

Semiramis spoke softly to reassure the animals and encourage them to walk deeper into the cave, but they had just gone a few yards when the dark space echoed with the thudding noise of many hooves. Fatigue and the reverberations in the cave had distorted her usually sharp hearing and the queen remained silent, trying to decide where the sounds came from. Then she heard Ninyas shouting as the winds gusting through the mountain pass carried his words into the cave. She felt certain that the winds would have helped cover the tracks her chariot had made. Yet Ninyas sounded close.

She moved a little more deeply into the cave. Sounds and shadows, formless and black, bounced around her, playing tricks on her mind. She stopped and waited: listening. When her eyes adjusted, she groped her way along the side of the cave until she found a pile of earthen jars in a crevice. Many travelers became lost trying to navigate the rugged mountain passes and were forced to take refuge in the caves. This was why the queen had commanded that the route through the mountains be marked.

She picked up one of the jars. Its shape was not familiar but it contained what she had expected: sesame oil. She lit the oil and stacked the remaining jars in the back of the chariot. The voices were nearer, although she could not recognize the words that overlapped and danced off the rocks. Then it came together in her mind. They were speaking the language of her enemy, the Urartu. *Ninyas speaks their vile tongue all too well,* thought the queen.

She urged her horses deeper into the mountain, relieved when she found a side tunnel broad enough for the chariot to pass. Something about the tunnel made her think it had not been formed naturally, but she had no time to dwell on that now. The tunnel opened into a large chamber, big enough to shelter many horses and chariots. For now, this was what she needed.

As she was tying the horses to an outcrop of rock, her foot hit something metallic. *This floor has rings imbedded in it, just as I have in my own courtyard. Yes, this grotto has served this purpose before.*

After securing the horses, Semiramis took a spear from the back of her chariot and retraced her steps to the mouth of the cave. Peering outside, she was relieved to see the area was deserted. Hugging the rock wall, she slipped out of the cave and dropped down into a wadi. Her ears strained for the sounds of men approaching. Then she heard Ninyas' angry voice screaming orders. The queen climbed out of the wadi and up the side of a rocky knoll to investigate the area below. Inching herself up onto a stone ledge and lying flat, she peered over the edge.

Below her was Ninyas and ten of his bodyguard. Their words floated up to the queen's ears and she was appalled at what she heard. Ninyas had made a bargain with the King of Urartu who was sending a large armed force to exterminate the last of the Assyrians loyal to Semiramis. Ninyas would rule and Assyria would become a province of Urartu.

The queen had difficulty controlling her anger. What a fool her son was to give the Urartu free entry into Assyria. She recognized the man he'd addressed as his captain as an Assyrian soldier that she had rejected for service in her army.

She listened as Ninyas tried to goad his men into continuing the search for her.

"It is important that we bring the queen's body back to the people to show them they have no one to help them. Then they will follow me without resistance," said Ninyas.

Outraged, Semiramis hurled a spear down at Ninyas. The tip of her spear became imbedded in the floor of Ninyas' chariot, inches from his foot.

Ninyas' head snapped back and he looked up and spotted her. He screamed through clenched teeth. "Mother! You are already dead. Do not prolong this foolish chase." He shook his fists at her in frustration.

His venomous words stunned her. She was taken aback by the depth of his hate. Looking down at her son, she cupped her hands around her mouth to be heard over the wind and projected her voice. "The search for one's quarry is the best part of the hunt."

She pulled back from the ledge, out of view, as arrows glanced off the rocks where she had stood. When the barrage stopped, she peered over the edge, ready to flee, but saw that the men below were no longer focused on her. The Captain was pointing at the sky to the north and Semiramis gazed in that direction.

This was the end of the rainy season that nourished the fertile land between the Tigris and the Euphrates. Soon the great hot dry winds would arrive from the northwest, heating the surface of the land. They would bring unpredictable storms with them. As Semiramis' eyes focused on the distance, she saw why the Captain was so agitated. A gigantic storm was approaching at a frightening pace.

Ninyas had no choice but to order his men to temporarily abandon the hunt. With one last icy stare at his mother, he led his men in a hasty retreat. The glare said everything. He would never give up; he would return to kill her.

Nature's violent display mesmerized the queen as she stared at the approaching storm. When the first drops of rain stung her face, she realized she had stayed too long and the danger was almost upon her.

A violent, wind-driven rainstorm came at her from the west. It was a Sharqi, notorious for forming enormous wind funnels that swallowed men and animals. This was not the warm wind she expected at the end of the rainy season. Every Assyrian knew the patterns of the weather, for they dictated the proper time to plant and harvest. This storm was not a nourishing one.

At first, Semiramis believed the storm was a sign that the gods were helping her, but now the temperature plummeted and icy sheets of rain pummeled her skin. By tradition, the high priests of the palace had relayed the thoughts of the gods to her, but now she was experiencing the power of the gods first-hand. The display frightened even the battle-hardened queen.

Ninyas and his men whipped their horses furiously and turned east toward Lake Van and away from the approaching storm in an attempt to escape from its path. But the dangerous funnel-shaped torrent suddenly turned and followed him as if it were hungry for horse and man. Moonlight glinted through the twisted distorted storm. Within seconds it overtook the men at the rear of Ninyas' band. At least two men and their horses were swallowed by the ravenous red funnel.

As hail pelted the queen, she stood watching Ninyas retreat. She cheered the Sharqi, for she hoped it would wipe out her enemies. Then, in one terrifying move, the storm shifted and veered toward her. Leaping down from the exposed ledge, she raced for the shelter of the cave. Rocks, sand, and hail pounded her body. She was knocked off her feet several times as the wind picked her up and threw her down. On hands and knees, she struggled toward the shelter of the cave. She feared the storm that had saved her from her enemies might now take her life in payment.

She was soaked to the bone and shivering when she crawled into the shelter of the cave. Exhausted, she lay in the cold mud inside the entrance, trying to catch her breath. Before she passed out, she promised herself that Ninyas would never be king. Again and again she shouted it: "Never!" After a while she fell into an exhausted and fractured sleep.

She awoke with the chilled air rushing over her, whipping her tattered wet cloak and tunic against her bruised body. She forced herself to stand, then walked stiffly further into the cave. The storm still raged outside, but it lacked the ferocity it had possessed earlier. She knew she had not slept long when she looked at the night sky. A glimmer of morning approached. Her golden crown lay in the mud. She retrieved it and cleaned away the dirt with the ragged edge of her cloak. With the death of her son, she thought, she would wash away the filth and disgrace he had brought to Assyria.

The warrior rose within her and forced her to prepare for a different type of war. *This cave will be my battlefield. I will be part of the darkness, attacking when and where they least expect.* She wondered if one warrior could save an empire.

She ran to check on the horses. The exertion warmed her exposed arms and legs and the circulation began to return to her hands and feet as her fingers and toes tingled in response to the blood pumping through her veins. As she approached the grotto, she heard the hooves of the nervous horses dancing on the hard rock. The crystal pool had already started to expand as the torrential rain swelled the underground river. She cut the traces that attached the horses to the chariot. It was unfortunate, but she would have to leave the chariot behind so she and her beauties could move faster through the maze of tunnels. She removed what was left of her long wool cloak and wrapped it around her bow, arrows, armor, and the small jars of lamp oil and then secured the load to her back with a strap of leather. Slipping her short sword into her belt, she grasped her long sword in her right hand in case some wild animal lay hidden in one of the passageways. Before leading the horses out of the grotto she turned for one last look at the chariot. Until now she had taken the chariot's beauty for granted. She had planned for it to be placed in her tomb for use in her next life, but realized now it was possible the cave would become her tomb.

She ran her hand over the golden dove that adorned the front of the chariot. A vision of the king handing her the reins of his gift flashed through her mind. The wings of the dove stretched around to the sides and caressed the golden image of Ishtar that was carved into the wooden side panels. Her fingers traced the symbols and she sighed. "Thank you, my husband," she said, then turned and broke into a trot, leading the horses from the lower chamber.

The flickering light from the small flame she carried danced off the cave walls. The shadows reflected an image in ragged garments but the light of the flame shone upon a royal visage and she thought, *I am still your teacher, Ninyas, and you have one more lesson to learn.*

Chapter 8

The Dove—Tongues of Hate

(Unknown location)

The trees surrounding the playground cast long tangled shadows across the dewy grass. The half moon's glow glanced off the cloud cover, allowing a few precious rays of moonlight through to mingle with the black of night. A cloaked figure floated along the mottled path. She liked the darkness. It was safe and she welcomed nightfall to her as if it were a living being, a warm companion.

Her black cloak made it easy for her to become part of the night and concealed her form from any casual observers. Her hair was tucked under the hood which was pulled forward to shadow her face. Under the deceptive garb she wore soft, flesh-colored silk slacks and shirt that clung to her body. She was part of the shadows around her and she mused at how shadows were like her lives, each different and unique, each taking on a new shape to meld with the environment. No one would ever guess how many lives she led.

She arrived at the rendezvous point on time. She frowned. Where could he be? Concealed beneath the branches of a giant olive tree, she stared at the outline of a statue. She had seen the statue before. Her eyes focused on the figures in the middle: children feeding birds. *Chil-*

dren? It was a question she chose not to answer, a painful memory that she forced out of her mind.

An RV pulled up to the curb near her. The interior of the van was dark, but she did not hesitate to enter when the side door opened. Once inside she did not speak, but followed a shadowy figure to the back of the moving vehicle. While she could not see his face, his strutting gait was very familiar. He opened a door at the rear of the mobile home and she entered the small traveling bedroom. The shades were drawn. The furnishings were cheap and ugly. She heard a click behind her and knew the door had been locked.

Her silk clothing rustled as she turned and faced the man in the room.

"Tariq," she spoke the name in a whisper. The promise of something sexual lingered in the silence. A soft smile touched her lips.

The masculine figure took a step closer. "Ah, my Dove," he said. "I have been too long away from you." He reached between the folds of her cloak, anxious to touch the breast just inches from his grasp. The eager look in his eyes sent a quiver of anticipation through her body but, at the last second, he merely fondled the image of a dove that hung from a heavy gold chain between her breasts. "Is this a lover's gift?"

"My lucky charm," she smiled and pulled from his grasp. "It is a token." She moved closer so that her body brushed against his.

He embraced her; his tenderness was a surprise. He pushed back her hood and stroked her hair. Then he helped her take off her cape.

"My Dove, how long can you stay?" Tariq guided her to

the bed and they sat down. An outsider looking in on their interaction would have wondered what game they were playing. But the intrigue of the sport and the trophy was what kept them engaged, one against the other. Their relationship was a concert in seduction and intrigue.

Her fingertips brushed down his cheek. The low rasping sounds of her nails across the black stubble on his face echoed in the silence before she answered. "We have all night, if you wish."

He moved toward her, anticipation in his eyes. She placed the palms of her hands against his broad chest to curb his lustful progress. "First, how is the boy?" She always called their child the boy. She used the term to remind her that she had no maternal ties to the adolescent.

Tariq sat on the edge of the bed, both hands on his knees, and spoke with a father's pride, his voice husky. "He is strong and very shrewd, like his father." He pointed to himself and sat ramrod straight, his chest puffed out.

Tariq was a block-shaped man and on the short side, but his frame expanded when he spoke of his son. He stared at his son's mother, his Dove, and deep furrows formed across his narrow forehead, linking his bushy eyebrows and hiding his unemotional brown eyes. His drooping coarse black mustache accentuated his cruel mouth. Soon he would once again dress in the uniform of the old guard, the same olive drab fatigues that he had worn when he was a soldier with Hussein. For this clandestine meeting, however, he was wearing jeans, a white T-shirt under a brown plaid, long-sleeved flannel shirt with the sleeves rolled up, and polished combat boots. His weapons were hidden under the shirt and in his boot. His short-cropped black hair made him look very military, even in blue jeans. His thick muscular forearms were covered with the same coarse black hair that protruded from the neck of his shirt. "My son will be a credit to me."

The Dove stared into nowhere, then she took his hand in hers. "We were never children. I am glad the boy has that chance."

Tariq stood, gesturing with his hands as he spoke. "Growing up in the camp was good training for us. My father did the right thing by sending me to the camp when I was a disrespectful teenager. The boy is getting similar training from me."

Tariq had been her first love and she had tried hard to overlook his verbal and physical abuse. After the birth of their son, Tariq insisted she return to the United States and to college. She had no model of how to be a good mother, but she remembered being hungry as a child and didn't want her son to suffer the pangs of starvation she had endured. So she had abandoned him to Tariq's family in Baghdad.

Right after graduate school, she had been summoned home. When she returned, she was a different person. Everything she had endured for fifteen years mingled and twisted her into the formidable woman she was today. Fluent in English, Arabic, various Kurdish dialects, Hebrew and French, she was proficient in hand-to-hand combat and had an extensive knowledge of small arms and explosives. Sophisticated and cultured, she could converse with anyone on a wide variety of disciplines, from science to literature. She had been one of the best of an elite group of Saddam's terrorists. The beatings, isolation, and abuse she endured as an orphan in Saddam's youth camp instilled a fear in her that no amount of time could erase, and so she always obeyed. Yet with her education and maturity came a realization of the power she possessed to control men, to be invincible to their lies and manipulation. She wondered if Tariq knew that she saw the real meanings behind his lies.

An anxious expression crossed her face. "You didn't tell him about me, did you, Tariq? Our enemies could use him against me and our plans."

"I have done as you wished. He doesn't even remember you." He sat back down next to her and held her hand. The soldier in him cautioned him not to let emotions interfere with his duty. They now walked separate paths. He liked the feeling of power and the surge of adrenaline and he wanted that power back. He had once been a friend to Hussein and he had prospered. Hussein's vision was the only thing dear to Tariq.

A united Arab nation, something Saddam had not accomplished, and the return of Iraq to the Ba'thist régime would be Tariq's greatest accomplishment. The woman sitting next to him had provided the means.

"Through some creative computer theft, I've recovered the funds I secreted away in France. It was enough to purchase all we will need to get things started." Tariq slipped his arms around her waist and kissed her earlobe.

"Stop." She stood, withholding favor from him as she paced back and forth in front of the bed. A trail of her perfume, Pink Jasmine, floated in the air. "My trip to Australia was successful." Tariq's eyes flashed. He leaned forward. She enjoyed watching his anticipation build and she paused before saying, "I delivered the package."

"Details, my love. Give me the details." He licked his large lips, his mustache glistened.

"After everyone was aboard the plane, the cabin crew would follow their usual routine of going through the cabin closing all the overhead doors. My little package had sticky tape on both sides so that the moment the overhead door was closed the package would stick to the door and the side of the compartment. The next time that overhead compartment was opened, the seams of the airtight packet would break open, dispersing virus all around the lucky passengers in and near seat 21B. Putting it in the large economy section will be a good test of dispersal. Because of the new air-handling structure with those HEPA filters in the air re-circulation system, we only had a chance for first encounter infectivity. I made sure there was over ten times the lethal dose of the virus in the packet, but we have no way to know how many passengers will pass through the virus cloud and be exposed to a lethal dose. Then, of course, there will be secondary infections among their loved ones."

This was what he wanted to know and the real reason for their meeting. A malicious, satisfied smile distorted his bristly mustache.

"I've set things in motion. The virus is our catalyst. The first insertion of the virus was extremely easy. It will be five to ten days after initial exposure before most primary cases turn up in the hospitals and then secondary cases will start sprouting up from those. We will erode their infrastructure and throw them into such chaos as to divert their eyes from the East," she took a deep breath. "Tariq, how close are you to having the location of Saddam's hidden stores of WMDs? I've got enough virus left for phase two. But, I will need more if we have to make good on our threat."

"Now that I have the money, it won't be long," said Tariq.

"Not good enough." The sweet music of her previous voice disappeared and a cold wind oozed from her mouth.

"Do something! The time to make our final move gallops toward us."

Tariq grabbed her shoulders. "It is within my reach," his hands massaged her arms. "Then those who betrayed us will pay, including those inspectors. I will have personalized gifts for many of them, especially Dr. Swift. He kept everyone searching and destroying precious stocks." His hands again tightened. "But be assured, I know they did not find all the storage facilities." He smiled and let his hands drop to his side.

"I remember," her face hardened. "Swift was with one of the UNSCOM teams. He was part of my assignment. I would also like to meet him again. But, you digress, Tariq. Are your troops ready? Do you have enough men with strong backs and weak minds? Soldiers ready to die? After all, that is their purpose and the weaker the mind the easier they are to manipulate."

Tariq savored the malice in her words. She was a vicious soldier. That was the part of her that had first attracted him. It aroused him. It was always her passion that excited him. He had never met anyone like her. There were so many different sides to this woman. *But,* he thought, *if I cannot control her, it will be as she has often said: "soldiers die, that is their purpose."*

He turned her to face him, then guided her back to sit on the side of the bed. He sat down next to her, his bulk making the bed sag and screech in protest.

"These are the locations for the next virus insertions," Tariq unfolded a map and spread it out on top of the cheap bedspread. He pointed out their choices, five yellow circles on the map. Even this was a turn-on for him tonight. He watched her full lips as she spoke. They were still moist from the passion of her previous tirade.

"I have agents working at all these places." She agreed with his choices. "They will deliver the packages."

"You are my scientific specialist in this matter. I leave that part of the operation in your competent hands," he stroked her ego and body at the same time.

"The virus will be delivered two weeks from today," the Dove stabbed a finger at each city on the map for emphasis. "As usual, the packages will be postmarked from Israel." She relaxed and moved into him, her silk-covered body slid tantalizingly against his.

She was very excited, even though—or perhaps, because—she did not trust him. Once she delivered the last of the virus in her possession, she knew he would make his move to eliminate her. This game was dangerous, but she was an excellent player.

"Come to me," he said as he lay back on the bed. His words were warm and alluring, but the cruelty still twisted his smile.

She closed the gap between them and put her arms around his neck. He responded by kissing her lips. She pulled him to her and slid beneath him.

Their lovemaking accelerated. His hands were more gentle than usual. Tariq was amazed and confused by the unusual fervor in her response, but he was ready to take advantage of the dreamy look in her eyes. His ego told him he was the man in her dream. When he was finished, Tariq left her lying on the bed. As he closed the door, he saw her smile and stretch out her naked body and caress the pillow. Tariq grinned, thinking of the effect he had on his Dove.

And, indeed, the Dove continued to enjoy her dream—but it was not Tariq's face she saw.

Chapter 9

London, England—Gog and Magog

During the crossing, Matt went over in his mind again and again the last time he had seen his mother: she'd been healthy and so full of life. The image of her in a critical care unit was unacceptable to the physician in him. *I know she's eighty-five years old and sometimes illness comes unexpectedly to the elderly but this doesn't make sense.* He tried to calm himself by meditating and eventually drifted into a broken sleep.

The captain's voice over the plane's intercom roused his fitful slumber. "Prepare the cabin for arrival."

Matt looked over at Wayne. "Thanks," he said.

"No problem," Wayne replied.

After collecting their luggage, Matt and Wayne exited through the Nothing-to-Declare green lane of British Customs and into the mob of relatives and commercial drivers seeking their fares.

Wayne spotted Olivia before Matt did and thought to himself, *My god she looks terrible.* Her hair had been neglected and her clothes were crumpled as though she had slept in them. Her slim frame looked even smaller than usual. He waved in her direction and she waved back. Wayne gave her a quick hug and pecks on both cheeks and then Matt took Olivia into his arms. She tried to control her emotions. As Matt held her, though, that resolve melted and she began to cry, hiding her face in her husband's shoulder. Matt's eyes also filled with tears.

When they pulled apart, Matt put a reassuring arm around Olivia's shoulder and kept it there as they moved off to the car. On the drive to the hospital, Matt turned to Olivia and, struggling to keep his voice steady, asked exactly what had happened.

"Martha called me three days ago and said she hadn't been feeling well for a couple of days and that she thought she had the flu. I went over to take her to the doctor. When I got to her apartment, she didn't answer the door. I used my key and found her on the bathroom floor, unconscious. She came around in a few moments. I'd already called an ambulance. When they came, one of the ambulance men asked if she was an epileptic because she appeared to have had a seizure. I told them that she wasn't." Olivia dabbed at her moist eyes.

"Go on, dear," said Matt.

"Dr. Hartford, at the clinic she frequents, had her taken to King's. He managed to find a consultant at the hospital who listened to his plea that she be admitted for observation. He said it was not serious—just the flu—but he wanted to be sure because of her age and the potential for head trauma after her unobserved fall. Martha was actually in good spirits and didn't want the fuss. Then they called yesterday, around two in the morning, saying her condition had deteriorated. Matt, I would have called you when she first became ill, but she insisted I should not bother you because she'd be back to herself in no time. I'm so sorry I didn't call sooner."

"Olivia, don't blame yourself. I'm sure she expected to be on the mend, just as she said." Matt patted Olivia's hand.

Olivia felt relieved now that Matt was home. He wouldn't let anything happen to Martha.

"If you don't mind, Matt..." Wayne indicated that he wanted to ask Olivia a few questions.

Matt was grateful his friend was with them. He needed someone with a clear mind, someone he could trust to ask the right questions and think of alternative diagnoses. He was too personally involved to think objectively.

"This is very difficult for you, Olivia. I know how much you love Martha," Wayne smiled warmly before he went on, "have they done a CAT scan or EEG? Did they mention if they had done a lumbar puncture?"

"Yes, all of those and some others but I don't know what the results are. I'm sorry. I should have mentioned the tests." Olivia pulled her shaking hands through her hair nervously as she tried to remember all the tests the doctor had rattled off.

As they entered the hospital parking garage, Matt felt an urgency to get to Martha quickly. The nurse in the intensive care ward recognized Dr. Rogers as he burst out of the elevator. She hurried to catch up to him before he entered the empty room that had been Martha's, but Matt's long strides took him to his mother's room first.

Matt's heart sank when he saw the empty bed. He was too late. He fell back against the doorframe with a thud. When Wayne and Olivia caught up to him they too stood frozen in their steps next to Matt.

The nurse hurried in. "Please don't be alarmed, Dr. Rogers. They've moved Mrs. Rogers to the isolation unit on the fourth floor."

Olivia thanked the nurse as she and Wayne again hurried to catch up with Matt.

Impatient, Matt wouldn't wait for the elevator and ran to the stairs. He had an eerie feeling that if he didn't get to his mother's bedside soon he would not see her alive.

He took the steel gray steps three at a time and burst onto the infectious disease ward on the fourth floor just as Wayne and Olivia were exiting the elevator. All heads turned and looked at Matt. The foreboding sterile atmosphere was made even more dismal by the look on the faces that greeted them. The unit head, Dr. Williams, and Martha's clinic physician, Dr. Hartford, stepped forward. Matt dabbed clammy perspiration from his face as he hastily introduced Wayne to his associates. "Where is she?" he asked.

"Please come this way," Dr. Hartford said, escorting them to a colorless observation area next to Martha's room.

Matt stared at the pale woman beneath the stiff white sheets. His mother looked so very small and vulnerable. An assortment of various colored wires connected her to an array of beeping equipment. Tubes in her nose and rectum traveled across the starched sheets to deposit blackened fluid into plastic pouches at the bedside. Both arms had IVs running, one with clear fluid and the other with a fresh supply of blood. Martha stirred and tried to smile when she saw her worried son behind the window. The fingers on her left hand lifted slightly in a feeble attempt to wave.

Matt knew she recognized him by the smile in her eyes. When he was a small boy and did something devilish, she would put her hand under his chin and tilt his head up to her face. "Matthew," she'd say, "you're the smile in your mother's eyes." He hoped she could see the love in his eyes now through the tears.

On the inside, Matt was horrified by his mother's condition. He had paled when he first saw her and it took him a moment to compose himself. She was much worse than he could have ever imagined. "I will see my mother first, and then we can discuss her case," he said in a shaky voice to the doctors.

The ominous whoosh of air as he released the handle and entered the prep room magnified his fears. When he helped design these suites, he never expected to see a member of his own family in them.

After securing the door to the airlock, he jumped into the waiting isolation suit and attached his air hose to the outlet near the door.

King's was one of the few hospitals in London that had such isolation suites. This room was at biological safety level IV, the highest level of containment. Negative pressure inside the room created an inward pull like a vacuum for clean air to be sucked into the room, preventing infected air from escaping. All the air from the room itself passed out through HEPA filters that trapped even the smallest microbe. Since access to the room took so long, it was equipped with the latest equipment in medical technology for bedside care. Physicians could do major surgery, laboratory studies, and radiological studies within this containment area. Results were displayed on monitors and, along with room video, could be transmitted anywhere in the hospital or to any of the 120 consultants on-call worldwide to help manage these types of patients. The system had been government-funded after the U.S. and French anthrax scares during the Bin Laden-Hussein reigns of world terrorism.

Matt took a deep and controlled breath, then let it out, trying to still his rapidly beating heart and limit the condensation that typically formed on the inside of the face shield of the suit. All of this technology gave him no comfort in caring for patients or, now, visiting his mother. The protective suit took away the sense of touch—so important to the art of medicine—and to feeling close to his mother. Nevertheless, he shuffled over to his mother and sat down beside her bed.

He noticed the dark red, almost black, blood coming out of the nasogastric tube and draining into a container on the floor beside the bed. The EKG monitor confirmed the irregular rhythm and very fast heart rate. He could see she was struggling for every breath, even with the oxygen mask over her mouth and nose. He was intensely aware of his mother's pain and discomfort; it seemed to fill the air. Yet, she sustained a loving smile for her anxious son. She had numerous red lesions over her exposed arms. Matt knew similar lesions covered her entire body. The bleeding under the skin was a sign of deeper hemorrhage, but from where? Olivia's description of a possible seizure clearly indicated meningitis, but this rash was not the rash of epidemic meningococcus, the most common form of meningitis that had devastated Britain before the new vaccines had been introduced. Besides, Martha had received those vaccines less than a year ago.

Matt cleared his mind of medical matters. He knew too much and he simply couldn't be the savior-physician, for it meant that he had to turn off his deep love for his mother and he had no clue where that switch was hidden, if it existed at all.

Like most mothers, Martha knew what her son was feeling. It took all her strength to hold Matt's oversized double-gloved hand. "Matthew, the time has come...for me...to join your father." Martha fought for oxygen, her breath coming in shallow gasps. "Don't blame yourself...for not being able to save me. If you want...responsibility for anything...let it be for the joy in my life.... Please, remember...you, Olivia and the boys...have given me so much love...and I love..." she gasped, "I love you all...but it's time to let me go."

Matt broke down and laid his head on the bed. From just this few minutes with his mother, seeing her life draining away into the collection of plastic containers surrounding her, he knew she was right. He was helpless to save her. Martha laid her hand on the helmet covering his head and gently patted him.

Wayne and Olivia watched through the Plexiglas barrier as the emotionally charged scene inside Martha's room settled in their hearts. Wayne turned away, tears in his eyes. He felt he was intruding on a private moment. Tears streaming down her face, Olivia closed the curtain covering the observation window and turned off the intercom.

Wayne needed to do something, anything. He decided that he would find answers to some of the questions Matt would be asking later. Wayne went in search of the doctors he'd met on his arrival—Hartford and Williams—and found them at the charting area in the nurses' station. He told them a little of his background as a medical doctor and microbiologist, so they could relate details to him in medical terms without the translations necessary for lay people. They'd heard of his unique field—biocriminology —and were relieved to have such an expert on hand.

Dr. Hartford suggested that one of the nurses give Wayne Martha's electronic chart to review. The two doctors admitted that they were baffled and worried because now they had two more cases with similar presentation in adjoining isolation rooms. Dr. Williams had contacted London's public health department and alerted other consultants through the EPIdemic-Support and Technical Operations Program network, or EPI-STOP as the doctors called it among themselves. Ironically, Wayne was part of EPI-STOP and he was sure a message was waiting for him back in New Mexico.

Dr. Williams noted that all of this had happened so fast. Now, with a total of three cases, his team was at alert level omega, one stage below alpha. If the situation worsened and was given the alpha designation, the government would open Emergency Preparedness and Management System headquarters and begin citywide quarantine procedures.

Wayne clicked onto the chart's DDX icon, to review the differential diagnosis: viral meningitis was coded in red as the primary diagnosis with intracranial lesions, subdural empyema and effusion, intracranial neoplasm, brain abscess and vascular lesions coded in shades of yellow as lesser diagnoses. As Wayne clicked on each diagnosis, relevant images from CT and MRI scans, X-ray, and microthermal and cytokine imaging appeared on the right side of the split screen with running text of the radiologist's notes and live chat room comments from EPI-STOP. While the data would have been confusing to a lay person, to Wayne it was as familiar as a stock broker reading the tickers on the cable business network. Wayne did not bother turning the audio stream on as he found this function disrupted his own thought processes. In spite of the physical bruises and scrapes he had suffered in the cave and the unseen impact of sleep deprivation during the frantic trip from New Mexico, Wayne was in full mode as the biocriminologist, a unique hybridization that made him an international commodity. He reviewed the many layers of the chart, noting that the obvious alternatives had been ruled out by the various scans.

Wayne's scanning stopped. *Hold on, what do we have here?* The trackball mouse was awkward and he cursed the old technology. He had grown used to the homegrown, voice-interactive system a friend's son, Mike, had installed. *Here they are: complement fixation, hemagglutination inhibition and antibody titers on the blood icon submenu. Damn it, no results yet. Why not? Not another chip problem? These are two mysteries too many. I wonder what the CDC serology gurus are thinking.* They were asking Wayne the same question by e-mail and his silence was as much a concern to them as the lack of data.

Wayne prepared to bring up the chat room index and sort by the keyword *serology* when a nurse interrupted him, telling him that Olivia was asking for him. The cursor blinked, waiting for Wayne to provide further instructions and he glanced up at the clock, noticing that he had been reviewing Martha's chart for over ninety minutes.

Cursing himself for leaving Olivia alone for so long, he hurried to her. He knew the moment he saw her that Martha was gone. Wayne had never been part of this kind of family scene of mourning before and, when he walked into the observation room, his lungs instantly constricted as if he had breathed in all the pain and grief saturating the air. He held his arms out to Olivia. She clung to him, her sobbing almost out of control. Wayne glanced at the monitors and heard vital sign alarms blaring inside Martha's room.

Wayne coughed to clear the lump in his throat. He looked past Olivia and into Martha's room. "What is Matt doing?" he asked.

"The heart monitor straight-lined over five minutes ago, but he hasn't moved. He *must* hear those hideous alarms, but he hasn't budged from her side," Olivia dabbed at her eyes and nose and walked around Wayne to stare at her husband. "I tried to talk to him over the intercom, but he acts like he doesn't hear me."

Wayne pushed the talk button on the intercom. "Matt?"

There was no sign that Matt heard him. He had his head resting on his mother's chest, her hand clasped tightly in his. "Matt," Wayne said softly, "say goodbye. Let her go." Martha's pale lifeless hand slid from Matt's grasp.

Wayne heard Matt's lament through his helmet microphone. "'They may kill the body but not the soul. Come to me and you will find rest for your soul.'"

Wayne looked curiously at Olivia. "It's a Bible verse," she explained. "Martha read it at Matt's father's funeral."

Matt raised his head, stood and, as if in a daze, turned off the blaring monitor alarms. He reached down and touched his mother's face and then gazed over at the observation window. He saw his own hollow reflection looking back from the polished glass. He just stood there with a blank expression, staring and then his sunken eyes turned cold. Anger for this senseless death began to creep into the restrictions of his containment suit.

Olivia walked forward and placed her hand on the window. Matt finally came out of his trance when he saw Olivia's hand reach out to him and touch the window. Her hand was on his heart in the mirrored reflection. Matt mouthed the words, "I love you." Tears streamed down Olivia's face.

Matt shook off his grief but, when he spoke, there was steel in his voice. "I'll be right out. Let me shower and change. Don't move her yet. Wayne, we need to talk."

Olivia knew her husband. His response to stress was to face it head on. That was what he was doing now: the physician had questions and would demand answers. He would use every possible means to find the reason for Martha's mysterious illness and untimely death.

His hair still wet from the shower room, Matt exited the isolation unit in blue surgical scrubs and went straight to Olivia. They went into the deserted waiting area, its stiff gray plastic chairs were not very inviting, but the space provided them with some much needed privacy. They held each other and talked for about fifteen minutes. When Matt came out, he was composed. "Wayne, I'm going to take Olivia home. Then I'll be back with some questions."

"I'm working on some answers," Wayne said. "When you're ready, I've set up a meeting with the physicians and someone from London's public health department."

Eight days later the medical and public health teams knew no more about the mysterious illness that had thus far taken three lives than they had when they started their investigation. Four more cases were admitted shortly after Martha and then things quieted down. With no new cases in the last five days everyone relaxed with the exception of Matt and Wayne.

Returning from Martha's memorial service, Wayne took off his borrowed jacket and tie and sat down at the walnut dining room table in Matt's South Kensington home. With his elbows on the table and his head resting in his hands waves of sorrow mixed with happy memories flashed through his mind. It had been difficult for him to say good-bye to Martha. More difficult still to see the pain her passing had caused his friend.

He thought about Miryam and, to stave off another bout of tears, got up and walked to the window. It didn't help. Different location but the same grief returned. He stared into space. The weather matched his mood, dreary. Olivia came into the room with a tray of hot coffee and sandwiches. Wayne didn't noticed until the rich smell reached him. He thanked her with a brief hug and sat down to pour himself a cup of the steaming black brew.

Olivia called to Matt, who was in the living room with their sons. "Coffee and sandwiches are in the dining room. Can I do anything for you before I make something for the children?"

Matt's bloodshot eyes looked from the sad faces of his sons toward the dining room. "No thanks, luv."

With a long sigh, Wayne let some of his own tension drain away. He knew the worst was yet to come. He took a deep breath. The past few days had been hectic. It had taken all of Matt's influence to get his mother's body released for cremation so they could finally put her to rest. Wayne and Matt had met several times with local health officials and, via webcast, with EPI-STOP infectious disease specialists. All the meetings were about the same thing: to review the possible cause of Martha's death. Dr. Theodore Davies, one of the patients whose symptoms were similar to Martha's, had died that morning and the other three were not expected to live. The hospital had done an excellent job with the press. If the cause of this illness was what Wayne thought, keeping a tight seal on information would continue to be essential.

Matt walked into the dining room, his head and shoulders drooping from physical and emotional fatigue. Shadows hung under his eyes and in the hollows of his cheeks. Olivia and Wayne were in quiet conversation when Matt joined them. Exhaling, he removed his black suit jacket and draped it over one of the chairs. He fidgeted, straightening his jacket before he sat down opposite Wayne. He smiled at his wife. "If you don't mind, Olivia, I need to go over a few things with Wayne. Would you keep the kids out of our hair?"

"Of course," she said. "Call if you need me." Olivia kissed her husband lightly on the cheek as she got up and left the room.

Matt turned to Wayne. "I'm glad the funeral is over. If one more person had said to me, 'now you can have some closure,' I'd have punched them in the mouth." Matt glared at the silver tray, picked up a sandwich, decided he wasn't hungry, and slapped it back down. He walked to the kitchen and returned with a couple of glasses of stout. He sat down and slid one across the table to Wayne. Matt took a long drink and sank lower into his chair, stretching out his long legs under the table. He looked from his drink to Wayne and then pulled a letter from the pocket of his trousers. He handed it across to Wayne. "My mother is still surprising me. I received this letter in the morning post. Read it aloud, I don't know quite what to make of it."

Wayne unfolded the letter and read: "Dear Dr. and Mrs. Rogers, I don't wish to intrude during this time of mourning but I must tell you what your mother did for me and my son. Although I did not spend a lot of time with your mother, her warmth and compassion touched me." Wayne paused and looked up at Matt. "This is incredible," he said before continuing. "She watched my son and me board the plane in Australia and noticed how tired and uncomfortable we were. I am also pregnant and this likely made me appear even more uncomfortable. She did the most remarkable thing. Perhaps you were not aware that your mother gave my son and me her seat in the first class section of the plane? As I sat in that seat on the way to our new home, I was encouraged, thinking I had made my first new friend. I was very sad to read of her death. I would like her family to know that her kindness touched me deeply and I hope that hearing this will, in some way, comfort you and your family."

Wayne's brows rose as if he was remembering some special moment. He smiled. "Martha was a special lady, Matt." Wayne handed the letter back, wondering if this was the right time to tell Matt what else that letter meant. He decided to go ahead. "If my theory is correct, she may have done more for that family than they will ever know."

Matt wiped his eyes with a handkerchief from his back pocket. He was puzzled by Wayne's comment. "You want to bring me up to speed on what is going on in that strange mind of yours? And you can start by explaining that last remark."

"I've been trying to find a common link between your mother, Dr. Davies and the others who've been taken ill. Until now, the single thing all the victims had in common was that they had been in Australia at the same time, or at least left at the same time. They all walked through the same airport and flew on the same airplane when they departed. I researched all of the places they'd visited to exclude mosquito or tick contact. Nothing matched except that Dr. Davies and the other victims sat near each other on the plane. The passenger list had your mother in first class. Until now I'd crossed the plane off my list because she didn't sit near them and there were no secondary cases in first class. But ... after reading that letter," Wayne leaned forward, "I'd bet the farm that Martha was seated near the other victims and they were all exposed to the virus on the plane. By the way, I talked further with Kathleen Daly, London's public heath officer. She sent the additional tissue samples to CDC in the States and they are giving them the highest priority."

Matt was caught up in the conversation, nodding as he followed the logic of Wayne's words.

"The first tissue samples have come back with a preliminary ID consistent with an arbovirus. They're trying to match the RNA analysis with the strain collection at CDC and cross-referencing with the American Type Culture Collection in Manassas. They are, however, certain it is an arbovirus. I had a hunch it was arbo from some of Martha's symptoms. Matt," Wayne hesitated, then seemed to push forward, "I know we haven't had this kind of conversation in a long time, but Martha wasn't anywhere near the arboviruses that circulate in Australia and she didn't have the classic joint pains. Also, what I'm reading in the CDC data is that the RNA sequences look like they've been tampered with. Matt, I think your mother was the victim of a combination of biological agents deliberately planted on that plane."

Matt's mouth fell open. "Are you saying this was a biological attack? So who are they after? Me? One of the other passengers?" Matt was silent for a moment thinking. "My God, do you think it's my family?" Matt sprang to his feet. "The kind of enemies I've made would find this appropriate payback." He bent forward with both hands on the table, poised for action.

"Martha's death was an accident," Wayne said in a calming voice. "Remember? She changed seats. No one would know that in advance. Unless the criminals were on the plane to directly infect her, the collateral cases would have been in the first class section, not coach. Relax, focus ... you're the virologist. I could use some help."

"Give me the rest of it. But..." Matt waited.

"But... I am thinking this was a terrorist attack," Wayne looked at Matt intently.

Matt paced up and down the carpet, occasionally rubbing his forehead as if to stimulate his brain. "I know where you're going. Why haven't the terrorists taken credit? The government hasn't received any claims of responsibility or I would have been the first to know."

Wayne walked to the dining room window and stared out at the wet pavement and the flowers beginning to bud in the window boxes along the street heralding spring's late emergence.

"Wayne, what is it?" prompted Matt.

"I was naive to think we'd abolished biological weapons. My lack of vigilance and foolishness may have given our adversaries time to develop even more virulent weapons." Wayne's face paled and in a trancelike voice he quoted, "'Satan will be released from his prison, and will go out to deceive the nations in the four corners of the earth, Gog and Magog, to gather them for battle.'"

Matt was perplexed for a moment. "Revelation," he said at length. He walked over to stand near Wayne. "Why were so few infected? Why haven't we seen secondary cases? It would be stupid for a terrorist not to take advantage of the opportunity to kill more people. Do you think they didn't have much virus? That would be too much to hope for."

Still deep in thought, Wayne replied, "Maybe it was a test run. Maybe the HEPA systems on the plane really *did* work. I just don't have enough information." Wayne's mood then lightened as he turned to Matt, "Your next step, my friend, is to take care of your wife and kids while I do my Sherlock Holmes' impersonation, starting with the plane."

"Wayne, if the plane was used to disseminate the virus, don't you think it's a little dangerous to return to the scene of the crime? Let the bio-response team do it," suggested Matt.

"What bio-response team? Have you forgotten the world is free from this type of threat? The U.S. has a token response team that used to be part of the FBI but has been staffed by CDC personnel for the last three years. You and I and damn few others, except Rich and Miryam, are the only old dogs left who've seen and have direct knowledge of this type of disaster medicine. I talked to your infectious disease institute and they're willing to furnish me bio gear. We were lucky. The plane was taken in for maintenance right after its return to base at Heathrow. With Dr. Daly's help, it's been quarantined. But, if I'm right about the plane, then we could see more victims before this is really over."

Matt rubbed his chin, trying to digest everything, and was thankful his mind and heart were occupied with something other than grieving. "It's damn curious that there haven't been more people admitted."

"It could be a weak agent or something rapidly inactivated it," Wayne said, thinking out loud.

"Listen," Matt said, "Martha may have been a bit old, but her immune system was strong. This was no weak, half-baked agent. It had to be potent stuff. It came on too fast. It was made to be lethal." Matt shifted focus and continued, "As you've pointed out, I'm one of the old dogs, so I'll be tagging along to help with the plane investigation." Matt rubbed the back of his neck, "I take any attack on my family very personally and I want the head of the one responsible stuck on a pole outside my door." It was the most bitter tone Wayne had ever heard from his friend. Matt sounded calmer when he added, "besides, I know more about vaccines and delivery systems than you do, remember?"

"Revenge can get in the way of finding the truth, my friend. I'm glad to have you along, but be careful your emotions don't get in the way. I'm hoping for a natural culprit, but I think it's unlikely. If I'm right—that this is a genetically engineered infectious agent—chaos is exactly what the people responsible for this attack are hoping for. We have to play this close to our vests and pray that the media doesn't get wind of our investigation. I'm thinking of looking up the rest of our old UNSCOM team in case we need reinforcements. We can count on Miryam, but I don't know where Rich is or how to get in touch with him. He's one of the best tech agents the CIA ever had; we were lucky to hook up with him on our first inspection trip to Iraq. His experience on the Hazmat Response Unit, combined with his engineering skill with explosive devices, would be invaluable. Remember how he used the Iraqi's own explosives to destroy the Al Hakam anthrax facility?" Wayne laughed, "it was beautiful."

Matt had never accepted Richard's roughshod methods. "I don't know if we'll need Blitz. He's so… I don't know, unpredictable. When in doubt he blows things up. I also remember when they wouldn't let us into the Al Manal facility because the officer with the keys couldn't be found? He blew the damn door off the hinges! We didn't make any friends *that* day."

"Oh, come on, Matt, we all thought that was great. He was just responding to another one of their delaying tactics. We'd heard that excuse a hundred times. And after he blew up the door, we never heard that excuse again, did we? I know what bothers you: his dress code."

"He doesn't have one," Matt smiled despite himself.

"Yes he does," corrected Wayne. "It's jeans and Harley T-shirts. Who cares? He's the best and we may need him."

Matt had to agree that Rich *was* the best. He gave Wayne the last number he'd used to contact him. "I think he's still in northern Iraq with the Kurds...spy stuff. Whoever answers the phone will know where to find him."

Chapter 10

Washington, D.C. – Service

April 13th – Wayne and Matt were quiet during the flight to Washington via JFK International Airport. It was amazing how fast the State Department had tracked Wayne to Matt's home and summoned him to the White House. Minutes after Wayne's call, Matt received a similar request from Britain's Prime Minister to join his colleague on the trip to Washington.

Wayne knew the PM was pleased that the investigation into the mysterious deaths was being moved off his turf. The cover story in the London papers describing the illness as food poisoning was holding up, but the PM worried about leaks to the press.

For the two of them to have been called, it was obvious that the United States had its own reasons for being interested in seeing this potential terrorist event sorted out as soon as possible. So far, no one had said what those reasons were. But one thing was sure: if the President of the United States called such a hurried and surreptitious meeting, it had to mean that the nightmare had indeed begun again.

Wayne had a magnificent view of the Washington Monument as their plane passed nearby on its approach to Reagan National Airport. Being at the hub of vital operations in his country's government was something special for him, although he felt embarrassed by his feelings of pride and patriotism. He could never understand why he felt like waving the flag when he visited Washington, but the same feeling came over him every time.

In silence, the pair left the plane. As they walked side by side, Wayne glanced at his friend and saw the deep lines of sorrow etched on Matt's face. *Martha, Martha. It will be a long grieving period for us all.* Wayne cleared his throat and fought to focus on the reason for their trip in an effort to regain control of his emotions.

The moment they left the shelter of the terminal they were assailed by the oppressive humidity of an abnormal spring heat wave. In their rush to get to their hotel and still have time for a quick shower before their meeting, Wayne and Matt grabbed the first cab available. As they drove along the Potomac basin, they realized their taxi was not air-conditioned and the interior temperature was in the high nineties.

The driver talked nonstop. "This is unusual weather. All of a sudden, bam, it's hot. Happened overnight. Maybe something to do with that global warming stuff, I don't know. Is this your first time in D.C.? Are you guys lucky. This warm weather forces the cherry trees to bloom. You've gotta see that! They just pop open overnight. It's a beautiful thing."

Wayne ignored the cab driver and stared out the window. The cab passed the east lawn of the White House. Wayne watched the tourists straining to see the home of the president. Many held to the fence and just stood there staring. Wayne wondered if they thought the edifice held some mystical power that might radiate out to them.

The cab stopped unceremoniously in front of their hotel and both men lurched forward. The driver stuck his hand out the window for his fare and had the car in drive almost before Wayne and Matt had a chance to grab their belongings and exit the cab. Both men were exhausted, grumpy and drenched in sweat as they trudged up to the reception desk at the Carlton Hotel. Wayne carried a backpack slung over his shoulder, while Matt had a small suitcase with a couple of changes of clothes. Not just the employees of the Carlton but guests passing by gawked at their scruffy and wrinkled appearance.

After registering, they rushed up to their rooms to shower and change shirts. In thirty-five minutes they were back in the lobby and opted to walk to their meeting because the afternoon traffic would make them late if they took a cab.

The shower and air conditioning had finally brought Matt out of his sullen mood and, as they walked down L Street, he asked "What kind of man is the president? I came here to get answers, not to play politics."

Wayne quickened their pace. Even in the heat, it felt good to be exercising after the cramped six hour flight to New York and one hour flight to DC. He was concerned about Matt's mood. Even though he had confidence in his friend's abilities, with the death of his mother, diplomacy was not going to be Matt's strong suit. "I've never met the president," said Wayne. "I think, like most events in Washington, this one will start late and I'll have a chance to at least dry out in an air-conditioned hallway somewhere while we wait our turn to say our piece."

"I didn't abandon my grieving family and come all this way to sit in a hallway." Matt began to walk even faster. As they turned onto Pennsylvania Avenue he pulled ahead of Wayne.

"This isn't a race, my friend," said Wayne. "And, why aren't you sweating? How do you always come off looking so pressed?"

Matt smiled and let some of the tension he was carrying dissolve. "It's my James Bond method of packing. You know Bond could cross the ocean hanging from the bottom of a plane and when you see him next his tuxedo doesn't have a wrinkle. It's all in the packing, old chum."

As they drew closer to the barricaded portion of Pennsylvania Avenue on the west side of the White House, near the back gate, they heard a stream of chanting voices. When they rounded the corner they were surprised to see a large group of poster-carrying demonstrators. The posters read "NO U.S. $$ for aid to Iraq," and "Iraq will stab us in the back like Japan." A large circle of protesters marched and chanted as the television cameras recorded every shout and song.

"How long has this been going on?" Matt asked.

"I don't know. I've been out of circulation. No TV at the farm. The last I heard they were debating a bill to send more financial aid to Iraq," said Wayne. "I guess it passed."

"It's the same in Britain," Matt replied.

"Some think it would be another fiasco like the reparations to Japan after WWII. You know that later, those we helped come back and charge us exorbitant prices for the technology we gave them." Wayne smiled, "Personally, whatever the politicians decide won't make a difference in my life. I worry about the Americans who don't and will never trust the Iraqi people because of the bloody Ba'thist. They could mess up all the good will our soldiers created when they were in Iraq. Saddam in particular left a bad taste in the mouths of Americans. Unfortunately, many Americans lump all Iraqis in the same basket with their former dictator."

They walked up to the security gate and identified themselves to a very cordial guard. "You gentlemen are expected," the guard said after the formalities were dealt with. "This is your escort."

A husky Secret Service agent appeared and looked them up and down, then, his square jawed face devoid of expression, he introduced himself. "I'm Agent Letterman. Please follow me."

Wayne and Matt stifled their smiles. "Excuse me Agent Letterman," Wayne asked, "how long have these demonstrations had been going on?"

"Since Congress voted to send more financial aid to Iraq three weeks ago. It's getting worse every day. Some of the newspaper articles are worse than the demonstrators."

"What do you think about all this?" Wayne asked.

"I have no opinion, Sir," the agent said without cracking his stern facial veneer.

"I don't think I've ever met anyone who had no opinion," Matt whispered to Wayne as they followed behind their FBI agent. "So much for your country's famous freedom of speech thing." They laughed, but discreetly.

Dropping back a few paces behind their escort Matt asked, "Do you think he's a relative of that amusing David Lettermen on American television?"

Wayne smiled. "The Secret Service takes guarding the president seriously. Any attempt at jocularity will probably be lost on this guy. Tread lightly, Matt."

"The man doesn't have a sense of humor, that's all I'm attempting to point out. And you Americans talk about our dry British humor. At least we have one. Perhaps these Secret Service blokes have their humor genes removed when they join up."

"Remember, 'Humor is odd, grotesque, and wild, Only by affection spoiled; Tis never by invention got, Men have it when they know it not,'" quoted Wayne.

"I give up. Who said that?"

"Swift," Wayne answered.

"Bloody hell," chided Matt. "So, now you're a poet?"

"No. Jonathan Swift is the poet."

They followed Letterman through a back entrance and down a narrow corridor that opened to a wider hall with worn red carpeting. They walked past several closed doors and came to a halt in front of an unmarked door.

"We must be the poor relatives coming in the back door," whispered Wayne out of the side of his mouth.

The agent indicated that they should prepare for the customary search and scan for weapons. They were annoyed, since this was their second such search.

"By the way, Mr. Letterman is indeed a member of my family. However, no one has yet found a genetic link for humor," said their secret service escort as he finished.

At last the agent stepped to the side and motioned for Wayne and Matt to join another agent who escorted them into an elevator. It opened into a more luxurious area and they found themselves outside a heavy ornate door.

"Gentlemen, please go right in. They are waiting for you," said the agent.

Wayne and Matt looked at each other, awed. Their feet felt frozen to the carpet. They were bewildered, wondering who "they" were. Neither man had really expected to meet the president: just a middleman who would later fill in someone else who would boil down the final version for the president. Were they really standing in front of the Oval Office? It looked an awful lot like it, if the movies were correct. Wayne was not totally ready to meet the president. His usual bravado melted away as seconds elapsed, barely enough time for both men to compose themselves and surreptitiously wipe their sweaty palms on the legs of their pants.

"Well, old boy, since he's your president, you go in first."

Wayne opened the door and entered the Oval Office, Matt followed a few steps behind. All conversation stopped and they felt like intruders as heads swiveled in their direction.

President Salinski rose from his chair and everyone else followed suit.

"Ladies and gentlemen, now that our stars have arrived, it seems our number has outgrown the Oval Office." The most powerful man in the world shot a scowl at the director of the CIA and his operations director, who had both brought too many aides.

"Let us adjourn to a larger conference room," the president's chief of staff, the scrutinized Thomas Yamoto, the first of Japanese descent to occupy a position on a president's staff, whispered in the president's ear and then motioned for the president to lead the way. Wayne and Matt were still standing just inside the door, staring as the president and the others in the room filed past them. After the Oval Office had emptied, they followed the crowd down the hall.

"I guess we know the answer to at least one of our questions," Wayne whispered.

Matt looked over his shoulder at Wayne, puzzled.

"The president called us stars. At least someone around here has a sense of humor."

Wayne and Matt were the last to enter the large plush conference room. They waited until everyone was seated and then took the chairs in the back of the room against the wall, trying to be invisible. Wayne took a deep breath and looked around the room. He noticed that he was the only one not wearing a tie.

While they waited for the president to start the meeting, Wayne identified the people in the room for Matt.

Around the table sat some of the most influential people in Washington, all part of the president's inner circle. First was Vice-President Ivy Martingale, a plump, five-foot two-inch woman who looked decidedly jolly. She was in her mid-fifties and her rosy cheeks accentuated her black hair dappled with white, pulled back into a cluster of curls at the nape of her neck. She was the American version of Golda Meir: tough love was her modus operandi.

Next to her sat Attorney General Howard Aminson, a short, overweight bald man who looked a couple of decades older than his forty-seven years. His belly bumped the side of the conference table as he leaned back to give his assistant some files. Wayne could see the perspiration glisten on the back of his hands as he extracted a white handkerchief from his breast pocket and dabbed at his dripping forehead. Wayne seemed to be the only person in the room who found Aminson's incessant fidgeting distracting.

Secretary of Defense Joshua Acker; Secretary of State Jose' Alveriz, and Chairman of the Joint Chiefs of Staff Tony DeMarco, huddled together at one end of the table, a low hum emanating from their whispering circle. The director of the CIA and his aides sat behind the group and generated their own buzz. To Wayne it looked as if their main function was to exchange numerous pieces of paper.

The national security advisor, Pearl Sugarhill, was the matriarch of the group and the last to arrive. She went straight over to the president and whispered in his ear. He responded with a faint elevation of his thin brown eyebrows, but his square tan face gave no clue to the nature of their exchange. Pearl had served two other presidents, but in different capacities. Ex-Navy, she had strong opinions that guided her political party. When she spoke, people listened. Wayne thought she looked like someone's favorite Aunt Bessie in her frilly lilac-flowered dress and matching lilac shoes, but he had heard she was far from a timid, auntie profile. She was respected throughout the world as the national security advisor with clout. Many had endured her tongue-lashings, which had been rumored to include language that even a sailor had never heard. Wayne noticed the large gold cobra brooch on her collar and wondered if it was, perhaps, a symbol of the woman's inner self.

All the busy chatter stopped when non-essential people were asked to leave the room and the president addressed the group. "There is no reason to guard my words with political rhetoric. Once again we are facing a formidable threat from an unknown assailant or assailants using the scourge of biological weapons. For reasons that will be obvious after this briefing, the information presented here must be kept in strictest confidence. Mr. Alveriz, would you please update the group."

The thin secretary of state stood and, in a voice surprisingly deep for such a small man, began to speak. "Yesterday, I received a message from the health and human services secretary that the head of CDC was requesting an urgent meeting with President Salinski. Dr. Mackey arrived that same evening with the news that samples sent to CDC from England by Dr. Swift and samples received from another source were identified as a sort of viral cocktail. One is a brain virus, tick-borne encephalitis, often referred to as TBE. The other is Rift Valley Fever, a hemorrhagic agent. There is also a third agent or additive present but, at the moment, it has not been identified. Drs. Swift and Rogers,"

Mr. Alveriz acknowledged them with a nod, "were on the front lines during the battle against weapons of mass destruction, starting during Desert Storm, and they continued their involvement through Operation Iraqi Freedom. Dr. Swift has led many of our biological inspections and is a prominent scientist in his own right as well as the world's foremost biocriminologist. Dr. Rogers is an eminent virologist and an expert in vaccines. Dr. Swift will continue the briefing."

As if everyone's head in the room was controlled by one touch of a remote, the President and his council swiveled in unison and looked at Wayne. Wayne was thinking ahead three moves now that he was back at the chess game of bioterrorism. He marveled at the matter-of-fact way Mr. Alveriz spoke about such potentially deadly news. As he rose from his chair he tucked in an errant flap of his shirttail. "I would like to verify my conclusions," he said to the group. "Mr. Alveriz, did the other samples come from Australia?"

The president raised his hand to silence Alveriz and answered for the secretary of state, as if to remind everyone that this was his meeting. "Yes, that is correct, Dr. Swift, but I would like to know how you know? I just received that information from Mr. Yamoto seconds before this meeting."

Wayne had given every waking hour and then some when he should have been sleeping, trying to mold the events into a plausible scenario. In the last week he had formed many theories, but always came back to his first hypothesis. Now, with this one small piece of information, the puzzle was complete.

His analytical mind was way ahead of his usually shy personality. This was what biocriminology was all about:

tracking down the villains by scientific methods and, of course, a dash of Sherlock Holmes' sleuthing. Wayne was in his element. He started pacing and talking as if he was thinking out loud.

"The first victim was Martha Rogers. From the beginning she had all the symptoms of both a hemorrhagic and an encephalitic illness. As she was in her 80s: she's not a fit for either Strumple-Leichtenstern encephalitis, which is found in kids, or Hurst's disease, seen in 30 to 40 year olds. The lab studies also ruled out any vascular or autoimmune causes and we found no telltale signs of toxins.

"Then, when the other cases came in with the same combined bleeding and nervous system symptoms, we had to consider an infectious source. Since Mrs. Rogers' immunizations were up to date for all the common bacterial causes we focused on viruses, it was easy to rule out herpes because of the lack of inclusion bodies in the brain tissues and the samples didn't react to common agents like LaCrosse. Since she had been traveling in Australia, we broadened the scope to look at the nasty bugs that reside there and we began to consider that it was possible, although unlikely, that she was infected with two different viruses."

"While the CDC was doing its thing with tissue samples, I investigated all the backgrounds and movements of those infected. I could not find a common link, until my colleague, Dr. Rogers, and I obtained evidence that the common link was the 767 they traveled on back to London." Wayne moved nearer to the president and cocked his head to one side, "I assume the victim in Australia was on that plane?"

"You are correct," the president answered. "The deceased was a steward aboard the plane and we have been asked by the Aussies to help them. They don't know about the London cases. By the way, I had a call this morning from the British prime minister and he told me that three people from the airline's maintenance crew have been hospitalized. Please continue."

Wayne regretted that he had not had time to check his EPI-SPOT messages before getting to the White House. He never liked being behind the information curve and liked it even less when a politician knew more about something than he did. Not to be undone, Wayne continued. "Dr. Rogers and I inspected the plane. We started in the seating area. To be exact, coach section rows eighteen through twenty-two. I won't bore you with details about the technical equipment we used, but, stuck to the storage compartment above where Mrs. Rogers we found a minute piece of transparent film and a matching piece adhering to the compartment door. The bio-package, as we have come to call it, was cleverly fixed to the side wall of the overhead compartment. We suspect that the device was attached to the bin prior to the passengers loading and that, after the cabin crew came through and closed the compartment doors before take-off, the other side of the package adhered to the compartment door. The next time the compartment door was opened, the package tore open and the contents were released, spreading a small invisible aerosol cloud above row 21."

"The air currents in the cabin and the movement of the passengers then spread the virus. It's obvious and we're fortunate that only a small amount of virus was used because there would have been a greater number of victims and it would not have been easy to hide behind our veil of an outbreak of food poisoning. Specimens of the bio-package as well as the contents of the garbage collected in the plane, the cleaning equipment used on the airplane, and the HEPA filters from the plane have all been sent to CDC. The plane is now being decontaminated. This has been handled well, and, I might add, discretely by the British government."

"Dr. Swift, what did you mean by saying we were fortunate a small amount of virus was used?" The question was from defense Secretary Acker.

"I don't want to sound dramatic, but are any of you familiar with a little exercise Johns Hopkins did back in June 2001?" asked Wayne.

National Security Advisor Sugarhill was the only one who nodded that she had.

"Enlighten us, Dr. Swift," instructed President Salinski.

"The exercise was a simulated bioterrorism attack. The agent was smallpox. Initially, twenty-four cases were identified in Oklahoma City, then some in Georgia and Pennsylvania. The exercise called for ring vaccination to prevent the spread of the disease. That means they sent in the National Guard and Army troops to quarantine the area around the sites of the outbreak and to vaccinate everyone within that area. The available twelve million doses of vaccine were used in the ring immunization. This was not enough vaccine and the smallpox infection continued to spread, resulting in three million infected. One million of those infected were dead within four weeks of exposure. Fortunately, it was a simulation."

The quiet room exploded with questions until the president silenced everyone. "Please continue, Dr. Swift, although," he said, "I can guess what's coming,"

"The simulation found that there was total collapse of interstate commerce. Public unrest, to put it mildly. Martial law was declared." Wayne sat back down, adding again, "It was a simulation."

A heavy silence hung over the room. Jose' Alveriz attempted to laugh, breaking the somber mood.

"Doctor," said Mr. Alveriz, "that was an interesting fairytale, but still just a fabrication of someone's imagination. I don't mean to make light of the scientific community, but it was just an educated guess. An exercise."

It took great effort for Wayne to hold his temper, but then he had had a lot of practice. He remembered all the others like Mr. Alveriz who had rejected his warnings. Alveriz's rebuke was reminiscent of the frustrations Miryam told him she had faced in Israel. The unwillingness of politicians to believe the experts was the reason he had stepped out of government service. Everyone rejected the reality of bioterrorism, as if hiding their head in the sand would make them immune.

The room began to buzz with conversation. Wayne stood, scrapping his chair on the marble floor and the talk stopped. Everyone looked in his direction.

"Dr. Rogers and I have seen TBE and Rift Valley fever in their natural environments. Devastating as they are individually, an attack with these agents in a combined cocktail that was modified to enhance the infectivity and spread of the viruses, and then disseminated in several locations in Britain, the United States or any country would be devastating. That is a fact, not a hypothesis or fairytale."

"Dr. Swift, I assume the intent of such an attack might be to extract a ransom?" Alveriz asked.

"Yes, that's a possibility. But a concoction like this might just as easily be a first-strike weapon, intended to stretch our military and medical resources, create confusion, rendering us vulnerable while our attackers remain at a distance. With limited capacity to diagnosis the cause, no effective antivirals or vaccines, we would be defenseless as the infection spread and our infrastructure was extended beyond its capacity. Such a strike, on a large scale similar to the smallpox simulation, would totally disrupt our communications and logistics."

A few seated around the table whispered to one another but Wayne continued anyway. "The urgency of such a situation would stress all our resources beyond their limits and cause us to recall our forces abroad, leaving our allies unprotected and vulnerable."

Wayne walked to his chair and sat down next to Matt, resting his head in his hands. Then, as an afterthought, he raised his head and added, "Keep in mind, Mr. Alveriz, not everyone wants money. Some just want to, kill Americans. For some it is a mantra they have heard from birth. They are the really dangerous ones."

The room was filled with words, one flowing into another as the president asked preparedness and option questions of the Joint Chiefs. Wayne shut out all the voices, lost deep in his own thoughts. Something had tickled his neurons while he was talking and he needed to think it through.

"The United States has retained strategic nuclear forces sufficient to deter any hostile foreign influence that might act against our vital interest, including asymmetric means such as chemical or biological weapons," Secretary of Defense Acker reminded the group.

Colonel M. L. Marshal from the Marine Corps suggested alerting U.S. forces abroad to be ready to support a swift response once the source of the threat was discovered.

The national security advisor's soft but commanding voice asked the president about the "Joint Vision for 2010" prepared by the Department of Defense. "Wasn't that blueprint put forth in 1998 in preparation for an event like this? It required a new level of proficiency and an improvement in our technology to combat such a threat as a joint venture with our allies and coalition forces. Surely we have the technology that can detect, treat, and defend against any possible agent thrown at us? No pun intended. That posture was to be a deterrent."

"Budget cuts," the CIA director said as an answer to the national security advisor's question. He added that it was too early in the investigation and would say no more.

"Excuse me," Matt spoke for the first time but had to repeat himself and raise his voice to get everyone's attention. "Mr. President. Excuse me, but I'd like to remind this group that there has been no attack on the United States. The first strike has been against Great Britain, and I am here to enlist your aid in the event of further attacks and to ask your cooperation to find the criminals. I think we are all going beyond the scope of this event. For all we know, it could have come from some cult group. It doesn't necessarily follow that a threat to the international community exists. I suggest all has not gone down the drain and cool heads and a measured, deliberated defensive response—not military action—would be the most appropriate reaction. If a response is needed, I'm sure my country will discuss options. Unless you know something we do not? I assume all intelligence information between our governments has been shared?" Matt waited but no one answered his question.

"That's it!" Wayne yelled, jumping out of his chair.

A silence fell over the room. President Zigmund Salinski recognized Wayne. "Dr. Swift, would you like to share your revelation?"

Wayne's face lit up. He was animated, walking back and forth gesturing with his hands, thinking to himself, paying no attention to the others in the room.

"Dr. Swift?" the president said again.

"Sorry. But something was missing, the picture was incomplete." Now Wayne circled the room. "It didn't make sense that more people haven't been showing up sick from secondary exposure. This attack doesn't follow the Hopkins simulation. I mean, we're not up to our necks in additional contact cases. But we should be. So, we need another explanation. Perhaps this bio-weapon has been engineered *not* to be transmissible. It is possible that the third unidentified agent acts like a brake on the system. The question is, why would someone do that? Perhaps this event was meant to get our attention or maybe someone didn't know what they were doing, but I doubt that. If the first possibility were true, then it would follow that the British prime minister—or someone—would be getting a call for a large ransom to forestall further attacks. Of, course, there's always the chance that the perpetrator was simply a crackpot and used up all the virus in this one attack and we won't be hearing from them again, like the first anthrax letter attack in the United States." Wayne walked over to the door and started to leave the room.

"Dr. Swift, may I ask where you think you're going?" the president asked.

Wayne suddenly remembered where he was and was more than a little embarrassed. "Excuse me, Mr. President. I was going to check out my hypothesis about the third, unidentified agent. This might be something new that we haven't seen before. Or it could be more dangerous than I thought."

"I would take it as a personal favor if you would remain for the entire meeting," the president said wryly.

Wayne walked sheepishly back to his chair and sat down.

As if he needed permission, the president continued, "If I may be allowed to sum this up? We have identified at least two agents in this terrorist biological attack. The source remains unknown. Best case, this was a sick prank and, because of the lack of secondary transmission, a limited one, as Dr. Swift has pointed out."

"Mr. President. That is not what I said. I..." Wayne was silenced by an irate look from the president.

The president raised his voice and seemed to be projecting in Wayne's direction. "*Our* intelligence network may find the answers we are all looking for, Dr. Swift. In the meantime, I would like you and Dr. Rogers to probe more deeply into the virus cocktail used to start this turmoil," he swished his hand through the air as though he were mixing martinis, "and for you to track the culture to its source. That is what a biocriminologist does, correct?" The president's eyes locked onto Wayne's. Satisfied that Wayne had learned his lesson and would remain silent, he continued. "Customs and other law enforcement agencies are to be put on high alert by Homeland Security. I would like to remind everyone here that this is a very delicate time for us in our relationship with Iraq. We must not—let me restate that—we *can* not let one word of a possible biological weapon attack leak to the public. With Iraqi's history, whether they were responsible or not, they would be the first to become suspect. The Middle East is at a very fragile stage. The public and my political enemies would be more than happy to find Iraq guilty before asking any questions. It would be difficult to defend them in the present atmosphere of distrust. The other Arab states would see it as another excuse for us to occupy the area. It would mean the end of any possible chance for us to exert our influence in the Middle East as Iraq works toward democracy."

In her ladylike, Southern manner, Pearl Sugarhill asked if she could have a few minutes. Everyone turned their attention toward Madam National Security Advisor.

"I just want to remind this esteemed group that history has documented many instances that verify Drs. Swift and Rogers' position. Further, there is another scenario that has been overlooked. A disease or biological agent—I apologize if my terminology is unscientific—could be made to infect only the person primarily exposed. Wouldn't that mean that after, say, all military forces had been exposed and fallen ill, anyone could walk in and take over without fear of becoming infected?"

Sugarhill is right on target, thought Wayne. He was about to respond when the president abruptly, tapping his pen on the table. Everyone in the room with the exception of the guests knew this was his usual tactic when he wished to drive home a point.

"That is another very interesting scenario, Pearl, but conjecture is irrelevant at present. As Dr. Rogers has pointed out, we have not been attacked. We are helping at the request of the Australians and the British. Therefore, all this is clearly conjecture. It is necessary and prudent to be prepared for any eventuality, however, at present we do not have a real threat. The vice-president will form a committee to investigate all possibilities, including our readiness to handle a terrorist attack."

The president seemed to think carefully before he continued. "Let's keep our minds on the primary issue here. Everyone at this table knows this is the first opportunity the U.S. has had for a foothold in the Arab world," his voice grew louder and more urgent, "and I'll be damned if I am going to be known as the president who lost the greatest opportunity the free world has ever known. Free huh, that's a joke. We all know nothing is free, especially not oil. I have no intention of giving that up." Regaining control of his escalating temper, the president straightened his jacket sleeve, and cleared his throat to compose himself. His face, that had reached a deep plum color as he spoke, slowly returned to its normal ruddy complexion.

A tidal wave of silence crashed over the assembly. Usually the president kept his emotions under tight control. This unexpected glimpse of his zealous plans for role of the United States in the Middle East was surprising. The president recovered quickly and sought to downplay his heated words by emphasizing that the role of the U.S. would be that of a supportive nature for the new Iraqi government.

"We can handle the political side of this situation without your help Dr. Swift. You and your colleague will limit your thinking and investigation to the scientific aspects. We will take care of the rest of the world. You will have no comment, in any of your interactions concerning this matter. This meeting is over."

It was a subdued group that filed out. Thomas Yamoto followed President Salinski into the Oval Office anticipating his need for a private conversation.

"Yes, Mr. President?" he said when they were alone.

"Thomas, I think we may have a problem. I want you to keep your eyes on Dr. Swift. Not as an active analyst, but behind the scenes. I want to know his every move and that of anyone with any connection to him. The man has an independent streak and has a history of being a loose cannon. We can't afford that right now. My Middle East plan is vital to our nation's survival. I want you to prepare our international friends by downplaying any inquiries pertaining to this questionable outbreak in England. I don't want any suspicious fingers pointed in the direction of Iraq. I don't care how you handle it, but don't involve the Iraqis."

"How many men do you want me to put on Swift?" asked Thomas.

"Keep it low-key. Send one man. Someone so ordinary he's invisible. Dr. Swift is not without friends in high places, so you'll have to be careful. And I don't want this to come back at me. Understood?"

Thomas nodded.

"Put that little fellow on him. Everything goes through you. I don't want to see a report. You can brief me verbally; give me the bottom line." The president circled his desk and as an afterthought, said, "Contact Jenkins, the head of our embassy in Iraq. I put him there, so he's loyal to me. Fill him in. I want him to know this has my highest priority. I need his eyes and ears to keep me informed of any changes in the climate there."

The president's chief of Staff Thomas Yamoto acknowledged that he understood with a half bow as he left the Oval Office. The fewer of his words that were recorded the better. That was one of the first lessons he'd learned when he came to the White House. Elliot, the weasel, would have Dr. Swift under surveillance within the hour.

A light blinked on the president's desk intercom. "Yes, Chris," he said.

"Your national security advisor is here and she insists on seeing you immediately."

"Ask her to come in. Tell Thomas to arrange a meeting with the Cabinet and the CIA. And Chris, get the NSA director in here. I have to do something about the information that Dr. Swift may have circulating on the Internet."

Pearl marched in. She did not mince words. "Three prominent officials in the new Iraqi government have died due to questionable illnesses and you didn't think that it was worth mentioning during our previous meeting?" Pearl refused the president's offer to take a seat.

She could have said, "I made you an apple pie," from the calm expression on the president's face.

"Pearl, I've called the Cabinet, the National Security Advisor and the CIA to meet in the ready room in five minutes. People die in Iraq under questionable circumstances every day."

"Not all in *one* day," Pearl said. "It's as if they were all infected at the same time."

When Wayne and Matt got back to the Carlton, they were happy to see Hal waiting in the lobby. Even Matt smiled.

Once in Wayne's room, they realized how long it had been since they'd all eaten and they ordered dinner from room service. While they waited for the food to arrive, Wayne and Matt opened the minibar and snacked on expensive nuts at the government's expense. Hal sat on a small, beige loveseat, staring at the dull colored carpet as Matt and Wayne filled him in on all that had happened since they'd left him in New Mexico.

At a knock on the door, they stopped talking. It was the waiter and Matt let him in. The pimply faced youngster arranged the meal on a small table, but there was so much food that some of it had to remain on the cart.

Matt looked at Hal. "You can't possibly eat all that," he said.

Hal smiled. "Get what you want while you can."

The three ravenous men sat around the table eating and, with each mouthful, their tension was replaced by relaxed smiles of satisfaction.

"This coffee is great, hot and double strength. Just the way I like it," Hal said.

Wayne toasted Hal with his coffee cup. "Glad you could make it." He had called Hal before he left London and asked him to bring some of his gear. He didn't trust the airlines to transport it in one piece. "Besides, I think you should tag along in case Rich is unavailable." Wayne pushed his chair away from the table, wiped his unshaven chin with his napkin and leaned back, sipping his coffee, waiting. Little pieces of the paper napkin still stuck to his chin.

Matt threw Wayne a cloth napkin. "James Bond you're not."

Then Matt turned his attention on Hal. "If we are going to work together, tell me about this thing you do."

Wayne looked at Hal. "He needs to know," Wayne said evenly.

Hal took a sip of coffee, stood and walked to the window. He opened it and breathed in and out two or three times as if making a decision that required divine guidance. Then he turned and approached the table. His prominent handsome features and immense muscular frame loomed over Wayne and Matt.

"When I was five years old, my family made a sacred journey with other members of our tribe and camped on the plains near the sacred mountains. We were there about three days when some of the elders of our tribe went into a cave for a special ceremony. I stayed with my mother and played with the other children."

Hal's face took on a faraway expression as he relived the event. "I remember we all heard and felt a rumbling from the earth under our feet. I thought Mother Earth was speaking to us, for I'd heard the medicine man tell us many times to listen to our surroundings, the trees and the rocks. But I was wrong. Suddenly everyone was shouting and running toward the cave. At the cave entrance we saw a cloud of dust and falling rocks. When the dust settled, a sense of hopelessness fell over everyone. It was an earthquake and it had totally blocked the entrance to the cave where all the men from our tribe were meeting. Resigned to their task, the women and older children began to remove the rocks. When night came, they went back to the camp for food and water. I heard them say it would take too long to reach the men. That they would die before we could get help. My father was trapped in there too."

Hal took a swig of his coffee before continuing. "Two teenage girls hopped into one of the vehicles and went for help. It was forty miles to the nearest phone. It would probably be hours or maybe even days for someone to get heavy equipment into the remote location. After the girls left, the rest of the women returned to the collapsed cave entrance and their hopeless task. The older children took care of the young ones and put us all in one camper to sleep. The women decided to work in shifts all night, trying to create a tunnel so the men could crawl out."

Hal swallowed hard, walked over to the loveseat, and sat down. He looked tired, as if this explanation was taking some effort.

"Go on," Matt urged after a short silence.

"When I woke up, it was still dark. I climbed over the

other children and went outside. I had to pee," he chuckled. "I was looking around to make sure no one could see me. And that's when I saw it."

Matt was enraptured. "Saw what?" he asked.

"It was a brightly lit path. It was as if the sun was shining in just one spot in front of me. I followed it. I could see the rabbits hiding in the bush and a snake eating a field mouse. I didn't know if I was dreaming, but as a young boy I was taught that dreams were important. I walked away from the camp and around the other side of the mountain from where the women were digging and saw an opening in the side of the mountain partially hidden by rocks and bushes. Don't ask me why, because, to this day, I don't know why, but I crawled into the cave. I was not afraid." Again he laughed, "Maybe I was just a dumb kid."

"Go on," said Wayne.

"I thought the sacred mountain was helping me see in the dark, like one of the old medicine man's stories. Once inside the tunnel I walked about a mile and then stopped by a small pool of water to have a drink. The tunnel had several branches but I always seemed to know the correct turn. I walked a very long time, then got tired and stopped to rest. I fell into a deep, deep, sleep and dreamed. My father was holding me in his arms and, as he walked, we sang songs. We were in a beautiful open grotto with shiny teeth-like rocks coming up from the floor and down from the ceiling. Many of the other trapped men were there with us."

Hal paused and sat his cup on the table. "When I woke up I started walking again. I remember wondering how long I was expected to walk, but I continued. I enjoyed the cave. Soon I came to a dead end and I couldn't walk any further but I knew I was meant to go on. I picked up a rock and started hitting the mud wall in front of me. The dirt fell away and then I saw a hand and then a face. The beam of light, like sunlight, returned and was shining over my shoulder. I saw my father's face on the other side. But he couldn't see me because of the light, I guess. He asked who it was and I said, 'Hal.' To say my father was shocked, is putting it mildly." Hal chuckled at the memory. "My father enlarged the hole and pulled me through and hugged me fiercely. When I looked around, I saw it was the cave in my dream, the one with the shiny teeth. My father said the mountain brought me, and he had faith that I could find the way out. Some of the men were frightened. They kept talking about how we would get lost in the dark and it was best to wait where they were until rescued. My father convinced them that I could lead them to safety. They tied their belts together to make a rope to hold onto so they wouldn't get separated. My father and I sang as they followed me back the way I had come. I showed them the pool of water and they all drank and we rested. The men in the tribe began to talk about me as being something special, filled with a spirit," Hal shook his hands above his head. "We crawled out into the sunshine four days after I had entered. The tribe had a special feast and renamed me Cavemouse, 'Little one who sees without light.'"

The three men sat in silence. Matt tried to find a logical way to accept what he had just heard. He didn't doubt for a minute that it was true. After what Matt's British sense of proper etiquette said was an adequate interval of silence, he said, "But Cavemouse?" He looked Hal's gigantic frame up and down. "I can't imagine you even little. Mouse-sized is a bit of a stretch."

They all laughed.

"That went better than I thought," said Hal.

Wayne smacked Hal on the knee. "OK, you're in. One who is obviously not 'in' is the President. He's not the man I thought he was. He's smart but he's absorbed with oil. 'Integrity without knowledge is weak and useless, and knowledge without integrity is dangerous and dreadful.' He is dangerous."

"Rasselas," Matt offered up. "1759." He slyly added elbowing Hal. "The man has a quote for every occasion, if you haven't noticed. I'd forgotten how annoying your little game can be, Wayne."

Their conversation was interrupted by a knock at the door. Matt jumped to open it. Their mouths fell open at the sight of Pearl Sugarhill. "Aren't you going to invite a lady in for a drink, boys?" she asked.

Matt gave a half bow and made an inviting motion with a sweep of his arm signaling for Mrs. Sugarhill to enter.

"Charlie, you and the boys can wait outside, I'm safe with these gentlemen," observed Pearl, her Southern accent slid in to the room with her as she waved a hand dismissing her Secret Service detail. Matt closed the door behind her while Wayne and Hal stood fixed at attention.

"Now, gentlemen, I'll take that drink. Is it all right if I sit down?" asked Pearl.

Wayne came out of his trance. "Of course."

Pearl's evening gown rustled as she brushed passed Matt and sat down at the table. She pushed the dishes away and looked expectantly at Wayne.

Suddenly, it dawned on him, "A drink? Yes, of course. What may I get for you, Madam Advisor?"

"First, the name is Pearl. I didn't choose it, but I'm stuck with it, so I'd like ya'll to use it." Mouths fell open and eyebrows formed curious peaks. "I'm just glad I was the second girl, my sister is Goldie. Just a little personal trivia, after all, I think we're going to get to know each other quite well and long titles can hamper a friendship. Second, I'd like bourbon, straight up. I'm on my way to the opera and could use a little fortification."

Wayne fixed drinks from the minibar for everyone except Hal, who declined and settled for more coffee. An anticipatory stillness fell over the room.

Pearl was the first to break the silence. "Before we talk business, I need to know something about this big man," Pearl said, waving her drink at Hal without spilling a drop. "I've read about all the medals you received as a Navy Seal and I've investigated your civilian background. If you can't tell yet, I'm on your side. Let's be honest with each other. What I need to know is: why you are interested in this matter?"

Wayne started to defend his friend's privacy when Hal answered for himself. "The history of my people is riddled with poems and death songs recording the plagues brought down upon them by others. The first recorded epidemic was in Massachusetts in 1630, when the Algonkins were decimated by smallpox brought to North America by European explorers and colonists. Between 1630 and 1640, the disease moved back and forth through New England and west to the St. Lawrence and Great Lakes, reducing the population of the Huron and Iroquois by half. The Cherokee and the Catawba, who once numbered in the thousands, fled west with less than half their population left. By the end of 1800, two-thirds of the Omahas had also disappeared. Have you ever heard of the Mandan tribe? No one ever will. Not one person of that tribe survived the infection. The indigenous people had no resistance to the virus."

"My God, I had no idea." Matt was astounded.

Hal lifted his head higher and continued. "During the war of 1763, we supported the French so Sir Geoffrey Amherst of the British command ordered smallpox-contaminated blankets distributed to the Indians. They hoped that annihilation of the native population would make winning the war easier. This was not a tactic whose target was limited to soldiers. The young and the old, women and children suffered and died."

The small room grew cold with Hal's grim words.

"I realized after Wayne's call that we could be facing a bigger and more deadly but similar problem. This is why I have chosen to tag along. To repeat history's blunders by purposely letting a lethal virus loose on an unprotected civilian population is a crime against humanity. If I can do anything to prevent history from repeating itself, I will. There you have it, the reason I'm here." Hal finished the requested explanation without fanfare and stretched his long legs out in front of him, the tips of his size fourteen cowboy boots pointing up.

Everyone waited for some comment from Pearl, who didn't hesitate. "Be careful, that Princeton education of yours just slipped out Mr. Cavemouse," she smiled. "Those are good enough reasons for me, let's get on with it. I do not share the president's vision, exactly. Oh, I want the oil too. After what happened in England, the possibility of a biological attack—who knows where—is too real." She finished off her bourbon and motioned for Matt to refill her glass then rose from her chair and sashayed around the room, stopping in front of Wayne. "I've heard good things about you, Dr. Swift, pioneer of this new branch of science, biocriminology."

"Thank you," said Wayne, showing his embarrassment.

"And, Dr. Rogers, I have to assume by your close association with these men that you are a man of equal integrity. What I'm about to tell you must never be repeated to another living soul. If any of this leaks out, I will not support you in any way. In fact, I'll help the government bury you." Her hazel eyes took on a cold glint and her manner changed from that of a gentle Southern belle to a fierce hard politician, coiled and ready to strike. Brushing back a strand of her hair, Pearl's voice softened. "Come sit with me around the table."

Matt, Wayne, and Hal obeyed without hesitation.

"I've received intelligence information from a source inside Iraq of a rising militant presence outside the government. They're gathering the worst of Saddam's leftovers and they're independent of Bin Laden's terrorists." She sipped her drink, savoring their obvious anticipation. "This is the punchline, gentlemen. Our madman, Tariq Mohammad Saeed, is one of Saddam's men. He worked at a bomb-filling station for biological weapons. He's been making friends with some interesting people. A Dr. Bossem for one. Do any of you know him?"

Wayne, Matt and Hal all nodded. Wayne looked at Hal curiously.

"I was in South Africa," Hal explained. "A seal mission."

"I, and a few others," Peal continued, "want this Iraqi situation to disappear, quietly."

The atmosphere in the room thickened. When Wayne spoke, it was almost a whisper. "The attack in the U.K. was a preemptive strike by this Tariq? And you want us to do the president a favor and take care of this guy for him? We're not your hit squad Pearl. Send the CIA."

"Our inside source speculates that General Saeed is working with a terrorist out of Israel, code-named the Dove. They have also discovered that the Israelis have taken away the security and laboratory clearances of Dr. Miryam Stollar, a prominent research scientist who had access to Israel's deadliest viruses. I need to know how Israel is involved. I want you three to follow the virus to the source and see if there is a connection. Another trifling thing the president did not mention was that tissue samples are on their way to CDC from three highly placed officials in the Iraqi government who died under mysterious circumstances, all on the same day." Pearl smiled, perhaps in an effort to warm the chill that had fallen over the room. "There are too many questions. I want answers. This is right up your alley."

Wayne started to object but Pearl stopped him. "Let me continue," she said sharply. "I know you were close to Dr. Stollar, Dr. Swift. If you're so sure she isn't involved—and your face tells me that's what you think—then prove it. She worked with similar viruses in her laboratories and, of course, we know that the Israelis are no strangers to the seduction of biological agents as weapons. Unfortunately, the president may try to use this morsel of information to pin the event in Britain on Israel and divert attention from Iraq. I can't let our relationship with Israel break down. It would be a disaster of international proportions. Besides, I have personally guaranteed that such a thing won't happen. I'll support you in any way I can as long as our connection is not leaked to the press and you don't jeopardize my position. Are we clear?" For a moment her jaw muscles tightened.

Pearl watched them then added, "I'm asking you to put your reputations on the line." Pearl's expression was as hard as stone.

"We'll sort it out," said Wayne, his voice weary, but

firm. "We won't get anywhere without your support. So we'll play by your rules."

Matt had heard that quiet voice of determination from Wayne before. Nothing would stop him now, especially when Miryam was implicated.

Wayne's tone softened. "It's always bothered me that there wasn't the volume of agents to match the production equipment and documents we found in Iraq. I trust you, Pearl, even though you are foremost a politician, but covering for the president ... I don't know."

"Wayne, honey, we were all deceived. The president was under a lot of pressure to keep his promise and get out of Iraq, returning the government to its people." Pearl flashed her sweet Southern belle smile at the grim faces surrounding her. "I want you to work for me. The president doesn't know anything about this meeting." Wayne did not respond and Pearl went on. "No one made a bigger mistake than he who did nothing because he could do so little."

Wayne didn't hesitate. "Edmund Burke," he said.

Matt scratched the back of his head as he turned away from Pearl. "She's got *your* number."

Pearl adjusted her gown with a satisfied tweak. "I think we'll make an awesome team. How about 'Crescent Veil' for your mission name? It sounds ... mysterious."

Rocking back on the legs of his chair, Wayne smiled. "I like it," he said.

"Let me know when ya'll are finished in Atlanta. I have friends in many places, so don't hesitate to ask the impossible. This is between us. We need solid proof before I go to the president. I'll handle him. He wouldn't be in that chair if it weren't for me, darlin'."

One of Pearl's security men entered and handed her a

note. Pearl frowned and stuck the message in her handbag.

"Oh, we'll be working with another friend of ours. His name is..." Pearl broke in before Wayne could complete the sentence.

"I know. Mr. Lee. I've worked with him before. I'll give you a case of Twinkies to take to Arbil for him."

The heads turned and surprised eyes questioned her.

"Yes, someone is always watching. You can bank on it." She put a finger to her lips. "Gentlemen, you will be in the Middle East very soon." She paused. Her serious face vanished, replaced by her misleadingly sweet smile. "But I must be on my way," she said. "The night is young and should prove to be enchanting. Ah, to be forty again. Ya'll enjoy the rest of the evening." She threw an envelope on the table, her smile devilish, and with a swish of satin, left.

Matt examined the envelope's contents. "There are two first class tickets to Atlanta, one first class ticket to Adana, in Turkey, a cell phone and some phone numbers and a note that says, 'Keep in touch.' I guess I better call Olivia and say I'm going to be occupied a little longer." He picked up the cell phone, hesitated, looked it over for bugs then shrugged and began to punch in his home number.

"What are we doing?" Matt said when he'd completed his phone call.

"We'll take it one step at a time," Wayne said rubbing his hands together. "My palms are itching to get a good look at this bug. And you," he pointed to Matt, "need to take a look at the records at CDC and the tissue culture repository."

The three friends gathered around the small table and decided that Hal would return to New Mexico and gather supplies, then travel to Iraq, entering through the back door that Pearl had set up for them. They would rendezvous with Hal at Richard's if the trail led to Iraq.

"'The game is afoot, Watson,' if I may cite one of my favorite philosophers," said Hal. They all laughed.

Out in the hall, Pearl patted her handbag as she hurried along, checking to see if the message had burned a hole through the silk purse. She was far more worried than her cavalier manner had revealed.

The latest communiqué from the Israeli ambassador was a warning. "If America considers Israel responsible for the terrorist attack in England, our long-standing friendship will be stretched beyond its limit."

Pearl wondered who on the president's cabinet was leaking information to the Israelis?

In the room next to where the three companions made their plans, a weasel of a man sat hunched over a receiver listening to their conversation. He was content. The microphone he had planted when he removed the dirty dishes had gone undetected.

Chapter 11

Assyria, 811 B.C. — Cradle of a Lost Civilization

Semiramis' legs quivered from long hours of walking without rest. She was pushing herself beyond her limits. There was a purpose to her being in this cave at this time—it was not merely for shelter. She was determined to unearth the mystery of the powerful presence surrounding her.

For a short time, the water she had salvaged from the pool in the grotto helped her maintain a rapid pace, but it was gone now. With her continued exertion, she was quickly becoming dehydrated. The damp cool surroundings chilled her to the bone.

In this underground environment, she was not aware of the power of the storm outside or that it had raged for one full night and all the next day. During that entire time, the queen had been walking and wondering where Ninyas was and what he was planning.

She didn't know that Ninyas had taken refuge close by or that he had lost half his men. But her keen mind was already strategizing. He knew where to find her and that was his advantage. Yet the queen was sure Ninyas could not return to Calah for reinforcements. He would not want to show weakness to his new master and risk forfeiting his own head. His greedy need and diminished force were her advantage.

She looked at her horses and knew her fondness for them was a weakness that Ninyas would exploit if given the chance. He would look for a cave large enough to accommodate the chariot and the animals. She stroked the horses, still glad the animals were with her.

Semiramis walked beside her beauties, helping them through the tight spots. Countless times she fell onto the unyielding rock, tripped by the uneven terrain and hampered by inadequate light. She held tightly to her horses' reins but she was not cognizant of this action. Her fingers were frozen into a tight fist around the knot of leather and her breathing came in loud, ragged gasps.

The subterranean passages felt like an endless abyss. When she first started her descent into the twisting tunnels, she was alert to every sound and her mind searched the darkness for a place to meet her son and his bandits in combat. She needed terrain that would give her some advantage, but the cave had not revealed the battleground she was looking for.

Her weary mind began to wander. Now she was unaware of her movements, lost in the need to keep her body in motion. Like a sleepwalker, she stumbled forward.

The flame she was carrying flickered, then died. Carefully she removed her cloak, which held all her possessions, and laid it open on the stone floor. In the pitch blackness, she bent over to search for another jar of oil but could not find one, even though she knew she had several. Her legs shook, then gave way and she fell to her knees. Holding onto the horse's reins she pulled herself to her feet. Her fatigue and the darkness began to play tricks on her and it felt as if her mind no longer worked in concert with her body.

Until it was gone, she had not realized how much she depended on the small sputtering flame as a link with reality. Panicking, she felt around again for a jar of oil and she stumbled, her legs collapsed. Trying to break her fall she extended her arms and her left hand jammed into the empty oil jar, shattering it. Broken pieces of pottery were driven deep into the palm of her left hand, but she was numb to the pain. The endless hours without sleep wrapped around her like a shroud. She could not think clearly. *There, I see it, that shadow, black on black.* "Is that you my son?" *She jerked away, what was that?* She brushed feverishly at her legs.

"Is someone there?" she shouted at the darkness. *They are all around me.* She drew her short sword and stabbed left and right at imaginary villains. Reaching out with her empty hand, she felt along the tunnel walls, shuffling a few feet sideways on her knees. As fate would have it, she found a damp crevice large enough for her to back into it so she could defend herself. "Come out and face your mother," she cried. No one answered. Her mind and body drifted. It was time to take a momentary respite from the battle that would soon burst upon her. Finally, Queen Semiramis let herself fall into the blackness and she slept.

As soon as the storm subsided, Ninyas ordered his men to return to the area where they had last seen the queen. They found her tracks just a few feet inside the entrance of the third cave they searched. "I told you the gods were with us. The storm didn't cover all of her tracks," said Ninyas.

The troop was excited to find some sign of their quarry for the soldiers believed it meant the wealth they had been promised was close at hand. In Ninyas' warped mind, it meant the death of the person who was responsible for all the failures and humiliations he had endured throughout his life. He had this one last mission to complete—kill his mother. With her death, at last he would be king!

He had decided a long time ago to take the power and wealth he wanted by treachery if necessary. But it wasn't until he was approached by the King of Urartu that he was given the means to gain both of his goals. Eliminating his mother was a bonus. She was like a festering wound that he had finally found a way to heal. If he had to, Ninyas was prepared to kill his mother with his own hands and rip Assyria from her heart.

Ninyas noticed the captain staring at him. "What is it you want, you insolent ape?" Ninyas challenged.

The brutish captain grinned. The boy's insults meant nothing to him. He was after the treasure he had been promised and it gave him a chance to settle a personal score with the queen besides. "We await your orders, my king."

King, yes, that is as it should be. "Of course, my dull witted friend. Find shelter for the horses near the cave's entrance and distribute the supplies among the men."

After everything was organized, Ninyas gave the order to take the torches from their packs and light them. The troop followed as he led them into the cave. He marched at the head of the group, thinking scornfully, that it was easy to be a leader of men. You just had to pay them enough.

Two levels below them, Queen Semiramis lay on the floor as if dead. Dreams—mysterious, supernatural dreams—held her in a deep sleep. She was lost in her dreams, destined to wander aimlessly. Had the gods forsaken her? The people in the dreams were all strangers except for one familiar face: Hazael. She reached out to him and his features dissolved. A sharp pain jerked her awake, a creature attracted by the smell of blood— perhaps a bat—had bitten her bleeding hand.

"I am not dead! Demons of the cave, did you hear me? I am not dead!" Semiramis shouted. She crawled around on the craggy tunnel floor until she found her woolen cloak. This time she found one of the remaining oil jars and lit the wick. The sleep had not renewed her; she needed food.

She pulled herself to her feet, stretching her arms and legs, and her sore muscles objected. She was unaware that she had slept for several hours, but it made little difference: time stood still in the darkness.

She gazed around. The horses stood nearby. Their nostrils flared at the sudden illumination, but they were comforted by the touch of their mistress' hand.

Standing near the animals for warmth, Semiramis paused to gather her thoughts. She reached out to grip the horses' reins and felt an excruciating surge of pain through her hand. Placing the lamp on a flat rock nearby, she examined the gash across her left palm. It oozed blood and there was dried black blood all over her hand and along her arm. After being in so many battles she knew the danger signs of excess blood loss and felt neither faint nor weak. She was confident that her ability to fight would not be hampered.

She examined the wound more closely, found a pottery shard still embedded and pulled it out. The wound began to bleed again and she tore off the ragged hem of her garment and bandaged her hand tightly to staunch the flow.

Her two middle fingers would not respond when she tried to bend them and she knew the tendons deep inside her hand were damaged. She bound her four fingers together so the injured fingers would not get in the way. This injury would lessen her fighting ability with two swords, but she was a master with the long sword so the short sword or dagger would be worn on her belt to be used only if the long sword failed her. The queen was confident that, even if she was weakened by hunger and injuries, her skills and experience would be sufficient to overcome Ninyas. She sneered; at best, her weakness would even the odds.

She renewed her trek knowing she would not be alone long, Ninyas would find her. A final confrontation was inevitable, and desired, but it would be on her terms. She began to strike marks and the number fifteen at measured intervals on the side of the walls with a white chalk-like rock she picked up. At least she would be able to find her way back to this area and, she sneered, perhaps Ninyas needed some help. She held the lamp high above her head in an effort to shine more light over a greater area of the tunnel. She noticed how this part of the cave was very different from the upper level. The sides of the walls were damp to the touch and her fingers sparkled like silver from the residue on the smooth surface. *Smooth walls? Man made?*

For hours she had been aware of spiraling deeper into the mountain. The dampness and type of rock on the walls at this level were different. The dust and dirt on the floor had gone undisturbed until her intrusion, but it was smooth. *Smooth?* Could it be that many feet have traveled this path? She had the soothing feeling that ageless companions walked beside her.

She led her horses into a broad side tunnel slanting off to her left. It ended in a wide domed room with a small pool of water in the center. Semiramis allowed the horses to sniff the water. When they moved forward to drink, she knew the water was untainted. She took a long invigorating drink and licked her lips. "Umm, such a sweet taste." The queen sat down next to the pool and rested her head against the rock wall.

Semiramis decided that the horses were slowing her down and that they would be safe here. The parting was difficult. She removed their bridles, placing them carefully on the floor. If she were slain, they would be free to try and find their way back to the surface without hindrance.

"My beauties, I shall never abandon you. Be patient. I will return." She hugged and patted them.

Semiramis walked out of the grotto feeling very much alone. Her meager belongings were slung over her shoulder, wrapped in her cloak. Her decision to leave the horses behind proved correct as the tunnel began to narrow.

Suddenly she vomited. Wiping the acidic spit from her mouth with the back of her hand, she leaned against a rock, waiting for the dancing lights in her head to retreat.

Gradually her energy returned and she looked down at the floor for the first time. "These are steps! Man-made steps!" It was incredible. "They have been chiseled out of the rock," she said in amazement.

She stood and held the lamp high above her head and ran her hands along the wall. It was smoother than the upper part of the cave had been. She brought the lamp closer to the rock and discovered a torch set into the wall. Elated, she pulled the torch from its holder, felt the tip and smelled her fingers as she rubbed the oily substance between them. All aches and pains were forgotten. She put her tiny light to the torch and it burst into flames. It gave off a warm glow that illuminated a large area of the tunnel.

Holding the larger torch high above her head, she inspected the walls on both sides of the path. She spotted another torch in a bracket in the wall just in front of her. She hurried to light it. Now even more of the passage was illuminated. Yes, she was right: human hands had shaped this tunnel. Torches were mounted on both sides of the passage in a staggered manner. The steps curved down and off to the right. In a small rock outcropping was an altar dedicated to the god EnLiL, the wife of NinLiL. She recognized the statues. They were like those in the temples in Calah. Quickly, she ran back up the steps to retrieve the wool cloak that contained her supplies and weapons.

Delighted with this small discovery, she sprang down the passage with her pack over her back and the torch in her injured left hand. She did not feel pain or exhaustion. Her body was numb but her spirit was alive. Now she was most eager to continue and to see what—or perhaps who—was at the end of the tunnel. She quickened her pace.

The spiral steps widened and the descent became more gradual. Here the torches were closer together and ornamented with brass fittings. On the left side of the steps was a well-oiled wooden railing with carved symbols in cuneiform writing. Semiramis rubbed the mold away and brought the torch closer to decipher the script. It was evident that the railing had been polished smooth by many hands. The steps were finely chiseled, not the roughhewn stone used in the upper region. Narrow, man-made side tunnels branched off from the broad main passage every ten feet. She investigated the first few and found that they were about six feet in depth and ended in one or two small cells, probably living quarters for the priests or people that inhabited the cave.

Inside one cavernous space, Semiramis saw a storage bin. It was overflowing with moldy grain. Decaying baskets of petrified bread and dried, desiccated vegetables lay on the floor. Clay jugs filled with oil, covered and sealed with waxed hides, were the only things left unspoiled by the mold that covered everything else in the chamber. Hides from goats and sheep hung from the walls. She grabbed a couple of the sheepskins and shook the dirt and mold from the fur, then wrapped them around her chilled body.

She stuffed some of the moldy grain into her mouth and chewed the distasteful seeds. *How curious that, with all these delicacies to choose from, there are no scavengers of any kind?* She made a pouch in her robe and filled it with grain. Not a feast, but it would have to do. When she returned to the main passage she felt a slight breeze crossed her face. It felt wonderful. Better yet, it tasted like fresh air. But from where?

She retched and all the grain she had savored a short time ago was spewed onto the tunnel floor. Doubled over and waiting for the next wave of nausea to assault her, she stared at the vomit on the floor. Grain—grain mixed with blackened blood—lay at her feet.

"No, No. It can't be. The demons are inside me!" She squatted down, waiting for the turmoil in her stomach to pass. Though they were hallucinations, what Semiramis saw was demons dancing all around her. She imagined she was in her own tomb and the demons were with her. She squeezed her eyes shut and put her hands over her ears to shut out the screeching voices. She imagined hands clawing at her; they were all over her. She was frightened—really frightened—for the first time in her life. She backed away, pulling the imagined hands from her face, arms, and legs. They wouldn't let go! She covered her head with her arms and tried to conceal herself in a crack in the rock wall.

"Please! Please go away!"

If the distressed queen had been clear-headed, she would have remembered the priests talking of others who were crazed as she was now. It could either be demonic or divine. In actuality it was neither, the queen was experiencing the effects of ergot poisoning and the moldy grain she had eaten was the culprit.

Fortunately, she had thrown up most of the poison, so the effects would be transient. The visions would soon dissolve now that she had emptied her stomach. The lethal Rift Valley virus demon she carried, however, would remain.

Semiramis tried to rub the images away by massaging her temples. She paused in the darkness and reached out to another woman dressed in unfamiliar garb. Her features were like her own and for an unknown reason she felt drawn to her. "Run! Run to the mountains," she shouted to the woman. "I will be there to help you."

Chapter 12

Kurd Territory—Desertion or Betrayal

Costumed in the same full-flowing dress and headscarf as the rest of the Kurdish women in the offices of the Kurdistan Democratic Party in the city of Arbil, Ghariba blended right in. Some of the women at the office adopted Western dress but still maintained the required Muslim demeanor with ankle-length skirts and traditional head coverings. Some added a few Western accessories. Not Ghariba. Her sole accessory was a small handgun, strapped to her thigh. Like many of the other women in northern Iraq, she carried a Russian Kalashnikov for protection while traveling to and from work. The barrel of a gun propped nonchalantly by a desk was a common sight all over the office.

Although the Kurdish homeland was officially under international protection, it was still a tribal society. Factions were scattered throughout the rugged mountains to the east and north of Arbil. Feuds between clans could and did erupt, particularly with the Patriotic Union of Kurdistan, the KDP's chief rival for control of the Kurdish land. The Kurds still tried to solve their disputes—especially political differences—with guns.

Ghariba sighed as she thought about how glad she would be when she completed this assignment with the disorganized Kurds. She hated their clan mentality and the constant bickering that inhibited decision-making. The region's reorganization process was slow and the repeated delays grated on her nerves. But, in truth, most of her restlessness was self-induced. Every day the discord within her grew stronger. The reason for this attack of conscience eluded and annoyed her. Perhaps her judgment was being corrupted by her relationship with Richard.

Her superiors had warned her to sever the connection with the American, but she hadn't been able to. The emotions he evoked in her were new. Reconciling her many lies with the usual rhetoric did not work as well as it used to, especially when she was around him. Of late she found herself unable to recognize and separate her own genuine feelings from those she feigned. Was it love? Love, she reminded herself, was not welcome. She tried to control the exciting new feelings Rich aroused in her, but she was losing the battle. It seemed that, now that these strange and wonderful emotions had been awakened, it was a struggle to put them back to sleep. Like a junkie, she needed and—if she were truthful with herself wanted—more. Much more.

Ghariba forced herself to stop thinking about her relationship with Rich and focus on the objectives of her mission. Shielding her paper from prying eyes, she jotted down the names of Iraqi refugees and dissidents to be included in her report, then gathered the documents she had copied and the added material she had collected during her travels in England, Australia, and Israel. Her job as official interpreter and liaison for the new Kurdistan territory was a perfect cover for her clandestine activities. *The world is held together with secrets,* thought Ghariba. She found it amazing that most foreigners were so poorly educated on the inner workings of this small country, considering the global impact the Kurds could have on the world's oil market.

As a translator with top-level clearance, many doors were open to Ghariba. At social functions and business meetings translators were always present, but seldom noticed. Ghariba enjoyed her anonymity. This was as true here in Arbil as it was abroad. Even now, her mind listened to the numerous conversations going on around her, translating the Persian-laced language of the Kurds and sifting through it for key words that might prove worth further effort. Convinced she had enough information to satisfy her superiors, she went back to her desk.

The cleaning crew arrived at her office just as she finished her report and she glanced up to check the time. Five p.m., everyone else had left the office two hours before. If she didn't hurry, she'd be late making her weekly drop. She locked her desk drawer, placed her report in a brown, internal office envelope and sealed it, then wrote the number seven very small on the upper left corner of the envelope. She walked over to the department mailbox and dropped in the report.

Back at her cubicle, she was surprised to find an envelope marked with the number fifteen—her number—on the desk. It must have been placed there only moments before, yet she'd seen no one in the area.

Ghariba looked around cautiously before picking up the envelope. Perhaps, like her, one of the cleaning staff had more than one profession and had left it on her desk. Reminding herself that there were spies everywhere, Ghariba bent forward, letting the loose ends of her headscarf fall forward to conceal her movements. She opened the envelope and removed the plain white paper. Two words were printed on it: Crimson Winds. It was a warning. She was in great danger.

Ghariba's hands shook and she buried them in the folds of her skirt. Forcing herself to regain control, she gathered her things and left. With her Kalashnikov comfortably cradled in her arm, she mingled with the throng of workers crowding the street. She glanced over her shoulder one last time before jumping onto the bus for the ride home.

❧

Rich pushed himself away from his workbench, glancing out the window at the corner bus stop. He had a good view of the whole town from the third floor of the apartment he and Ghariba shared in a poor section of Shaqlawah, northeast of Arbil. He checked his watch. It was about the right time.

He gazed at the mountains to the east that loomed over the gray, crate-like buildings of the city. At the base of the rugged peaks he could make out dots of green wheat struggling to take hold in the scattered limestone rubble. It struck him that the whole country was a patchwork of stark contrasts: the old and the new, the living and the dead. He knew that, on the other side of the mountain range, was Iran, yet another extreme.

He heard the squeal of brakes and looked down at the street. A huge smile spread over his face when he recognized Ghariba's silhouette leaving the bus. No amount of traditional dress could disguise that sexy figure.

Every day he was impatient for her return, even though home was a cheap two room apartment that had come furnished. This meant it had a small table, two wooden straight-back chairs, a bed—a mattress on the floor—one very lumpy faded green couch and a small propane-powered refrigerator. They cooked on a hibachi grill that Rich had rigged from scraps. He had also built a kitchen area on one side of the room, complete with shelves and a sink.

The walls were cracked and pitted so badly that no one could tell what color they had been originally. The best feature of the place was the sunlight that streamed in through two windows, both of which were intact, a rare commodity in the war-scarred city.

The apartment was in the tallest building in the town and had almost six hours of unobstructed sunlight every day, a bonus since electricity was rationed. Their section of the city had three hours of electrical power from six a.m. until nine a.m. and another three hours from six p.m. until nine p.m.: the commuting times. The fact that the windows faced the street gave them what Rich lightheartedly called a "charming view of the neighborhood."

Rich's workbench sat in front of the windows. The last rays of sunlight highlighted a jumble of gadgets, wires, and switches strewn over its surface. Rich loved tinkering at home. There was separate housing for American consultants and there was Tent City, but Rich and Ghariba were happy to take lesser accommodations in order to maintain their privacy.

Rich had gone against the rules by becoming involved with Ghariba. But he didn't care: she was worth the risk. He marveled at how lucky he was to have such a beautiful roommate as Ghariba, his foxy lady. Soon she would step into the room and remove her scarf and her shimmering hair would spill down over her shoulders. Her arrival always made him feel as if a movie star had walked into the apartment. He leaned against the wall and imagined, for the thousandth time, her entrance, the slight rustle of her garments brushing against soft translucent skin, across a body that any model in a Victoria's Secret catalog would die for.

He heard her footsteps approaching and a tingling

spread through his body. Ghariba opened the door and looked questioningly at Rich as she removed her scarf and hung it on a hook behind the door.

"I knew you hadn't shopped while I was gone so I picked up supper." She raised the woven grocery bag she held, "are you going to help me with these groceries or just stare at me?"

"Hey, you've only been home a few days, I'm still in my fantasizing stage." Rich took the groceries from her. "Baby, you must be out of shape. You don't usually work up a sweat walking up three flights." He kissed her cheek and put one arm around her waist. "It's been a long day without you."

She pushed him away playfully. "First the food."

Rich and Ghariba had been living together for the past nine months. They had met years before during the UNSCOM days. Rich still worked for the CIA and Ghariba was a defector, like many others in Kurdistan. She had fled Iraq and found sanctuary in Arbil, where they had met again and, against all the rules, fell in love.

They came from contrasting worlds, maybe that was why they were attracted to each other. Rich had grown up pampered by affluent parents. Ghariba had come to maturity in a world where every day was a struggle to survive. He had no formal education but was brilliant, whereas she was lucky to have a college education, even if studying was terribly hard for her. He was tall and lanky with blond curly hair, hazel eyes, and fair skin. Ghariba was the exact opposite: small framed, long darkish hair, olive skin and golden eyes with thick black lashes that tickled Rich's cheeks when they embraced. Neither culture approved of their association.

Ghariba was gratified that Rich accepted her when

other Americans did not. But then, Rich was a naive man in some ways. That was one of the things she liked about him.

Ghariba moved over to the hibachi and lit it in preparation for dinner. "Rich, stop. Why are you staring at me with that silly grin on your face? It's embarrassing."

"I like to watch you." Rich winked at her and his eyes sparkled.

She gave him a wave of her hand that said, "you're crazy," and continued her efforts at the hibachi, blowing gently on the small flame. When she succeeded, she opened the window to allow the smoke from the coals to escape and walked over to a row of cabinets.

"I'm my usual charming self," Rich said playfully. "Why do you question your good fortune to have me around?" He embraced her from behind in a playful bear hug, rubbing his face in her hair. "You smell good."

"What's put you in such a good mood? It's something more than my homecoming. When I left, you were worried your government was planning to send you home and you were trying to think of a way to stay. Did we find more explosive devices for you to dismantle? I know how much you like blowing things up."

"You're beginning to sound just like an American," he rubbed his hand over his day old beard and, fleetingly, wished he had shaved. "You'll never guess who called me today."

Since the warning in the note, Ghariba's nerves were on edge. She was in no mood to play games. "I'm tired after all my traveling this month, please just tell me so I can get on with dinner."

"Wayne Swift. Remember him from our UNSCOM days?"

Ghariba's face flushed and she turned away, hoping Rich wouldn't notice.

"I'd been wondering what he was up to. He wanted to know how available I was in case he needed to put the old team together. All of us, Wayne, Matt, Miryam, you and me. What do you think? We had some good times together. There's always excitement when Wayne's around."

"How did he find you?"

"Through the agency, I guess. I didn't ask. Why does it matter?"

Her paranoia came thundering back and Ghariba turned to peek through the boards covering a hole in the wall over the sink. She checked the street to see if she was under surveillance. Added to the warning she'd received earlier, this unexpected news changed everything. She didn't want anything to change, but with Wayne Swift back in the picture, she knew her time with Rich was coming to an end. Wayne had disliked her right from the start. She'd tried to seduce him, but he'd resisted her enticements. Now he was coming back and would pose a real threat to her completing her assignment.

No one on the street was watching the apartment, and Ghariba turned away from the wall to stare blankly at the bare wood floor. She walked into the combined living room and sleeping area. Rich followed close behind, sensing her unrest. A newspaper was spread out on the lumpy green couch. She picked it up to make room to sit down.

Rich sat down next to her and held her hand. "What's the matter? This is just what I need to extend my stay. I thought you'd be happy."

"When I saw Matt in Australia, he didn't say anything about coming here." Ghariba pulled her hand from Rich's, got up and walked to the window and parted the flimsy curtains. Again, she scanned the street. She wondered if Wayne could be the reason for the Crimson Winds warning.

"Relax, Ghariba. He'll let me know the details later. He just wanted to know if I was available, that's all." He waited but Ghariba didn't respond. Rich went over to her and folded her into his arms, kissing the top of her head. He loved the way she felt in his arms.

She relaxed for a moment and then pulled away. She couldn't think with him so close to her. He was confusing her. "By the way I was never part of your little group," she said through clenched teeth. "Didn't he tell you anything more?"

"No. Well, yes. He told me a little, but it's secret stuff, baby."

"Wayne has always been against me." There was a fire in her eyes that Rich had never seen before.

"Look, Ghariba, if you think Wayne will get between us, you're wrong. I make my own decisions when it comes to whom I love. Besides, the past stays in the past."

"Then why can't you tell me anything?" Ghariba relaxed against Rich. He felt taut muscles beneath her garments.

He closed his arms more tightly around her. "Sorry, baby, I can't. It's just conjecture at this point. Hey, what's up? The cloak and dagger side of my life has never bothered you before."

It took her only a second to respond, she was so used to lying. "You're right. I was worried about you, but I know you can handle yourself." She turned and embraced him. Then abruptly she pulled away.

"Rich, I have to go out for awhile. Don't wait up. I forgot to do something important at the office." She was already at the door, slipping a scarf over her head and shoulders.

"Wait. The fire's almost ready for me to start cooking. Eat first, baby."

She looked at Rich without seeing him. Her mind was racing. Without a word in response, she opened the door, ready to walk out, when Rich grabbed her elbow.

"I'll walk you to the bus stop. We can talk."

She stiffened and frowned at him.

"Can't whatever it is, wait until tomorrow? You've been working 24/7 plus traveling so much. How much do they expect of you? Ghariba..." Rich tightened his grip on her arm trying to guide her back to the couch.

She tore her arm from his hand. "What's wrong with you? How dare you question me as if I were a child?" Amazed by her own words she stopped. The hurt in Rich's eyes made her heart ache, but she needed to get out and report. "I'm sorry," she said, her voice softer. "I'm under a lot of stress at work. I told you, I just remembered I left something very important unfinished."

Rich grabbed her by the shoulders. "Wait."

"Let me go," Ghariba yelled. She pulled away and grabbed her Kalashnikov.

"Don't leave! The streets are too dangerous after dark," Rich pulled her toward him. "I'll go with you."

Ghariba reacted instinctively, knocking Rich's legs out from under him with a sweep of her left leg. Taken by surprise, he went down with a crash and lay sprawled on the floor, shocked. Then he grinned. "That's a new move. I'm glad you didn't try it in bed."

"I don't know what's wrong with me. Forgive me, Rich."

Tears streamed down her face as she turned and flew down the stairs.

Rich jumped up and yelled down the hall after her, but it was too late, she was gone. He was stunned and confused.

Ghariba hurried back to her office to add this new information to her secret report before it was picked up. As she was unlocking the office door, a dark figure appeared behind her in the unlit corridor. One hand clamped over her mouth, the other grabbed her hand to prevent her from reaching her weapon. Her arm was twisted behind her back and she was dragged into the shadows, away from the door.

When she didn't come home, Rich went looking for her. He found her keys still dangling from the lock on her office door. He searched for Ghariba for three days but, despite his CIA connections, he found nothing. The police added her name to the long list of the missing.

Chapter 13

Aski Kalak, Iraq — Succession of Fear

Tariq picked up a large red marking pen from his desk and walked over to his calendar. With one bold stroke he marked this important day. *Ten days since the virus was liberated, and three members of the new democratic inner circle were successfully eliminated.* He whispered under his breath, then, out loud, to release some of his pent-up joy: "These are exciting times."

It may also be the right time for goodbyes. My beautiful Dove is becoming unpredictable. Tariq looked at himself in the mirror and was surprised that his eyes appeared sad. It was faintly discernible, a sagging of the eyelids and moisture gathering in the corners. He sat back down behind his desk, resting his elbows on the cushioned armrests and dabbed his eyes with a handkerchief. He laughed out loud and marveled that the emotion looked sincere in the mirror.

The orange light on the general's secure phone blinked. He picked up the receiver and said nothing, waiting for the caller to identify himself. He fidgeted, his right leg bouncing up and down, keeping time to music only he could hear. This could be the most important call of his life. It took forever before the caller gave the proper code word.

"Desert Hawk," said a deep male voice.

"Continue," replied Tariq. He licked his lips.

"I have confirmed that the packages were delivered and will be prepared by the date you specified."

"Excellent." Tariq almost clapped his hands in his excitement. The Dove's most recent trip, of course, was to deliver the virus for phase two of his plan. Now that her task had been completed, she was obsolete. It was time for Tariq to deliver her to what had always been her fate. With her death, he would have shed any direct link to the bioterrorism attacks. "Continue. The other matter?"

"I have my objective under surveillance. The Americans are beginning to mistrust and hate Israel almost as much as we do." There was a slight laugh before the speaker continued. "I have also found the location of her nest. I am awaiting further instructions."

"Well done, sergeant. Captain Arif, will join you shortly. Keep her under surveillance. Assist the captain. Arif has specific instructions. They must be followed to the letter."

He hung up the receiver and rubbed his hands together, satisfied. *The captain is a reliable assassin. He has never failed. Now that Rijah has confirmed my suspicions, Dr. Stollar's opportune death will give Israel what they have been looking for: the notorious Dove. You have meddled in my affairs for the last time, doctor.* Tariq rubbed his hands together excitedly.

A demure voice announcing a guest interrupted Tariq's daydreams. He rubbed the back of his stiff neck and, irritated by the interruption, snapped: "Enter."

Abu al-Tubar, still dusty and dirty from his trip, walked in, beaming.

"Yes, report."

The hatchet man spoke: "I have found your treasure and secured the location. We were not detected by the Kurds and, with the schedule of the satellites which you provided, I am sure we were not seen. The prize is yours, my general!"

Undisguised joy erupted from Tariq. He grabbed the

colonel and hugged him, laughing with maniacal enthusiasm.

"I had every confidence in you, my old friend. How vast is the supply?" He tripped over his words as he tried to squelch his excitement. "Come over here to the map and show me where it is located. Coordinates?" Putting his arm around his old friend's shoulder, Tariq guided him to the wall charts.

"My general, the supply is immense." Almost in a hiss, he repeated himself for emphasis: "Immense! Intact and deep in a cave, here," he pointed to a location on the map. "It is in these mountains in the northwest, Kurdish territory. The American's bombing had collapsed the entrance, that's why they didn't find it during their inspections. But with the coordinates I found it easily and recruited some farmers to reopen the tunnel." He lowered his voice to a whisper. "It is but a few hours from here, near this dam. These are the exact coordinates." Proudly, he handed the general a slip of paper.

Without looking at it, Tariq put the paper in his breast pocket and zipped the pocket closed. Later, he would memorize the information. "What do you mean by immense?"

"The stockpile fills one large cave and several small alcoves. I found several filing cabinets containing an inventory of each area's contents. Chemical as well as biological weapons stand in bombs, ready to be delivered with little preparation on our part. Defunct freezers with biological seed stock and liters of chemical agents await your nurturing touch. I also found research documents."

Breathing deeply to check his euphoric dizziness, Tariq walked on shaky legs to the chair behind his desk and sat down, lowering his head. He had often dreamed of this moment, but the reality of the power now in his hands made it hard for him to speak. Like a faithful dog, Abu al-Tubar sat down opposite him, waiting.

Tariq's head rose to face his old friend and he smiled. His eyes never left al-Tubar as he slid open the top left drawer and felt for the Berretta 92 pistol. His fingertips fondled the cold steel of the gun barrel while he looked at the photo in a silver frame on his desk, a gift from al-Tubar. Two proud young corporals, arms around each other's shoulders, it had been taken in the youth camp. Then his gaze shifted back to the devoted servant sitting motionless opposite him. *He is like a submissive family pet waiting for a bone. He doesn't have a single thought of his own in that ugly head of his.* His hand moved past the gun and instead removed a wad of money from the drawer and threw it on al-Tubar's fat lap. Tariq's voice cracked and he cleared his throat before he continued. "Arrange to have six of the biological bombs delivered to the farm's underground facility. Everything else will stay where it is until I inspect and inventory the cave's contents."

"Yes, my general."

"Just in case people—the Americans or the Israelis—are foolish enough to question my courage to use the weapons, I must be ready to make an example of them. The rest of the stockpile is safest where it is for now. Get yourself cleaned up and rest tonight, my friend. Soon you will be very rich and I will be very powerful!" They laughed and evil mirth shined in their eyes.

As al-Tubar left, he paused and looked back over his shoulder through the opened door at Tariq and the officers gathered in the conference room. An uncharacteristic impish grin stretched his rubbery jowls white when he thought: *a wealthy future is secure either way.*

Though he didn't want to interrupt the on-going discussion, when Tariq stepped into the conference room, his smug uncharacteristic smile signaled to all the officers that the time to reap their promised harvest had come. An anticipatory silence filled the room.

Tariq raised a hand that the colonel should continue speaking as he sat down at the head of the table.

"After anonymously leaking to the American press that the food poisoning in Britain was a cover-up, an account of the terrorist attack dominated the headlines world wide. We have infected the world with fear without a single finger pointed in our direction." The media was spreading panic even faster and further than Tariq had planned. The colonel continued: "The current implication is that Israel was the possible source. That was enough for the European community to tighten border security in an effort to isolate themselves from the fallout between Israel and Britain and of course their best friend, the United States. Terrorist and splinter groups are sending threats and fighting has escalated in Israel's West Bank. The Palestinians are crying out for protection before the Israelis use the virus on them."

The colonel picked up a pointer and explained the plan to the officers present. He gestured at the map on the wall where small clusters of blue, yellow, and red push pins were located. "The red are political targets; yellow, communications targets and the blue, our foot soldiers. Small units designated red and yellow to coincide with their targets, are in place at critical locations and our blue units are on our borders." A special division—which Tariq called his sand men because they had trained and survived in the harsh conditions of the desert—supported by 24 MIAI Abrams tanks, were hidden in the mountains. "Our sand men await the signal to annihilate the Kurds once and for all. This will give us complete control of the northern supply routes."

Restrained chuckles of agreement spread around the room. "The units along the frontier will act as sentries. As we all know, our army, though few in numbers, was not formed for a conventional battle. Each group has specific assignments and works independently. The Baghdad units will neutralize the government and take over the communication networks. Who is there to stand against us when they have proof of our power?" All the officers applauded.

Tariq glanced at the damage assessments someone handed him. The analysts had been very thorough. They had estimated both civilian and military casualties in Israel, where their first strike would be an example for the rest of the world. Even if the international community complied with his every wish, Tariq intended to bomb Israel. It had always been his favorite fantasy. Smiling he took a second glance at the estimate. The losses were acceptable, with civilian numbers the highest, but this would be a relatively bloodless battle once he used his weapons of mass destruction.

General Tariq Saeed nodded his approval and agreement. "Yes, this is very good. What did Stalin say? 'One death is a tragedy but thousands are a statistic.'" They all laughed.

Then, in a serious voice, Tariq said, "Let this be clear: I will not tolerate any aggressive action. If the United States or anyone takes a retaliatory posture, a biological warhead will be our immediate answer. The world powers must know we will meet all threats decisively." His voice swelled. "One week from today, we will control the world."

Tariq's new secretary knocked on his door. "General,

the television—CNN—is broadcasting an emergency situation in the United States."

Chapter 14

Assyria 811 B.C. – Revenge

Staggering, Queen Semiramis followed the scent of fresh air and found herself in a large open chamber. As she filled her lungs with the clean air, the fetid fog and ghostly images that lingered in her mind after the moldy ergot slowly began to evaporate. She held her torch high above her head and searched the shadows behind her. No one followed. The voices in her head grew quiet at last.

She walked deeper into the chamber, again inhaling and filling her lungs. Her torch flickered in the breeze. It was wonderful and impossible. How could there be fresh air so deep beneath the earth? She took another step forward. Her torchlight reflected off the walls in strange patterns. She rubbed her hand on the walls and inspected them. That same glittery substance that covered the walls now covered her hand with a rainbow of color. Holding the torch high, she could see part of a luminous mural painted across the surface of the wall. At the base of the mural were troughs filled with oil, similar to those used to light the temples in Calah. She lowered her torch to the oil. Her eyes followed the flame as the oil ignited, encircling the chamber with warmth and light.

Her eyes rebelled at this sudden explosion of bright light after the virtual darkness. She covered her eyes with her hands and tried to let light in a little bit at a time. At first it was painful and blinding, but gradually her eyes adjusted.

Cautiously, she lowered her hands from her eyes, wiped away the tears and squinting while she looked around.

She was standing in the middle of a huge domed chamber, and it was like nothing she had ever seen before. Colorful bas-reliefs and inscriptions covered every wall; even the dome was covered with them. Semiramis was astonished to read the history of the ancient inhabitants of this cave. One area depicted their customs and exploits of war, artistically blending the two aspects of life using a rudimentary form of the present-day cuneiform writing and pictures.

Semiramis' mind was swimming; she found every detail fascinating. On one wall, enclosed in a circle, was a map of the entire complex. With her finger she followed what she thought was the path that led her to this spot, obviously the town center. *Yes, this will be an advantage. While Ninyas thinks I'm wandering through the tunnels, I will be leading him.* She went over the map again. Like a hunter, her mind memorized every curve in the passages. She noticed the tunnels that led nowhere and then came across the symbol for bird: she knew it meant a secret passage.

She left the pictogram and walked around. Something had caught her eye. She found distortions in the way the mural was formed at the back of the grotto. She could tell that something wasn't right, though at first she couldn't place it. She stepped closer to the rock walls to investigate.

Looking closely at the walls she could see steps carved into the sidewalls. "By all the gods," she exclaimed aloud. The steps cut into the walls blended so well into the murals that you could not see them until you were upon them.

It felt as if she was walking into the scene in the mural as she followed the narrow steps up to the multiple levels of the beehive-like dome. Along the way she passed holes cut at odd angles into the wall. These openings were also hard to detect because they blended so well with the designs on the wall. Each opening led to a cell large enough for two or three people. Household items, pottery, bedding, and furs were scattered about on the cold floors. When she reached the top of the beehive and stood on a balcony that overlooked the town center, the layout was clear in beautiful symmetry. The people who had created this place had been fantastic builders.

She retraced her steps, returning to the lower level. The stone floor looked marred where her footprints had disturbed the dust. She leaned down and ran her hand across the surface. It felt so smooth and, where the dust was disturbed, an intricate mosaic was exposed. *But why haven't I found any bones? Where did they all go?*

Once back on the main level, she noticed a large well in the center of the hive. She hurried to it, eager to wash away the sour taste in her mouth and the raw feeling in her throat. A large terracotta jar, intended to draw the water, sat by the wall, but the rope to lower the jar had rotted long ago. She tore strips from her cloak and tied the line she made to the jar. She lowered the jar inches at a time. Then the jar began to spin and swing and it shattered. As the queen stared down the well thinking of another way to get to the water, muffled voices echoed through the cavernous space. Licking her sticky lips, she abandoned her attempt to reach the water and ran to listen to try pinpointing Ninyas' location.

Reassured that the voices were probably above her by at least two levels, she decided she had plenty of time to continue her reconnaissance. She had not yet discovered the source of fresh air which might also provide escape from Ninyas and the mountain.

She peered into many of the side tunnels that branched from the town center like spokes of a wheel.

"That wonderful breeze, I feel it again," she murmured and followed the air current. Once in the tunnel, her curiosity intensified when she saw the walls were covered with red and blue mystical symbols. Further in she discovered the source of fresh air. Holes had been dug in staggered intervals in the ceiling of the tunnel. She imagined they extended up to the surface of the mountain. But they were too small for a person to fit through; only about the size of a small melon. There was no exit, no escape to the surface.

Disappointed, she returned to the place where she had seen the magic symbols on the walls. "Painted by priests and magicians." Her fingers traced the symbols and tingled when they ran across Ishtar's secret name. When the tunnel came to a dead end, she bent down to examine the well-worn footpath and vomited. It was more of the same black blood. She paid no attention to the blood and wiped it from her nose and mouth with the back of her hand as she continued searching. She did not fear the demon working its evil inside her.

When she stood, she noticed the torches surrounding the wall at the end of the tunnel. *One of them must be a lever to open a hidden door*. Semiramis had many such burrows in her own palace, and all the treasure rooms had such secret entrances. *Could there be a treasure on the other side of this wall?*

One by one, the queen tried to move every torch, but none budged. She examined the adjoining walls. Again, no lever. *By all the gods, what am I missing?* In desperation, she sunk down to the floor and leaned against the wall. Then she saw it, a clay tablet in the wall covered with thick brown mold. At first the cuneiform writing made no sense until she remembered that the tablet had to be turned ninety degrees to the right to decipher the forms. She had forgotten what every child in Assyria knew: the script was written in wet clay from top to bottom in parallel lines but was read from right to left. The scribe's hand often smeared the preceding column so the tablet would be turned and the signs written in horizontal lines running from top to bottom.

Her mind adjusted the tablet's angle and she recognized the pictographic form for water. She whispered the words as her finger traced the symbols: "d en kid lil sum-ma gir-pad-du a- wi-lin is-te-bi- ir gir-pad-du su i se-eb-bi- ru... They will break his bone." It was a warning. She skipped the rest and let her fingers trace the last line. "Birds. No: Doves," Semiramis exclaimed.

Impatiently she searched for the doves and found that the symbol was repeated four times along the bottom of the wall near the floor. She placed a finger on each symbol and pressed. A lever slid out from the wall. Grasping the handle with anticipation she pushed it down. She waited. Beads of sweat glistened on her face as the seconds ticked away without anything happening. Then a low thick vibration began to tickle the bottom of her feet. As the vibrations flowed up through her body, an ear-piercing grinding noise filled the tunnel as the whole wall—some eight feet high by six feet wide—began to swing open ponderously. As the opening widened the dank smell of decay sprang from the darkness. As the stench washed over her and filled the passage, Semiramis grabbed her sword and held it ready as the opening widened.

Ninyas most certainly had heard the stone door opening, so she had to hurry. As she walked in she wondered if this could be the home of the gods. A few yards into the tunnel she saw a faint, rosy glow radiating from the other end of the passage. The glow warmed her, and she slackened her grip on her sword, pointing the tip at the ground. Her shoulders drooped. She found herself tiptoeing as if not to disturb the gods. *I belong here.* She felt both relieved and repulsed.

Reverently, she walked into the space. Dark, shadowy figures loomed around her. She could sense their presence but she heard not a sound, not a breath. Not even the noise of water was audible, yet the symbols had indicated it would be found here. Her nausea threatened to return at any moment and she was desperate to see the lay of what would most certainly be her last battlefield. She knew where to look for the torches by now and quickly moved to the walls. After lighting them all, she waited a few seconds for the greasy smoke from the burning oil to dissipate. When the smoke cleared, she saw that this was indeed the most holy of holies: the home of the gods. They were all there to welcome her. In the very center of the ornate cavern stood the statue of EnLiL, god of gods, in all his glory. His regal head almost touched the ceiling, thirty feet above. He was covered in gold and his ten pairs of horns were made of silver and studded with rubies. His blazing eyes were gleaming emeralds and they stared at her. Ishtar's statue was just as bejeweled and when the queen saw the goddess, she fell to her knees and chanted the ancient words that glorified the gods.

"EnLiL, whose command is far-reaching, lofty his word and holy,

"Whose pronouncement is unchangeable,

"Who decrees destinies unto the distant future,

"Whose lifted eye scans the lands,

"Whose lifted beam searches the heart of the land,

"When father EnLiL seats himself broadly on the holy dais, the lofty dais,

"When he perfects lordship and princeship,

"The earth-gods bow down before him,

"The heaven-gods humble themselves before him...." [2]

After her prayers, she walked toward the glow at the far end of the chamber. There, she discovered a huge shimmering pool of midnight purple. It stretched as far as she could see. The gypsum crystals covering the columns hanging from the ceiling and rising from the floor exaggerated the torchlight. It blinked back and forth across the underground lake, spilling a dawn-tinted hue over everything.

The scent of decay was strongest on the far shore of the lake. The queen walked toward the odor and soon discovered the bloated body of a horse on shore. She thought, *probably a victim of the storm. There must be an underground river that feeds this lake.* But she knew she did not have the strength to risk the swim to find it.

She returned to the far side of the lake, knelt down and scooped up a handful of the clear water. It tasted sweet but, no sooner had the water passed her lips a second time, than the retching started again and her nose ran blood and she thought, *I must hurry before all my strength abandons me. My son knows by now that he, too, has been infected, so this battle will be to both our deaths. Assyria will be the victor.*

She saw a trough of oil that ran around the perimeter of the lake and lit it. Then she laid the remnants of her once regal cloak, together with all that was left of her worldly possessions, at the side of the pool.

From a leather pouch at her belt she withdrew a small

round ball of soap. It was more of an abrasive than soap, made from ashes mixed with oil and pure clay. With the graceful movements of a dancer, she stepped to the edge of the water and began to remove her soiled clothes, leather belt and arm bracelets. Her naked body cast a serene silhouette over the glow of the lake. The chill of the water did not slow her progress into the deeper waters, nor did her stomach cramps and severe headache delay her advance. Her only thought was to prepare herself.

She submerged her entire body in the frigid water. When she reemerged, she scrubbed the blood and grime from her skin before leaving the lake. She could see bleeding beneath the skin where she had rubbed her arms too vigorously, but she continued the ritual anyway.

She walked onto the rocky beach and laid open the leather pouch and set aside the contents. She examined her body and was satisfied that it was as clean as she could be under these circumstances. It was part of a warrior's ritual to purify one's self before battle.

She removed a small vial of perfumed oil and anointed her naked body and hair. This custom was observed by even the very lowest in society. It served the dual purpose of both softening the skin in the arid Assyrian environment and destroying the irritating vermin that were so common in the hair.

When she had completed her preparations, she wrapped her chilled body in the salvaged sheepskins and at last laid down to rest. *Yes, Ninyas is close. I can feel his hatred.*

She fell into a deep sleep. Hazael's strong face and encouraging words found her. "I will give you my strength, and you will win the day."

Then she heard the king calling her name: "Come, come,

my warrior queen, join me in battle. We fight for Assyria's future together." She could hear his deep coarse laughter above the sounds of the swords clashing, but could not find him on the dust-clouded battlefield.

Now a different battle—that between a mother and her son—invaded her dreams. They ran toward each other with a purpose born of evil intent. The dreams and reality mingled together in that twilight time before one comes fully awake. She awoke confused. She wished one of the priestesses with the gift of prophecy was with her to interpret the dreams. But, like all Assyrians, she understood that dreams were how the gods communicated with mortals. Assyrians regarded a dream as the equivalent of reality. Her dream was a present and future truth and it included a dark, beautiful lady. Their essences mingled and became intertwined.

The woman's name was as beautiful as she: "Miryam," whispered the queen into the darkness. "Your name means rebellion."

Chapter 15

Vortex

The continuous ringing of the telephone reverberated in Wayne's mind like the annoying beat of a drum. He covered his head with his arms, trying to obliterate the intrusion.

The ringing continued.

He jerked and his legs fell off the chair where they had been resting and landed with a thud on the floor. He twitched at the sound, but still was not ready to open his eyes.

Raising his head from the table that had been his pillow, Wayne stretched his arms out in front of him and gripped the edge of the table, then pushed back. Papers stuck to his arms and, when he opened his eyes, he looked at the offending white pieces strangely before he pulled them off and threw them back into the disorganized mess. The ringing drummed on and on. On wooden legs, he walked to the phone, rubbing his face, trying to wake himself up.

Matt and Wayne bumped into each other as they converged on the offensive phone. As they got closer, their noses twitched in response to the odors their unshaven, unwashed bodies were giving off.

Wayne picked up the phone and answered with a dry rasping: "Yeah?"

Still in a semi-comatose state, Matt wandered over to stand in front of the air conditioner. He turned the fan on high and waved his hand in front of his face in an attempt to clear the air, then turned his back against the wall and slid down to sit on the floor, not far from the spot where he had slept for the last three hours before sunrise. He rested his elbows on bent knees and cradled his head in his hands. "I can't remember ever being this tired," he muttered to no one in particular.

Wayne listened to the person at the other end of the phone for a few seconds and then hung up without a word. Sluggishly, he staggered to the table and sat down. He caught Matt inspecting him. "What? Don't look at *me*, buddy. You don't smell so great yourself. Your stink is worse than mine."

"You have what my sons' call swamp breath," said Matt, scratching his uncombed head. He stretched his arms above his head, revealing stains under the armpits of his last clean shirt.

"You could use a little cleaning up, yourself. The James Bond thing is slipping." Wayne walked into the bathroom and turned on the shower.

Matt got up and walked into the bedroom and stopped in front of the two neatly made beds. Last night had been intense. He was worn out beyond all comprehension. They had been in Atlanta for eight days working non-stop with the CDC to track the strain of virus and its ultimate nesting place. Finding the point of origin had been more complex than they had anticipated. A convoluted route had been ingeniously planned to conceal the scientist who had ordered the samples. Matt had spent days weeding through the computer files at the tissue culture repository. Meanwhile Wayne had worked in the laboratory to identify the precise strain of the viruses and research his hypothesis about the unidentified third agent.

At last Matt had made a breakthrough. Hidden deep

in the computerized shipping records at the repository he found the order for the virus that had killed his mother. According to the shipping documents it had been sent to a non-existent research facility. All the documents lead to just one person and one place. That person had received the exact strains of Rift Valley fever and tick-borne encephalitis viruses that they had identified as the agents used to kill Martha and the others.

Matt's rage regarding his mother's cold-blooded murder had not subsided, but the work channeled his anger. When he first told Wayne that Israel and Miryam were involved, all hell broke lose. Matt knew Miryam and had hoped the information Pearl had given them was a false trail. That hadn't proven to be the case: the deeper he dug, the more often Miryam's name surfaced.

Wayne and Matt had argued most of the night. The two friends had almost come to blows. Then, when Matt showed Wayne the British intelligence information he'd received the previous night that confirmed that Miryam had ties in Iraq, the situation worsened.

Disillusioned and confused, Wayne still rose to defend Miryam. "Someone could have planted that information to camouflage their involvement. You know Miryam: she's not capable of killing that way. She's a physician."

"She's a soldier like us," said Matt.

"Exactly. She's *not* a terrorist," Wayne insisted.

"I know what you think: The Jews hate anyone they feel might threaten them. Britain has a large Muslim population now and the government is obliged to respond to them and they see Israel as a viable threat. Parliament has cut back on their support of Israeli business in our country and that will only be the beginning." Matt hated to hear the venom in his own voice, but he wasn't going to turn away from the facts, no matter how good a friend Wayne was. His mother was dead and he wanted the guilty party to pay.

"Matt, look again: this is bogus. You worked intelligence. Can't you smell a rat?"

The pain in Wayne's voice threatened to halt Matt's unrelenting accusations. But then he thought of his mother's agonizing death and his own pain bit back. "What was Miryam doing in Iraq anyway? That was never in her background information until now. Don't all these little bits of new information that keep surfacing make you wonder if you really knew Miryam? Stop thinking with your heart, Wayne! If it was anyone else, you wouldn't hesitate to pronounce them guilty. The facts fit! And I know she had the knowledge and expertise to do it. Remember, you told me not to let my emotions get in the way of the facts. Maybe we should ask someone more objective like my mother, the lawyer, where the evidence points. Oh, I'm sorry, we can't do that, she's dead!"

They went over and over the evidence and Wayne would still not accept the results. They were both too stubborn to give an inch.

One was venting his rage concerning his mother's senseless death, the other defending a lover. Emotions spent, they agreed to reserve judgment—or at least sentencing—until they had spoken with Miryam.

Even so, Wayne still would not give up. He continued to search the records all night for the smallest hint of something that would exonerate Miryam.

Matt was glad that endless night was over. He stretched out on the bed, waiting his turn to use the shower. *This is strange, we were going to ask Miryam for help, and now we find out she's the cause of everything. I wonder how Wayne will react when he sees her.*

He pulled the last of his clean underwear out of the suitcase Olivia had sent him. When he heard the shower stop, he stripped off his smelly clothes, grabbed his clean underwear and walked into the living room just as Wayne was coming out of the bathroom, a towel wrapped around his waist.

From the open bathroom door, Wayne watched in fascination as the trail of steam from the bathroom was drawn toward the air conditioner. "I owe you an apology, Matt. Sorry I was so hardheaded last night. I can't deny where or to whom the paper trail leads and I will confront Miryam. But please, let's give her a chance to explain. I like to think there are always possibilities."

Matt smiled. "Star Trek? Spock?"

"Right," his wily smile returned briefly. "So let's keep our minds open."

"There's one more thing: I need a favor, Matt. I don't want anyone else to know about Miryam's possible involvement until we have a chance to check it out." Wayne looked pleadingly at his friend.

"I can keep it under my hat for awhile. But remember, I'm here on behalf of my government. The clock is ticking and I won't jeopardize the rest of my family or anyone else by not passing on information that might save lives. But I'll give you some warning before I go public. Agreed? "

Wayne wiped his forehead with the back of his hand. He noticed he was already sweating again, but he managed a smile and stuck his hand out to Matt. "Agreed," he said as they shook hands. "By the way, that was Hal on the phone earlier. He had a message from Pearl. She wants us in Israel as soon as possible. Everything's been arranged. Hal is on his way to hook up with Rich. We leave tonight on a cargo plane from Atlanta."

"How did she know that we'd need to go to Israel?"

"My guess? Madame security advisor has a great network of spies. Or our room is bugged."

"I don't even want to think about it. I need a shower and some strong coffee before my brain melts down." Matt ambled into the steam-filled bathroom and closed the door behind him.

An hour later, Wayne and Matt sat opposite each other in a booth at a diner. Wayne was on his second plate of hominy grits, eggs, and thick-sliced ham. He had filled the jukebox, and the jaunty songs of the Beatles, the Four Tops, and the Everly Brothers flooded the diner.

Over breakfast, Wayne and Matt debated Wayne's theory that the foreign gene was not natural, but had been inserted in the matrix of the virus. It was something no one had seen before.

"I know no one's been able to classify the third agent," Matt said, "but why call it a suicide gene?"

Wayne shoveled in more food as he spoke. "Don't you see? That's the only explanation for there not being any secondary infections from contact with the people exposed on the plane. That's what saved Olivia and the boys. But I know what you're going to ask: why would anyone want to do that?" Wayne chewed and thought, his fork making circles in the air. "The reason is still percolating." He shoveled grits and ham into his mouth. This idea would not let go of him. Ever since the briefing with the president, he'd had the idea that the virus had a purpose beyond death and destruction, but just what that might be, he couldn't say. Perhaps even more importantly, someone out there—not Miryam—wasn't afraid to use it.

Matt swirled the last few drops of coffee left in his cup

around and around, thinking about what Wayne was saying. The waitress came and Matt ordered a third cup of coffee.

The waitress returned with a steaming pot of black liquid and filled Matt's cup. "Wild night out, huh, sweetie?" She winked. "Looks like you could use this, honey." Her eyes sparkled at Matt. "Don't you worry. Margo will take care of you." She moved on to her other customers with a seductive swing of her hips, glancing at Matt over her shoulder.

"I think Margo wants to be your friend," Wayne said.

Matt smiled at Margo, who was keeping her eye on him. "OK: just for argument's sake, say that there *is* a suicide gene. How would it work?" He relaxed back into his seat, sipping his coffee, waiting for an answer.

"Let's keep what I'm about to say under our hats. I need to get a few more answers in Israel first."

"There's not a lot of space left under my hat, but I'm with you. Don't let our disagreement last night make you question my loyalty. We're in this to discover the truth. I'm not looking for just anyone to use as a target for my revenge. I don't want the almighty U.S. of A. getting into a war with the wrong people, old boy. So tell me what you're thinking."

Wayne began, a cocky smile on his face. "I think the virus goes through an abortive replicative cycle in peripheral cells. Isn't that interesting?"

A few of the men sitting behind Wayne looked at him as if he had spoken a different language.

He grinned, lowered his voice then continued. "I think the host becomes infected, but by the time symptoms show up, the virus growth cycle has been completed. Maybe that's why we haven't been able to culture anything in the lab. Could it be that it's temperature-sensitive?"

"No," Matt replied. "If it was sensitive to high temperatures it wouldn't have grown in the brain and caused the encephalitis symptoms. Besides, the CDC tried to grow virus from the samples at a whole range of temperatures. They didn't find anything. We could study this for years," continued Matt, "but I see where you're going. And that would explain why the hospital personnel and other contacts, like Olivia, were not infected. Thank God!"

"Remember when Dr. Daly and I went to the hospital isolation laboratory to look for virus under the electron microscope and do a smear and genetic testing? We found genetic evidence of a viral infection but never found virus. While we were there, I noticed one of the lab workers had a bandage over his hand and was very nervous. With some encouragement he told me that when the first samples came to the lab for identification, he'd broken a tube containing some of the samples. The glass cut right through his gloves and he had a large gash on the palm of his hand. He was waiting to get sick but hadn't and was too frightened to tell anyone what had happened."

"Don't you see?" Wayne enthused. "We treated the samples and our patients as if they were infectious, but in reality they were not. And that poor laboratory guy's experience clinches it: the virus didn't have the ability to cause secondary infections. This is so cool."

"Don't lose your perspective, my friend," snapped Matt. "It's diabolical! This 'cool' bug causes death. Real people have died. And more may follow if we can't figure this out. And we still don't know why, or do we?"

"You're right. But I think I know at least the why. There are two possibilities. The first is that it's some experiment that went awry. The other is, like you said, to cause panic, but on a limited scale." Wayne finished his meal and hailed their waitress for more coffee. "To find the genetic material but find out it's not infectious points to the presence of—for lack of a better label—a suicide gene. If that's the case, it means that someone was genetically manipulating the virus, perhaps to make a new form of biological weapon. Think about it."

Matt stared at Wayne. Slowly the last statement sank in and he shuddered. "So the possible scenarios are that the virus kills off everyone exposed to it and the terrorists walk in and take over, without a fight, and without fear of becoming infected. Or—and this is even scarier—if the terrorists removed the suicide gene from the virus and threaten populations with secondary and tertiary infections. We have to figure out where it was manufactured and how much more of this new biological ordnance is around."

They both stared into space thinking. Matt broke the silence first. "What if the virus considered the suicide gene as extraneous material? Unnecessary garbage. There would be no advantage for the virus to keep it, which could cause the virus to find a way to delete the suicide gene on its own."

"You're right. Remember: nature can surprise us with its own mutations. We don't know if it's possible for this virus to do its own site-directed mutagenesis and override the suicide gene. Mother nature often finds a way to undo man's meddling,"

"Even worse, it could combine with some other virus and reconfigure the human host genetic material." Wayne leaned in closer to listen to Matt. "Bingo: a new virus no one's ever seen before. It would spread unchecked, infecting whole continents as it devoured most of the world's population. What's even worse is that no one would recognize it and there'd be no treatment to stop it. It would be like the return of the plague that killed a third of Europe's population in the fourteenth century."

"This reminds me of something I read in the *Annals of the New York Academy*," Wayne said, newly alert. Matt's words had clearly sparked something. "It was about what chaos theory calls a bifurcation point." Matt looked confused. He added, *"Jurassic Park?* The movie?" Still no recognition on Matt's face, Wayne continued. "According to Hedén, 'It is a critical junction at which a system may either move to a higher state of order or degenerate into chaos.'"

Both men stared bleary-eyed into their coffee cups. The implications were terrifying.

Now that Wayne had voiced all of the fears he had held in check since day one, he felt worse, not better. Once again they were caught up in a possible biological tidal wave that threatened to wash over and consume millions of unsuspecting innocent people.

Matt gave his cup another swirl but he did not drink. Bringing the cup closer, he stared into the black liquid.

Matt answered Wayne's unasked question in a whisper: "Don't worry, I can handle it. But I don't mind telling you that I had hoped after Saddam's downfall that we'd never have to discuss one of these doomsday scenarios again."

"I'm sorry to have brought you into this," Wayne said, meaning it. "Maybe you should be at home with your family. As we get closer to the terrorist, we could be stirring up a contagious hornet's nest."

"I'm here *for* my family. They know that. But now I understand why you were reluctant to disclose everything to the government." Matt leaned back into the vinyl seat of the booth, "I'm with you for the duration of this… whatever you want to call it."

Matt picked up his coffee cup and drained it. His lot had been cast with his friend and he swallowed his fear along with his coffee. "Besides, you need me. Who else has first-hand field experience handling these kinds of biologics? You're more of a lab rat. And there might be an upside to this suicide gene thing. It might help us develop better vaccines."

Just then a young man with fair hair wearing jeans, sneakers, and a bright white T-shirt approached their table. From his carefree appearance, Wayne thought he was selling candy bars for the Boy Scouts. When he walked over to Wayne and Matt and spoke in a strong decisive voice, Wayne was surprised.

"Which of you is Dr. Swift?" he asked.

Wayne raised his hand like a child asking to be excused to the bathroom during math class. "Now what?"

"I've seen pictures of you, but it never hurts to check. I have a message from a friend of yours." He hesitated and slid in next to Wayne. "Pearl says, 'Leave right now.' A plane is waiting. Gentlemen, I am your escort. We are going to Israel."

"Who the hell are you?" asked Matt in his stiffest British tone.

The young man had a disarming smile. "A friend," was all he said.

"What about our clothes and papers?" asked Matt.

"All of your things are on the plane. We saved you the trouble of packing." He stood and motioned for them to get up and follow him.

Wayne was not surprised by Pearl's message and put up

his hands to surrender, threw some money on the table, and motioned for Matt to follow.

"What? They packed all our soiled clothes in with the clean ones? Abominable." Matt was jesting, but couldn't resist getting in one more shot. "Obviously we have different hygienic standards in the UK than you do here in the States. I say it is positively unsanitary." He talked as he threw a big tip on the table for Margo and then stood and followed Wayne.

"Tone it down," Wayne whispered. "Remember Letterman? Genetic mutant?"

"From the same mold?" Matt asked.

Wayne nodded and laughed, "besides, we didn't have any clean clothes."

"Well, then," Matt smiled his agreement, "I suppose you're right." They left the diner and fell in behind their escort who headed toward a waiting van with the motor running.

While they walked, Wayne took a closer look at their escort and noticed the hard lines around his mouth and the way he walked. That walk spoke volumes. The young man's hands rested at his side but did not touch his body. He was ready for anything.

"Doctors," the kid motioned to two other soldiers waiting by the car, "this is the rest of your team. I'm Lieutenant Gibbs, this is Cordy, our desert expert and the guy in the back seat is Jack, we call him Flash Jack, demolitions. We will be accompanying you to Israel and wherever you need us to go. Our purpose is to support your mission."

"So are those your real names?" asked Matt.

The three Marines smiled but didn't say anything.

Wayne smiled. "Well, this evens the odds..."

Matt frowned. "So, the five of us go up against Israel

and the rest of the world? There is only one person who would love those odds..."

Matt and Wayne supplied the name in one voice: "Rich."

"'No one made a bigger mistake than he who did nothing because he could do so little,'" Wayne quoted. He waited for Matt to respond.

Lieutenant Gibbs answered instead: "Edmund Burk."

Then, like Houdini, Lieutenant Gibbs made two rings appear in the palm of his hand. He extended his hand to Matt and Wayne so they could get a good look at the jewelry as he said: "A gift from Pearl. As you can see they are duplicates of your Rutgers college ring, Dr. Swift, and of your wedding band, Dr. Rogers, with a slight addition." Checking his watch, Gibbs, suggested he explain all the details on their way to the airport so they jumped into the van.

Cordy drove as Gibbs turned to face the back seat to finish explaining. "Your rings each contain a computer chip with coded information identifying you both as special envoys of the President of the United States. The rings will give you carte blanche access all over the world, or most of it," explained the lieutenant. "When you pass through the security scanners at the airport—say in Israel—the chip will omit a signal that security personnel will recognize, giving them the green light for you to enter without going through customs or any of the usual inquiries and searches."

The lieutenant passed out the counterfeit rings and collected the real ones, promising to keep them safe. Matt's was a little loose. "I'll be in the dog house if my real wedding ring gets lost," warned Matt.

The lieutenant smiled. "You mean the sexy poem engraved inside? Look closer, doc. It's still there."

Wayne moved over to try and get a look at the poem. "There's a side of you I didn't know about," quipped Wayne.

Matt pushed him away. "How did you find out about that?" he sputtered. "That's a bit over the top."

When Lieutenant Gibbs turned around to face Wayne and Matt he smiled for the first time. It was a nice smile, a reassuring smile, warm and friendly. And it did the trick. Who could ever believe the kid was warrior?

Chapter 16

The Captain

It was dark by the time Miryam finished her work in Ha Gosherim. She was weary as she drove south to her home in Rosh Pina, an agricultural community north of the Sea of Galilee.

She was certain of two things: there would be another attempt on her life and—her instincts told her—someone had been following her all day. She had taken precautions, expecting these events. After all, she had been trained by the best spies in the world, the Mossad.

She had made many enemies and some of them were Israelis. And she had made mistakes. One was when she had drawn too much attention to herself over her concern with chemical and biological weapons. After the scientific committee turned her down, she had gone to the newspapers. The public forum had angered the government and damaged her credibility. Miryam wondered if they thought she was a security risk. But she knew that, if the Mossad was after her in earnest, she would already be dead. *A tiny ricin pellet injected from a needle-tipped umbrella as I passed by on the street, that's more their style.*

The strong wind whipped up dust around the car as she turned off the main road. Miryam strained to see out the front window through the powdery mist. The sand and dirt settled on the road, camouflaging large sections, making it difficult to tell where the road had been cut through the arable land. She gripped the wheel with white knuckles. As night fell, the light of her own headlamps bounced off the dirt particles suspended in the air and glared back in her face. Fighting fatigue, her eyes watered and her lids grew heavy as she strained to penetrate the illusive foggy tunnel that now surrounded her. The monotony of the drive and lack of sleep the night before was taking its toll on her concentration. She fought to stay awake.

She rubbed her tired eyes and leaned forward to see. Then something astonishing and unexpected happened. There, in the dim glow from the dashboard lighting, a vision took form on the windshield in front of Miryam. At first she saw only her own reflection. Long shadows under her eyes, nose, and mouth made her into a macabre figure, but it was still her face. Transfixed, she watched in fascination as the image wavered and began to change. It was still her, but she was dressed differently and she could hear herself speak in the Assyrian language: "Beware of the Captain."

She was jerked back to reality as lights from an oncoming car blinded her and extinguished the face in the windshield.

Frustrated, she stamped her foot on the accelerator. She checked the rearview mirror and noticed that the same car she had seen earlier today was behind her again. Once she hit the city limits of Elifelet, she easily lost the car following her in the rush hour traffic and only then did she decide it was safe to head home. She parked several blocks from her apartment and switched to another vehicle she had waiting

The work at the lab went well that night. The excitement of being followed had awakened her mind. When she returned to her apartment she fell, exhausted, onto the bed and into her dreams. An indistinct image drifted in and out of her rest, mingling with Miryam's own image. Eventually, she fell into an undisturbed sleep. The corners of her full lips turned up in a serene smile and then down in a feminine pout. Miryam was sleeping and, for the first time in months, she was also dreaming but not about the Assyrian queen. Anyone seeing her then would have recognized the look of love that lit her face. In the dusky light, the outline of her voluptuous body was visible, stretching beneath the thin bedcovers. Light from the street lamps filtered through the slats of the blinds and rippled across her body. The faint ribbons of light enhanced the curves of her breasts and thighs as the thin cotton sheet rose and fell with each gentle breath.

The sensual woman languishing in the small bed was of special interest to the leering eyes that watched. He fantasized about perhaps having a beautiful woman like this one for his own one day. He held his breath as one lovely bare leg slid out from under the sheet. With regret, he returned his attention to jimmying the lock on her window, his frustration and sexual excitement rising.

From his usual sleeping place at the side of her bed, Strider came to attention and a low growl rolled into the static air. Miryam's guardian was alert, waiting and watching the shadowy figure outside the window.

A whimper escaped the sleeping women's lips and she whispered: "Wayne." She swooned in response to something or someone in the dream. Strider gently nudged the graceful arm dangling over the side of the bed. She resisted his attempt to awaken her from this rare and peaceful sleep. Strider prodded her again, and licked his mistress's arm. In a sleepy voice, with eyes still closed but mind now waking, she spoke to the dog in hushed tones. "Strider," she said sleepily. She groaned and stretched, opening her eyes to look at him. "I was dreaming. Wayne and I were together, lying in the warm sun on our beach."

Pulling the nervous dog closer she thought about the dream. *How many lives ago was Wayne a part of my life? I'll be glad when this charade I've been living is over.* Another voice from within promised peace and a new beginning. Like a wisp of smoke, her misgivings were gone and the queen was back with her, part of her.

"Oh, my beauty," Miryam whispered as she moved to the edge of the bed. She placed a bare arm over the dog's shoulder and then sensed his tension. His body stood rigid and alert next to her. The queen whispered in her mind: *"The Captain approaches."*

Now that Strider had all of Miryam's attention, he growled and looked back and forth between the window and the bedroom door. Danger was close by. She froze and watched in the dim light. Strider lowered his head, sniffing at the bottom of the bedroom door. Another, more menacing low growl rolled from his curled-back muzzle. Like quicksilver, she threw on a T-shirt and crawled over to the dog and gave him a hand signal to be silent. Dog and owner huddled together in the darkness, still as statues, listening.

As she stroked the dog's white fur, she heard a slight scuffing sound. Her body became taut.

She waited, listening to the darkness. She could be very patient. Her razor-sharp hearing identified another person's shallow breathing just beyond the door.

Silently, she slid her arm away from Strider and returned to the bed for the two throwing knives attached to the back of the headboard. She watched the dog and read the signals of his body language. The dog's head swiveled around to the window. From where she crouched by the bed, she could see the shape of a solitary figure breaking the light pattern made by the blinds. Strider was correct: one intruder was in the apartment and another was outside the bedroom window.

She sneered, thinking, *I guess it's a compliment that two men were sent to kill one woman.*

Moving through the shadows, she reached the bedroom door and placed her fingers lightly on the knob. She felt it turn slightly in her hand but she was not turning the knob. She signaled Strider to move behind the door next to her.

Suddenly, the window shattered. Strider's full weight was thrown against her legs as one of the intruders crashed through the window from the fire escape, slamming into Strider. The dog's weight pushed her up against the bedroom door, preventing the man on the other side of the door from entering. She threw the steel bolt on the inside of the bedroom door to stop the second attacker's entry.

Miryam crouched and threw a knife towards the place where the assailant had landed when he jumped through the window. The muffled thud and shriek told her she'd hit her mark and at least wounded him. Strider was sluggish at first but recovered quickly and tore into the intruder, growling and snapping. She was about to help him finish the man when she heard the bedroom door splinter. She rolled into the bathroom, pulling the door shut behind her and locking it. From the commotion in the other room, she knew Strider remained in a fierce battle. Miryam smiled when she heard Strider's opponent curse in Arabic.

Then she heard a low, piteous whimper and silence, *Strider, that was Strider.* She wanted to go to him but knew it was just what the assassins wanted. She flattened herself on the bathroom floor and peered out under the bottom of the door. In the small square of moonlight shining through the tattered blind she saw her beloved companion lying as still as death on the bedroom floor. At first glance she was terror stricken. Then she saw the dart lodged in the fur near the back of his neck and she watched the rise and fall of his chest. He was breathing. He was all right, just sleeping. Relieved, she rolled onto her back and took a moment to calm her rapidly beating heart. Then it occurred to her that a dart gun was a curious weapon for assassins.

She could use a second weapon. As she cracked open the door, she saw her bloody throwing knife, just inches away. Then she heard a dull thud and felt the door vibrate. It was another dart. She jerked back, abandoning the knife and locking the door. *One knife would have to do to kill two men. But why the darts? Why not just shoot me?* Then she saw Tariq's plan as clearly as if he were speaking to her. *He wants to make it look like suicide to the Israeli authorities. I am to be remembered as a traitor—and what else? Possibly a terrorist? Perhaps he hopes I'd write a farewell confession?*

She thought of Strider lying peacefully on the floor. If it weren't for his warning, she'd be hanging from a rope or maybe something worse.

She heard one of the men whining about Strider's attack. "No one said anything about a dog, damn it. He nearly tore my arm off before I got the dart in him. And that cursed woman's knife got me in the leg."

Footsteps crossed the room. She listened. A deep voice berated the man who'd crashed through the window. "You idiot, we've lost the element of surprise. It's an advantage not to be squandered. You've much to learn. What good are you to me wounded?"

The younger man answered in Arabic. "But, captain, I had her in my sights. I don't know how I could have missed her. And this will not slow me down." He tied a scarf around his wound.

Ah, the captain has arrived. Miryam crouched out of sight, barefoot, on the rough wooden floor beside the bathtub. *Interesting, I recognize the same fear of failure in the wounded man's voice as I heard in the man in the park.*

She was clad only in underpants and a T-shirt. *Excellent. All the better for fighting.* She grabbed a bottle of ammonia from under the sink. She punched the cap with her knife. The potent smell made her eyes tear.

Now she could hear them searching her desk and computer. The captain instructed the other man to take all her computer disks and that the fire would destroy everything else.

The general isn't sure how much I've learned. The knob on the bathroom door rattled. "We know you're in there, Doctor," purred the Captain.

Miryam did not answer. She was thinking about the panel behind the tub that the plumbers had cut into the wall when she'd modernized the apartment. The pipe conduit ran inside the wall from the bath into the kitchen and living room area. If she could make her way along the narrow tunnel inside the wall, she'd come out under the kitchen sink, behind them. Before making her move, she listened at the locked bathroom door.

Now that there was no need for silence, the two men talked openly. The captain was still worried about arousing suspicious neighbors. He wanted to hurry and finish the job.

"Captain, we have her cornered," the other whispered.

Just a boy, what a shame he will not get any older, the warrior in her thought.

"Silence," whispered the captain through gritted teeth.

"Use your night-vision glasses. There's no way for her to get out of that room."

Miryam smiled to herself as she crawled into the tunnel. *It'll take them a while to remove the bathroom door.* Her bedroom doubled as her office and was the largest room in the apartment. The room was cluttered and cramped. It would take time for them to sort through it all. *It pays to be messy*, she laughed to herself.

She was making steady progress crawling along inside the wall when her knee came down hard on the tip of a protruding nail. She stifled a cry of pain and pulled her knee off the nail. Wincing, she tested her wounded leg by flexing it out behind her. It hurt, but headroom was limited so she had no choice but to continue crawling on the bloody wound.

The younger of the two intruders cursed as a stack of books toppled over onto him. "Shit," he cursed.

"You're useless," the captain fumed. "I'll start working on the bathroom door. You backtrack into the living room and make sure she doesn't get by you. No stupid stunts. Let's finish this. It's almost dawn."

Miryam paused for a second, amused. She knew exactly what had happened. *Crashing through the window was a childish act of bravado.* The younger man's clumsy movements further emphasized his inexperience. *Children should not play adult games,* she mused. Then she decided he was an easy target and would be her first kill. Neither fear nor anxiety nor even indignation at the assassins' intrusion invaded her thoughts. She was not dreaming now. She steeled herself: the danger was real and upon her and the queen was with her, replacing fear with strength.

It was easy to find the opening under the sink and pull herself onto the kitchen floor. When she emerged, her body was coiled and tensed, every muscle ready to react. Her bare feet moved silently on the wooden floor as she quickly moved to the circuit breaker on the wall. Experience told her the assassins had turned off the power and her plan needed illumination. Remembering that she had turned all the lights off before going to bed, she safely threw the breaker switch to the on position.

"I'm telling you, she's not in the bathroom," said the captain.

"Then where did she go?" asked the young assassin.

"Stop talking, you fool," the captain grunted. "She has to be somewhere in this apartment, stupid."

That was going to be the last thing the soldier ever heard. *What a terrible time to die, with the words, "Stupid fool," floating in your head*, thought Miryam. She saw the young soldier's silhouette as he hesitated in the doorway between the bedroom and the living room. His night-vision glasses were in place and his dart gun hung loosely in his hand at his side. He strolled into the kitchen and living room area, his guard relaxed. He was beginning to wonder if the figure in the bed that he'd lusted over earlier had been an apparition. Now, he was opposite her hiding place, the broom closet. Only about four-feet separated them. He paused, looked from side to side, then continued walking toward the door that led out into the hall. When his back was fully exposed, Miryam sprang up from her hiding place and blinded him by turning on the light.

He grabbed his night-vision glasses and tore them off. He never had a chance to turn or even protect himself. The knife entered the back of his neck between two cervical vertebrae, cleanly severing his spinal cord. The boy crumpled. Before his body hit the floor, she had plunged the room back into darkness.

If her other opponent had seen the malicious smile on her face, he would have cringed. But a sample of her pitiless nature was clear when he heard her hiss. "Now the contest begins."

The more experienced captain had jumped for cover behind the bedroom door the instant the light came on. The next thing she heard was the slamming of the door and the popping of light bulbs in the bedroom.

Fool. I've something else planned for you. A humorless laugh slipped from her lips in response to his actions. "To make the first kill in a contest of life or death is exhilarating, don't you think?" Her lips, soft and inviting during her dream, were now drawn taut across clenched teeth.

He heard her searing comment and wondered what kind of woman killed with such enjoyment and skill. He had come to do a job and kill a woman. Murder or assassination—whatever you wanted to call it—had always been a relatively simple task for him. He was quite capable and sometimes he even enjoyed his work, though most of the time he felt nothing. He was strong and expert with his weapons. His confidence, even now when he knew he had lost the boy, was high. Perhaps it would take a little longer than he had thought, but he would succeed. After all, he was a trained soldier. He had no doubt he would prevail against a woman.

She heard the scrape of the bedroom door as it inched open. He spoke in the hopes that she would relax her defense. "Excellent execution in this poor light. You are an interesting adversary. Come, let us meet, one soldier to another."

He received no answer. They waited and a hushed anxiety permeated their battlefield.

In the dark she remembered the many hunts she had

enjoyed with the king. This was very much like those hunts. That old sensation of danger and excitement roared through her veins. She could actually feel her opponent's eyes searching and stalking her like one of the lions in the mountains of her homeland. She had learned much from the wild animals of Assyria. Patience and courage, like the female lion. *Let us see how long this man can control the fear building inside him.*

Warriors and hunters for thousands of years had played the game being played this night. The question was, which one was the hunter and which the hunted? Miryam was prepared to show this intruder that she was the predator and he her prey.

"Come, one soldier to another," he repeated his challenge. He waited. No reply. "Very well, it shall be a stealth battle. But remember, soldier, the last kill is the sweetest." She knew he was trying to bait her. She ran her hand up the wall by the door and felt for the thermostat. She turned down the thermostat low enough for the air conditioning to come on. The night-vision glasses depended on body heat and if she could lower her skin temperature it would confuse his sensory perception through the glasses. It was to her advantage to keep the apartment in darkness now, since she knew the layout better than he.

Again he taunted her, trying to draw her into the dark bedroom.

But she was not so foolish as to give away her hiding place by responding to his baiting.

Using the furniture as a shield, she crawled over to the boy's body and swiftly removed her knife from his neck. She still had the bottle of caustic ammonia with her and she risked a second lunge for the night-vision glasses the boy had been wearing. Inspecting the glasses, she noticed that they were equipped with a microprocessor that sent signals to a terminal at some distant location. *Interesting,* thought Miryam, *there is a television camera on one lens*. Someone was watching as this assassination attempt unfolded. She held it at arms length in front of her. *Smile pretty for the camera.* Then she mouthed the words: "I am coming for you, general."

As she put the glasses on she thought about her situation. If she could capture her opponent alive, she would send another kind of message to Tariq. She reached for the dead boy's dart gun but abandoned the effort when a dart from the darkened bedroom whizzed by her head. Graceful as a gymnast, she vaulted over the kitchen table, pulling it down on its side to use as a shield.

It was fascinating that all the knowledge that Miryam had acquired in espionage training was now mingled with the queen's own field-won experience. A modern day warrior with the cunning and tenacity of the ancient Assyrians made a formidable soldier. She smiled in the darkness.

Absolutely sure she had the advantage because he had to follow Tariq's plan and could not kill her outright. Miryam was a little more daring than usual.

She began to scan the apartment. She searched every corner of the room then moved along the inside wall that separated her from the bedroom and her assassin. She was sure he was behind the bedroom door, waiting for her to enter, so she would oblige. Peaking through the half open door, she scanned the bedroom. Although the dog's image was distorted by the ambient light from the street and the chilled air, she could see Strider's blurred form on the floor exactly where she had last seen him. She stepped in closer and kicked the door against the wall to crush anyone hiding behind it, but no one was there. She scanned the room, straining to see into the corners and behind the toppled furniture and books. Using all her senses she smelled and tasted the air. Something wasn't right. The patterns were wrong. The smell was wrong. She began to think her instincts had betrayed her and he had fled. Then she came upon his form in the most unexpected place.

Like a menacing ghost from a forgotten world, an eerie green-blue figure uncoiled from under Strider. The tactic surprised her and she froze. In disbelief she kept staring at the apparition as he smiled at her in a jaunty, disarming manner.

Almost too late, she saw the gun rise to meet her gaze. She had but a second to admire her assailant's ingenuity when the dart exploded from the gun. She threw the ammonia at his face as she sprang over the bed.

The captain wrenched the glasses from his face, screaming with pain and rage, trying to wipe the ammonia from his eyes.

She came up quickly and threw the knife where she thought he was. Ducking back, she crawled to the head of the bed and waited. The pressure on her injured knee sent a searing sensation of heat through her body; the agony took her breath away. She had almost been too slow. There was a dull thud and a dart splintered the wood of the dresser. She took off the glasses and threw them aside, depending on them instead of her natural abilities had nearly cost her life.

Flattening herself onto her stomach, she ventured a look under the bed to see if she could locate her opponent in the light that filtered in from the street. She searched for unnatural distortions in the gray shadows. She'd been sure of her aim when the knife had left her hand, but had not heard the heavy thump of it hitting the target or the cry of his pain as she had hoped. Perhaps he was strong enough to deny her the joy of knowing the knife had hit home.

Straining to listen for breathing or some movement to reveal the exact position of her challenger, she wondered how many darts he had left. She could make it to the door and escape, but she couldn't leave Strider behind. His love and loyalty was her one and only weakness.

She heard a noise near the window to her left and she crawled to the edge of the bed. Even from under the bed she could feel that the air had been disturbed. A faint breeze brushed against her cheek.

The night was getting old and the approaching dawn would soon elongate the streaks of light coming through the ripped blinds and illuminate the room. Drawing in a deep breath and letting it out, she focused all her inner energies on finding the captain.

Her eyes were closed as she searched with her other senses. Something was different. She no longer sensed his presence. He was dead or no longer there. As she started to pull herself out from under the bed, her left hand touched something wet on the floor. She sniffed at her hand. Was it ammonia? She doubted it. She would have detected the pungent odor instantly. No, it wasn't ammonia: it was thick and sticky.

She was elated. That sticky thick fluid was very familiar. It was blood. Yes, she had hit her mark! She rolled out from under the bed on the far side, away from the assassin's pool of blood. This battle was over. It was now time to get Strider and leave. She would never return to this place. The bodies would be left behind for someone else to take care of. She reached into the living room and flicked on the switch to shine light into the bedroom. Immediately, she fell to her knees, oblivious to the pain the action caused her. The captain was not lying in a pool of blood on the floor. Strider lay there in his place.

She dragged herself to his side, caressing his white fur and stroking his head. Her pain was intolerable. Flinging herself over the animal she cried out. A long, wailing sob was torn from her throat. She lay with him for what seemed a long time, but it was only a few seconds. Then she rose with clenched fists, gritting her teeth. Strider's throat had been cut while he lay sleeping off the effects of the dart. The captain had escaped.

Enraged, she hurried to the window and tore the mangled metal blind from the wall. She looked out onto the fire escape. Puddles of blood dripped from the landing and steps. Her eyes followed the trail. It was then that she saw a glint of light, a reflection off something metallic. Across the street, holding up a knife for her to see, was a shadowed figure. He raised the knife to his forehead and saluted her, then turned, clutching his arm, and disappeared into a waiting car.

There were no tears. With utter clarity of mind Miryam had the last piece of the puzzle. Major General Tariq Saeed was close to finding Saddam's biological weapons. That a madman would find the weapons that she and the other inspectors had never found had always been her worst fear. It was the reason she had returned to Iraq to search. Now it might become a reality. Desire for revenge flowed through every part of her as she glimpsed flashes of her life: Wayne, a love snatched away; the Israeli government spurning her warning and destroying her career; and her faithful and only friend, Strider—no longer with her. Everything that had given her reason to live was gone.

Rays from the rising sun shined on her hands and she rubbed them together as if to spread the light over them.

She felt oddly detached from her movements. Taking a deep breath, she straightened her spine and raised her head. She looked every inch a queen, despite her bloody garments.

She gathered her belongings quickly and stuffed them into a backpack. The continuous knocking and yelling of the old man who lived on the second floor made her work even faster. She put a clean cotton blouse and khaki pants on over her bloody undergarments. She opened her medical bag and removed the laser wire. The wire, about twenty inches long, was hair-thin and very flexible and as sharp as any surgical scalpel. A self-contained laser beam that ran on a minute power cell fitted in the handle. She used it for amputations and cauterizing wounds when she was doing field surgery. With a practiced flick of her wrist she activated the unit and touched the beam to her bleeding knee. The flesh sizzled and smoked, but the bleeding stopped. With practiced movements, she bandaged her wound and threaded the wire into a pouch concealed in the waistband of her pants. She stuffed a few bandages into the backpack and threw the pack over her shoulder. She took one final look around the room. Her eyes fell to her beloved Strider. "This contest is not over, captain," she hissed. She ran to the window and was down the fire escape before the rest of the few residents in the apartment building could be roused.

As Miryam left the city, shrill blasts from the air-raid sirens exploded into the early morning. She drove on faster and faster as though hounded by the sirens. A voice in her mind urged her on, ever faster. *Hurry! The moment you have been waiting and training for draws near. You must get to the cave before it is too late.*

"What cave?" she asked herself. *You know. Search your mind and see the mountains where once you played and hunted.*

"Yes, I see them." The mist in her mind lifted and she could picture the whole area as if she were there at this very moment. With astonishment she said out loud: "I remember everything now. The killing, the blood and oh, so much suffering." Tears poured from her eyes for the first time in centuries. *Be strong, I am with you,* said the inner voice.

As the sky grew brighter it amplified a new danger. A long line of cars passed her, heading south: the direction opposite to the one she traveled. She slowed as she approached the last checkpoint near the city of Dan before passing into the western frontier.

A stern-faced young guard checked her papers, then insisted she park and accompany him into the office.

Miryam sat ridged on a metal chair close to the door, opposite his desk. She was wondering if the police alert for her capture could already have reached this remote location.

The soldier wiped his brow with the back of his hand. "Are you aware that a state of emergency has been declared? Why have you ignored the warning sirens?" He didn't wait for her to answer. "What is the nature of your business?"

"As my papers show, I'm a doctor. I have an emergency."

"There have been terrorist attacks in the United States and Great Britain. The Americans are blaming us."

Miryam was shocked. "Biological?"

"Yes, biological attacks," said the border guard. "I can't let you through, doctor. We're closing all borders."

Miryam knew her mission was now even more urgent. "That is not satisfactory," she said firmly. "My patient may die during transport without proper care, and you, my incompetent young man, will be responsible for his death. Closing the borders for those who have clearance was not part of your orders." She had to think quickly and not give him a chance to call his superiors for advice. "I can be there and back within the hour. Time is of the essence and you are wasting mine. You've seen my papers; you don't have the right to prevent me from going anywhere!" With great effort she lowered her voice "I'll tell you what, why don't I take your medic with me? That should satisfy your orders and my medical concerns." Her hands slipped from her pockets. She moved a foot forward and leaned seductively on the desk.

He thought for a moment—her smile was enchanting—and ignored the ringing phone. "I suppose if you were accompanied by one of my men it would be all right." He returned her smile and spoke into his radio to the guard at the gate. "The doctor may pass. I'll be right out." Then he came around the desk to escort her to her car. His smile disappeared when he saw blood stains on her hands. He started to ask for an explanation when she knocked him unconscious with a chop to his neck. He collapsed on the floor.

Casually, she walked back to her car and waved toward the office door. She pulled up to the gate, waited her turn, and drove through. As soon as she had passed around the next bend, she left the road and, throwing the Land Rover into four-wheel drive, climbed up into the mountains, heading for Arnah, in Syria. From there it was a short walk to the remote village where Isaac, a friend, would provide her with transportation—a small one-person helicopter—for the next leg of her journey.

She knew the area and would be in the air and on her way quickly to Silopi, near the Syrian-Iraq border. She would cross into Iraq near her uncle's farm and would travel from there by boat to the mountains near Tariq's farm.

She searched the horizon. Without warning the captain's words rang in her ear: "The last kill is the sweetest."

She drove on, not oblivious to the possibility that he might be near, but rather reassured by the idea of his presence. The final judgment would be incomplete if the captain were not present.

Chapter 17

Broken Shield

Wayne's agitated voice speaking to someone on the plane's telephone pulled Matt into consciousness long before his tired body was ready.

"How could that happen, Pearl?" Wayne's face seemed paler than usual. "Yes, I'll put you on speaker. Go ahead: we're all listening." He pushed the speaker button, replaced the headset, and sat down, too stunned to remain standing.

Pearl's grim tone alone filled the still air with crystal clear meaning. The worst had happened. "Our first count today, over six hundred people were exposed in the main terminal at LAX. Fortunately—and I say that tongue in cheek—we'd been on alert after a warning from the French government that a biological attack might be imminent. Our snooper near the security inspections picked up the virus, but it was too late by far. Those devices were supposed to detect virus being carried onto planes or from planes. We never expected it would have to pick up virus already circulating through the air."

Wayne ran his fingers through his graying hair and attempted to clear his throat. "What's being done?" he said.

Matt paced, hands in his pockets, now wide awake as their Marine escorts moved in closer to hear Pearl's details.

Matt heard the soldier named Cordy say that his wife and kids lived near the airport.

Pearl's voice was hushed. "LAX was sealed off immediately and an entire ten-mile radius around the airport has been quarantined. It's a mess. The people at the airport are being held in hangers and wherever they can find space. It looks like an internment camp. We have no idea how long the device has been spreading the virus through the terminal or how many others were exposed coming and going through that area. They found the virus package in an air duct. Maintenance worked on that area of the ventilation system five days ago, it must have been planted after that or during. Who knows? Riots and fights are breaking out at the airport and in the city. It's escalating beyond what the National Guard can handle. The army is isolating the city in an effort to prevent the possible spread of the illness. Fear of infection has caused some healthcare workers to refuse to treat those who've already become ill. Some hospitals have refused to admit any patients in an effort to keep their own facilities safe and free of infection."

"Anything from Britain?" Matt asked.

"After we discovered the device at LAX, they searched and found a similar device on a sweep at Heathrow and also another one in Taiwan and Reagan National, but no cases yet. Since we're already seeing illness scattered throughout the country, the public health officials think LAX was the terrorist's first stop. The president has closed down all non-military air travel."

"Is anyone attempting to verify it's the same stuff we found in Britain?" Matt sighed.

"Not yet," said Pearl wearily.

"Clever and unexpected. It's the best way to disseminate

an aerosol virus to a great number of people. We should have put the snoopers..." Wayne mused.

"Sorry to interrupt. Wait a moment," Pearl said. "They just found a similar device in Israel. This is going to inflame and accelerate things. Before you ask, no one knows how it got into the terminal and frankly, my darlings, I don't give a damn. We don't have time for Monday morning quarterbacks. I don't know where the other packages were found but they appear not to have been activated. I want this terrorist found and the threat eliminated."

Wayne and Matt could hear the fatigue in Pearl's voice. Nevertheless, she continued, "We were lucky that the air duct they chose at LAX fed only a small section of the terminal, but with air being circulated throughout that wing, who knows? Having the military handling the matter makes it worse. People and the press resent the military pushing them around. The president is playing it tight-lipped. The people that have been quarantined are frightened, the rest are mad and looking for someone to blame."

Matt turned on the television. The words *Special Report* showed in red across the bottom of the screen as the commentator spoke. "The National Guard has sealed off the city of Los Angeles and no one will be allowed in or out. Please do not try to approach or contact those in the quarantined area. A telephone number will be forthcoming for information. The governor has called up the reservists, and the president has placed the military on full alert and recalled some of our forces stationed abroad. Regular programming has been canceled. This station will continue to provide ongoing coverage. The president will address the nation in thirty minutes, please stay tuned." The announcer began to repeat the message when Matt walked over and turned down the volume.

"Wait," Wayne put up his hands.

The reporter's voice droned on as the camera stayed with a long-range shot of the Reagan National Airport; the Jefferson Memorial in the background. "Just in," the announcer said, "a second bomb has just been found at Reagan National Airport and, moments ago.... We have breaking news that a bomb has just exploded at Metro Center station in D.C. It's 5:15 p.m. in the east, folks, and that would make it rush hour in D.C."

"Okay, Pearl, give us the rest." Wayne stared at the muted television as he listened.

A transient quiver entered Pearl's exhausted voice. "The president may shut down the borders. If he does, it will be the first time in America's history that a president has had to declare a state of martial law. Every psycho on the planet is getting into the act. Similar problems are being reported all over the world. Israel has had several bomb threats and three terrorist explosions along their border in the north. They think Lebanon is responsible and is preparing to invade Israel."

"We're getting close. Don't let them stop us, Pearl." Wayne sounded desperate. "We traced the virus to that scientist living in northern Israel you mentioned. She's in a small town near the Golan Heights. Wait, Pearl, did you hear that? The pilot just came back and told us they wouldn't let us land in Israel. Can you do something about that?"

"I can get you in, I can't do anything else." Pearl's voice was breaking up. After a brief silence, they could hear Pearl shouting orders to her aides, then she was back on the phone. "Things are getting complicated. Now for the bad news, which will help explain the defensive posture you'll be facing in Israel."

Pearl's voice cracked and she cleared her voice: "The president has been made aware of your suspicion that the virus originated in Israel."

Wayne and Matt stared at the phone. "How?"

"Clearly, he's been monitoring you both and laying a foundation to point an accusatory finger at Israel."

"Someone is spying on us?" Wayne was outraged. "Why, that son of a..."

"Right now you've other concerns" Pearl said. "What you need to know is that the president has warned Israel that any further aggressive acts on their part will be met by retaliatory strikes. He's playing the wounded ally. He told Congress that he was appalled by the use of biological weapons against one of Israel's closest allies. By the way, his daughter was on her way home during college break and is now quarantined at LAX. He's madder than hell that she's in danger and even he can't get her out. The insiders in D.C. are leaking that Israel may be responsible and that they were looking to blame it on Syria as a rationale to expand their borders again. Israel's taking a lot of hits and is on full alert. Both Syria and Lebanon are sending more of their troops to the Israeli borders to bolster their positions. They're posturing as if they were already at war. Tread lightly, boys. You're being allowed into the country because I personally vouched for you. So don't make any waves or you might get arrested and become POWs. Take a good long look at Israel. I'm not changing my mind, but I don't want to be wrong on this one."

"I'm sorry, Pearl, but I still don't believe Israel is involved. It's not their style. What do you hear from Iraq?" asked Wayne.

"I don't trust Israel, but this is beneath them and there's nothing for them to gain from such an attack. Here's another tidbit to add to the puzzle: France has invested large sums of money in a farm in Iraq that produces genetically engineered food. That farm is owned by someone we thought, until now, was a minor player, Tariq Mohammad Saeed. We took another look at him and a deeper probe into his finances and found out that he has convinced a few of Russia's old biological weapons scientists to come work at this farm. He's made questionable equipment purchases with more money than he should have. Presumably, he grows genetically engineered vegetables. The farm's in the north, east of Mosul. Check it out. You're the experts. He's been spending more money than he should have from his farm operation. Satellite photos show a large gathering of equipment and personnel at his farm. It's hard to keep track of his movements since every terrorist seems to have the schedule of our satellite pass-overs. That leaves a lot of room for unobserved movements. The new government says it's all above board, but I think this place is worth visiting. Take down this cellular phone number in case you run into problems in Iraq. If Israel does pan out, get out as soon as you can.

Matt grabbed a pen and wrote down the number. His eyebrows rose when Pearl told him it was that of the new Iraqi president.

"Gentlemen, I'll give you one day in Israel. Rich and Hal will be waiting for you. Once you're in Iraq, you're more or less on your own. The new president is my friend, but he doesn't want to look like he's bending to the U.S. He won't bother your discreet investigation, but it will have to be something monumental for him to support you openly. Sorry, that's the best I can do. Oh, I almost forgot. Our ambassador in Iraq, Arthur Jenkins, is someone you can trust and count on for help. Rich and Hal will have more information by the time you arrive in Iraq. Lieutenant Gibbs will take care of your travel arrangements. "

"Thanks," said Matt.

"The situation is critical," Pearl's voice quivered. "The bad and the ugly are taking advantage of the disorder. Hold on." They heard background talking then Pearl's voice, a distinct undercurrent of agitation in it. "A bomb just exploded and killed a theater full of people in London. This affair is deteriorating rapidly."

Matt turned up the TV as the words *Urgent Warning* flashed across the screen. "It is reported," the commentator explained, "that the president has issued a warning to Israel and suspects them of the terrorist attack at LAX. As a frightened world points an accusing finger at Israel, the Middle East has become a volcano ready to explode. I repeat..." Matt turned off the television. "What the hell," he said, "there's only bad news."

They could hear Pearl take a deep breath. "The world is moving toward chaos. Don't disappoint a sweet old lady. We'll handle the home front. You give me the terrorist and I'll broadcast the truth."

As soon as their plane entered Israeli air space, jet fighters buzzed around them like agitated wasps. If they had any doubts about the sincerity of Israel's threat to repel aggressors, they dissolved at the sight of the missiles hanging beneath the jet fighters surrounding them. Although it seemed impossible to be any tenser than they already were, their anxiety turned up another notch after they landed and saw the tanks, anti-aircraft artillery and hundreds of armed soldiers swarming around the airport.

In spite of the virus package found earlier at the terminal, upon their arrival at David Ben Gurion airport, it was business as usual. Wayne and Matt passed through security without a hitch. Their rings got them in, but their military escorts watched every step of the way, trigger fingers at the ready.

Within forty minutes, they were introducing themselves to a nervous Israeli government official. The woman's attitude toward Americans was clearly expressed in her clipped words. "If it wasn't that many of us owe Pearl Sugarhill, you'd have been detained the moment you got off that plane. I suggest you make your visit short, or even Pearl won't be able to get you out. I think you Americans would be uncomfortable in my country if there was a war." When she smiled, her eyes were as hard as coal.

It was the same with everyone they met. None of the soldiers or officials bothered to hide their hostile feelings, and there was no doubt outsiders, especially Americans, were not welcome.

As they were driving away from the airport, Wayne nudged Matt and pointed at an irate crowd booing a group of people trying to get into the terminal. Their military escort, an army major, explained: "So many Americans trying to get out of our beautiful country. I wonder why?" Matt and Wayne saw his face in the rearview mirror. The smile was ice cold, the disdain in his voice was chilling.

"As you requested, I'm taking you to Dr. Stollar. There have been some developments," their escort announced.

"What kind of developments?" Wayne asked.

Their escort ignored the question.

The soldiers lining the streets seemed to scrutinize every car. Every street corner was occupied by a squad of soldiers. Tanks and mobile missile units, heading north to guard the border, clogged roadways. They passed families heading for the shelters carrying a few possessions and even small children carried gas masks.

Matt found this especially disturbing and wondered how his sons would react to such a frightening scene. "Look at this place. They have their fingers on the trigger, ready to start a war."

They stopped at a low white building and a grandfatherly man, plainly dressed in a wrinkled gray suite, jumped into the front seat next to their driver.

He introduced himself as Jacob Horshien, a low level government representative. He filled them in on what he had found out about someone he referred to as Dr. Stollar's alter ego, the Dove, and her reputation as a skilled spy. Her laboratory had been discovered and with it the evidence Israel needed to end the potential conflict brewing between his country and the U.S. The evidence included specimens that might match the virus found on the airplane that Matt's mother had flown on, as well as other virus which might have been used in the terminal in the U.S. Samples were already on the way to CDC in the U.S. to confirm their findings.

Wayne was bewildered and could not or would not believe what they were being told. "Let me get this straight: Miryam, a dedicated physician, is a terrorist and planted biological bombs in the U.S. and all the other places?"

Jacob Horshien nodded. "I'm sure she had help. Her passport records validate her visit to Australia and the United States shortly before both attacks. It will take time but I am sure we'll find passports under other names she used."

Wayne rubbed his hands together, hoping to dry his palms. He shook his head. "No, I can't believe she's responsible for these attacks. This is a mistake. Didn't she work for the Mossad? Wouldn't that be why she had that activity on her passport?"

"Yes, we trained her. She was one of our best," he added with some pride. "But it wouldn't be the first time one of our associates switched sides to a more lucrative game. Her bank accounts verify this. In the last few years, her behavior has been somewhat eccentric. We began to doubt her sanity."

"You thought she was a risk so you've been spying on her?" Wayne snapped. "But she still kept her lab secret?" Wayne smirked. "You screwed up. She's smarter than you."

Matt put a hand on his friend's shoulder and squeezed to remind him to be careful.

"Finally, the notorious Dove is revealed," said the stout, self-satisfied Jacob as he turned and faced to the front, ignoring Wayne's comments.

Wayne's neck turned red and his hands tightened into fists. Matt whispered in his ear: "Do you know who you're insulting? He's the commander of their covert operations. The Mossad doesn't jump to conclusions. Don't push this guy, he has a nasty reputation."

Brushing Matt's warning aside, Wayne began to question every piece of evidence. In his enthusiasm to defend Miryam, he ignored Jacob's growing anger.

It was not a grandfather but a cold inquisitor who started firing questions at Wayne about his relationship with Miryam.

Their escalating debate was interrupted when Matt pointed out the window. "Look, there's a crowd up ahead."

Jacob stared at Wayne when he explained, "That's the traitor's apartment house."

Finally, Wayne started thinking with his brain instead of

his heart and shut his mouth down. But it did not stop him from locking eyes with Jacob and in doing so telling the man that he would not be intimidated.

Several blocks later, the car came to a stop and they climbed out. Wayne and Matt followed Jacob's lead. The Israeli equivalent of a SWAT team was dispersed around the building and sharpshooters were positioned on surrounding roofs. Several armed vehicles and a special biohazard unit were moving into position.

Wayne saw a small hyper-incendiary bomb being taken out of a military van. The soldiers started to attach it to the Auto-Robo RMA-46 and Wayne knew exactly what was going to happen. He ran over to where they were loading the bomb. "Wait! Let me go in and talk to her. This is all wrong," Wayne pleaded.

They were going to sacrifice her, innocent or guilty. She was the way out of the escalating dilemma with the United States. The crazy scientist would be the scapegoat, and any evidence of her innocence would be consumed along with her. He pulled Matt aside. "Do you see what they're doing? She hasn't got a chance! I need to get in there, Matt!"

In the background a young soldier, the operator of the robotic device, explained to Jacob how it worked. "The RMA-46 has a video camera and lights fitted above each of its three arms. It gives the operator an unobstructed view. We call her MA. MA always gets the job done, sir."

Jacob seemed satisfied with the explanations and turned away. He whispered into the commanding officer's ear and then stepped back.

"Wait. Wait! Let me go in and talk to her," pleaded Wayne. He looked to Matt. "Damn. They're going to fry the place! You know she won't have a chance."

The senior SWAT team leader stepped forward and

pulled Wayne back. "We cannot take a chance on her releasing a biological agent."

His bureaucratic tone infuriated Wayne. Matt grabbed his friend's arm. "Come on, Wayne. Take it easy." Matt's commanding voice and strong grip were all that stopped Wayne from decking the patronizing officer.

Wayne whispered to his friend. "Matt, help me."

Matt looked at the other man. He wanted to help, but his mother's agonizing death wasn't far from his mind.

Wayne saw his friend's hesitation. "We've used these devices, Matt. You know what they do. The heat builds to incredible levels, incinerating anything and everyone in the building. She doesn't deserve this!"

Wayne was running out of options. He turned to Jacob. "How do you know she's even in there?"

"I don't answer to you, Dr. Swift. But as I told you, we've had her under surveillance and she returned late last night. No one has seen her leave. A man across the street heard noises from her apartment around dawn. She's in there."

Wayne glanced at Matt, gave him an imperceptible nod, shoved the policeman closest to him aside and ran for the apartment, calling back: "I'll bring her out."

The officer next to Matt drew his pistol and aimed at Wayne. Matt whirled around and kicked his right arm, sending the gun flying. The officer was furious and about to retaliate but one look from Jacob brought him under control.

Matt smiled at the injured man. "Sorry, old boy, I slipped and must have hit your hand."

Wayne turned and gave his friend a salute of thanks before he ducked into the building.

Several soldiers took up position around Matt, who just smiled.

"Wouldn't you really prefer to capture her so you can interrogate and torture her?" Matt asked Jacob.

When Jacob spoke, his tone was unemotional and flat. "This changes nothing. By going in there your friend may have come in contact with the virus." He signaled for the team to continue. Matt watched as MA laboriously maneuvered up the steps and into the front door.

"Wait a minute," protested Matt. "If you set that thing off," he pointed at the bomb attached to MA, "it will be murder."

Jacob didn't acknowledge Matt's comment but turned to the uniformed officer at his side, pointed at Matt and said: "Shoot him if he moves."

Matt's escorts moved in closer. He had no where to go. Images of the inside of the apartment house came up on a video monitor. Jacob and Matt leaned over the shoulders of the young man controlling the robot: they were seeing what MA saw. A small picture of Miryam was displayed in the upper right-hand corner, MA's target. The robot rolled up to one of the vagrants who hung around in the halls of the building and grabbed the man's arm. The robot scanned him, checking its memory banks to verify if this was the fugitive it was seeking. If the answer was no, the operator would tell the machine to let go. MA was overzealous and grabbed too hard, "a glitch in the computer system," explained the operator.

Matt flinched. "Did that thing just break that man's arm?"

Ignoring Matt and speaking to Jacob, the robot's operator announced: "The injured man was negative for biologics, Sir." He returned his attention to his console. "We're on the second floor and moving into her apartment now, sir."

Matt tensed. He was ready to do whatever it took to prevent them from detonating the bomb while Wayne was still in there. Plastering a fake smile on his face, he edged closer to the operator. The smile dissolved when he saw what was on the monitor. A body lay on the kitchen floor. It wasn't Wayne.

Matt, like Jacob, hovered over MA's monitor. The robot rolled the man over and checked to see if he was dead by placing one of its digits on his chest. The words, "no pulse, no respiration, and clean," flashed across the screen. Scanning the room and using its sensors, MA moved through the kitchen and sitting room area and approached the bedroom door. In another situation it would have been comical to see MA raise two of its arms in the universal gesture of peace: hands in front, palms open and forward while the bomb remained in the third hand. But in this case, peace was not the intention. The robot was using the microwaves in its fingers to scan for the presence of any life force.

"One intruder present," was the information the display flashed and Matt winced at this conclusion: *That means either Wayne or Miryam is dead.*

As the robot moved further into the room, its monitor showed a macabre scene in red and gray. Wayne sat on the bedroom floor amidst tumbled furniture and a jumble of books. He cradled a dog that had once been white but was now red, saturated with blood. It was a rare moment when Wayne's emotions were visible to the world, but they were now: his shoulders shook as the tears and torment seeped from his body. When he became aware of the camera, he rose and turned away. "Miryam's gone." They couldn't see Wayne's face, just his hand when he held out a small micro snooper that detected virus for MA to check. "No virus," he said as he stood. Strider's head rolled to the side and lifeless eyes stared up at MA.

Chapter 18

Assyria, 811 B.C. – Mountain of Death

Semiramis was jolted awake by the sudden onslaught of incredible, twisting abdominal pain. She doubled over and vomited. The black blood no longer surprised her. She vividly remembered the agonizing deaths of the slaves. Their death would be her death. That was fitting. But not until she was sure Ninyas entered the underworld before her. He was a traitor and the penalty for treason was death.

She staggered into the underground lake to refresh herself. *Yes, that was better.* She stepped away from the water and, picking up one of the sheepskins, dried herself, before throwing it in a heap beside the pool.

From the hem of her tunic she tore several long strips and wove them between the cut and swollen fingers of her left hand, binding them securely. She tested her handiwork with practice stabs and parries with her short sword in the injured left hand.

At first, gripping the sword caused a searing pain to bolt through her left hand and travel up her arm. Once that shock was over, only a dull throbbing remained. What she had not counted on was her inability to let go of the sword. The injured fingers would not relax their grip. She had to pry open the hand to remove the sword. She knew that this could be a blessing or a curse. Resigned to letting destiny take charge, she laid the short sword down and returned to her battle ritual.

Her hair was anointed with oil and still wet from the bath she'd taken earlier. It seemed almost to glow in the diffuse light. It was awkward, but she combed her loose hair with the fingers of her strong right hand. Carefully, she plaited each tress into the woven combat style, just as her maids would have done before a battle. She placed the golden band with its rosette motif across her bruised forehead to keep her hair in place.

Next, she removed her armor from its leather sack. With the soft inner side of her garment, she wiped the dust from each article. Then, over her wool thigh-high undergarment, she slipped on a purple linen tunic. The richly embroidered garment was hemmed with metal threads that formed a resplendent gold fringe. When she smoothed the wrinkles from it with her hands, she did it absently. *How many times have I worn this into battle? The king thought it foolish of me to stand out as a royal during a battle. But the first time I wore the purple, the men saw me and rallied. It gave them courage to win the day.*

Reverently, she continued her ritual. She slipped spiral silver bracelets on her upper arms. The open end of each was decorated with the head of the mighty ibex. She placed a heavy ring-shaped earring on each lobe. A cone decorated in thin leaf metal and studded with agates dangled from each gold earring.

Every piece of apparel was always put on in precisely the same order before battle. With meticulous care to detail and without rushing, she prepared herself the way she had been taught, chanting small prayers to various gods for victory in battle.

"Ishtar, great goddess of Mother Earth, who created the

mountains and this cave, hear my words. Let your anger burst forth through me and shake the land. Tear open the earth and let it swallow the demons that walk among us. I will sacrifice the fat rams and goats to your name..."

As she chanted, she raised the leather breastplate above her head and slid it down over her chest, then tied the laces on each side. It was thick and heavy but she was accustomed to the weight; it gave her comfort. Metal plates were sewn into the front and back and the star of Ishtar was embossed in the center of the front breastplate. She passed her hand over the star, which gleamed crimson in the eerie light of the underground temple.

In the distance she heard scuffing sounds. She paused for an instant, thinking *yes, search each passage, Ninyas. You must be careful not to let me slip away.* She was not startled by the sound. Indeed, the intrusion brought a smile to her serene face. *Good. Very good, I won't have to wait too much longer.*

On her left hip, she strapped the baldrick, a scabbard that held her short sword. This was balanced by a flat-bladed dagger, engraved like her short sword with a rosette motif. She placed it on her right hip. Next, she lashed her quiver of arrows onto her back and affixed leather guards to her forearms and shins. Last, she placed the leather, conical-shaped helmet on her head, it rested comfortably inside her golden crown. The leather flap extending from the back of the helmet down to her shoulder protected her neck, although now it irritated her sensitive skin. Cuneiform writing denoting her as the ruler of Assyria was etched across the helmet in gold lettering. Like all her armor, it was decorated with mystic protective symbols lettered in blue.

She picked up her long sword and turned it over in

her open hand, balancing it lightly in her palm. The light danced on the blade as she flicked the weapon back and forth, testing her skill, like a surgeon before an operation. *Today I will be like the lioness depicted on the hilt of my sword, a ruthless hunter.*

Her weapons were razor sharp. Hazael had once commented that the blade gleamed from being honed on the bones of the queen's adversaries.

She slid her left arm and head through the curve of the bow and let it rest on her right shoulder. The bow's name was Lord of Justice, or *Samas bel dinim* in her language. It was made from a pale yellow wood, and the ends were tipped with ivory and carved in the shape of duck heads. Like a bright golden sash, it lay draped across her chest.

At last, she was ready. Then, she remembered that this was the month of Nisan and the beginning of a new year and perhaps a new Assyria. A few drops of blood ran from her nose and she picked up her dirty tunic and wiped away the blood. When she stood erect over the pool to check her reflection in the tranquil water, she was satisfied. She saw a warrior.

What she did not see was the bleeding under her skin: the oozing scrapes and cuts and the way her organs were preparing to melt away. She saw what would give her strength. "I will lay down a scent that you cannot resist, my son, and it will bring you to me."

Her last task was to go to the treasure hidden behind the statue of Enil and scoop up a handful of gems. She thrust the gems inside her tunic and ran off to meet the enemy, her son.

Chapter 19

Joining of Heroes

Rich stared up the steps expectantly as the door of the small transport plane opened and was locked back into position for cargo and passengers to disembark. He wouldn't have been here on this day had it not been for personal requests from Iraq's new president and the U.S. Ambassador to Iraq, Arthur Jenkins. The old Habbaniyah military airport, northwest of Mosul, was on the fringe of Kurd territory and never used. But Rich assumed that, with the world situation being what it was, there was a good reason for the person he was meeting to come into Iraq through the back door. All Arthur Jenkins had told him was that the person he was meeting had connections to Wayne.

So here he was when he should be looking for Ghariba. Rich got out of his jeep and slammed the door. He wondered about the identity of the person he was meeting. Wondering, who is this guy? It had to be someone special for the Iraqi government to give him a get-out-of-jail free card with no limits on his access throughout Iraq. Rich reflected that the company didn't even have that kind of access. On the other hand, he'd stopped trying to figure politicians out long before. He knew he just had to play along and not get kicked out of the country before he got the change to find Ghariba.

After fifteen minutes, Rich had grown tired of standing

in the hot sun waiting for the visitor to make an appearance. His attitude was becoming more hostile the longer he waited.

Waves of heat rose off the tarmac; people and objects in the distance took on the watery appearance of mirages. Rich stared at the shimmering images as they mingled with the stifling air around him. His mind wandered as he waited. It had been seven days and still no word from Ghariba. To make things worse, he had discovered she'd been leading two separate lives.

Rich had used his CIA connections to try and find Ghariba. The trail led to an apartment he knew nothing about. But when he searched the place, instead of finding answers, he found more questions, like receipts for trips to places she didn't tell him about. He knew that people disappeared all the time in Iraq and most were never found, but he wasn't going to let Ghariba's disappearance be swept under the rug. This country was still dangerous, but he couldn't figure out where to look next. She had no close friends at work and no family.

He paced back and forth on the black tarmac. The heat rising off the runway made the soles of his feet feel as if they were on fire right through his cowboy boots. Rich heard movement inside the plane and turned toward it. Hal stepped out, squinting at the harsh sunlight. He stretched.

Rich took in the ponytail and high cheekbones as Hal walked down the steps. They looked each other up and down. Rich's scowl turned up into a smile. He stuck out his hand. "I approve of your tailor. Welcome to Iraq."

Apart from the difference in their hair color, the two men were quite similar in appearance. Both men wore T-shirts, Wrangler jeans and cowboy boots. Rich grinned and indicated that Hal should follow him. "This way, I have my jeep waiting."

"I've got a bunch of supplies to unload and take with us," Hal said. "That's what took me so long. These guys aren't too careful. Wayne and Matt will be here by nightfall."

Rich was puzzled. "Hold on. Wayne and Matt are coming here?"

"Is there somewhere private where we can talk?" Hal dropped his voice to a whisper. "There are things going on in the outside world that the government here in Iraq doesn't want their people to know."

He placed his concerns for Ghariba on the back burner. From years of living and working in this restless world, he knew something major was about to happen. The terrorist attacks in Baghdad, the biological weapons attack in Los Angeles, and the CIA alert had some connection to Wayne and Matt's hasty arrival. A tingle of electricity surged through him.

Rich thrived on being on the edge. He inhaled, filling his lungs with the high octane that he imagined filled the air. He liked the uncertainties and the sensation he got in the pit of his stomach when he was betting his life on his skills. It was a lifestyle few experienced and even fewer survived.

Rich helped Hal organize the supplies and had them loaded into his jeep. He recognized most of the equipment but didn't comment.

The two talked through dinner at a small local restaurant and quickly got to know each other. They had a lot in common. Hal had worked with explosives and sensory equipment as a Navy Seal and was very interested in Rich's gadgets. Both had also worked as ironworkers, walking the high wire during summers in New York and Boston.

Hal filled Rich in on the death of Matt's mother in England. When they started discussing the LAX attack, Rich—as a CIA operative—knew more about it than Hal.

Hal told Rich about the meeting with the president and the private meeting with Mrs. Sugarhill. "If it weren't for Madam Security Advisor, we'd have been frozen in our tracks. She's been running interference for us. She got us out of the States when the airports closed." Then, as if it were an afterthought, Hal dropped some shattering news. "The president—our president—is covering any tracks to Iraq and letting Israel take the blame for the attack at LAX."

"I'll tell you, Hal, when I add your information and Pearl's to what I've already gathered, the situation is beginning to make sense. It's hard to explain the politics in this country, but the new government bends over backward not to step on anyone's newfound freedoms. Meaning they're very careful not to accuse or harass people without proof. They don't want any similarities between the new government and Saddam's secret police. We—the CIA that is—have had this Tariq Saeed on our watch list for quite a while. I made contact with someone who works for him on behalf of the U.S. and Iraq. I usually handle the more delicate stuff that involves electronic sensor-triggered systems and other junk, but this guy's story intrigued me. I know what Tariq and Wayne are looking for. The CIA has continued to search for the same thing."

Hal looked at Rich curiously.

"Yeah," Rich continued, "that BBC announcement—'The United States confirms it is no longer looking for

WMD in Iraq'—didn't stop the hunt. If you had ever seen chems or bios. in action, you'd never stop looking."

They didn't talk while their glasses were being refilled. When they were alone again, Rich took a sip, let out a weary sigh. "Back to this farmer. As I said, he was a colonel in Saddam's army, didn't play an important role, so after the war, we let him go. I've been working with a man inside his organization. He's been feeding me information that has checked out. Last Friday, when we made contact, I gave him an added incentive to move to our side of the fence: bonus money and a promise that the U.S. of A. would keep him safe if he's threatened. Then he starts telling me how he'll be out of contact for a while because he's going on a special mission for Tariq. This is the interesting part: he said Tariq was mobilizing all his forces. He said General Saeed was about to secure his trump card, which everything else depended on."

Hal wasn't sure what to think. "He didn't give details? What the mission was or where Tariq's forces were going?"

Rich shook his head. "He *did* say some of Tariq's men would be making deliveries moving important supplies into the farm. Then he got spooked and left." Rich kept talking while he signaled for the bill. "The colonel is still holding back information so he can get the highest price. If something is happening, I'd know about it. I put the word out. Damn it, part of me thought he was just putting me on. You know: trying to get money out of me by making up a story. I was going to check it out with the sky watchers, but then you arrived. I did pass it on to one of the guys on my team as a routine follow-up. After we pick up Wayne and Matt, I'll see what he's got." Rich stood up to leave.

"Do you think there are still biological weapons hidden

here in Iraq and this nut has gotten his hands on them?" asked Hal.

The waiter arrived with their check and Rich didn't answer until they were alone. "Yes. Wayne, Matt, Miryam: all of our inspection team always thought we hadn't found all of Hussein's biological and chemical stash, but there wasn't anything we could do about it and Saddam had eight years without inspectors around to find the just the right hiding place. Everybody knew the numbers didn't add up. But the politicians were doing their friendly thing and we were told to back off. My gut says that Miryam wouldn't get involved with a guy like Tariq Mohammad Saeed," he said with heavy emphasis. "That doesn't make sense. This guy is a real egomaniac and a nut case, even if he is smart, street smart. He learned a lot from Saddam."

They talked as they walked to Rich's jeep. Hal shook his head in dismay. "If Tariq is the terrorist, he's proven he's not afraid to use biological weapons. That makes him one sick psycho."

"His farm is our best lead. It's in north Iraq, near Kurd territory," Rich said. "Saeed has a strong security force there. He says he uses them to keep the farm safe from Kurds and bandits, but they look more like paramilitary than security personnel. Problem is, he's right. Bandits routinely hit and run between Turkey, Syria, and Iraq, so it's not safe for anybody. His farm feeds two thirds of the population here, so he's been left alone. Most Iraqis think he's a patriot. I think we should start there. It's a big area and backs up to the Kurds. There is a temporary truce right now as they negotiate over territory for their independent state with the new Iraqi president, so we may be all right."

"Are the Kurds at least still friendly to Americans?" asked

Hal. I don't know much about them, except that Hussein tried hard to exterminate them and never succeeded."

Rich looked at his watch. "We've got some time before we're due at the airport so I'll give you a quick history lesson. The Kurds don't trust anyone and with good reason. The League of Nations orchestrated a treaty in 1920 which gave the Kurds autonomy with the capability of becoming independent, but the area involved was disputed and nothing happened. In the aftermath of Mother Nature's own biological warfare agent—influenza—in 1918, the U.S. never got behind the League and, as it fell, so did support of the Kurds. We've let them down on more than one occasion, at least the CIA did. That's another fiasco and another story. Right now, we're on their good side. I could go on and on, reciting the broken promises made to the Kurds, but it all boils down to territory. No one wants to give part of their land to the Kurds, and the Kurds have very stubborn ideas about the boundaries of their territory. They've inhabited this area for centuries and can claim parts of Syria, Turkey, Iran, and a sizable chunk of Iraq."

"I didn't realize," Hal said, clearly fascinated.

"Most important is the fact that the disputed territory takes in the headwaters of the Tigris and Euphrates rivers," Rich continued. "Iraq needs those waters for irrigation and electrical power. Did I mention the disputed territory also takes in a couple of the oil reserves of Iraq, Turkey, and Syria? And an independent Kurdistan would control the rich supply of chrome, copper, iron, and coal found in the mountains. You can see why they fight so hard to keep the land. Every attempt to remove them has failed. Somehow, they always make their way back to the mountains. They are tough fighters, and skilled. Even Hussein recognized their fighting ability and put the conscripted Kurds in the frontline of battles. Their survival has depended on a combination of being cunning diplomats who are always prepared for deception."

"I like them already," Hal smiled.

Rich finished the lesson. "The Kurdish calendar dates back from the defeat of the Assyrian Empire at Nineveh, or present-day Mosul, by the forces of the Medes. The mountains have been their refuge for centuries and, some Kurds say, their only friend. Nobody enters the mountain country without their knowing. They survived Hussein's attempts to annihilate them and, since we're looking for biological and chemical weapons that were used on them, they might be sympathetic. But they will never trust us, even if they help us."

"As soon as Wayne and Matt get here, we should head to the farm you talked about," said Hal.

"I've enough clout to insist Tariq let us inspect his farm," Rich said as he reached for his computer. "You're right, we should leave tonight. I'll let Ambassador Jenkins know what's going on. We need to keep him in the loop in case we have to call for back-up. Suspecting this General Saeed of having Hussein's biologicals and using them is big news. If Saeed has the weapons, we have to act fast before he can use them again. Time can be an unforgiving enemy."

Hal and Rich sat in silence. Rich thought about the last few days; Ghariba's disappearance, his informant's report, all the bits and pieces of CIA intelligence he had gathered and, finally, the puzzle about Miryam. He wondered where the hell she fitted into this mess. His communications with Ambassador Jenkins complicated things further. He tried to form a coherent picture in his mind, but it was like a basket full of mating snakes—he could not get a clear picture of any one creature.

Rich didn't believe in coincidences. That meant Ghariba's disappearance had something to do with Wayne and this operation.

Rich's thoughts were interrupted when the old Beatles song, "A Hard Day's Night," sounded from his laptop signaling an urgent incoming message. It took a few extra seconds for decoding, but finally the message scrolled down the screen. It was intelligence reporting movement of some of Tariq's men to the western borders. And one of Rich's contacts had spotted the Colonel heading east, leading a convoy of three trucks to the mountains, toward the dam complex. "Hell," said Rich. "We better get moving. This happened hours ago."

On their way to pick everyone up, Rich stopped to add one more man to their group: Elliot. He was sent by one of Rich's CIA friends as a Kurdish interpreter.

At the airport, without many words passing between them, the group of eight men loaded their gear into the two Land Rovers Rich provided. Before they got underway, Wayne, the unspoken leader of the group, impressed upon them the gravity of the situation and instructed them in the goals of mission Crescent Veil. The Marines did not look quite so young when the briefing was finished.

As Wayne drove east in the lead vehicle, the night seemed like an void without end. They stopped at the occasional checkpoint to show their passes, but the road to Mosul was deserted and eerie. The small convoy generated the only noise and movement for miles. During the day, all eight lanes of the main thoroughfare into the city were clogged with noisy taxis, vans and delivery trucks weaving through the tangled jungle of bombed-out buildings and the skeletons of vehicles. For years to come, the Iraqi landscape would show the scars of the battles coalition troops had fought on behalf of the Iraqi people. At night, everything came to a standstill. There was no nightlife, and the present government had imposed a curfew to help maintain law and order during the transition to democracy.

"We'll head south on what was supposed to be the extension of Highway One that comes up from Baghdad," Rich said as he drove, explaining their route. "Once we're in Mosul, we'll turn east, toward the mountains. The farm is east of Kukujahni. Right after, we cross the Great Zab River."

"Hey, Rich, what's that over there?" Hal pointed out of the Land Rover at the bombed out shells of a cluster of buildings.

"The old Al Kindi ballistic missile facility. It was the only missile facility Hussein built in the north. Missiles launched from there could easily reach Israel."

As they drove, Matt tried to talk to Wayne but Wayne would not acknowledge him. On the flight to Iraq, all they had talked about was Miryam. After the visit to Israel, Matt was even more convinced of Miryam's guilt, though Wayne still wasn't.

Rich removed a map from his pocket, turned to Hal and Matt in the back seat, and pointed out the areas that the Iraqi president had under his control and those he did not. The northeast mountain territory, where they were headed, was not inside the boundary.

"Great," said Matt.

"The Kurds will be one of the states in the new United Iraq, so don't sweat it," remarked Rich in his usual cavalier way. "You know the Internet rumor is that President Salinski proposed they change the name to the United States of Assyria, U.S. of A.? How ironic would that be?"

As they rode along the black, unlit, highway the men

settled into sporadic conversation. Occasionally they could see the reflection of the dark waters of the Tigris River in the moonlight to their right. After passing through Mosul, they left the river behind and blackness surrounded them. They tried to relax in their seats, but the pockmarked road bounced them around too much.

In an arid, desolate stretch outside Aski Kalak, Wayne stopped to let everyone stretch their legs. They piled out of the Land Rover and mulled around, swapping complaints about the ride and its effect on their backs, kidneys, and bladders. The only man who stood aloof was the interpreter. While a couple of the marines were taking care of the vehicles, Wayne took Rich aside. "What do you know about this guy?" he said, pointing at Elliot, the interpreter.

"I haven't seen him around before, but that doesn't mean anything. I talked to him while we were waiting for you at the airport and he seems knowledgeable. He speaks Arabic very well and also Kurmanji and Sorani, which are Kurdish dialects. It's hard to find interpreters who know both languages."

As Elliot walked toward them, under his breath Wayne said, "Watch him, Rich."

Rich nodded that he understood. "It will be light in another couple of hours," he said to the group. "Many of the side roads are no more than dirt paths. This might be our last chance to get some sleep for a while, so I suggest we do it right here."

Wayne agreed and stepped over to Matt. "We've got three hours until daylight. OK?"

Matt smiled his thanks. "OK." They had made their peace.

As Wayne rolled over onto his side, trying to get comfortable on the hard ground, he elbowed Rich. "I didn't have time to say much at the airport, but it's good to see you. Matt told me you're settling down. Who's the lucky lady?"

"You know her. It's Ghariba and she's missing. After this is over, I could use some help finding her." Rich's tone mirrored his concern.

Wayne was so surprised that he answered without thinking, "Are you crazy? She's a spy." Then he softened his tone, "I hope you don't think I'm sticking my nose in your business, but..."

Rich didn't let him finish. "You're right: it's none of your business, but who better to marry a spy than a spy? I'm going to sleep."

Wayne didn't know what to say in response. Was Rich serious? While he was gathering his thoughts, he heard a faint snorting followed by the unmistakable swelling sound of Rich's deep breathing. The breathing quickly lapsed into full throaty snores. "Huh, same old Rich." He'd forgotten that Rich could sleep at the drop of a hat, anywhere and any time. A smile, the first in days, crept onto Wayne's face. At least he was the same.

Wayne rubbed his sore back and tried to get comfortable. He dozed fitfully until the faint light of the approaching dawn woke him.

The marines were already munching on ration packs when the rest of the group woke up. No one else had much of an appetite, so they piled into the Land Rovers. The sun was just making an appearance as they turned back onto the road. Rich pointed to the scarlet sunrise, "sailors take warning."

After three hours of driving, they turned off the main road onto a much smaller one, which quickly became hard to follow as clouds rolled in and the wind picked up, stirring dirt and sand over the road. The terrain began to change also. Jagged outcroppings of rock dotted the flat part of the landscape and became thicker on the right side of the road, where they could see the mountains. The farther north they traveled, the more the road deteriorated.

Matt was explaining to Rich that a Harley T-shirt was not considered formal wear when Wayne interrupted their banter. "May I have your attention, gentlemen? I think that is the farm on the horizon."

As if on cue, the wind swelled and began gusting and swirling around the vehicles. The whooshing sounds were loud and unexpected. Rich started to hum the theme from *the Twilight Zone* in an attempt to amuse himself, with the added bonus of irritating Matt. "As we move beyond sight and sound..." Rich mimicked Rod Sterling.

As they got closer to their destination, they grew silent. The building looked ominous. It was larger than they had thought. It was a sprawling one level concrete structure that covered quite a few acres. Above ground tunnel-like structures extended out from the central hub in all directions, they counted at least seven wings from their vantage point. "Hey, Rich, where are the fields of vegetables? This doesn't look like any farm I've ever seen," Wayne said.

"He uses hydroponics to grow his genetically enhanced vegetables. You know: one carrot can feed a family of ten."

Matt picked up his field glasses and examined the white limestone cliffs that loomed high above the back of the building, forming a protective barrier. The other two sides opened to flat land dotted with rocks and earth that had been scoured clean of any vegetation for as far as they could see.

Matt's communicator beeped. It was Lieutenant Gibbs in the other Rover. Matt repeated what the lieutenant told him. “Two fifteen-foot barbed wire and steel mesh fences, one inside the other, surrounding the complex. Surveillance cameras at every corner of the complex and along the electrified fence. The lieutenant said we can count on the ground surrounding the complex being mined.”

“Is the main road the only area not mined?” Wayne asked. Matt relayed the question. The answer came back in the affirmative. “It’s probably mined fifty yards out from the fence in every direction except the flat road, that’s the usual pattern.”

They rolled forward, one vehicle behind the other, careful to stay in the center of the road. Then, they saw the armed group of men guarding the entrance to the farm.

“Pretty stiff security for a farm,” commented Matt as he looked through his field glasses.

Wayne’s hand fingered the slip of paper from the Iraqi president that was supposed to give them admission to any facility in the country. It felt thin and worthless between his fingers. So much for the easy way, he thought. The area was so deserted, the men in both Rovers could be slaughtered and no one would ever find the bodies.

“If what we’re looking for is in there, this might get nasty,” Wayne said, breaking the silence. “Rich, how long would it take that back-up to get here?”

“Too long. If we wait, they could pull a Saddam and have the place cleaned out before we could get in.”

“It looks like we’re on our own, gentlemen.” Wayne’s crooked smile was not reassuring.

“Did anyone besides me ever notice how he always calls us gentlemen just before he asks us to do the most ungentlemanly things?” Rich asked.

“Look, over there!” shouted Matt over the rising howl of the wind.

All eyes flashed to where Matt was pointing. A convoy of three trucks approached on a small dirt road that intersected their path about a mile ahead.

"I don't think they saw us," Wayne said after a few tense seconds. "But I'd sure like to look in those trucks before they get lost inside that building. Rich, didn't you mention that your man was traveling east in a truck convoy?"

"Three trucks," Rich supplied.

"Pull over!" Wayne called over to Gibbs. He pointed to some rocks. Wayne leaned out, talking to Gibbs. "Take a good look at those trucks, lieutenant."

"What's so special about them?"

"We need to take a look in them," said Wayne, wondering if they could be so lucky as to find the items they had come for inside those trucks and outside the fortified farm complex.

"Yes, sir. I can cut them off before they get close to the farm, where they'd have gun support from the towers."

"Hold on, kid," Rich shouted to be heard over the wind, "before you ride off half-cocked, remember to be careful not to damage the trucks. If the virus is in there, we don't know how it was secured for shipping. Let's be cool."

Looking out his window at Wayne and the others, the lieutenant nodded his understanding. The one called Flash Jack stepped out of the Land Rover and handed Hal and Rich two AK-47 assault rifles before jumping back in his vehicle as Gibbs gunned the engine.

Oblivious to the fact that they had visitors, the trucks continued forward at their lumbering pace.

Hal took his weapon and inspected it with expert hands. Rich handed his to Matt, saying, "I don't need this."

Through the swirling dirt, they saw the main gate open and an armored vehicle come out. "We've been spotted,"

Rich yelled. "Hang on to your hats, here we go." Wayne closed in on the marines and the interpreter riding with them.

Bullets pinged off the Rover. The wind intensified, sweeping under and around the vehicle, threatening to push it off course. Steadily increasing, and now at gale force, the dirt and sand obscured their view. In an effort to see, Wayne turned on the wipers and they winced at the screeching sound of sand grating against the glass.

It was still nearly impossible for Wayne to see anything. The convoy, the marines, and the armored truck disappeared in the dirt. Visibility was zero. Automatic weapon fire seemed to be coming from every direction. Despite the dense clouds that surrounded them, Wayne continued on what he thought was the convoy's original course.

Suddenly, the front window shattered as a series of bullets cracked the reinforced glass. Wayne swerved in response, then fought against the wind and sand flying in his face to come back onto what he thought was the road. His heart was racing as fast as the wind and flying shards distracted him. He strained to focus on the location of the trucks. If they were going to have any chance to examine and, if necessary, destroy the contents of those trucks, he had to catch up to them now, before they entered the mine field.

Rich was having a good old time. "Ride 'em, cowboy," he yelled as the Land Rover bucked and twisted in the wind.

One by one, Wayne's passengers got off the floor where they'd taken cover. "Rich, has anyone ever told you that you're a bloody barbarian? I suppose you think this is cool?" Matt yelled.

Rich put his sunglasses back on with a flamboyant gesture and pulled his neckerchief out and tied it over his mouth, then yelled back, "I love it when you talk sixties."

Wayne brought his handkerchief up to his nose and mouth, pulled his hat down low over his forehead and put on his sunglasses to help shield his face. The others followed his lead and covered up as best they could. The roaring of the wind made communication all but impossible.

"Ready?" Wayne yelled at the top of his voice as he slammed his foot down on the accelerator. The Land Rover lurched forward, propelling them into the turmoil.

Matt leaned over so Wayne could hear him over the wind. "What the hell are you doing? You can't see a damn thing!"

"We have to get to those trucks. The marines will need our help, especially if the trucks are carrying the virus."

The combination of the wind and the barrage of gunfire all around them were confusing. It was like being in a dense fog with a freight train. The sound of weapon fire had escalated and now and then the sound of small mortar fire vibrated through the Land Rover. The big question was, which direction was it coming from? Everyone held on as the Rover rocked from the impact of a mortar round hitting close by.

"Sounds like that armored truck from the farm has joined us." Rich cocked his head to one side, listening. "I'd say it's an old Bushmaster with a 30-mm cannon. We're dead meat if it hits us. It can go right through the armor on this thing. The good news is, it sounds like they're shooting over us. Either they can't find us or we're going in the wrong direction, away from the fight."

"Great," said Matt.

Without warning, the gray blur of a wall materialized directly in front of them. Wayne slammed on the brakes and veered sharply to the right to keep from hitting it head-on, trying at the same time to avoid veering off the road and into a land mine.

The heavy Land Rover was well grounded and didn't roll. All four wheels dug into the sand, trying to grip the road surface. They slid sideways and came to a full stop about eight feet from the wall. The wall turned out to be the bottom of one of the trucks in the convoy they had been chasing.

Bullets cracked off their vehicle. They leaped out and got down low behind the Land Rover in the shallow trench the vehicle's slide had carved out. "Is that what I think it is?" Matt yelled.

"Yeah, I'm pretty sure it's one of the trucks in the convoy," said Hal. "It must have flipped. Maybe the Marines shot out the tires."

"Let's gear up," Matt shouted. He crawled back into the Land Rover for their protective gear and emerged dragging a couple of packs. "We better get in that truck and see what we're sitting next to. If the containers holding the virus are in there and were broken open in the roll, there's no telling how far the virus could spread in this wind storm."

Wayne pulled on his protective gear. "Matt, get your sampling kit."

"Wait a minute," said Rich. He scurried back into the vehicle for his pack but came up empty-handed. The other three men were huddled together trying to get their supplies ready when they saw Rich disappear under the Land Rover.

"We're caught in crossfire," Hal had to yell to be heard over the wind. "Stay low. The marines must be in front of us and the bad guys over there." He pointed to the other side of the Land Rover.

"Where's Rich?" Wayne's question was answered when Rich popped up.

"Sorry, guys, I had to get my bag of tricks," he held up his pack for all to see. "It fell out the broken window." He rummaged around in the bag as Wayne filled him in on the plan.

"Matt and I will take a look in this truck. If the virus isn't there, we'll need to find the other two vehicles while you and Hal hold back the hordes. Matt is going to take some samples, just in case."

"That's the big plan?" Rich asked.

"Is there a problem?" Wayne said.

"If the stuff is in there, I've got something that will make it fast food." He handed Wayne three small, cauliflower-shaped objects about six inches in circumference. "Remove the plastic wrapper and put the sticky side against the container. I can detonate by remote. One for each truck will be enough to turn everything into toast. Here, take a pair of glasses."

"You're giving me sunglasses?" Wayne pointed at his eyes. "I'm already wearing sunglasses to protect my eyes."

"These are some of my specialty items. You'll be able to see body outlines even through the dirt and sand, plus there's a range finder display in the upper right corner of the right lens, and a built-in compass in the lower left. They'll help you get back here." Rich handed Matt and Wayne each a pair. "Don't forget the secret password: 'Crescent Veil' Hal and I are not looking to make any new friends here, so don't come up on us too fast."

"Right." And then Matt added, "And if they don't know the secret handshake, I'll shoot them. OK?"

Wayne and Matt moved off into the swirling dirt and Matt called back, "I see you're back in business, Blitz."

Hal and Rich moved over to the protection of the Land Rover.

"Who's Blitz?" Hal asked.

"Me," said Rich.

"Don't bother to explain, I've a suspicion Blitz fits you."

Rich handed Hal a pair of his special sunglasses. "No one gets left out. The glasses work off air patterns and body movement, not heat images and they double as cool evening wear."

Hal looked confused until Rich explained. "Night vision. You can use them instead of the old heavy night vision goggles."

Hal put on his sunglasses and crouched. He and Rich sat in silence at the rear of the Land Rover, back to back, legs bent, arms resting on their knees. Hal had his weapon ready. He focused on the images he could now detect moving around. They remained at a distance.

Rich fished around in his bag of tricks again and came out with a strange-looking short shotgun which he showed to Hal.

"It has two barrels, a large bored one on top of a small rifle-bored barrel. The small barrel shoots .38 magnum steel-cased bullets," Rich turned the gun over, giving Hal the guided tour. "The flat square box on the top barrel feeds the large bore barrel. The sight mounts on top of the box and is calibrated for both barrels." Rich handed the gun to Hal.

"What do you call it?" asked Hal, looking at the gun admiringly.

"It's a her: Sleeping Beauty." With a gentle hand he

reached across and patted the wooden stock. "Either barrel puts them to sleep. The top barrel shoots a grenade a little larger than a 12-gauge shotgun shell. When the grenade hits the ground, it spins and explodes, disbursing thin, needlelike, armor-piercing explosive projectiles in a fan array about three feet off the ground. They're like mini-missiles and they cover a ninety degree radius."

With his free hand, Rich dug deep into his pants and came out with a pocket watch. He held it to his cheek then said, "it's still cool, that means it keeps on ticking," and took his gun back from Hal.

Hal looked at him, one eyebrow arched, so Rich clarified, "it's a jamming device. I flicked it on when I saw the trucks coming at us from the farm. With this little electromagnetic pulse device, we don't have to worry about them calling reinforcements." Rich explained how he had redesigned the old electromagnetic pulse equipment. "My enhancement creates a force field around..."

"Watch where you're aiming that thing," Hal said, moving back.

Rich heard voices and tensed, his eyes focusing ahead of him. Hugging the side of the Land Rover, he moved forward, then flipped up his sunglasses and brought the scope of his gun up to his naked eye. He had spotted four figures crawling toward the Land Rover. "I might need help in a minute," he called to Hal.

He waited until the men were in his line of fire, then sent a rifle shot over their heads, just to let them know he was there. Through the storm, he heard someone curse, then say, "Crescent Veil." The three marines and the interpreter crawled around behind the Land Rover and took refuge. The marines took up guard positions along the sides of the Land Rover.

The lieutenant explained that, while they were in pursuit of the convoy, they took fire from a large group near the rocky steppes, which were now at their backs. "Before we knew it, one of our tires hit a land mine. Hell, visibility was zero, we didn't even know we were off the road. We flipped, and hit the second truck in the convoy. The last truck," he pointed to the one about eight feet in front of them, "overturned trying to avoid hitting us and the mined field. The first truck got away. We couldn't follow it on foot without getting lost in the storm."

Rich grabbed the lieutenant by the front of his uniform. "What's in the trucks?" he demanded. "Are there CBWs in the trucks?"

"The marks on the bombs matched-up with the symbols Dr. Swift had showed me," Gibbs said, tracing a symbol in the shifting sand.

Rich held his breath. "Anthrax. They're filled with anthrax. Damn." Rich explained what was going on to Hal. After a few words to his men, the lieutenant disappeared around the front of the Land Rover to look for Wayne and Matt.

As if someone had asked if things could get any worse, the storm intensified. The sand stung their skin right though the layers of clothing they wore. "I've got bandits at three a clock," Rich called to the two remaining marines and the interpreter.

"At least a dozen coming in at nine o'clock," Hal called back. "They're coming down the road to catch us between them."

"Here they come," someone yelled and, before he finished speaking, they were assailed by a hail of automatic gunfire that flew over their heads and bounced off the Land Rover. One of the marines was hit.

"Our turn," Rich yelled, jumping up and firing in front of him and then again in the direction where Hal had sighted movement. His grenade gun made an awesome roar that was easily heard above the howling storm. His companions drew back in awe when the shotgun went off.

"I have to work on that," he yelled as he hunkered down, waiting to see what would happened next. In seconds, they heard the howls of their wounded adversaries.

"That will hold 'em for a while," said Rich. "Let's see what they come up with next."

An eerie calm blanketed the battleground as all gunfire ceased. The sandstorm blotted out the sun and day seemed to turn into night within seconds.

With some urgency, Rich suggested they get into the Land Rover. "The storm is getting worse. The vehicle will provide us with some protection, even with a window out."

The marines wanted to stay outside as sentries, but Rich insisted that everyone get in the truck. Hal and one of the marines busied themselves covering the broken window with a tarp while the other marine kept watch. The interpreter pushed into a corner of the back seat and curled up. He didn't offer to help.

"It's late in the year, but I think we are in the middle of what the Iraqis call a Sharqi," Rich explained. "It's a violent, dry dust storm with gusts up to eighty kilometers per hour. Sometimes the columns of dust rise several thousand meters into the air. Believe me, whoever's left out there will have to find shelter fast or they'll be in trouble."

The corporal's left ear had been nicked and Hal bandaged it. "You'll be fine," he said.

"Thank you, sir," the fair-haired young man replied, returning to his post by the tarp that now covered the window.

"Kid, are you the one Gibbs calls Flash Jack?" Hal asked.

"No. Cordy, sir."

Hal asked, "Rich, what do we do now?"

"Hunker down, just like they're doing," Rich replied pointing outside. "We'd better hope Wayne, Matt, and Lieutenant Gibbs find a safe place to wait until this storm blows over. One good thing is that the storm will slow everyone down, including Saeed. I'd get some rest if I were you. We can take shifts with the kids," he said, pointing at the marines.

"OK," Hal turned and reached out to take the gun from Flash Jack sitting near him. "I'll take first watch. You rest a bit." The boy began to object when Hal noticed the awkward way he was holding his gun.

"What's wrong with your arm, son?"

"Nothing, sir. I bumped it when the Land Rover crashed."

"Let me look at that." Reluctantly, the boy let Hal roll back his sleeve. "Damn, kid, you've got a broken arm! Rich, take a look at this."

Hal felt the bones in the soldier's arm. "The ulna and radius are both broken. I can straighten the bones and put a splint on, but that's it. It must hurt like hell."

Hal got busy. Jack didn't flinch, and once Hal had worked his acupressure techniques, the marine said the pain was reduced to a dull throbbing. As Hal closed his medical kit he wished he could do more, like give Jack a dose of morphine, but it would make him too drowsy and they had to stay mobile in case of an attack.

Rich winced and turned away as Hal replaced the morphine syringe in his medical kit. *I'd never live it down if Matt knew I fainted when I saw a needle,* he thought.

Hal applied an air cast to the kid's arm. "Don't be such a hero next time," he said when he was done. "Ask for help. In the long run, it's better for all of us. What if you had to fire your gun?"

Jack smiled. "No disrespect, sir, but I *have* been firing my weapon. Thanks for fixing the arm."

"You get some rest," Hal said. "I'll take the first watch. He raised a hand to silence the young marine's objection and said. "Don't worry: I'm not so old that I don't know which end the bullets come out."

Rich motioned for the boy to sit next to him. "Thanks," Jack said as he settle down. "I'll sit but I don't need any sleep."

That was the last thing the boy said. Hal reached over and applied pressure to specific points on the boy's neck. Flash Jack drifted off to sleep instantly. Hal smiled at Rich. "He'll be out an hour or so."

"Can you teach me that Vulcan thing you just did?" Rich didn't wait for Hal's response. He made himself comfortable in the driver's seat, his shotgun sticking out of a gap in the makeshift barrier. They'd had trouble keeping the tarps in place around the shattered windows until Rich found his extra roll of duct tape in his bag of tricks. Hal was amused. *I wouldn't be surprised if he pulls out a couple of glasses of icy Kool-Aid.*

The inside of the Land Rover grew quiet and the whine of the wind and the dirt hitting the truck took on its own voice and rhythm. The storm droned on and on. If it were not for the occasional large rock hitting the Land Rover, it would have been easy to let the tempest lull everyone inside the vehicle into a false sense of security.

Chapter 20

Northern Iraq, Near the Syrian Border— No Return

A gnarled old man was dozing in the cool darkness. He sat in the dirt resting against the doorframe outside a run-down shack. When Miryam stepped out of the night, her uncle opened his eyes but was not shocked. He was used to her sudden appearances. He wondered what trouble brought her back to Iraq. But, from living for years on the edge of death, he knew it was safer for both of them if he did not know her business. His poor farm lay just across the Syrian border, outside Faysh Khabur, where the Tigris entered Lake Buhayrat Dahuk. He knew Miryam often used the river to travel deep into Iraq, and he provided provisions for his niece and a safe haven during her many clandestine journeys.

They embraced briefly, then walked to the river. They had begun loading supplies into a battered fishing boat when he turned and faced her.

Her uncle's withered brown hands reached out to take hers. Holding Miryam's hands in his, he shrugged and looked deeply into his niece's troubled eyes. Sadness filled his heart. He embraced her and then stood aside to let her go. His emotions had been stunted from years of brutal oppression, during which he'd had to hide his feelings to keep both of them alive. This time was different. He felt the end was near for both of them. He would welcome the chance to be released from the drudgery of this life and the burden of hiding his thoughts. He suspected Miryam sought the same relief.

Miryam climbed into the boat and started the engine. The boat was an old friend and the outboard sparked to life instantly. She could not let sentiment weaken her, so she forced herself to pull away from the riverbank quickly. One last time she looked at her uncle, watching until his small frame melted into the darkness. Then, she faced into the wind and became part of the river.

The Tigris was as familiar to Miryam as her own hands. Disguised as a fisherman she blended in perfectly. Time slowed on the river. Hours passed before she was forced to slow down to navigate the passageways around the two dams on the river above Mosul. She traveled south, with the rapid flow of the swelled Tigris to help her along. She would stay on the Tigris until it intersected with the Great Zab River below Mosul. Then she would turn north and have to fight against the current of the Great Zab. Once she passed Aski Kalak, she would have to go on foot to Tariq's farm. She hoped she wasn't too late for Rijah.

Thinking of her friend, she said a silent thank you for the map Rijah had provided of Tariq's complex. With the map, she would be able to search for chemical and biological weapons much more efficiently and she'd have a better chance of finding her friend with the map to guide her.

What concerned her more than anything was that the farm was located at the foothills of the al Jazira mountain range and that was a Kurd stronghold. She would have to be careful.

It was two in the morning when she docked the boat. The ground felt familiar the moment she stepped out of the boat and set foot on land. She slung her backpack over her should and let instinct guide her through the darkness.

She marveled that the area had not changed all that much in two thousand years. She slipped back into thinking in her native tongue. *There's some erosion and a slight change in the course of the river through the mountains, but on the whole, not much has changed. The mountains have retained their nobility.*

Miryam had been in this area many times before, but had never felt the intense connection she now felt. "I'm home," she whispered into the night.

She took out her water bottle and took a long drink, then stood relaxing in the warmth and peace of her surroundings. Impulsively, she reached into her blouse to hold her necklace, then remembered her talisman was not there.

When she was a child and terrible things happened, she would grasp the image of the dove that hung on the chain. For some inexplicable reason it always gave her strength. It had been her solace and helped her get through the hell of the youth camp. She had never understood the significance of the dove or the ancient symbols on the necklace, but the comfort it gave her had been significant.

Although her amulet was missing, its magic stayed with her. Overjoyed to be back in her homeland, she closed her eyes and lingered, letting her imagination take her back to her beginnings. Ancient images raced through her mind's eye: the king, Hazael. Another image pushed itself to the surface. A boy—her son— barely a man, but thinking he was a king at sixteen. He was a shade taller than she, with dark brooding features. She spat out his name: "Ninyas." His dark hair curled softly and made her reach out into the emptiness to touch the vision. *Are you also waiting for me in the mountains, my son?* Then the queen spoke to her mind: *Remember the cave. That is where Tariq and Rijah are.*

The image faded and she felt a chill. "Yes. Not the farm, the cave. Of course," she murmured. She opened her eyes and for an instant thought ancient Assyrians encircled her. Then she felt a sharp pain and a veil of emptiness.

Miryam was jolted awake by gut-wrenching abdominal cramps. She rolled over onto her side and vomited. A damp rag and a pan of water lay on the floor within her reach. Picking up the rag, she moistened it and wiped her face. When her inner trembling and sweating subsided, she pulled herself into a sitting position. The vomiting returned and brilliant stars danced in front of her eyes. She leaned back against the cool rock wall with the moistened rag on her forehead. The nausea diminished and she made an attempt to stand, but dizziness overcame her. A black tunnel spiraled toward her and her vision began to narrow. She passed out, sliding down onto the cold stone floor in a crumpled heap. When she awoke again, her body was shaking. She wiped the cold sweat from her eyes with the back of her hand and lay still, waiting for the room to stop spinning.

From her prone position, she opened her eyes and thought back to the last thing she could recall. *I remember seeing the ancient ones, then nothing.* She looked up at the ceiling: it was hand-hewn rock, like the walls and floor. It looked like a cave, but harsh light and a crisp breeze filtering through a barred window near the ceiling told her she wasn't below ground. She heard voices in the distance but couldn't immediately identify the language. Then it came to her: they were speaking a Kurdish dialect. *If only I could pull myself up to the window and have a look out.*

Her first and second attempts failed and were accompa nied by more nausea. Her stomach was empty so she was unable to vomit, but the spasms deep in her gut persisted. Her head swam and the room swirled around her. She reached up and touched the back of her head. Sharp pain accompanied by flashes of light danced around the room and then disappeared into the gray stone. Her hand came away with fresh blood smeared between her fingers. *OK. So, I have a concussion. That explains my headache, nausea and the lightshow. Nothing but an earthly hand could have inflicted the blow that did this damage.* She reached up and touched the back of her head again. The physician in her examined the area with her fingertips. *I don't feel any depression, that's good.* She picked up a rag and dampened it, then placed it over her wound. *At least whoever did this cared enough to leave these.* She washed out the rag and reapplied it to her wound.

She sat for a while and rested, then, when she got up, she was careful to be see if her legs would hold her. The rock beneath her feet felt firm, not like before when she could have sworn the floor was moving. Regaining some of her strength and senses was encouraging.

As her mind awoke, she noticed all of her gear was gone. She felt the waistband of her slacks and found the familiar outline of her laser wire: it was still secreted in the waist band of her pants.

She circled her prison cell, finally moving to the windowless, solid steel door and examining it. The hinges were on the outside and the lock was inaccessible. *No way to escape there.* Miryam continued to inspect her prison inch by inch. The window was three feet above her head and she could hear activity outside. She grasped the jagged rocks that protruded from the wall and, in spite of occasional dizzy spells, managed to pull herself up to peer out the barred window. She was amazed at what she saw.

She was in a veritable fortress high in the mountains. She saw horses and men dressed in flowing robes with head coverings. But instead of carrying swords, as her dreams of the ancient queen would have dictated, they carried a variety of modern-day weaponry. Armored vehicles were parked in rocky recesses and artillery, covered with camouflage, was positioned at strategic lookout points.

She also noticed clouds drifting by at eye level and she could see the tops of mountains in what she thought should be the east. Home: she was home and in the mountains not far from Lake Urmia. The cave was nearby and, although things had changed a little, she would have recognized the silhouette of this area against the Assyrian sky anywhere. She had noticed the small camera near the ceiling the moment she pulled herself up to the window.

When the steel door burst open, two rugged, sun-bronze-d men entered, pointing Russian Kalashnikov automatic rifles at her. One pulled her down from the window while the other stood back, ready to shoot if she tried to escape. They shoved and prodded her along the hallway and across the busy courtyard. She was pushed into a small room that contained an old steel desk, a modern computer and sophisticated communications equipment. The sidewalls and ceiling were part of the mountain: solid rock. A small door in the back wall was the only other exit from the room. Miryam kept her expression neutral, but her mind was alert, looking for a means to escape. She stood alone in the middle of the austere room while the guards watched her.

Standing in the well-lit room, she was aware of how shabby she must look. Dirt and sand coated her skin, hair, and clothes. She began to brush herself off then, unashamed, smiled at the guards and removed her shirt to shake the dirt out. She untied her long hair and let it fall to her shoulders. When she fluffed it and a dusty cloud rose from her beautiful tresses.

"Well, well. Do you think your womanly charms will persuade one of my men to help you escape?" The perfect Hebrew came from a block of a man with a face as heavy as his body. He had just entered. When he looked at her and his brow furrowed his forehead disappeared into prickly looking eyebrows. "These men are my 'peshmerga,' those who face death," he continued. "Your enticements will not tempt them." He sat down behind the desk and the two soldiers who accompanied him moved to stand on either side of him. Red patterned headscarves covered their faces, except for a narrow slit through which their dark expressionless eyes watched her. The sound of the wind twisting around the mountain peaks hummed through the room. Sand began to filter in through the open door, eddying round them in the small room like mist.

When she saw how low the sun hung in the sky, Miryam realized she had been unconscious for most of the day. The soldiers whispered to each other as she shrugged back into her shirt and tied her hair. She checked her shirt pocket and noticed the map of the interior of Tariq's farm was gone. She stood waiting for her inquisition to begin.

It was obvious who was in charge: the guards jumped to take up positions by the door when the block of a man barked a command.

"I have many questions," he began, staring hard at Miryam. "The first concerns your presence in Kurd territory."

She glanced around, buying time, listening to the conversations in the courtyard and ignoring the big man's question. *That's very interesting.* Her Kurdish was elementary, but the words she grasped had to do with an ambush gone wrong. She also heard Tariq's name mentioned. *Curious*, she thought as she casually walked to the door and smiled sweetly at the guards; all the while listening to a man outside giving urgent orders to his men.

The door was slammed shut in her face. Its thud made her head throb worse than before. The man behind the desk became persistent. "I'll try some other questions. What is Israeli's legendary spy, the Dove, doing in Iraq? Who sent you?"

She flashed him a beguiling smile when she replied, keeping her answer vague. "I was lost and wandered into the mountains by chance." Her throat was dry and, even to her own ears, it sounded raspy. She eyed the tray holding a decanter of water and cups that a young boy had brought into the room and placed on the desk while she spoke.

Her interrogator followed her gaze. "Where are my manners? You are thirsty after your ordeal. Please, help yourself."

The water refreshed her parched throat. It also tasted familiar. *Fascinating.* She licked her lips. *It is a taste from the past?*

Her interrogator spoke again but, instead of Hebrew, this time it was Arabic. "We are a well informed and educated people. It would be childish to try and hide the truth. We've been following you since you entered Iraq. You were on a fixed course. It was no small task to find the hidden path to this fortress through the foothills as you did." He did not raise his voice but his look was threatening, "It was no accident. Come, maybe we can help each other. We Kurds are honorable people."

"I am sorry but I don't understand what you want." *A partial truth may be more helpful to me than a lie.* "Many years ago I lived and hunted in these mountains, and I simply returned for a visit."

"Hunting, you say? There've been no animals to hunt in these mountains for centuries. Don't you mean your own government is hunting you? If you cooperate, it would be so much easier for both of us. We have a lengthy account of your career, doctor." He rattled off where she had been educated and the government positions she had held, including her role with UNSCOM inspections and added details of the widespread alert sent out by the Israelis in the effort to apprehend her. "What is your connection with Saeed? We found the map."

She was stunned that he knew so much about her, but tried hard to show no sign of concern. "That is all in the past. I have nothing else to say." *There is too much at risk and time is of the essence. Let him shoot me or let him put me back in my cell where I can plan my escape.*

He pressed further. "We monitor the Israeli communications and picked up your description and the direction you fled across Syria and into Iraq. If you do not confide in us, perhaps we could make a deal with the Mossad. They are most anxious to get their hands on you. We would be gentler than the Mossad. Think about it. We may be able to help each other if you would confide in us. Now, how did you find your way to this secret stronghold? And who was the man on a path parallel to yours? Was he another defecting spy like you? Or is he a member of the Mossad? Perhaps this is all a ruse?"

"What are you talking about? I was hit on the head and woke up here. I didn't find you, you found me!" Her voice was agitated and shrill. She wanted him to think she was upset and confused. Which was true, for she had not known someone was following her. She rubbed the back of her head and exaggerated the pain her touch produced. "Ouch!"

"You were found by our guards a short distance from this place," her interrogator said firmly.

"I didn't know anything was here. As I said, it's been some years since I've been in this area. I became lost then someone hit me on the head and..."

His smile disappeared. "Silence! Lies! Was the man with you part of the Mossad or one of General Saeed's? We've followed your movements for a long time now and we've seen you with one of Saeed's associates. You have also made several trips in and out of Iraq. Speak! I want the truth!"

She hesitated, feeling bewildered. "When you apprehended me, why didn't you grab this mystery man? Then you could have asked him these stupid questions! And I don't know any General Saeed. My scientific and medical work occasionally brings me across the border, but that is all."

A soldier came in with a message.

Abruptly her interrogator ordered guards to return her to her cell. "A storm approaches," he told them. "We must prepare." He walked over and thrust his face inches from hers. "We will talk again, but I warn you, it will be under less pleasant circumstances. We may have other guests arriving later. Maybe they will encourage you to remember."

As they moved her back to her cell, Miryam's mind was swimming. *Other guests? Who? Not Tariq, I could see the hate in the leader's eyes when he said Tariq's name. If he thinks I work for Tariq I could be in big trouble.*

They tossed her in her cell, slammed the steel door and left. A few minutes later she heard the key in the lock. She moved back against the wall. The door swung open and a slim figure entered. She recognized it as one of the guards who had been in the office moments ago. She prepared herself for what she thought was an assassin, but lowered her guard when the scarf was removed and a familiar face emerged.

"Do you remember me?" The voice was soft and calm.

"Yes, Ghariba," Miryam answered, her tone hard, "I remember you." Polite conversation was out of the question. Miryam had always despised Ghariba and the passing years had intensified her hatred.

"I'm here to do you a favor and I suggest you take advantage of my good nature. Only our past friendship has kept you from being tortured." Ghariba crossed the cell, brushed dirt off a three-legged wooden stool, and sat down.

Miryam sat on the mattress on the floor opposite her visitor. She eyed Ghariba warily. "I thought there was something familiar about the glint of red hair of the guard who jabbered in the leader's ear. Is he your latest conquest?"

Ghariba's jaw tightened. "That was my brother. It was Qassem's idea. He is very protective. I'm happy I've found him after so many years."

"Does he know about your past?" Miryam's question sounded more like a threat. She moved on, not giving Ghariba a chance to answer. "You've changed, Ghariba. There's a hardened look about you. Sorry, dear, it's not very attractive. And by the way, we were never great friends."

"You spoke on my behalf when I had that little problem during your last inspection tour in Iraq. That is not a matter I take lightly. I could have been imprisoned if not for your support. Saddam was a cold and unforgiving dictator, Miryam."

Miryam relaxed, this was going better than she had first thought. "Do you mean when Dr. Swift caught you rummaging through his luggage and I lied for you? You incurred no debt with me. I think we'd both be better off if our pasts remain ancient history. I would, however, like the answer to one question: When did you start working for the Kurds?"

"As you wish, the past is nonexistent. To answer your question, I have always worked, as you say, for the Kurds. I was born here in these mountains..." Ghariba stood and gestured toward the barred window and the expansive vista outside. "Not too far from here, in a cave. My mother was hiding from Hussein's troops, who were attacking our village with chemical weapons."

"That's a fascinating story," Miryam's voice was laced with irony. "I haven't kept up with current events so I guess I missed your repentance and transformation. So you're a spy for the Kurds now? The last I heard you were helping Iraq's new democratic government. And let's not forget how entrenched in Saddam's organization you were. Great performance," Miryam said, clapping her hands. "I bet you even fool yourself. It must be hard to keep it all straight when you change sides so often."

Gharиba leaned forward, her eyes meeting Miryam's intently, as though she really wanted the other woman to understand. "I grew up quickly. Soon after I was born, Saddam's police murdered my mother and the rest of my family. I didn't know until recently that my brother had escaped. I was captured, deported to the south and re-educated. Have you forgotten our shared beginnings?"

Miryam stood and moved toward Ghariba menacingly.

"We have shared nothing! As I remember, in the camp you were a bully and a willing participant in the torment of the other children." Miryam's pain and hatred dripped from every word. "I was taken from my family and persecuted because I was a Jew. You took delight in finding new ways to humiliate me in front of the other children."

"Yes, that's true, but you must understand: I had to play the game to survive. You weren't there as long as I. You don't know what I suffered." Tears gleamed on Ghariba's cheeks.

"Crocodile tears? Appropriate, but they have no effect on me. Save them for some poor man you want to seduce. The only thing you've proven is that evil can be beautiful."

Unruffled, Ghariba faced Miryam, a compassionate look on her face. She placed a hand on Miryam's shoulder. "Forgive me?" As she stood, the folds of the scarf wrapped around Ghariba's neck fell open.

Miryam shoved her hand away. "Now it is time for justice to be served." A wicked sneer accompanied the word justice then, in a blur of motion, Miryam tore the silver dove from Ghariba's neck. "This is mine," she raged, and the intensity of her words forced Ghariba to take a step back. "How did you get this?" She held the necklace close to her chest as she spoke. "Perhaps I was wrong. We've something in common, Ghariba. We have both learned how to hate with a vengeance."

Ghariba began to step forward but Miryam's words stopped her.

"I am no longer a weak child you can torment. If you want to try and take it from me, I'm ready! I have looked forward to this moment, come on." Miryam crouched, assuming a fighting stance.

"Miryam, it's a trinket of little value. It was a gift. Until now I didn't recognize it as the necklace you had with you in the camp. Listen to me: I have a new life now and a chance to do something good. Keep the necklace." Ghariba stretched out her hands as if in prayer.

Miryam relaxed her stance but remained ready in case Ghariba attacked. "I'm not taken in by this mask of kindness. You are and always will be the kind of person whose heart changes with every beat." A deep silence filled the chamber as Miryam paced to the other side of her cell. "What exactly do you want from me? Or is it too early in your attempt to become my sister in tragedy for me to ask?" Miryam's scathing words hung in the air. "I have no patience for these games you like to play."

Ghariba stiffened. "Years ago, I thought I saw something in you that reminded me of my own suffering and I felt we shared a certain torment, but perhaps I was wrong. You too have changed and I'm sorry for you." Ghariba sat back down on the stool, picked up the canteen she had brought and offered Miryam a drink of water.

Miryam kicked the canteen from her hand. "I don't need your pity!" Miryam stood over Ghariba, hands on hips.

"Calm yourself," Ghariba said in a whisper. "There are eyes." Her head titled toward a camera in one corner of the cell. She waited while Miryam went to the mattress and sat down. "Very well, we'll do it your way. We want the exact location of the chemical and biological weapons. I can promise you your life if you cooperate."

"What weapons?" Miryam bent her head to hide her surprised expression. *How could they know?*

"You've been working with the CIA for years. I am well aware of your affair with Dr. Swift. They sent you here after their advisor's last communication." Ghariba waited. Miryam made no comment. "We intercepted a message from a man known to be a CIA agent saying he'd trailed one of Saeed's men, a Colonel Abbas, to the place in the mountains where Hussein had hidden his biological and chemical weapons. Then nothing, he disappeared. We assumed he'd been discovered and murdered by Saeed's men. That was three days ago and now you show up."

Miryam clapped. "Nice speech."

Ghariba recognized a strength in Miryam she had never seen before and wondered what had happened to change her so drastically. "We've heard about the threats the United States is throwing at Israel. It's all over the news. We are well aware that the U.S. and Israel like to play games with our lives and would use the weapons as a bargaining chip." Ghariba stood and walked toward Miryam. "When the CIA sent you here, what information were you given about the location of Hussein's weapons? We know Americans are in these mountains right now searching also. My brother and his men will not allow either Israel or the U.S. to have the weapons. It is futile to go against us."

When Miryam laughed, Ghariba was taken aback by the insanity she heard in that laughter. Miryam stretched her legs out in front of her and leaned back against the wall. She saw the small eye of the video camera contract. *Ghariba is playing to an audience.*

"We Kurds are as patient as these mountains," Ghariba said, standing. The authority in her voice was clear. "But this is one time we will not stand by and be pawns. Our loved ones have had firsthand knowledge of the inhumane results of these weapons and we will not let chemical or biological agents leave these mountains. We mean to find and destroy them. My people have a chance with the new democratic government here and we would all give our lives for this opportunity. Justice has been too long coming!"

"Justice?" screamed Miryam. "You know nothing of the pain and sacrifice justice takes. Do you know what it is like to be the cause of the death of a nation or see your own son betray his birthright and plot your murder? Are you a warrior? Could you kill your own flesh and blood to save your nation?" Miryam turned and mumbled something under her breath. Her many lives had blended confusingly in her mind.

"I'm finished bantering," Ghariba said. "Unless you prefer painful interrogation, tell me where the weapons are located."

"Foolish child," Miryam said with disdain. "Do you think I fear any of *you*? Leave me. Go back to your people and tell them I follow my own path. If we meet again I will cut those venomous lips from your lying face. I know who you really are, but never think for a moment you know me. I am a warrior like none you have ever seen!"

Ghariba had faced the blood and gore of battle and many other terrifying events in her short, eventful life but nothing had sent such a foreboding chill through her as completely as did Miryam's pitiless words and cold eyes. She backed away and left the cell without saying another word.

Miryam was glad to be rid of the intrusive Ghariba. She started to examine a section of her cell's rock wall as inconspicuously as possible. She thought she'd seen something earlier, but had been hurried away by the guards before she'd had the chance to investigate.

Shouting from the courtyard interrupted her search. She pulled herself up to the bars and peered out. Everyone was running and yelling, but Miryam was too far away to make out what they were saying. She could see a man shouting orders and pointing to the west. She lost her hold on the rocks and fell down to the floor. She dusted herself off and, in spite of her discomfort, climbed back up to the window. This time, she looked to the west. A giant swirling funnel of dust was heading straight for them. She could feel the temperature dropping. The sky, so clear moments ago, was turning gray at the approach of the storm. It was huge, much more than an ordinary sandstorm.

Nimbly, Miryam jumped down from the window, scanning the six-by-six -foot cell for the best place to sit out the storm. She decided that the supporting beam in one corner of the outside wall was the safest place to take refuge. The beam protruded into the room a few feet and would provide at least a small barrier against the debris that would come in through the window. Already the wind was driving sand through the bars and the air in the cell was becoming thick with sand. There was little time to prepare and Miryam hurried to gather up the rags and water. The danger was not the powerful wind, for her stone prison would withstand heavy gusts, it was the choking dust in the air. She curled up in the corner behind the beam with the rags and canteen on her lap. She soaked one of the rags with water and tied it over her face. The harsh sounds of the windstorm reverberated around her and she covered her ears with her hands to block out the shrieking sound.

As nature battled outside, Miryam pulled the shirt she was wearing up over her head and brought her knees up to her chest to protect herself. Patiently, she waited.

When the room was filled with dust, masking the camera that watched, she escaped.

Chapter 21

Assyria, 811 B.C.—Demons Strike

Semiramis moved, catlike, into the labyrinth in the mountain. She did not question her plan, not even for a moment. She believed the gods were working through her and that they had inspired her path to revenge.

Like a phantom wind, her breath extinguished the torches she had lit earlier in the passages near the town center and temple. *The darkness is more suitable for killing*, she thought.

Now that she knew the meaning of the symbols, she could use the secret passages to move from level to level and get behind or ahead of her quarry.

But first she had to find out how many men Ninyas had with him. Surely her son had lost a few of his men in the storm? She hoped many. She wished he had come alone but, after their last meeting, she knew he would not be that foolish and risk another scar on his pretty face.

She dismissed the idea of a one-on-one meeting for another reason: her son was a coward. Ninyas was at his bravest when others did his fighting. She slowed her pace as voices approached from a nearby passage. When she turned the next corner and entered the main tunnel, she saw the light from their torches and heard Ninyas' angry voice.

He was in a rage. "We must continue. I have promised my benefactors her head and I cannot go back without it!

Remember, we are in this together. If we do not succeed, he will take all of your heads. The King of Urartu does not take kindly to failure."

"She could not have survived this long," she heard Ninyas' Captain answer. "All her men have already died of the illness and she was with them in the slave pens. It is foolish for us to continue this futile search. We must go back or we will become lost in these caves forever."

"How dare you question your king's orders," Ninyas shouted. "I tell you, she's still alive. I can feel her presence! Calah is ours. She's the one person who could dispute my claim to the throne."

They ranted among themselves until the captain stepped forward to speak for the troops. "We'll search for one more day, then we will leave you and your wretched mother to rot in this hole forever."

Semiramis listened to the grumbling soldiers and determined that there were five of them, not counting Ninyas. It was hard to call them soldiers. His army was made up of thieves and murderers, and the scum were dressed in the uniforms of her honorable soldiers.

She got down on her knees and put her eye to the small hole she'd been listening through. She recognized the one Ninyas addressed as captain. He had been a soldier in her army. He had been caught stealing from his comrades and she had ordered him flogged and thrown off the palace grounds. *Huh,* thought the queen, *I was too lenient. I should have had him flayed.*

At first she thought she could frighten some of the five into running away, but now she wanted them all to die, if for no other reason than for dishonoring the uniforms her noble men had once worn.

As if walking on velvet, she silently moved down to their

level and slid into the shadows of a side passage, waiting to see which fork in the tunnel they would take.

The troop continued searching the broad main tunnel. She followed carefully staying outside the circle of light from their torches. Ninyas stopped once, lifting his torch high above his head to search the darkness. He looked around the back of the column and inspected the side tunnels nearby. "I know you're near, mother," she heard him whisper through clenched teeth. "I'm coming for you."

By the light of the torch, Semiramis could see his face and the maniacal look in his eyes. Poor boy, she thought, even the gods seemed to have abandoned him.

Once the men had decided on their route, she darted into a hidden passage that would allow her to come up behind them.

She waited in a deep dank crevice just off the tunnel where they would soon pass by. Her breathing slowed to less than a whisper. She remained as still as a lioness stalking a much needed meal.

The troop's noisy footsteps grew steadily more loud. Torchlight splashed the rock walls. It grew ever brighter, then began to dim as they passed within inches of her hiding place. She fell in behind the last man and melted into his shadow. He never heard her approach or sensed her presence. She slid her dagger from its warm home next to her body and thrust it into her injured left hand and with her right hand forced her fingers to close around it. It immediately began searching for a new source of heat for its home as she crouched down and crept closer.

It was all too easy. With swift, practiced movements, she placed her right hand over the rear guard's mouth, slit his throat and stood cradling the limp dead man in her arms as the torchlight of his still living comrades vanished down the tunnel. Quickly, she discarded the body in a side passage.

It wasn't until Ninyas called a halt to refresh himself that he discovered that one of his men was missing. "I told you she was still alive. Now do you believe me?" He paced and mumbled like a frightened child as he waited for the captain to return.

The captain, who had been investigating another passage, returned smiling. He and Ninyas moved away from the others. The captain spoke in whispers as the young prince giggled as he listened. When the captain had finished, Ninyas grinned wolfishly. "Do it. Leave no way for my mother to escape if she gets by us."

The ugly captain nodded his understanding, took one of the torches and went back into the passage he had just exited. The rest of the band grumbled, their nerves on edge, when Ninyas ordered them to continue their search of the cave.

After the queen had made her first kill, she moved into the passage that ran above and parallel to the route Ninyas and his troop followed. Semiramis found the going difficult, for she had to stoop to walk in some of the tight spaces. Nose bleeds and dizziness caused her to pause frequently, but she still managed to resume stalking Ninyas and his troop. "Four left and then it will be just you, my son." Her voice was contemptuous. She moved confidently without the assistance of light, now quite comfortable in the total blackness. The darkness was, in fact, a soothing companion.

Suddenly, shrill cries violated her tranquil darkness. The sounds surrounded her. They were horrible. They whipped through the cave, pounding her senses. She put her hands over her ears. Then, just as suddenly as the awful screams had started, the cave fell back into total silence.

At the next opportunity, the queen moved down to the same level as Ninyas. She crept along the passage, almost bumping into the captain as he came hurrying out of a side tunnel. She jumped back just in time as he rushed by to catch up to Ninyas and the others.

She moved down the tunnel he had just left and pulled one of the small oil jars from inside her tunic. When the flint sparked and ignited a small flame, she noticed that the area looked familiar. She broke into a run. Strange, her feet felt warm. *Yes, warm and wet*. She looked down and, to her terror, found she was standing in a river of thick red blood. It was streaming out of a broad side passage. With a trembling hand, she raised the fragile flame high above her head to cast more light over the grotto as she entered.

Her mind screamed, *No! No!* But there on the rocks near the edge of the water were the heads of her beautiful white horses where they'd been thrown after being savagely hacked from their bodies. The last of their life's blood drizzled into the cool pool of water that they had once shared.

Semiramis was stunned by the brutal way the animals had been dispatched. She caressed the still warm flesh and smoothed their flowing manes. When she was unable to contain her agony, she screamed. "Ninyas!" and then again, "Ninyas!" As she struggled to regain her composure, through gritted teeth she promised that the captain would also die an agonizing death.

Ninyas and his men stopped in their tracks as her bloodcurdling cry filtered through the cave. At first Ninyas was shocked and then he looked at the captain. Depraved smiles spread across both their faces. "I think my mother has received our message."

"I have no doubt our missing comrade was the first to find my mother," Ninyas said to his remaining men. "Don't get any ideas about trying to make it to the surface alone. Be vigilant or she will make sure you also become permanent residents of this cave."

The frightened men stared at their would-be king. His twisted expression alarmed them. Even worse, they feared he was right.

"Find her!" Ninyas screamed.

Semiramis broke into a trot when she entered the main tunnel ahead of the group, her grief igniting her diminished energy. When she found where the chiseled steps started, she entered the first passage that led to the granary. She removed some of the gems she had stashed in her tunic and spilled them on the cave floor at the beginning of the passage, then scattered the rest on the ground every few feet. A grain chute that led to a lower level proved just large enough for her to fit through. It would provide her escape route.

When the trap was set she waited in the shadows of an alcove at the beginning of the side passage. Her breathing was ragged and she was sweating profusely. A bloody tear of sweat ran down her cheek.

Soon she saw their shadows playing on the cave walls. One of the men pointed to the marks she had made on the wall. Their spirits buoyed as they drew nearer. Their torchlight became brighter and she backed up, moving more deeply into the shadows.

The gems on the cave floor sparkled tantalizingly in the torchlight. First Ninyas and then the captain went past the side passage and she feared her plan would not work. But the next man stopped: something had caught his eye. He bent down to pick it up. "A ruby, I've found a ruby!"

Excited, the rest of the troop gathered around the man who had found the jewel. "We'll share equally in all treasure found," Ninyas shouted, "just as I have promised. Now let me see what you found." Ninyas held out his hand to the young soldier. "Give it to me," he commanded. The man hesitated, then he gave Ninyas the stone. Ninyas' eyes glowed as he inspected the jewel.

Now Ninyas was in his element. Semiramis thought to herself, that if there was one thing her son excelled at, it was calculating wealth. It was clear from the look on her son's face that his greed had sharpened this skill.

He placed the stone in a leather pouch around his neck and tucked it into his tunic. The young man protested. "Hey, I found that. It belongs to me!"

Just then, one of the other men called in excitement: "Here are two diamonds."

Ninyas eyes sparkled with the prospect of this new-found wealth. "You two men come with me. We will search this side tunnel. Captain, go back to the entrance and stand guard." Ninyas pointed to one of the men. "You, go with the captain. Keep a sharp watch."

Crouching in the darkness, Semiramis smiled. She knew his weaknesses so well. She doubted Ninyas had ever used his powers of observation for anything that did not bring him personal gain.

The three men started down the tunnel, Ninyas in the lead. Their attention was focused on the cave floor. It was like a game. Every time a stone was found, Ninyas would grab it, caress it, then place it in his pouch. They were ecstatic, believing the passage must lead to a storehouse of treasures. After they found the last of the stones Semiramis had planted, they hurried to the storage area at the end of the passage. All they found was a mound of rotting grain. Disappointed, Ninyas quickly commanded them to return to the main tunnel.

When she heard their footsteps returning, Semiramis moved to the middle of the passage, blocking their escape route. She swung Lord of Justice from her shoulder and placed three arrows in a row against the rock wall on her right. When she saw the light of a torch approaching, she went down on one knee and notched one of the arrows into the bow. Ninyas was in the front carrying the torch as they rounded the first bend in the winding tunnel. *Excellent,* she thought. All three were heading straight toward her, heads bent to the ground, still searching. She did not rush her shot. The eye of the queen who was about to kill her son did not waver as she took aim at her son's heart. She pulled the bow back to its fullest and let go the first arrow and had the second in the air before the first hit its target.

Just as she let the first arrow fly, Ninyas bent down to pick up something that lay gleaming in the torchlight. His greed saved his life. The first arrow found the heart of the soldier behind him. Ninyas was pinned face down on the floor when the dead soldier fell forward over him. The second arrow went through the neck of the happy young man who had found the first stone. The attack was silent and so unexpected that it took Ninyas several seconds to recover. Laying prone, pinned on the cold stone floor by fear, he began screaming like a frightened child. "Captain," he shouted, "we are under attack!"

Semiramis cursed her son's good fortune in averting death. As the captain approached, she slipped into the grain chute, placed her bow on her chest, and slid out of sight and down to safety.

By the time the captain reached Ninyas, there was no one to confront. "Where, my king? Where is she?" the captain asked as he searched.

"You fool. She must have gone right by you in the tunnel."

The captain called to the man guarding the main tunnel. He had seen nothing. The surviving soldier ran to Ninyas and the captain. "There are ghosts and demons here," he cried when he saw his dead comrades on the cave floor. "We must leave this haunted cave, this is the home of the gods and we have angered them!"

The captain knew the man was ready to bolt. He picked up the arrow the queen had left behind. "It is no ghost we fight. It is only a woman. Surely we can overcome one woman? We will stay together. No more splitting our forces." He grabbed the terrified soldier by his tunic and propelled him down the tunnel. "I'll guard our rear. No one will get by me."

The last remaining soldier's voice quivered, "But captain she is the warrior queen."

"If you try to run away, I'll kill you myself," Ninyas bloodshot eyes bulged as he spoke but the frightened man was silenced.

They returned to the main passage. Ninyas paused long enough to open his pouch and show the captain what he had found. "These alone can buy us a kingdom anywhere in the world." The two men grinned. The dead men were already forgotten and the attack was less important then the promise of more riches. Their greed drew them deeper into the mountain. Within moments, Ninyas was forced to stop, doubled over with abdominal cramps. Long, painful spasms racked his body as he tried to hide his pain.

"What's the matter, your majesty? Have you not seen

death before?" The Captain spoke with an air of compassion even though he was planning to slit Ninyas' throat and keep the treasure. He bent over the boy who would be king and patted him on the shoulder. In a fatherly manner, he helped Ninyas to his feet and guided him to join the remaining soldier.

Ninyas' pain was easily soothed as thoughts of the wealth and his glorious future trickled through his distorted mind. *I will kill my mother and recover the treasure. This great fortune will ensure my treatment by the best physicians in the world. There's nothing enough wealth can't buy.*

Chapter 22

Zagros Mountains, Northeastern Iraq—A Noble War

The eerie silence jerked Rich awake.

"I was getting ready to wake you," Hal told him. "The storm has either blown itself out or moved on."

"Yeah, weird isn't it? Let's get outside and see what's going on."

Hal tried the Land Rover's passenger door, but it wouldn't budge. Sand had covered it. It took Hal and Rich's combined strength to get the rear side door open wide enough for them to slip outside.

The bright sunlight made their eyes water. They grabbed their sunglasses and slipped them on. The marines and Elliot emerged one by one behind them and began to dig the vehicle out while Hal and Rich kept watch.

"There doesn't seem to be much else to do until the boys come home," Rich said. "You'd think they would have at least sent us a Hallmark by now."

Without warning, a hail of bullets flew at them from all sides—behind as well as in front—and, to a man, they hit the ground.

"Damn," said Rich. He snatched up his weapon and peered through the scope. "Why the hell don't they just come in and finish us off? They've got us surrounded. It's damn irritating. They just sit out there and play with us!"

Hal silenced Rich with a cautioning lift of his hand and gestured for them to listen.

Flash Jack had heard the same thing that had alerted Hal. He signaled Cordy to take one side of the truck as he took the other. The marines' youthful faces turned combat tough. Weapons were raised to their shoulders and ready. No one moved.

Rich held his breath, waiting. Then he heard it, too. Someone was coming up on them through the overturned truck. Rich pulled a stun grenade from his pocket and cocked his arm back, ready to throw the grenade into the truck as the others backed away and took cover.

The flap on the back of the truck shifted. Rich pulled the pin on the grenade and motioned for everyone to get ready. "Crescent moon," someone whispered. "I mean veil, damn it," and Wayne stuck his head through the canvas. "Expecting someone else?"

"You almost got your head blown off," said Rich.

Wayne backed away, hands up in surrender.

Then Rich remembered the grenade. "Oh, I forgot." He tossed the grenade over his shoulder, out into the desert. "Where's Matt?"

"Why? Were you worried?" asked Matt as he climbed down from the truck behind Wayne and dove to the ground when the grenade exploded.

"Good to see you," said Rich, smiling down at Matt sprawled on the ground and spitting sand.

Next Gibbs jumped out of the truck. Rich slapped the man heartily on the back. "What's up kids? Did you have fun at the prom?"

Wayne called for everyone's attention and began to brief the group. "The lead truck got away, but broke down in the storm about three hundred yards ahead of us. We couldn't get to it." Wayne signaled over his shoulder. "This truck and the one we could get to have filled bombs on board. I rigged them both to blow. None of the anthrax inside escaped. We've got samples. Here's the plan."

"Is it better than the last one?" asked Rich with a smile.

"Yeah, you'll like it. It has a high blast factor," explained Wayne. "Rich, contact the Iraqi president and have him send some men up here to reinforce Gibbs and his men."

He turned to Gibbs. "You and your men are going after the lead truck to prevent them from off-loading the bombs until reinforcements get here. Then you'll blow the last truck."

"The rest of us are going to storm the farm," Rich interrupted, "find the other bioweapons and destroy them. I love it," said an excited Rich. "An awesome challenge, and a noble cause. Of course we'll be out numbered one hundred-to-one but hey, what more could you want?" His speech abruptly ended as gunfire erupted behind them once again and they hit the ground.

"Listen up," Wayne said as they huddled together. "We found a map in one of the trucks. It's in Arabic." Elliot put his hand out for the map, but Wayne indicated that Rich should take a look.

"How stupid can they be?" Rich laughed as he examined it. "They circled their pick-up site."

"So, the rest of the weapons aren't at the farm," Wayne said, jabbing his finger at his map. "They're in these mountains? That doesn't make sense. We would have found any buildings Saddam erected during our inspections." He looked back at the map Rich was holding. "Rich what's this word written in the margin?"

Rich thought for a moment and replied: "Cave. It's perfect. They're in a cave."

Matt pulled his hat down further over his forehead, rolled his eyes. "Great," he said dryly. "It had to be a cave."

"The cave isn't far from here," Wayne continued. "Once the marines are in place at the third truck, they'll draw enemy fire and we'll make a run for those foothills," Wayne indicated a rocky area at the base of the mountains behind them. "We'll take refuge behind those rocks. When Rich blows this truck and the other one during the confusion, we make for the cave. It should be dark in another couple of hours and that will help. Clear?" Without waiting for an answer, he said, "Let's do it."

"I think I should go with you, Dr. Swift," a meek voice said from the rear of the group, "just in case you run into locals and need an interpreter."

Wayne looked at Elliot, and debated letting him come along. Pearl had warned them that President Salinski had sent a spy to infiltrate them and it was fairly obvious to him that it was Elliot. He decided to leave him behind in the custody of the marines and was about to expose Elliot for the spy he was when Hal spoke.

"Yeah, it's a good idea for him to come with us," said Hal.

Rich sidled round to Wayne and whispered, "I got through to the Iraqi president's assistant. He said they're having a bit of a problem themselves. More than half of the new cabinet members have been assassinated."

"Damn," Wayne's voice had lost some of its optimism.

"Never fear. We white hats will not be left to rot in the sun. I can assure you that the marines will get help. By the way," he said, lowering his voice so that only Wayne could hear what he said, "What did I miss over there between you, Hal, and the rodent?"

"Not now," Wayne said as he ducked down. "I'm counting on you, Rich. I hope you can deliver those reinforcements!" He positioned himself behind the tailgate of the truck and began returning fire.

As Rich picked up Sleeping Beauty, Hal elbowed Matt. "Wait until you see this. Get ready." Matt flinched at the first explosion from Rich's gun.

Rich turned forty-five degrees and fired again and then again and again in rapid succession, until he had come around full circle. "That should hold 'em." He cupped a hand to his ear. Automatic weapons were still firing in the distance, but not at them. "What the hell? Who could that be? It's coming from over there," Rich said, pointing to a spot between the base of a mountain and the farm complex.

Gibbs clambered up onto the truck and scanned the horizon through his binoculars. "Hey, the farm's under attack!"

Rich grabbed his binoculars and scanned the area. "Look at them going at each other."

"We don't have time to figure this out. Let's take advantage of the diversion," Wayne said, addressing Gibbs. "Now's your chance. Good luck. Remember: that last truck has to be destroyed. We can't take a chance on any of those bombs getting away."

The young lieutenant nodded with assurance and pointed at Flash Jack. "You're up."

Flash Jack picked up the hot-spot bombs Rich offered and stuffed them in his shirt like they were apples he'd take along in case he got hungry.

"Believe me, you'll be reinforced," Rich said, slapping the kid on the back. The three marines took off without a backward glance. Rich noticed Flash Jack supported his weapon with his splinted arm. He was a tough kid. Rich hoped he made it.

Flash Jack must have sensed Rich's thoughts because he turned and grinned at him before disappearing around the side of the truck.

"Can we make it to those rocks at the foot of the mountain?" Wayne asked dubiously once Jack was gone. He pointed to a spot about eighty yards to their right. "Rich, does it look mined?"

Rich put a small device to his eye and scanned. "I'm not showing that it's mined, but the storm might have interfered with my readings."

"Great," said Matt. "If you're that certain, then, of course, let's go." The five men dashed across the sand toward the foothills, vaulting over the bodies of the sleeping men Rich's gun had taken out of action. Rich was astonished when the interpreter passed him, sprinting for the safety of the rocks.

Once at the base of the mountains, they crouched down behind the rocks for protection. Wayne used his binoculars to see where the marines were located. He wanted to be sure they were at a safe distance when Rich blew the trucks. It wasn't only the explosion they had to worry about: this type of incendiary bomb had to reach an extremely high temperature in order to destroy the virus.

"How far away is a safe distance for the marines?" he asked Rich.

"I designed these bombs to minimize collateral damage. It's actually an implosion, not an explosion. When it ignites, the intense heat sucks air in, preventing material—in this case Anthrax or nasty viruses—from spreading outward. And the oxygen pulled in feeds the reaction."

"Give me the short version," said Wayne. "What's a safe distance?"

Rich double-checked. "You put just two hot spots in each truck?" Wayne nodded. "If they—and we—are at least two hundred yards away from the blast, no one will have to worry about getting sunburned. Let me look." Rich confiscated Wayne's glasses and started to describe the marines' progress toward the third truck and away from the two trucks he was about to blow up. "They're almost there. They're rounding the final turn and coming up fast on the home stretch. The finish line is in view, and they turn the corner behind a huge group of boulders. And now ladies and gents the winner is..."

He pushed a button on the remote and a thunderous explosion vibrated through the air.

"...Us. Shield your eyes," Rich yelled as they threw themselves to the sand, arms over their heads for protection.

The earth shook and two brilliant ruby clouds in the shape of inverted tornadoes formed where the trucks had been. Orange and white waves of molten heat enveloped the already distorted forms of the trucks. Rich gave the all clear and they lifted their heads to watch. Their faces reflected the sickly orange of the melting trucks. Ripples of the billowing heat filled the air and crawled toward them, a quivering silent tidal wave.

"The heat's incredible," Hal shouted above the roar of the sustained explosions.

Sand flew through the air as it was sucked into the inferno. It felt like angry bees stinging the unprotected skin of their necks and wrists. The five men burrowed back and deeper into the sand behind their rock shelters for more protection.

When Wayne retrieved his binoculars he was relieved

to see that the marines were fine. Most of their opposition had fled back to the safety of the besieged farm and the other group—whoever they were—were running for the hills.

"The Marines have a free hand getting to the last truck and blowing it," Wayne called.

"I gave Flash Jack his party supplies: he's got a couple of hot spots for the truck and a few extras, in case he gets inside and wants to blow anything inside the farm. Their remote is set on a different frequency than ours so we don't blow each other up. They're golden." Rich was casual about his accomplishments, but was clearly pleased. Sometimes his toys didn't work as expected, even though he always exuded confidence. Wayne and Matt never knew what to expect.

"Kurdish bandits are everywhere in these remote parts," Elliot said. "I think they attacked the trucks and we happened to get caught in the middle. They hijack the trucks and sell everything on the black market between here and Turkey. I don't think we have to worry about them. We don't have anything that would interest them."

The remains of the two trucks smoldered. The twisted frames dripped white-hot tears of melting metal. The rubber that had once been tires pooled on the sand. The rapid ignition and resulting level of heat devoured everything in the bombs' designated heat radius. Soon nothing would remain of the trucks to tell anyone what had been destroyed. They could breathe a little easier knowing these bombs were dead. Rich likened this invention to a self-cleaning oven. "A few benign ashes are all that's left at the bottom of the oven. You could wipe them up with a sponge."

"Are you sure we're okay here?" Matt asked.

"Yeah, there's nothing to worry about," Rich said.

"You're in good hands. It's brutal and beautiful all at the same time. Just like the perfect woman."

The group sighed in relief and relaxed against the rocks to catch their breath and watch the raging inferno.

Matt absentmindedly wiped the sweat from his and sat down heavily on a mound of sand. He examined his dirty shirt. "Damn, I miss my pinstripes."

"Forever the James Bond, huh, Matt?" Rich teased.

Suddenly, armed men materialized from the rocks behind them, their faces hidden behind headscarves. Not a shot was fired as the cloaked soldiers herded the five astonished men together while they confiscated their weapons. Rich was about to resist when they jerked his supplies off of his back, but Wayne restrained him. "It's too late. Chill."

The leader of the troop closed his cell phone after a brief conversation and turned to his captives. He said something in an agitated voice then, for emphasis, delivered a surprise blow with the butt of his gun to Rich's stomach. Rich fell to his knees, doubled over in pain.

Hal stepped between Rich and his assailant as Matt and Wayne helped Rich to his feet. They stood supporting Rich, stunned into silence. The soldiers seemed to enjoy pulling the plastic handcuffs extra tight on Rich's hands when they bound him and the others. The leader sent one of his men in the direction of the farm and motioned for a large contingent of the soldiers to again hide themselves among the rocks. He pointed up the mountain and he and the rest of the group started walking, herding their prisoners ahead of them like cattle.

Wayne decided these were not bandits as Elliot had suggested, but a sizable army and he wondered if Gibbs would be able to blow the other truck before he was overwhelmed. Cautiously, Wayne slowed his walking pace so that he was next to Elliot. "Do you recognize the dialect?"

"Yes, it's Kurmanji. They're Kurds. The leader of this battalion is Mullah Quazi of the Barzani tribe."

"Do you know anything about them? Are they friendly?"

"I know that the Barzani tribe was supposed to have been annihilated by Saddam. I didn't think any of the clan was left."

"Talk to them. That's why you're here: make yourself useful, damn it. Tell them we're here on an important mission and that we're Americans." Wayne nudged Elliot forward.

Elliot mustered his courage and walked faster until he was striding alongside the leader of the group. The other Kurds were amused to see the little man take giant strides to keep up with their colonel. Elliot spoke in a trembling voice, but the more he spoke, the calmer he became and the language eventually flowed with a certain impressive grace. "Colonel, we're Americans, here on a very important mission and..."

A strong, weathered hand grabbed the front of Elliot's shirt. "I do not play games with Americans," he warned.

Elliot began to speak again, but the rough hand was held up to silence him. "Save your flowery words for our leader. The only thing that stopped us from shooting you was that you were attacked by Saeed's men. They are our enemy also. You can explain your actions to our leader." Elliot was curtly forced to move back into line with his comrades.

Comrades? Elliott was furious. He despised the condescending attitude of his companions and their juvenile behavior. *These crazy men are not my comrades. I work for the President of the United States of America. They think I don't know that people call me weasel behind my back. Weasel! Well, this weasel will come out on top. They'll be sorry they kicked me around when I bring home Hussein's missing weapons. My payday is coming.*

"What did he say?" asked Matt.

"He said 'Americans always think only their business is important.'"

"What else?"

"If we speak without permission he will shoot us."

A guard stepped over to Elliot and raised the butt of his rifle. Elliot braced himself for the blow, but it never came.

The earth shook and the sky turned a now familiar tangerine. Their captors stopped in their tracks, but Wayne and his team ducked for cover behind the nearest rocks. A huge, ominous tidal wave of energy crawled toward them.

As the Kurds dashed for cover and Rich yelled: "Gibbs did it!" They all cheered. Rich's face screwed up as if he was angry. "I'll have to have a talk with Flash Jack. That was overkill."

Matt slapped him on the back. "It's a beautiful sight."

"Beautiful?" Rich whispered so that only Hal and Matt could hear. "Yeah, I guess you're right. It's beautiful because nobody will die from that poison. But never forget a bomb is still a device designed for destruction. You know I don't like killing, Matt. Even more, I don't like not having any other option." He walked forward, his face serious and his mind far away.

Hal stared after him and Matt explained. "In Rich's early days with the intelligence service he worked in their think tank and came up with some device that rendered the enemy unconscious with sound waves. Later, before he had done safety testing, he found out they used it during a mission. They set it off in front of a hotel and it worked perfectly. It knocked everyone in the hotel out cold for about an hour. The team walked in without a fight and got the hostages out with no loss of life."

"That's great... bloodless victories. Nothing wrong with that," said Hal.

"Wrong. A pediatric hospital was next door—every newborn in the hospital became permanently deaf, about twelve babies."

"I think I remember that in the news. They thought it was some kind of infection or virus. But how about that cannon he pulled out back at the Land Rover?"

"Did you see anyone dead?" Matt asked. "There'll be a lot of minor wounds and bad headaches from his special brew of sleeping potion. I think he fills the projectiles with Versed, it's a tranquilizer. I've used it to put my patients to sleep before surgery. But no one is dead and no one will die. He thinks it's a hoot because the enemy is convinced they've been shot. He just puts them to sleep for a while. Don't get me wrong: when necessary, Rich will mount a defense with lethal weapons, but that's his last resort, as it is for all of us. We three decided a long time ago that it was wrong and useless to stop violence with violence. For every person killed, there are ten more at home who will never forgive or forget who or what country was responsible for the death of their loved one."

Hal was confused, pleased, and interested in the outcome of this novel approach to the savagery of warfare.

"Unfortunately," Matt indicated Rich, Wayne and himself, "we three have seen more than most people could ever imagine in their worst nightmares. We will stop Tariq Saeed by whatever means the situation demands. But we'll try to do it with a minimum loss of life. Innocence lives."

Matt dropped back in line behind Hal before the guards got angry.

A soldier prodded Hal with his rifle butt to move more quickly. As he walked, he thought over what he'd just heard and his respect for his new friends grew. They were an unusual group, trying to wage a moral war against an immoral adversary. *They're either amazing or crazy.* He'd wait and make a judgment of their mental status later, if they survived.

The Kurds were chatting among themselves and Wayne pressed close to Elliot. "What're they saying?"

"They're surprised by the explosion," Elliot lied.

"Doesn't it prove to them we're all on the same side? Obviously, we don't like this Saeed and neither do they, or they wouldn't have been attacking his convoy and the farm."

In fact, that *was* what the Kurds were talking about. They had come to ambush the trucks and confiscate the weapons they thought Saeed was transporting. They hated him and knew the farm was a cover for his growing radical group. They had proof that, on several occasions, Saeed had used some of the small villages in the area for combat training for his troops stationed at the farm. The Kurds would not forgive or forget the needless murders.

Elliot would never tell Wayne exactly what he heard. He was not about to help Wayne and the others when his own fame was so close at hand. He could bring in a Seal team to secure the area and blow up the storage site if he wanted to. All he had to do was contact the president with the coordinates for the weapons before Wayne got to them. He had already memorized the map Wayne had taken from one of the trucks. This "little man" would not let them steal his glory.

A guard stepped up to urge him up the steep mountain path. When he saw the waiting trucks, Elliot knew his chance to escape would come soon. The sky was turning the deep purple that signaled the approach of night. That would, indeed, help Elliot's plan. He glanced around casually and spotted his pack slung over one of his captors' backs. He'd need his GPS and cellular phone. The rest he had sewn into his collar. *Rich isn't the only one who can do magic.*

At the bottom of the hill, they were herded into the back of a truck and their packs thrown in on top of them. One soldier rode in the back with them, two guards were up front. Elliot heard the soldiers say they were in a hurry to get back to headquarters.

Matt's complaints floated out from the dark interior of the vehicle. "Why did they have to tie us to the sides of the truck?"

The plastic cuffs rubbed painfully back and forth against their wrists as the truck jolted over the uneven dirt road. When they protested, their guard spit out a few threatening words and raised his rifle. No one needed an interpreter to understand his meaning. Later, Wayne tried a few words in Arabic but their guard either didn't understand him or simply didn't bother answering. Wayne called out to Elliot to ask the guard how much farther to their camp but didn't get an answer. "Hey, Matt, is Elliot sitting next to you?"

"Yes, he's right here. Why?"

"He must be asleep, like Richard." They all could hear Rich snoring as if he didn't have a care in the world.

Everyone was asleep when the truck pulled up at the fortress deep in the Zagros Mountains. The canvas was pulled back and a soldier jumped in to release the rope that had secured them to the truck. He signaled for the weary travelers to get out.

Rich was the last to exit. As he was about to jump down they heard the distant but unmistakable drumbeat of helicopter blades cutting through the night sky. "Must be five, no, maybe six Apaches," said Rich as he jumped from the truck.

Suddenly, streaks of fire ripped across the darkness as the choppers fired their rockets. After a slight hesitation, a fireball flashed the response they were waiting for: the rockets had hit their targets. Ground explosions started in rapid, ear-splitting sequence.

"I told you those marines would have reinforcements," said Rich. "It's the cavalry."

"OK, I give up," Wayne said, "what did you do? You said you couldn't get through to the Iraqi President."

"Right, but when I left him a message, I used an open line, counting on my friends in low places to get the message, just in case."

"Thanks for letting us know what was going on."

"What? You wanted details? There was no time, and besides, when didn't the CIA listen in on Iraq? Just because this country is becoming a democracy doesn't mean the spying stops. Give me a break. Have you been out of it so long, you've forgotten your basic spy stuff? We listen in on everybody!"

With the fireworks as a backdrop, they were herded into a dingy alcove carved out of solid mountain rock. Once the door was closed, the lights were turned on, temporarily blinding them. Wayne's eyes finally adjusted to the bright light and he looked around to make sure everyone was OK. He was startled to find Elliot missing. "Damn," Wayne whispered to Matt, "where's Elliot? He was right next to

you in the truck. When did you last see that little weasel?"
Wayne paused, listening to heavy booted footsteps echoing off the rock floors. The sound grew louder and stopped on the other side of a heavily reinforced door.

Matt was about to answer Wayne's question when a bull of a man entered and greeted them warmly in English. "Welcome to our humble home. I am Qassem." He bowed. At six-foot, four inches, he stood taller than most Kurds, with heavy muscular arms and the broad square shoulders of a weightlifter. "He looks like a WWF contender," Rich whispered to Wayne.

They all stared at Qassem's sun-bronzed face. His thick expressive brows hung heavily over lavish lashes as he stared back at them. His eyes sparkled with intelligence. He walked from person to person, his ample nose coming within inches of each person's face and he examined them as if he were a doctor with a group of new patients. It was not necessary for him to say he was the leader of this Kurd army, his bearing suggested no other possibility. His mouth was hidden behind an expansive curved mustache and no one knew if he was wearing a friendly smile or an evil smirk.

At this point, Wayne could not afford caution: their timetable wouldn't allow any more delays. His face turned hard, set in a granite-like scowl and he took two steps toward Qassem.

Soldiers instantly rushed forward to protect their leader. It was not necessary: he could take care of himself. At Wayne's approach, Qassem whirled around and, like magic, a knife appeared out of nowhere, the blade's sharp edge resting at Wayne's throat. The movement was silent and faster than lightening. None of the others—least of all Wayne—had time to react. The two men stood, their faces inches from one another. Wayne heard the blood pulsing in his head and, inevitably, was the first to blink. His lips parted to speak.

Qassem put a hand up to reassure his men and then he put a finger to his lips to silence Wayne. "We must begin as friends, not like this." The sugar-coated words were frightening.

His composure regained, Wayne didn't blink this time as he held out his bound hands. "Friends?"

With a barely discernible movement of his fingers, Qassem signaled the guards, and the cuffs were removed.

"Did you catch the hand signals?" Matt whispered as he elbowed Hal. "They use some kind of finger and hand movements for communication, but it's not any sign language I know."

Qassem did not miss this exchange. "No one has ever been able to decipher our battle language," he said as his full attention fell on Richard. Qassem's dull, faded fatigues rustled as he walked over to Rich and looked him up and down like a cannibal sizing up his next meal. Rich fidgeted, wondering what course he was going to be and what he had done to merit the honor. Finally, the Kurd leader leaned forward and whispered into Rich's ear.

Rich's expression changed from fear to bewilderment and then to joy. He leaped at the big man and attempted to embrace him in an impulsive hug but his arms wouldn't reach around the man. Qassem found Rich's effort amusing. He stepped back and guided Rich over to one side of the room where they chatted softly in Arabic while the rest of the group looked on with curiosity.

Rich was animated and firing questions faster than the other man could answer. Qassem's fingers and hand flashed a signal to the guards and Rich was pushed through a side door.

Wayne and the others protested and attempted to follow, but armed men barred their path. "What the hell's going on here?" demanded Wayne. The conversation had been hushed and too fast for him to make any sense of with the little Arabic he knew. Qassem turned to follow Rich. He gave Wayne a chilling look before leaving the room. They had no choice but to wait for their captor's next move.

"I hate this," complained Matt. "I saw him signal the guards, but who knows what they said?"

"I'm pretty sure he didn't tell the guards to shoot Rich or us," Hal said. "Rich looked happy."

"Is that intended to make me feel better?" asked Matt.

"I spotted the hand signals when we were first captured," Hal said. "It's a combination of finger and body movements. Kind of like a baseball coach, but not as overt. I think I'm getting the hang of it."

Matt grinned for the first time since their capture. "So, what did Qassem say to the guards before he took Rich away?"

Hal shrugged and remained silent.

Ten minutes passed and then half an hour. Wayne began to think that a peaceful solution to their predicament might not be possible. Perhaps at this very moment Rich needed their help, and they couldn't get to him. And what about Tariq? Was he already moving the weapons somewhere else, he had to be aware of the attack on the farm. If that happened, they might never find him or the weapons and they'd be right back to where they were after the war. An hour passed before a smiling Rich strolled into the room. To everyone's surprise, a beautiful woman clung to his arm.

Wayne and Matt recognized her immediately. Wayne gasped, then frowned as Matt elbowed him in the ribs. "Hello, Ghariba. This is a surprise," Matt said as he moved forward to give her a hug.

Wayne, however, had had enough. The terrorist attacks, Martha's death, the situation at Miryam's apartment, and a war with Isreal looming on the horizon, while he and his colleagues were stuck playing word games with the Kurds. He felt the clock ticking. He could take no more. He glared at Ghariba. "What the hell are you doing here?"

Then he turned, not waiting for her answer, and directed his questions to Rich. "Where've you been or did you forget the reason we're here?" When he saw Rich's arm tighten around Ghariba, Wayne realized he had to temper his anger. "We pictured you chained to a wall being tortured." Wayne rubbed his stiff neck and threw his hands in the air. "Well, Ghariba," he said. "You look right at home here. Now, would someone like to explain what the hell's going on? "

Rich spoke to Hal, ignoring Wayne's rudeness. "I'd like you to meet Ghariba."

Hal responded by smiling and taking her hand. A troubled expression crossed his face. Her touch had elicited some kind of response in him. Hal quickly recovered and smiled back at the young woman. "A pleasure to meet you." Wayne did not miss the concerned look that had passed over Hal's face.

Ghariba broke away from Rich's protective arms and walked over to Wayne and Matt, who had frozen in his steps when Wayne had first lashed out at Ghariba. "It's really good to see you both. I don't blame you for the cold reception, Wayne. I'm probably the last person you expected to see here. I know what you're thinking and, yes, I have a lot to explain. Rich has told me why you're here. You will come to no harm; I have vouched for you all."

Wayne, Hal, and even Matt could see Rich was completely under Ghariba's spell.

She can vouch for us, but I'm not ready to vouch for her, Wayne thought as he waited for her to speak.

"I'll explain everything," said Ghariba. "But first let us have some refreshment while we talk. Please come this way."

"We don't have time for a tea party," Wayne said. "If you want to help us, turn us loose."

"Please?" Ghariba dismissed the guards who had begun to inch forward in response to Wayne's hostility and pointed to the door. Rich gave Wayne a pleading look, and Wayne relented and followed the rest of the group into the adjacent room.

The rough rock floor was covered with luxurious red and purple carpets that muffled the sound of their army boots and gave the room an unexpected warmth and softness. Two comfortable sofas sat in the middle of the room, welcoming them. Even Wayne let down his guard and sat down, sinking into the warm cushions and accepting a cup of thick Turkish coffee.

"Thank you," said Ghariba as she sat down next to Rich. Ghariba's voice cracked a little as she announced, "I would like to introduce my brother, Mullah Qassem Barzani. He is the leader of the Kurds, as was our father, Massoud, and his father, the great Mustafa Barzani, before him." Qassem entered and sat down in a large armchair near them. Everyone stood in deference to the Kurdish leader who they had already met in the other room.

"Please sit down. Let us talk," Qassem began. "I know the urgency of your mission. Rich has explained everything. I can offer you my support. But I must make one thing very clear from the beginning: whatever is found, there will be no samples taken for study. Nothing will be removed from the site when we find the weapons; they are to be completely destroyed." His voice took on a deep and more dangerous tone. "Anyone who has another agenda will not leave these mountains alive."

Wayne and the others were surprised at Qassem's frankness. They sipped their strong coffee and listened.

"My people have suffered greatly from this abomination. Our land and my people need a rest from war. The weapons must be destroyed. You must decide now if you can abide by my rules. We want your assistance, but we are ready to go on our own if you have come here with another agenda."

Wayne stood and stepped forward. "You have my hand as a pledge of our sincerity. I can swear that each person here feels the same as you do: the weapons must be destroyed."

"What about the little man who was with you and escaped? Will you also guarantee his behavior?" Qassem said, not yet taking Wayne's hand.

Wayne stood, his empty hand still extended toward Qassem. "No, he's not with us. He is acting on his own. If you find him, hold him for the Iraqi authorities." Wayne was furious with Elliot. He could ruin everything. Wayne admitted to himself that he needed the Kurds to find the cave. "He's probably lost in these mountains."

"We will see," Qassem warned, clasping Wayne's hand in a vice-like grip. "We are watching for him and we will be watching you as well. The United States has not always kept its word to the Kurds, but Ghariba says you are an honorable man. Remember, my friend," Qassem squeezed

Wayne's hand even more tightly, "your hand is an extension of your heart. We Kurds take pledges very seriously. Let your hand do your heart honor or we will remove both of them so you cannot in future make another empty pledge."

"I don't need your threats to do my job," Wayne said without blinking, but releasing his grip. Wayne sat down next to Matt, flexing his fingers, hoping the circulation would return soon and trying not to let Qassem see how much his hand hurt.

"That's one big bloke to have mad at you," Matt whispered. "Could you please just vouch for yourself? I'd like to keep my heart and hand right where they are."

Rich motioned for Wayne and Matt to listen: Ghariba had a few things to say.

Her voice was apologetic as she began. "Many years ago I was captured and, like many other Kurds, forcibly relocated to the south when our mother and father were murdered. The government feared the Barzanis. That's why my parents hid my brother with a loyal family in Turkey until he could return safely. I escaped my exile but was free only a short time before I was again arrested while trying to make my way back to the mountains. The police placed me in one of Saddam's youth camps for re-education. I never knew until recently that my brother survived." She glanced over at him and smiled sweetly. "I grew up thinking only of revenge. While I was in the youth camp they recruited me to become a spy. The Iraqis educated and trained me, but for many years now I've been funneling information to the Kurds. It was very difficult. I worked with Hussein and this meant I was despised by my people." Tears filled her eyes.

Rich put his arm around her shoulder to comfort her.

"That is all in the past." Ghariba's voice grew stronger.

"The new government is willing to give us autonomy and my brother will be able to unite our people."

"She is a true patriot," Qassem said. "It's through her information that we found out about General Saeed's search for the weapons. We know they're in these mountains, but so far my scouts have not seen any of Saeed's men in the area or found the hiding place. I understand from Rich that you know the exact location?" It was half question, half statement.

Wayne aimed a disagreeable frown at Rich. "Yes, we found a map in one of the trucks we destroyed." He wondered how much more Rich had told Qassem.

Qassem began to speak, but a soldier came in with a message. Qassem excused himself and left the room, returning shortly with an air of urgency. "I have a report that General Saeed and a large complement of men have escaped his farm and are heading into the mountains. Obviously they're trying to secure the weapons after losing the trucks. They've slipped through without notice while our forces were busy at the farm. The underground complex there is huge and has many hidden exits."

"You're letting us go?" asked a grim-faced Wayne.

"Yes, but be patient, Dr. Swift." Qassem stood. "You'll need a guide."

Matt frowned, "Like who...?"

"Me," said Qassem. "My men will meet us at the cave and deal with Saeed's troops."

"We," Wayne pointed to Matt and Rich, "must make sure all the weapons containers have not been compromised. We are the experts here, Qassem, and I do not want anyone else near those biologics." Wayne was adamant.

"I'm not an uneducated man, Doctor. I agree. You are the WMD experts. We will, as you say in America, cover your backs so you can get in and destroy the weapons. But I must insist on being present to verify that everything has been destroyed."

Matt spoke up for the first time. "Get in? What do you mean, get in, and why do we need a guide when we have the coordinates?"

"From the information Rich has given me, it seems the weapons are hidden in a cave deep in the mountains not far from here. It is difficult terrain, but we know these mountains. You do not," Qassem said as he rose.

The skin on his face tightened and his eyes took on an intensity they had not shown before. "Never doubt our ability to see the world clearly. General Tariq Saeed is ruthless. This is war. We war against the inhumanity of his kind and all those who would perpetuate this type of biological atrocity." He paused to let his words sink in. "We leave in twenty minutes. Saeed's men are already in the mountain passes approaching the cave. The storm delayed him, but it will not deter him. The first thing they will do is secure the pass that leads to the cave. My men will attack him at the mouth of the ravine and keep his troops busy while we go over the mountain and get in the cave hopefully before him. All your supplies are ready. Prepare yourselves—it's a tough and dangerous climb, especially at night, so take only the necessities." His voice softened. "We make war, my friends, that we may live in peace."

Yes, thought Wayne. *I read somewhere that man is the only species that attacks its own kind when its survival is not threatened.*

"Did I hear him right?" Matt said interrupting Wayne's thoughts. "We're going into a cave to search for these weapons? And what about our spying weasel, Elliot?"

"I don't care about Elliot, as long as he doesn't get in our way," Wayne said.

"Don't worry, you're an expert caver now," said Hal as he smacked Matt on the back.

"Right," said an uncertain Matt.

During this exchange, Ghariba moved over to confront Wayne. "The person you knew before was just playing a part. You'll see. I'll prove I'm worthy of your trust and Rich's love. I'm different now." She stared at Wayne, hoping she'd convinced him of her loyalties.

Wayne wondered why it was so damn important for Ghariba to persuade him of her friendship. His instincts said this was all wrong and he trusted his instincts over Ghariba's words any day.

"I almost forgot," she said mischievously as she turned away. "We've a guest here I think you'll be interested in meeting."

Wayne was puzzled. "Who?"

He was shocked when Ghariba replied. "Miryam. Miryam is here. I've asked Qassem to have her brought to us. We thought she had the coordinates for the weapons or that the Israelis sent her to spy on us, but we can't get a word out of her. Perhaps now that you're here, she'll cooperate and tell us why she's here."

Wayne took a menacing step toward Ghariba, "If you..."

Rich stepped between them.

"We haven't touched her," Ghariba said.

Wayne's heart felt like it would burst from his chest. *At last. Miryam.* He could not restrain himself from pacing. The seconds seemed like hours.

Ghariba had a quick conversation on her satellite

phone. "I've contacted some of my friends, they will reinforce my brother at the pass," she told the group. Wayne and Hal eyed each other, keeping their expressions neutral. Ghariba kissed Rich and the two lovers whispered in private, their eyes darting from each other to Wayne every few moments.

Finally the door opened and Ghariba went over to the soldier she had sent to retrieve Miryam and he whispered something in her ear. Wayne stepped forward in anticipation, looking beyond the soldier for Miryam. "What's wrong? Where's Miryam?"

"Somehow Miryam has done the impossible," Ghariba said, controlling her anger and amazement. "She has escaped."

Chapter 23

A Taste of the Past

Miryam came out on the other side of the mountain, away from the Kurd stronghold, thanking the gods and the queen's memory for revealing the hidden tunnel through which she had made her escape. She had been traveling for hours under the cover of night to avoid her Kurdish captors. As she descended from the mountain, she moved by instinct, without the aid of a compass or GPS. Always traveling east, deeper into the mountains, she trudged along to keep her appointment with fate.

At last the trail she followed leveled out and the walking became easier. The meeting with Ghariba had enraged her and she cursed herself for temporarily losing her focus. She clutched the necklace that now hung from her neck.

The soft dirt at the bottom of the mountain was a relief on her bare feet. She relaxed and tucked the small rusty knife she had found in the escape tunnel into the waistband of her pants. The swishing sound of her pants along the loose earth soothed her, though her clothes were torn and dirty and thin for the cool night air. She would have to rely on her own physical activity to keep her warm. Water might be a problem. In ancient days, she knew the location of every pool. She resolved to find those pools again. If she didn't, there was the lake in the cave. Her ebony hair streamed out behind her and billowed in the breeze as she jogged along at an easy pace.

She slowed to a walk when the path narrowed. She was picking her way through a rock-strewn bend in the trail between fallen boulders when, without warning, she was hurled to the ground.

Her attacker had vaulted from the rocks above. She landed on her back and the wind was knocked out of her. He recovered faster than Miryam and rolled off to the side, coming to his feet to stand menacingly over her. Wisps of clouds, like the ocean's tide, filtered back and forth in front of the moon behind the silhouette man.

Miryam regained her senses and sized up her attacker from her prone position. From the weight of his body against hers, she surmised that her attacker was about five-feet, ten- inches and weighed 180 pounds; he was also bulky and slow with inflexible muscles. From the outline of his garb against the night sky, she was sure he was not a Kurd.

Her assessment took less than the five seconds required for her assailant to slide a large knife into his right hand. The glint from its jagged blade was visible and fatally familiar. With great effort, she tempered her passion for the ensuing combat and spoke to her shadowy stalker in Arabic. "Captain, have you been waiting long?"

"Our business is unfinished, doctor," he answered in the same language. "I admire your skills. Do not worry, my knife is sharp and quick."

He felt a ribbon of pain as Miryam rolled into him and slashed at his inner thigh with her own rusty blade. "Your arrogance may kill you today. You talk when you should fight." She stabbed at him as she jumped back onto her feet and assumed the crouched position of an experienced knife fighter. "I will give you the same measure of respect you showed my pet," her eyes darkened with anger when she thought about how this man had dispatched poor Strider.

The captain recoiled in response to her blade. He could feel that it was only a superficial wound. "Fool! Only a woman would display such emotion for an animal. My humiliation at the hands of a woman is not an option. Submit!" His mirthless laughter echoed in the narrow valley where they faced each other. "Death will prove who is superior," he jeered. With his free hand, he wiped the wound in his thigh and licked the dripping blood from his hand. "Let the dying begin," he said in a defiant voice.

He darted forward with a knife thrust to her body, but it was met by an expert block as Miryam swirled away. The two combatants danced in the muted darkness, each trying to gain the advantage.

When he circled toward the dark rock wall and his outline was obliterated against the sinister night sky, the sound of dirt and rock grating under the captain's heavy combat boots gave Miryam a target. Earlier, when she was climbing the rocky mountain, she had been thinking longingly about her desert boots, but the Kurds had taken them. Now she was glad the crunch of those boots was absent: it was an advantage. Her bruised and cut bare feet stepped lightly and silently. Using all of her senses, she searched the night for his essence. His musty smell permeated the night air and she wondered why she had not picked up his scent prior to his attack.

In the initial excitement of the contest she had been taking noisy, ragged breaths that her opponent might hear and use to locate her. Just as she got her breathing under control, a lucky hit grazed her left shoulder with a swishing sound that reminded her of a wasp's beating wings. She immediately attacked and felt her blade strike flesh, but the captain didn't give her the pleasure of hearing his pain

Their silent music played again and again and they

danced to its rhythm. She let him set the tempo and pursue her. Her plan was instinctive. It came from a hundred such battles she had waged in a time when warriors met face to face, swords singing the songs of war.

The excitement of the battle spurred the captain on. The drumming in his head intensified the beat as he closed in. His heart pulsed faster and faster as their steps quickened. She stabbed with the knife and kicked out with her feet in a surprise move, but one that he easily deflected. *Just a few seconds more,* thought the Captain, *and she's mine. It is too bad this contest will soon be over. Skilled opponents are rare. She is overextending herself and her movements are becoming predictable. On the next parry, you are mine, doctor.*

Miryam executed a front kick and followed it with a weak slash toward the captain's face. He brushed her leg aside with his own, then met her knife thrust with a heavy blow of his fist to her ribs. His reach was a significant advantage in the fight.

He pictured her pretty face, bruised and bloody. The image pleased him.

The air rushed from Miryam's lungs and a choking sound poured from her throat. She quickly backed away thinking, *any moment now.*

The captain had timed her movements and memorized her rhythm and now he felt her weakness. He expected her next feeble advance. Just as she made her move, he leaped forward and attacked her weakened left side. Sharp as the fangs of a deadly snake, his knife flicked through the skin on her right forearm. When she turned to guard her vulnerable right flank, he struck her already injured shoulder with a powerful kick.

The heat of pain filled her. Miryam staggered and fell back hard against the ground, stunned by the dramatic change in his rhythm. She emitted a long hissing breath, then gulped for more air. But she had no time to recover before he was on her.

He kicked the knife from her grasp, his heavy boot fracturing several of the bones in her left hand. When he stood over her with his foot grinding into her already slashed left shoulder, she whimpered in pain. He quickly squatted down over her and grabbed her hair, forcing her to roll onto her stomach as if she were a rag doll. As a horseman controls his steed by pulling back on the reins, so did the captain's hand grip her thick hair. He pulled Miryam's head back with all his might and was overjoyed to finally have her under his control.

Searing waves of pain snaked down her spine. She was afraid she might lose consciousness and all would be lost. He was talking, but her pain blurred her mind and she couldn't understand his words.

"Answer me, woman! Is a real soldier too much for you?" the Captain snarled.

His grip relaxed and she felt the cold edge of his jagged blade resting against the tender skin at her throat. Her mind now had control of the pain and her wits returned as she calculated her next move.

He sat astride Miryam's back, allowing her to read his position. His words and relaxed muscles conveyed a message of overconfidence. He had lost the edge and he didn't even know it. Something was triggered deep inside Miryam's mind. Her ancient language spilled unheeded from her lips in a low sizzling whisper.

As the first drop of her blood ran down her neck, he paused. He wondered, *what was she saying?* Her hair slid from his hand as he leaned forward, resting his now free hand on the ground for support, so he could be closer to his defeated opponent. He hoped she was asking for mercy. Those were words he did not want to miss. He would enjoy hearing her pleas again and again in his mind long after she was dead. He leaned forward—just a little bit more—to listen.

As she spoke, her fingers cautiously searched for the end of the laser wire still in the waist of her tattered pants. "It is too late for you, captain," she hissed in Arabic.

He hesitated for a second, pondering her words and straining to fully understand them. He was now off balance.

That was all she needed. In one motion, she sprang from her subjugated posture, flicked on the laser, and whipped out the wire. The thin white hot wire curled through the dark night like an avenging angel. It tightened around the captain's knife hand like a bullwhip and Miryam yanked with all her strength.

He screamed in pain as the wire sizzled and seared through tissue and bone. The knife and his hand still holding it fell away from his arm. Roaring with pain, he dropped to his knees. Reacting without reason, the captain searched in the sand for his severed hand and weapon.

Miryam was too quick for him. With one vicious kick to his spine, he was flat on the ground. Their positions now reversed, she gripped his hair and twisted it. He began to thrash and Miryam placed both of her knees on his spine and pulled. With all the strength her shattered hand would allow, she snapped him back, crushing his spine at the mid-thoracic level, rendering him immobile, but not dead. His body went limp. She rolled him onto his back. She wanted to make sure he could see her. His head lolled back and forth, his eyes wide open and alert. She watched his eyes and waited for the fear to come. But she could not delay for long. With his massive loss of blood, he would soon lose consciousness and she wanted to choose the moment of his death.

She scooped up the knife still locked in his severed hand and sat down on his stomach. His eyes flashed fear. She smiled and slowly tilted his head back to expose his neck. The time was right: his breathing was becoming labored. Lightly, with the control of a surgeon, she rested his own jagged blade against his throat. She could now see the terror in his eyes. They stared at her, transfixed. Then, with a pitilessly slow motion, she dragged the serrated edge of the knife from one ear to the other.

There was a bubbling sound deep in his throat. In his mind he heard the drum beat growing distant: he knew the dance was over.

Just before he faded into eternal darkness her lips skimmed his ear. "And so your dying begins," she murmured softly.

Chapter 24

Over the Mountain

When Wayne handed Qassem the coordinates for the hiding place of the WMDs, the big man showed them his warmest smile. However, once he had the map between his fingers, the smile faded and it was back to business as Qassem gave hand signals to several of his men while he thanked Wayne. Then he turned and waved for Wayne and the others to follow.

Rich leaned over to Hal. "Cool huh? If any one is listening you can..." he wiggled his fingers.

"I have a feeling that whatever he is saying," Wayne said as he walked by Rich, "it's not good for us."

Hoisting their gear onto their backs, Wayne, Matt, Hal, Rich, and Ghariba fell in behind Qassem. Night had completed its descent to darkness as they started out on a well worn path at the edge of Qassem's mountain stronghold.

The night sky was extraordinarily thick with clouds and the path they were walking on was barely three feet wide with a steep vertical drop off on one side. "How far to the bottom do you think, Hal?" Matt whispered.

"We are above the clouds," came Hal's cheerful reply, "so I'd estimate we are... pretty high. What difference does it make? If you fall," he laughed, "dead is dead."

"This is not the highest mountain in Iraq," Qassem interjected. "That would be Rawanduz at 12,001 feet. But this one is close, so be careful,"

"It's damn hard to see where we're going," Rich complained as he fished in his pack for a headlamp.

"No lights," Wayne cautioned. "Remember what Qassem said about being spotted by Tariq's men?"

"If I walk off the side of this mountain, it'll be a sure giveaway to our location," jested Rich.

"Follow the smell of my perfume," Ghariba suggested. Rich whispered something in her ear that made her laugh, a little too loudly, thought Wayne.

"Unless you want to give away our position, keep the talking to a minimum. Sound travels easily through the mountains," cautioned Qassem.

As they proceeded, Ghariba stumbled several times on the rock-strewn path, cursing and sending loose rocks over the edge. Qassem reprimanded her sharply. "Be careful, little sister. It has been too long since you traveled the mountains. Rich, help her."

They fell into a paced, rhythmic walk and lost track of time as they slipped silently down the curving mountain track. The threat of the unseen abyss, inches from their feet and hidden by the darkness, kept them sharp and alert. Their spirits as well as their sweat-soaked bodies were chilled further when the temperature dropped as the night deepened. They walked on, heads bent low, attempting to see the narrow path. The darkness became even less penetrable when a fine mist closed in as they dropped down into the clouds.

The pace slowed to a crawl and Wayne wondered if, even with the expert guidance of Qassem, they'd be able to get to the cave before Saeed. Despite his climbing experience, Wayne had never experienced a descent of this difficulty. First, he'd never climbed at night without the aid of some source of light and, second, the terrain was like nothing he'd ever encountered. They had to walk, climb, and crawl their way around and through the mountain. The horizontal and vertical climbs were to be expected but the diagonal ones were extremely difficult without the aid of light or the usual climbing gear. Their much-needed bio gear and Rich's toys were all they could carry with them, so toeholds, finger tips, and ropes were all they had. Their courage was tested again and again.

Although he was the unspoken leader of the group, Wayne had no illusions. He knew that without the combined strength of these men and their special talents mission Crescent Veil would fail.

The group climbed on and on, constantly wiping their hands on their clothing in an effort to grip the cliff wall more securely. On several occasions, each had experienced that sinking sensation of an impending fall as they lost their grip and scrambled to find another damp rock to hang on to. Minutes seemed like hours and, for them, the world beyond the mountains ceased to exist.

Finally the path widened and the walking was easier and shortly after they came to a spot where the path divided. The wider path went up, but Qassem had them take the narrower path that slanted down. "We do not use this trail often," whispered Qassem.

"I'm guessing the department of transportation doesn't come through here often to make repairs," Rich quipped as he helped Ghariba around a bend where the rocky path no longer existed.

A few stifled laughs escaped into the night.

Just when they thought there could be no more surprises, the path became steeper and narrowed from three feet to being scarcely wide enough to put one foot in front of the other. Loose pebbles and dirt made each step a survival contest as they inched their way along, holding onto whatever they could to keep from slipping.

Despite the obstacles the mountain threw at them, after two hours of strenuous hiking—Matt said it felt like ten—the band of six found themselves perched on a broad flat plateau overlooking a wide chasm between two mountains. An immense boulder blocked their path.

"We should rest here," whispered Qassem. He stood at the edge of the ledge and motioned below into the darkness. "There is a wooden suspension bridge about forty feet below us that will take us across the chasm. From there the path leads to a point above the mouth of the cave. But we will have to abandon this trail. A rock slide blocked it, so we will have to rappel down the last few feet onto the path that leads to the bridge."

"Great, for a moment I thought it was going to be hard," Matt panted as he dropped heavily onto the rock ledge to rest.

"Quiet!" Qassem's sharp reminder hissed through the darkness.

In silence, they rested and sipped from their water bottles.

Qassem rose and was about to speak when he was forced to his knees as the earth shook. To the west they saw the night sky light up as consecutive explosions rocked the ledge. They fell to the ground, trying to find protection from the falling rocks that had been jarred loose above them. After a few minutes, the earth stopped shaking, and they rose one by one and walked to the edge of the cliff to stare out at the sulfur sky that lingered beyond the mountains.

"It's Saeed's farm," Rich explained. Another explosion rocked them back. Several more followed in rapid succession. "He must have stored a lot of chemicals there," Rich said, pointing to the sky. "They give off weird colors when they burn."

The sky glowed with unnatural light. The colors intensified. "It looks bruised," said Rich staring at the sky. The burning chemicals tinted the clouds with hues of blues, yellows, and oranges that eventually mingled into a purple–brown color. It was an appropriate comparison for this broken and wounded country, Wayne decided.

"Quick!" Qassem motioned for them to move away from the edge as truck headlights lit up the ravine about a hundred feet below them.

"Everyone into your gear," Wayne said. "Leave the extra water and other non-essentials behind. We're going to be moving fast while the sounds of those vehicles muffle our descent. Let's go!"

"Wait a minute," Rich said. He pulled three small, round objects out of his shirt pocket. "Let's find out what they're up to below." Like a pitcher delivering a fastball at a baseball game, he wound up and tossed his walnut-sized stones into the air. He and Wayne watched until they disappeared into scrub brush near the cave entrance where a group of men in military dress stood.

Wayne smiled. "Good arm. Pick them up on five?"

Rich nodded. The communication devices that they all wore were multiple channel units. Rich turned the stem on his wristwatch and tuned his and Wayne's receivers to accept two channels. Everyone else was on channel 7 for person-to-person communication. Wayne and Rich also heard channel 5, which the stones—actually receivers—picked up.

The soldiers milling around at the cave entrance paid little attention to the loose gravel rolling down near their feet, their eyes were fixed on the explosions in the distance.

Rich's Arabic was better than Wayne's and he gave him the green light before Wayne had a chance to think about translating the conversation.

Everyone gathered their essential equipment and prepared to move out. Wayne disappeared over the side of the cliff while Hal was still checking Matt's knot on the line. Matt's fingers sprung back as Wayne's weight forced the line taut.

"Nice bowline," Hal whispered to Matt.

They all responded like a well-oiled machine that had been itching to get to work. By the time Matt, Rich and Hal moved to edge, Wayne was on the bridge, running across to the other side.

Rich leaned over to Qassem and placed a receiver in his ear and a small device like a straight pin on his collar. "Talk," said Rich.

Before Qassem could respond, Wayne's voice came crystal clear through his earpiece.

"Hey, the suspension bridge is falling apart. Don't risk it. I'm setting up a slide. Qassem, move a little more to your left."

Seconds after Qassem moved, there was a muffled sound and something whirled by him. Reaching out into thin air like a magician doing a trick, Rich caught and pulled in the wire Wayne had shot up to their location. "Just like Blitz," he said as he secured the wire.

Qassem asked why Rich hadn't given him the communication device earlier and Rich responded they were not needed until now. He didn't think Qassem needed to know that Matt, Hal, Wayne, and he had started the climb wearing them. *Rich wanted to say,* "We all have secrets," but he kept silent.

Qassem watched as each member of the group did his job. Rich secured the wire everyone would slide over on. Matt had finished his bowline knot and received a slap on the back of approval from Hal, who then slid effortlessly down the wire. Within seconds, Matt was in his harness and prepared to be on his way.

"You're next," said Rich as he attached Qassem's harness.

"Wait, that little thing won't hold me," complained Qassem. "I'll take my chances at the bridge."

"You'll never make it across. Don't worry." Contemplating his enjoyment of Qassem's discomfort, Rich smiled and pushed him into the abyss. He watched an angry Qassem slide down and reach out to Hal's waiting hand.

"Now, sweetheart, I've saved the best for last. But first give me a kiss for good luck." Rich grabbed Ghariba and pressed her close to him. She responded eagerly and her velvet lips were never more inviting.

"That was a sweet one. Don't worry, I'll see you on the other side," said Rich. He felt her tension and reassured her as they moved closer to the edge. "There's nothing to it. Let Hal catch you. Don't kick your legs around too much or you might hurt yourself on the overhanging rocks." Without hesitation, he pushed her out into the chasm directly over the soldiers gathering below.

As Rich watched the darkness swallow Ghariba, the wind through the canyon moaned and abruptly changed direction, increasing in intensity. The strong currents swirled around Rich, tossing dirt and sand into the air. He reached for his gear and felt the force of the gusts push against him.

The wire was stretched taut and sang an eerie song as the wind whistled through the gorge. Rich kept one hand on the wire to silence it. But he also knew that as long as it remained taut, Ghariba was OK.

Suddenly, there was a sharp "ping" and the wire whipped back at him, barely missing his face. He threw himself to the ground just in time to avoid the severed wire. The strength of the wind was enough to keep the broken wire in the air. *Lord, don't let anything happen to Ghariba,* was his silent prayer. Not waiting for a report over the communicator, he stood and activated his power suit. He would have to take a chance.

The experimental undergarment tightened against his body like a second skin. He felt the familiar tingle in his muscles as they tensed, expanded and grew stronger. Only seconds had elapsed, but he felt it took an eternity. He did not wait to test his new strength: waiting might mean the difference between life and death for Ghariba. He braced his feet against a rock at the edge of the precipice and pushed off into the black void, propelling himself in the direction of the rock wall that he estimated was thirty feet from where he had been standing.

Rich hit the rock face with such terrible force that he knocked himself out. Hal, the nearest person to Rich's unorthodox landing, grabbed for him. At first, Hal thought he had Rich safely in his grip but the weight of Rich, his equipment and the cumbersome suit which was still inflated, was too much for Hal. Rich began to slip through Hal's hands.

"Cut away his gear or he's dead," said Qassem. "It will drop into the gorge behind us. No one will hear," whispered Qassem urgently into his communicator.

"Hang onto him and his gear, Hal," came Wayne's emphatic voice through their earpieces.

Qassem's strong arms came out of the darkness to support Hal's effort and together they hauled Rich up onto the rock shelf. The next thing Rich knew, Hal and Matt were hovering over him. "Now I know why they call you Blitz," laughed Hal.

Rich blinked, wiping blood from his face. "Ghariba, is she all right?" Hal nodded. "How are you doing?" he asked again.

"I'm OK: a bump on the head, nothing that'll affect my strange brain," Rich tried to stand but was still too dizzy. Then he remembered to deactivate his power suit.

"What the hell were you thinking?" Matt was concerned but also angry with his friend. He was genuinely fond of this crazy guy, even if he constantly gave him grief. "You're lucky! Damn lucky Hal caught you before you rolled over the edge." Then he smiled. "By the way, I figure you just broke the Olympic long jump record."

Matt helped Rich get to his feet. "Damn, how long was I out?" asked Matt.

"About ten minutes," Matt replied.

"By the way, do you really think it was a record?" asked Rich smiling.

"The previous Olympic record was nine meters. You could have done better, but the mountain got in your way," replied Matt. They began to walk down the sloping path to the others. "So what prompted the giant leap for mankind thing you did back there?"

"I thought Ghariba was in trouble when the wire broke. I guess I misjudged the distance across."

"She was, but we managed. You're not the only hero on this team, chum. Now, tell me about this magic suit you're wearing. By the way, you're still bulging a bit," Matt chuckled poking at Rich's biceps.

As they walked, Rich explained the fundamentals of his muscle suit. "My entire body is interconnected to the suit via specific pressure points under the skin." The excitement returned in his voice as he talked about one of his toys. "A microprocessor initiates the electrical current that stimulates my muscles. Same theory as artificial limbs, but I've refined it. Not only does it enhance and increase my strength and endurance, it links into my communications network, so it's like carrying around a power generator."

Matt smiled. "But it's a little twitchy?"

"Yeah, it still has a few bugs. I can't quite gauge the depth of my enhanced capacity and I always seem to overshoot my targets." Rich rubbed his sore head thoughtfully as they walked.

"You mean you've jumped into walls before? Never mind, I know the answer."

Rich, Hal, and Matt inched their way forward until they came to where the others were taking refuge from the wind in a spacious rock crevice.

"What happened to you?" Wayne asked when he saw Rich's bloody nose. He had missed Rich's near fatal adventure. "Later, business first."

Rich reached out with a sudden need to touch Ghariba. "From now on you stay glued to me—forever." He moved over to Qassem. "For future reference, never, ever think about tossing my gear," he poked Qassem with his finger and the burly man looked ready to retaliate but Wayne interrupted the potential argument. "Gentlemen," he put his finger to his lips to silence everyone. Then, he whispered into his com link. "Qassem where's that sound coming from?"

"Power plant at the Dukan Dam, on the other side of the mountain," replied Qassem.

Chapter 25

Returning

The going was slow for Miryam after her clash with the captain. Her wounded body wanted to rest, but she denied her physical needs. She was a dismal figure as she labored toward her destination. Twice she heard the sound of trucks approaching and had to abandon the dirt road. To avoid capture, she decided to take the more difficult, but strangely familiar, path along the rugged mountain.

Traveling east she came across a small stream that in the past had been a wide, fast-flowing tributary of the Great Zab. It was a small channel now, with few of the fish that, in her previous life, had fed hunters and wild animals. She knelt and splashed muddy water over her face and arms, only moistening her lips for fear that the murky water would sicken her. She remembered there had once been a pool a short distance ahead in the cleft of the rocks and hoped the water would be cleaner there. Or would that be gone also? She could not risk waiting and took a few miserly sips. *Drink when you can*, was a rule of the wild.

The farther east she traveled, the narrower the stream became. In some places, the water was foul and stood in stagnant pools. Then the stream disappeared all together. She trudged on. After her fight with the captain, the need for water became more acute with every step. She stroked her dry lips with her sticky tongue and a sheepish smile filled her face. "I was a fool to have forgotten how cruel the gods can be."

She looked up at the cliffs as minute details of past experiences began to flow into her thoughts. The might of the land, the many gods she had honored, well tuned survival skills: all of these were part of her now and would be an awesome power. She lifted her eyes from the path and looked up at the unnatural tint that lit the night sky. And then she remembered, *it is the same color as when the priests burned all the bodies of the slaves.*

She paused, leaning against a rock. As she rubbed her tired eyes, something pricked her cheek. It was dirt. Tiny particles of dirt whirled through the air as a faint breeze made its way through the canyon. Miryam sat back on her heels and inhaled the hot air of the approaching Sharqi and enjoyed the touch of the wind as it brushed against her exposed skin. *The storm returns to me.*

The hot current of air gained strength and small pebbles flitted by her face and pecked at her ears. Miryam placed her hand on the rock wall and pushed herself away from her resting place. Her fingers brushed over carvings on the wall. Excitement rose within her, for she had hoped to find such marks, but feared they would have been erased by the winds through time. But here they were, precisely as she remembered them. Her fingers traced the familiar cuneiform writing. It took her only a moment to read the forms that she now deciphered so easily and then, following the directions she had read on the wall, she hurried forward, the wind at her back.

To her joy, a hundred feet ahead she found more writings. Climbing over rocks that blocked her path, she searched the walls of the canyon. Squeezing around a huge boulder, she found the next set of symbols and then, as directed by the message, slid around the rocks into a hidden fissure. Inside the cool damp cave the blackness was absolute.

She stood motionless and listened. Outside, the wind howled, but inside everything was quiet. *Now is my time. I must return to who I once was.* Her keen ears picked up the faint wet whisper of water dripping. With each step she sensed the mountain reaching out to her. Miryam felt around for the torch and the tools to light it: normally they would have been left near the entrance. A few feet in she found the niche she searched for and all she needed.

Although the torch had long ago dried out, she found a jar close by with remnants of oil and, using strips she tore from her sleeve, she lit the torch swiftly.

The light reflecting off the white limestone walls gave strength to the solitary torch. In the eerie light, she read the messages carved into the stone—graffiti from the past. Some of the stories were from travelers that had been lost in the mountains and lived; the rest, last words from people who had been lost and died.

One carving told of a family who had come here to hide from a great demon that attacked the people living in the city of Calah. The writing said they would try to hold out in this cave until their queen returned. "Our hope is with Queen Semiramis. She alone can save us from the demons plaguing our land and from the invading Urartu."

Many bones, large and small, and personal items were scattered about. It was impossible to make any sense out of the fragments that remained, although they told her the fate of the family that had sought refuge there, waiting, in vain, for her return.

Several low tunnels branched off the cave where she entered. Miryam did not hesitate. The smell and sound of running water tugged at her senses and pulled her deeper.

She chose the passageway to the far left where the smell of moisture was strongest. Ducking low and securing the torch in her injured left hand, she crawled into the tunnel. A short distance in, the tunnel ended and Miryam stood up, holding the light above her head to survey the surroundings.

The flare of her small torch revealed a great cavern with a cathedral-like ceiling. In the far corner, plumes of roaring water streamed from the rocks above, crashing into a stone pool several feet below the ledge on which Miryam stood. She edged her way along the slippery rocks to the water's edge. Carefully, she sampled the bubbling liquid. It was clean and cool. Colossal inverted peaks from the ceiling hovered over her while other similar sentries lined the floor, waiting in silence for their queen's commands. Her torn clothing was splattered with blood and dirt. Her once beautiful long hair hung tangled and dirty, clots of dried blood stuck to some of the strands. Dust covered her body from head to toe, giving her an ethereal appearance. She was not an angelic form, more a mixture of a ghoulish figure and avenging warrior.

Why Miryam stopped to cleanse herself she did not know, but she felt compelled to bathe. As if performing some long forgotten ritual, she removed all of her clothing and waded into the chilling water and immersed her entire body. Her long black hair fanned out in the water, framing her pallid face like the elaborate headdress of some ancient deity. On a shelf at the side of the pool she found a small ceramic jar. She lifted the fragile lid and extracted the remnants of a ball of ash and clay soap. The abrasive mixture was invigorating and the ancient concoction removed any trace of her previous bloody combat from her skin and hair.

The old ways must be honored, she thought as she continued her preparations.

Finally, her ritual bath completed, she sat at the edge of the pool, leaving her grossly swollen left hand in the icy water. When the throbbing ceased, she tore long strips from her trousers to bind the damaged fingers together and then wrapped a last strip around her wrist for extra support.

At the bottom of the soap jar, she found a patch of oil and massaged this into her hair. Combing out the tangles with her fingers, she plaited her hair into one long braid and secured it with another strip of cloth. She tore the ripped sleeves from her shirt and used them to secure the tattered remains of the garment around her waist, tunic style.

For thousands of years, the Queen of Assyria had been waiting for this day. Her destiny required that she pass sentence on the demons that once devastated her land and now threatened to return. She was here and her final battle was close at hand. She was both excited and weary to have this judgment day arrive. She must reach the main cave before Tariq, but how?

Miryam remembered that using the tunnels to travel through the mountain would save time and avoid the storm outside; a storm that would undoubtedly delay her rival. She began to gather her meager belongings, returning her laser wire to the waistband of what remained of her slacks and strapping the captain's knife to her leg. She placed the last few strips of cloth that would be useful as bandages and the small piece of soap that remained into a small make-shift pouch and secured the pouch to her waistband. One more time, she checked the map on the wall, chose a tunnel, grabbed the torch, leaving it unlit for now, and, without hesitation, entered a dark tunnel.

The passage narrowed as it spiraled down at a steep incline. The bleeding from her superficial shoulder wound had stopped, but she paused to reinforce the dressing anyway. As warmth returned to her left hand, so did the pain. And it bothered her more than any of her other injuries. She still had the use of her thumb, but the rest of her fingers on her left hand were useless.

Because she had to traverse much of the distance on her hands and knees, it didn't take long before sweat streamed down Miryam's face and soaked her clothing. With the back of her broken hand, she wiped the salty sweat from her burning eyes. She stopped, stretched her cramped legs out in front of her and rested her forehead against the rock wall. The wall felt like a cool hand on her weary wet brow. Old memories of her other life calmed and bolstered her spirit. Miryam relaxed, while both of her identities comfortably mingled in this mountain world.

A breeze brushed her cheek and Miryam shivered, startled more than chilled. Lighting the torch and holding it high, she searched in vain for the source. Then, out of the distant darkness it returned. Like a lover's sweet breath, it surrounded and caressed her. It lingered on her face, gently brushing her lips and kissing her cheeks. Her body was encircled by it and it swam about her shoulders and breast, spreading its heat. Gentle fingers moving over her. It was familiar. She leaned forward, straining to see. Out of the void an image, carried on this untouchable wind, raced toward her.

"Wayne! Wayne is here!" Miryam gasped. The sound of her own sharp breath frightened her. She recoiled against the rock wall and slowly reached out into the nothingness where the tantalizing face floated out of reach. Extending her hand, she lunged forward to take hold of the fading image but her fingertips struck only the unyielding rock wall beyond. He was gone.

Chapter 26

Assyria, 811 B.C. — A Welcome for Death

Semiramis reached the temple and the underground lake ahead of Ninyas. Climbing to a ledge above the entrance of the temple, she readied herself.

The climb was very difficult. The exertion left her legs weak and shaking. She was wise to have prepared her trap ahead of time, for right now she did not have the strength to move the large stones. With every second the malignancy within her consumed more and more of her strength.

It wasn't long before she picked up the sound of the voices of the approaching men. Like a bat in its lair, Semiramis sank deep into the shadows and made herself part of the cave. She heard the scuffing sounds of their sandaled feet on stone as they drew nearer, giving away their exact location. As they approached her trap she listened, calculating the number of men. Good: they were all together. She thought that the heavier footsteps must belong to the captain. How eagerly she anticipated his death.

As they drew nearer, their footsteps became softer, more cautious. Ninyas' black curly head passed beneath her hiding place and his mother thought it uncommonly brave of him to walk into the temple first. *But perhaps his insanity feeds his courage.*

She waited. Another head appeared below her. This man

was carrying a torch. She braced her back against the wall and pushed out with all the strength left in her legs. The boulders she had placed on the ledge over the entrance let loose and came crashing down with a hideous roar.

Ninyas swung around in time to see the man behind him engulfed by an avalanche of rocks. He looked up as though expecting to see his mother, but did not say a word.

"Welcome to our tomb, my son." She hovered above Ninyas, a weapon ready in each hand.

Semiramis looked down from the ledge and gestured at the pile of rubble below. "As you can see, I've been expecting you." A few of the stones on the top of the pile tilted back and forth and groaning could be heard from beneath the boulders. "This death is too good for you." Sounds of prayers and weeping now filtered through the pile of rocks as the buried man entered the final stages of his death.

Ninyas moved the torch to get a better look at his mother. When her form was in full light, he gasped. The voice was that of the queen, his mother, but her appearance was shocking. Then he remembered how the slaves looked in the pens and he knew that she was infected. He withdrew a few steps. "Stay away from me," he yelled. He thrust the torch forward and placed his other arm over his eyes as if to ward off an evil demon.

"Why, Ninyas, what is the matter? Perhaps you fear you are looking in a mirror?" She took a step closer to the edge of the overhang. The queen passed her arm down the length of her torso. "It is time to face your destiny. It stands before you, my son," she said, mocking him.

Semiramis jumped down from her hiding place, landing on her feet lightly in front of her cowering son. Just as her feet hit the rock floor, she heard the twang of an arrow leaving a bow. Instinctively, she yanked Ninyas around to use as a shield. At the last possible second she moved them both out of the way of the approaching arrow. It just barely nicked the skin on her right side. She touched the wound and held out a bloody hand to her son.

"Princes die last," she said, a maniacal smile spreading across her face as she circled. "And so the end approaches on the coattails of treachery." Her eyes were fixed on Ninyas, but her words were for the captain. "Just what I would expect from a coward."

Ninyas did not respond. The firelight on the metal plates of Ninyas' armor illuminated the reflection of the captain approaching from the shadows to the queen's right. She sneered and wondered if the pretend soldier thought he had a chance of sneaking up on her.

She looked her frightened son in the eye and grabbed hold of his tunic, yanking his face to within inches of her own, kissing his forehead and leaving a bloody imprint. "Your assassin has missed his mark. I think you should take his head for that mistake. That is what a real king would do."

A prickly sensation on her neck warned her that the captain was very near. She sneered at her quivering son, then pivoted like a practiced ballerina, blocking the captain's blow and forcing him to immediately give ground.

The captain was a large man: a head taller than the queen. His dark complexion, broad chest, and powerful arms reminded Semiramis of the western black-bearded barbarians. They were strong of body, but slow of wit, she reminded herself.

Instinctively, Ninyas backed away from the fight and into the shadow of one of the statues for safety. He drew his sword to defend himself or perhaps kill the queen if he saw her in a vulnerable position. His darting eyes followed every move. His sneer vanished as his mother feinted to the left and then attacked the right side of the slow moving captain.

"Watch your back," the frightened would-be king warned. "Watch your back!"

His words came too late. The queen's weapon sliced into the captain's sword arm. Ninyas called out encouragement to rouse his defender, but it wasn't necessary. The hulking captain had his own score to settle. He had never forgotten the humiliation he had suffered at the queen's hands when he was flogged and thrown out of the army. Now was his chance for revenge and he would kill her, ever so slowly. Mocking words sprayed from his mouth: "I was a better soldier than any of your royal guards and I will prove it. We will see how well you die, my queen," he laughed as he leered at her.

Her broad sword flashed in the torchlight, easily deflecting the lumbering captain's blows. Her movements were fluid and graceful as she danced past him and grabbed the torch from Ninyas' hand and threw it into the gutter of oil that surrounded the temple. The oil leaped to life, illuminating the entire cavern with a harsh, shifting light. The silhouettes of the two combatants—queen and captain—locked in mortal combat, leaped on the walls with the flames. The music of steel clashing against steel played off the ceiling and the vibrations caused some of the cone-shaped stalactites to fall around them. The cacophony of steel mixed with exploding limestone hitting the stone floor made a thunderous sound, but neither warrior faltered from the contest and only Ninyas jumped with each crash of stone on stone.

The duelers dodged the falling rocks, their footprints in the crystalline dust marking their path of battle. They roamed the temple, parrying around the fallen debris, their eyes riveted on each other. Around and around, back and forth, neither fighter gave an advantage or gained dominance over the other.

Both gladiators were now drenched in sweat and their failing strength was evident in the effort it took for each to raise their broad swords. Their blows were losing intensity. As Semiramis again pushed away from the captain, she paused as a wave of nausea threatened to overpower her.

Instead of attacking, the captain stepped back, breathing heavily. "Finish her," Ninyas yelled from his hiding place. "Kill her!"

The warriors knew the end was near for one of them, both were nearly spent. Each had given all they could and now it was time for the finale.

The captain was the first to speak. "What is the matter, woman? Is a real soldier too much for you?"

Semiramis raised her head. "I was overcome by your foul odor," she snarled, wrinkling her nose.

The Captain's face darkened at the insult, but a twisted smile curled up one side of his ugly face. "Perhaps I did choose the wrong ruler to support." He gave a slight bow of respect.

"It is too late, captain. I cannot forgive or forget the death of my beauties," said the queen. "Treason is treason. There is but one penalty for such an offense."

The captain's eyes hardened. "We all die. But which one of us goes first is the important question."

Ninyas was shuffling his feet nearby, but neither warrior turned to see what he was doing. The few words that had passed between the captain and the queen had not changed their mutual mistrust; their eyes remained locked on each other.

Semiramis acknowledged the captain's words with a nod of her head. They stood tall, facing each other and he saluted, one last time. Each of them shifted into the same semi-crouching position and circled like hungry wolves that knew the kill was close at hand. They stayed a safe distance apart as they moved around the perimeter of their battleground, each patiently waiting for the opening that would let one of them deliver the lethal blow and claim victory.

The captain knew he was slow and moved cautiously, mindful of his opponent's quick reactions and the strength behind the sword arm that had drawn first blood.

With lightning speed, Semiramis stepped forward and charged her opponent, raining blow upon furious blow, pushing him back. With the long sword in her right hand and the short sword frozen in the grip of her injured left hand, she attacked. Right, left and overhead blows pounded the captain. The clashing of their swords echoed in the underground temple as each sword protested the approach of the other.

The captain backed up to the edge of the lake, blood oozing from his face and side, wounds inflicted by her flashing blades. The earlier deep gash in his sword arm continued to bleed through his tunic draining his energy.

She had been careful to keep a sword's distance between them, but now he looked beaten and was gasping from his exertions to defend himself. Her sword sang out his death knell as she advanced for the kill. He went down on one knee as if unable to withstand her onslaught. Just as the queen raised her sword over his head to deliver the final blow, he pulled out the knife strapped to his leg and thrust it into her left thigh.

Stunned, she fell back onto the rock floor, dropping her

long sword. He stood over her and smiled, then grabbed hold of the front of her tunic and pulled her close to his face. “Well, my queen,” he snarled, “come closer and smell my sweet victory.” His words mixed with the saliva and blood dribbling down his chin. “You should never have treated me so badly. I will make you suffer for that.”

He waited eagerly to hear her beg and grovel at his feet. That was the revenge he wanted. But, instead of fear, Semiramis smiled. At this the captain began to wonder if the mother was as insane as the son.

“I was right. That foul odor *is* you,” said the queen.

The queen leaned forward and spat her infected blood-tinged sputum in his face. The captain growled at his captive and threw her onto the cave floor at his feet. He raised his sword above her and then looked toward Ninyas who continued to cower in the shadows, yelling for the captain to finish her.

The queen rose up on her elbows. “Perhaps you may be the victor in this battle,” she said, “but I have given you a gift that will assure you an agonizing death.”

The captain wiped her spit from his face with the back of his hand. His oiled black hair hung like dead eels around his sweaty face. When he leaned down, cheek to cheek with her, his repulsive hair crawled across her face. “You are about to meet the gods,” he said, his rubbery lips rested on her ear. “Beg for mercy.” He enjoyed having a queen lying helplessly at his feet.

“You are no soldier,” she taunted. “I see only a sweating, disgusting pig without enough brains or skill to ever be part of my army!”

Fire danced in the enraged captain’s eyes. Saliva and an unrecognizable guttural sound burst from his throat as he stretched to his full height, lifting his long sword high above his head to focus his full weight into the final blow that would cleave the queen's body in half.

She watched his sword in anticipation of the correct moment to make her last move in this desperate game. She saw the glint of steel starting its downward arc. As the captain bent his knees to complete the blow, Semiramis rolled to the side and came to her knees all in one motion. The dagger that had hung at the captain's waist was in her strong right hand. She plunged the weapon up to its hilt into his groin, while she thrust her short sword into the side of his neck. The short flat blade stayed embedded in his neck, half decapitating the horrified captain.

His dying body completed the last motion his brain had commanded and his sword chopped downward, ringing off the stone floor. As he fell onto his knees, the sword rolled out of his hand and the heavy hilt struck the hard rock. With a hollow sound of anguish, pink fluid foamed from the captain's gaping throat.

"No! No! You fool," Ninyas screamed as he ran into the shadows.

Semiramis watched Ninyas' crimson cape vanishing into the darkness before she turned her attention back to the ugly lump on the temple floor. Like one of the stalactites surrounding them, the vanquished captain was, for a moment, frozen in time. The stunned look on his face told the story. He had underestimated her again. The lifeless body slowly rolled off its knees and onto its back as watery sounds bubbled from its throat. The queen took a step forward. "Swift justice and a method of execution that befits the deed, captain," she said, her voice weak. "These are the attributes of a queen."

He could no longer understand, yet she continued. "I saw the death you inflicted upon my beauties. You enjoyed hacking off my horses' heads. You have brought out the ruthless side of your queen."

Semiramis' legs felt heavy and she staggered. She leaned over, put one foot against the captain's head and pulled the sword from the dying man's neck. In one last act of vengeance, with the toe of her boot she maneuvered his awkwardly angled head so that his watery eyes saw her. "Die alone. Your torment awaits you in the afterworld." She knew he had heard her icy words when his lips quivered.

She turned away, limping, blood dripping from her wounds. "Ninyas, Ninyas, my son," she called out soft and sweetly. "Do not hide from your mother."

Ninyas cowered in one of the niches surrounding the temple, in the shadow of a statue of dNin-Kur, Lord of the Mountain, a warrior figure. Ninyas tried to make himself small and invisible; hoping and praying someone would come to his rescue. His vision blurred as beads of sweat laden with fear dripped down his forehead and into his eyes. He wiped them with a corner of his regal cape as he cowered. His mother had spoiled all his years of plotting and planning. Tears mingled with his sweat and his nose ran. He wiped his face again to stifle his sniveling. In what he thought was a moment of clarity, he thought about drowning her in the lake. Every idea—and now there were too many darting through his twisted mind—appeared to him as a pearl of wisdom.

His eyes darted about frantically; his thinking grew more confused. *What should I do? Where should I go? They are all against me. I will go into Urartu, they'll help me buy an army, and I will return to Assyria as the rightful ruler. Yes, I still have the gems and there are more.* He felt for the leather pouch, hanging from his neck inside his tunic. *Now they are all mine. All is not lost, I am a rich man. But my mother will try to stop me. She always interferes. Why does she hate me? Spreading the disease among her troops was my idea, it was a brilliant idea. My war strategy was the best this time, not hers. Before all the people, I will be crowned king at last. I must get out of here and up to the surface. My kingdom awaits me.*

Ninyas was filled with fear. In hand-to-hand combat, he knew he couldn't beat the warrior queen. His deranged mind ran wild with ways to ambush her. Perhaps he could lure her into following him up one of the narrow steps that, like in the town center, circled the perimeter of the temple? *Yes*, he thought, *yes, this is good. I could hide in one of the priest's cells and grab her legs and push her over the edge. If that doesn't work, I can hide in one of these cells and kill her when she sleeps. Better yet, she is ill. Maybe she will die soon. I can do this*, he said to himself again and again. *I can do this. I can do this....*

Ninyas could hear his mother calling to him. "I wish she would stop," he whispered, covering his ears to block out her voice. Whatever cloak he had used in the past to conceal his insanity, it had been stripped away by his ordeal in the cave. Rational decision making was lost to him forever, and now he would indulge every fantastic thought that entered his troubled mind. He heard her footsteps and crouched lower, moving from shadow to shadow, edging closer to the spiral stairs along the side of the wall.

Semiramis stepped lightly, trying to pick up his trail. She saw that the dirt around the statue of the Lord of the Mountain had been disturbed. She looked around, expecting the unexpected from her sick son. "Come to me, my son. Your suffering will be over quickly." She took a few more steps and listened. She thought something moved to her left and turned in that direction. "Ninyas, I know this cave. Only I know the way out."

Ninyas dashed up the steps and plunged into the darkness of one of the side tunnels, rushing to conceal himself, hugging the cold stone wall, not daring to peer out and give away his hiding place.

She tried again to tempt him into giving away his location. "This is a beautiful place. It is like a giant beehive. I suppose the bees slept in those dark holes cut into the sides of the walls. Are you a busy bee, my son, trying to capture the queen?"

He giggled. His crazy mirthless ravings echoed through the temple.

She paused then spoke in a voice she never used. Her tone was compassionate and sincere. "I am sorry, my son, that we could not learn to love one another."

"Love, from you?" Ninyas screamed. "You have no right to use that word. You have shown me only duty and service. Everything I asked for, you denied me." Ninyas again giggled hysterically. "Duty and service to people who hated me."

Semiramis listened to the giggles of her damned son trying to pinpoint the origin of the sound. As she moved up the stairs cut into the sides of the walls, her eyes darted from burrow to burrow.

Ninyas heard her sandaled feet climbing up the steps and realized his mistake. He squeezed his eyes shut, hoping to be invisible in the darkness, or so his warped mind promised. He listened but could not hear her. The silence was unbearable, the waiting endless. As afraid as he was, he inched closer to the cell opening to see if he could locate his mother.

He made not a whisper of sound. *I'm smarter than she is. Did I not fool her into entering Memphis? I tricked the people and the priests. I turned them all, even the gods, against their perfect queen.*

The bizarre calculations of his mind bolstered Ninyas' courage. Inch by inch, he crept along the inner rock wall of one of the cells. He did not want his precious crimson cape to become snared on the rocks, so he wrapped it around him like a shroud. His insanity was all-consuming.

Eyes still pressed tightly shut against the possibility of discovery, he felt around with his hand and determined he was at the cell entrance. Forcing himself to overcome his panic, he began to open his eyes. *She will be easy to see with the light from the lake behind her.* Fear dripped from every pore.

The moment his eyes adjusted to the light and were fully open, he came face to face with his mother. They stayed frozen, neither moving.

What came next was in neither the mother's nor the son's plan.

Ninyas threw himself into his mother's arms. "Mother." They embraced, then wept. Tears rolled down Semiramis' cheeks. Ninyas' shoulders shook with emotion that had been held at bay for too long. At last she was ready to accept the role she had shunned during his childhood: that of his mother. She had no idea that his need for her was so great.

The embrace was more passionate than either expected. The queen had her back to the open stairs and the temple below. She was dangerously close to the edge. But she stood still, holding her son. Perhaps they had a chance after all. He would never be king, but she could help and protect him. "We were almost too late for each other, my son. I will care for you as long as I can."

In her weakened state, the weight of Ninyas' embrace was slowly forcing her back to the edge of the precipice.

She felt the rocks sliding from beneath her feet. Then, with all his remaining strength, Ninyas pushed her away from him.

She teetered on the edge, trying to get her balance. Her long sword fell, clattering to the stone below. Ninyas backed away from his mother, hugging the wall. He smiled and watched as his mother fell backward toward the cave floor. "Go home to your gods," he screamed.

Ninyas laughed and danced, circling in a jubilant frenzy. "Fools! Fools! There are so many fools in the world. I did it. I killed the invincible warrior queen."

He stepped closer to the edge and ventured a glance over the side to be absolutely sure she was gone for good. She wasn't there. Then he realized he had not heard the dull thud of her body hitting the floor below. Ninyas picked up the torch his mother had dropped and leaned out over the edge.

With her right hand, Semiramis had caught the edge of an outcropping right below the spot where she had stood a moment ago embracing her son for the first and last time. As he boldly stepped closer to the abyss, her free hand slid out and tightened around his ankle. He looked down the spiral steps and was aghast to see his mother hanging there.

"You're dead! You're dead!" he screamed.

"No, my son... we are dead," said Semiramis, as she pulled with all her remaining strength. Ninyas fell to his knees and clawed for a handhold. She crawled up and over his quivering body and hugged him tightly to her. Then taking him with her, she rolled out into the abyss.

Semiramis came to rest near the statue of Ishtar. Still alive she attempted to pull her broken body up onto her elbows to look for Ninyas. She found him impaled on the arrows in the statue's hand. The queen reached up and placed her hand on her son's foot and let the same sensation of warmth she had experienced in the temple in Calah envelope her once again. The pain was gone.

Chapter 27

A Message

As soon as the Hemmet-IV truck pulled up at the mouth of the cave, al-Tubar hurried out to meet General Tariq Saeed and his reinforcements. There were only three of them at the cave, including the general's sixteen year old son. As a result, al-Tubar had felt vulnerable and undermanned since hearing the explosions and learning the farm was under attack.

When he looked at the discolored sky his first thought was that the Kurds had orchestrated the attack, but he knew they didn't have the resources to mount an offensive of this magnitude. Even more puzzling, General Saeed seemed not at all anxious. Al-Tubar was unsettled. If the Americans were attacking, the hatchet man's strategy hinged on knowing Saeed's true plans so he could make a deal with the Americans, this time to save his life. In the back of his mind he hoped it was merely the troublesome Kurds so he could still cash in along side the general.

A soldier waved General Saeed's vehicle into the cave entrance and out of sight. A sergeant ran alongside the vehicle, shouting orders. "You four men stay here at the entrance to the cave. Keep alert and in contact. Let me know if you even smell trouble."

With brusque orders, the sergeant deployed the rest of his men to guard the entrance to the ravine. Tariq's eyes brightened when he recognized the sergeant and he thought to himself, *he is young, probably no more than nineteen, but he will do nicely*. As Tariq approached, the young man saluted smartly.

Tariq returned his salute. "I want you to take charge of security at the cave, Sergeant." *Yes, I thought I recognized him. He will do.* It amused him to think of what he had planned for the boy.

Tariq's thoughts were interrupted when he saw al-Tubar walking toward him. He smiled at his boyhood friend. The turmoil in the distance would not change his plans. He had prepared for just such an eventuality. It only meant he would have to deploy the missiles from one of the other locations. In fact, the attack at the farm might just turn out to be a good diversion.

"My facilities at the farm are on fire," Tariq said to no one in particular. "Colonel Abbas," he said, turning to the brooding hulk at his side, "I have reports that the trucks may have been captured when the Kurds attacked. It will be a bonus to eliminate them this time. But perhaps you already know all this?" For a heartbeat, Tariq stopped, tilted his head, and looked directly into the face of al-Tubar.

"No, my general," al-Tubar responded. "I lost communication with the trucks."

"Perhaps the storm earlier delayed them as it did you, my friend?" Tariq looked up at the sky. "And now the storm returns, again threatening delays."

"My delay was of a personal nature," al-Tubar feigned a smile that showed his rotten teeth. He winked at Tariq. "Will this delay your strike against Israel?" he asked, gesturing to the stormy sky.

The general raised an eyebrow at al-Tubar. "Nothing can stop me now. I have other launch sites prepared."

Wayne's group crouched behind a cluster of boulders directly above the cave entrance. Listening in through Rich's surveillance pebbles, the entire group heard the exchange at the cave entrance. Wayne had been worried when the trucks arrived, but he breathed a sigh of relief when he heard that most of the men had been sent back down the ravine, almost a mile away.

Rich signaled for Wayne to switch to a private channel. "The fat one," he whispered, "Abbas. He's my inside man."

Wayne returned to the open channel and spoke to the group: "Remember, we don't know how many more men were already inside before we got here. Everyone sit tight until Rich has more info. Dead heroes are useless."

"The men left to guard the entrance will take refuge inside the cave as the storm intensifies," Rich said, pointing below them. "I figure they'll cut out as soon as their superiors are out of sight. Let's give them fifteen minutes."

"OK," said Wayne. "Everyone get ready. We'll rappel down to ground level as soon as Rich gives us a go."

Shielded behind a boulder, Rich studied a pocket-sized computer monitor no bigger than his palm. Wayne squatted at his elbow. "OK, Blitz," Wayne said, "have you got a lock?"

"The four guards at the entrance are moving," said Rich. "They stopped about fifty yards in... on the right, in a small alcove. How cozy. They started a fire. Think they're going to roast marshmallows?"

The minutes ticked away and the guards remained by the fire. Wayne grabbed his gear. "It's confirmed," he said. "We go in the front door. Once we hit the ground, Rich takes the lead. Matt: you're his backup. The rest of us wait outside the entrance, out of sight. We don't want any soldiers wandering up from the ravine to spot us. Once inside,

Rich will take out the guards." He nodded in Rich's direction. "Rich, take us in."

Qassem wanted to ask how Rich was going to handle four armed men, but Wayne cut him short. "I'm in charge of this operation from here on," Wayne said. "And that means I'm in charge of you. Any interference and I'll put you down so fast you won't know what hit you. With the exception of Ghariba, I suggest the rest of you control your testosterone urges."

Qassem gave Wayne a curt nod of agreement.

Matt fell in behind Rich. "What's that gadget you have there?"

"You'd know if you'd come to the meetings," Rich smirked.

"What damn meetings?" Matt crouched down waiting.

Wayne inched over to Qassem. "Once Rich and Matt enter the cave we put in our ear plugs and keep quiet until Rich gives the all clear with a vibration in our earpieces."

Their best weapons had always been their brains, talents and the ability to improvise. Would it be enough to overcome the bullets and superior manpower this time? Wayne felt confident. He saw the excitement in the keen eyes of his companions. They had been down this road together before. Each man would be ready to step forward when he was called upon. The four men nodded to each other. Wayne knew that Qassem and Ghariba's actions were unpredictable, but his friends—even easygoing Rich—could be counted on to negate their interference.

Qassem gazed into the wind. "This is a strange storm," he said.

Until now, Wayne had not given the windstorm much thought. "It must be the remnant of the earlier storm."

"But it's concentrated in this area," Qassem said. "The

storytellers of my tribe speak of ancient ones, I think they were Assyrians. They could call up the wind. If I wasn't an uneducated man, I might think someone or something was trying to make it difficult for us."

Wayne thought for a moment. "Perhaps someone is trying to help us," he said after a while. "Don't forget, if the wind hadn't masked your sister's near fall when the wire broke, we'd be dodging bullets right now. Be optimistic my friend."

Rich scanned the area one more time, and nodded to Wayne. With a thumbs up from Wayne, Rich secured a rope to a boulder and repelled to the ground, landing lightly in the scrub brush at the side of the cave entrance.

While waiting, Matt spoke privately to Wayne, covering his communicator pin with his hand. "I've read extensively about ancient Assyria. This country is a mystery even to the people who live here. There's been very little research done here. It's always been a closed society."

"Get to the point," whispered Wayne.

"If this cave is as old as I think, we've got to be careful... traps, secret doors. The Assyrians were clever."

Wayne's bare hand brushed against the rock wall and he felt something. "I just want to finish this and find Miryam. I'll let you and Hal worry about the ghosts."

Matt noticed that Wayne was rubbing moss from the wall and looking curiously at it. He flicked on his penlight. "Cuneiform writing. It's got to be over two thousand years old."

"Can you read it?" asked Wayne.

"Yes, a little. It gives directions for travelers passing through the mountains. It seems a Queen Semiramis, whose patron goddess was Ishtar, had this type of map placed at strategic points to guide travelers through the mountains.

See this symbol?" The beam of Matt's light shone on a star followed by the number 15. "Ancient Assyrians thought it was bad luck to use the proper name of a god. It made it easier for a bad genie to find you, so the priests assigned numbers to their gods and sometimes even to themselves. Never heard of this one though, this Queen Semiramis."

Rich's voice came through their earpieces. "Where's Matt?"

"Go," Wayne motioned for Matt to rappel down.

Hal stepped forward to help hold the rope. "I think Matt's right, we have a bad genie in our midst."

Wayne had no time to think about Hal's comment, he had to get the team in place at the cave entrance.

Qassem and Ghariba slid down smoothly after Matt. As Wayne prepared to drop over the side, Hal whispered to him. "Ghariba's wire was cut."

Wayne slid down the rope thinking this was not the time or place to confront Ghariba or Qassem.

Once Wayne had touched down, he put his weight on the rope to steady it so that Hal—the last in the group—could slide to the ground. Searching his surroundings for anything unusual he thought, *I hate surprises. Ghariba wasn't supposed to be part of this group. Now Hal says she's hiding something, so does that include her brother? He seems passionate about his cause so why would he cut the wire and kill his sister? General Saeed is here and in the cave ahead of us. And Miryam must be around here somewhere. And where's that little weasel, Elliot? Damn! Damn! They better not get in the way. No one or nothing is going to keep me from destroying the WMDs.*

General Saeed was anxious to lay his hands on the weapons he had sought for so long. For the first time in Tariq's Muslim life he felt the kind of excitement he thought American children felt at Christmas. *Christmas in Iraq. I like it.*

They were deep in to the tunnel on the main level and Tariq raced out ahead of al-Tubar and his new bodyguard, the young sergeant.

"Colonel, give me more light," Tariq called out to al-Tubar.

With handheld flashlights, they followed the main tunnel in for about a hundred and twenty yards to where it curved sharply to the left and narrowed before it continued further into the mountain.

After rounding the bend al-Tubar switched on the portable generator and illuminated the huge tunnel with incandescent lighting. "Don't worry," he said. "The light isn't visible from outside. And we set up another generator and floodlights where the stockpiles are located."

They walked in another fifty yards and the tunnel abruptly ended. "Well, Colonel where are they? I see nothing but half-empty file cabinets and useless papers." Tariq was very agitated and began throwing the documents into the air. "Paper, paper!"

Al-Tubar grinned at the general's childish antics, but did not let him see his amused expression, "My general, the weapons are stored two levels below us, in a large natural grotto. If you will follow me, I will show you."

In fact, the tunnel was not a dead end, for a small dark tunnel branched off the back wall. It was cleverly hidden in a deep depression, and in his excitement the general had walked right by it.

"No games. Show me now, you ugly fool," cautioned Saeed.

The general's hatchet man was surprised by the unfamiliar edge in Tariq's voice. Ignoring the insult, he picked up a light and walked down a man made tunnel about thirty feet long and four feet wide. It ended at an alcove that was some fifteen feet in circumference. A bright yellow circle of light shone up from a hole cut in the floor of the alcove. A ladder protruded through the hole.

"Your treasure lies below," Al-Tubar's announced with a flourish. Tariq jerked the flashlight from al-Tubar's hand and climbed down the ladder.

"Why didn't you start moving the storage vessels up to the main level?" the general complained. When he reached the bottom, he gave an audible gasp. "This is no natural grotto, but a man made chamber. My guess would be some sort of ancient city and this is the town center." He looked around. "How did Hussein get them down here? Have you located the tunnel he used?"

Al-Tubar followed close behind Tariq. "I'm sure there's another, larger tunnel that leads straight into this huge chamber. Unfortunately we've not yet found it. Over the years, and due to the American bombings during the war, cave-ins have blocked many of the tunnels. The hole we came through is the result of such an event. This mountain is filled with tunnels."

The general was impressed by the sheer size of the underground city and even more impressed with the volume of the stockpile. He walked around smiling, weaving between the many crates and uncrated items, taking a mental inventory.

Two giant stone pillars supported the massive beehive-shaped ceiling and served as bookends for the crates stacked neatly between them. Like spokes of a wheel, bombs were stacked in a pyramid fashion around an abandoned stone well and along the walls. Forty-gallon plastic containers marked VX and Mustard Gas filled the vacancies between the stacked bombs.

Tariq rubbed his hands together in anticipation of the power now at his fingertips. He recognized many of the bombs. When he was in the army, he had worked at the al-Muthanna facility, filling and marking the bombs. "See here, colonel: the ones with the yellow nose cones are chemical bombs." He pointed to each stack as he spoke. "The aerial bombs that disperse biologicals are made in almost the same way. See the filler plug, sealed with a Teflon washer under the plug?" He pointed to the top of one of the bombs. "The fuse-well transit plug is here. The burster tube runs the length of the bomb down the center." Tariq continued his lesson. "The tail is more complex and contains a retarding parachute which deploys automatically when the bomb is released from the aircraft. The capacity of each of these bombs is one hundred liters." He rubbed them the same way he did his own stomach after an excellent meal. He was pleased. "All of these appear to be filled." His fingers danced lovingly over the top rows of the two hundred or so bombs stacked near the well and the others along the walls.

"These bombs are part of the R-400 and R-400A series and were reverse-engineered from Spanish aerial bombs. Our engineers in al-Muthanna called them Al-Tahaddi, the Challenger." Tariq's fist punched the empty air as he spoke. Then he pointed to the markings on each bomb.

Surveying the cache, al-Tubar saw that each bomb was marked with an Arabic A, B, or C inside a circle on the steel casing. The Arabic A, alef, meant it contained botulinum.

The Arabic B, bay, meant anthrax was inside and the Arabic Jeem, C, indicated agent C or aflatoxin.

"Some of these came from airfield thirty-seven," said Tariq, leaning over to get a closer look at one stack of the bombs. "We had a good thing going back in those days. Dr. Taha supervised the tests and suggested coating the internal surface of the bombs to prevent breakdown of the contents. The ones with the black strip are coated and those without the strip are not. We will use the black stripped bombs first."

Al-Tubar remembered that in the West they called Taha, Dr. Germ and he chuckled.

Tariq enjoyed reminiscing. "Did you know it was my idea to institute an award system at our production facilities? By the time Hussein had determined how many and what types of weapons he wanted, we already had an overproduction."

The three guards on duty came to attention. Tariq nodded at his son, who was one of them. "Start talking, al-Tubar," he said over his shoulder. "I hope you have a plan to get everything out of here." He waved his arm around the room. "It had better be a good one." The hatchet man followed behind Tariq as he continued his tour and passed several spray tanks used for aerosol attacks.

"Yes, my general. This chamber is directly under the main passage, but one hundred feet below it. I thought we could remove the filled bombs now and use them against the Israelis and later widen the entrance we came through to remove the remaining equipment and materials. Secrecy won't be a problem later, when we—I mean you—have control of the country, so we could use explosives to enlarge the tunnel and bring in heavy equipment." He stood at the general's side, waiting for a response.

"I fail to understand why you've not found at least the remnants of the passage Hussein used when he hid them here." Tariq touched the crates holding VX, his fingers following the writing. "Find out how Saddam got them in here!" he raged. "Sometimes you only think of the simplest and fastest solution." His face along with his mood became sour. "You would go fishing with a torpedo. You will never find the tunnel if you collapse all of them by bringing heavy equipment into this fragile cave system." He pointed at the gallons of deadly gas. "Did you ever think that this material may be unstable?"

The two men guarding the town center along with the general's son looked at Colonel Abbas.

"Find the passage. Go, all of you," Tariq ordered. "Search!"

Tariq never took his eyes off of his treasure. He saw that the most precious cargo, the virus seed stock, was secured inside fireproof titanium containers. *Saddam was so clever. The temperature in this cave is perfect for their storage. The waters from the dam complex above, on the other side of the mountain, keep it cool down here.* He fondled his bounty.

Chapter 28

Relics

Chips from the iridescent walls surrounding Miryam had rubbed off onto her hands, sparking a fragment of memory. She brought the torch closer to the wall. Something was scratched into the rock: a star, and the number 15 in cuneiform script. She ran her hands over the writings. The white silvery symbols were as familiar to her as the fingers on her hands. "I have been here before."

For the first time, she noticed the thick layer of dust on the passage floor. Something glistened through the dust. She bent down and picked up a small piece of cloth. It crumbled in her hand but shimmering gold threads remained on her fingertips. She smiled. "Threads from my tunic." She dropped the fragile pieces and quickened her step, excited to be near the end of her journey.

She hurried around a corner and barely missed coming face to face with one of Tariq's men. The man, head bent low, stepped around the corner just as she squeezed back out of sight and extinguished her torch. To her trained eyes, he was obviously young and inexperienced. His movements were awkward, not fluid and muscular like a seasoned fighter. He had the bearing of a pubescent boy, *perhaps a few years younger than Ninyas,* thought Miryam. He passed within inches of her and detected nothing. She crept up behind him, rendered him unconscious with a chop to the back of his neck and then expediently disarmed him.

She dragged him deep into the tunnel she had just exited and raised her arm to deliver a killing blow to the exposed area at his throat but something stopped her. She exchanged her torch for his flashlight and looked closely at her prisoner's face. Perhaps it was the guiltless sleep, but she decided not to kill him. *Enough innocent blood is on my hands.* She noticed he was not carrying a weapon and was disappointed. She bound and gagged him and left him where he lay.

Even though she risked running into another of Tariq's men, she had to return to the main passage to make up for lost time. The flashlight clearly showed the measured marks on the walls where she had struck them thousands of years ago and she easily moved through this familiar terrain.

Miryam tingled with anticipation. The foolish thought that her beauties were near and waiting for her return flashed through her mind as she ran to the grotto.

Crumbling bones of the horses, pieces of leather and, surprisingly, the smell of decay was all that remained in the grotto. The ghost-like skeletons reminded her that she, too, was a spirit from the past. Miryam picked up a round disk from the floor and blew the dust from it. The bronze disk with the cedar cone design had been a decoration on the harness of one of the horses. Tenderly, she pinned it to the front of her blouse.

As she turned to leave, a slight movement in the corner caused her skin to prickle. She stepped back thinking she was not alone. Miryam pulled the captain's knife from her leg sheath. She walked closer and shined the beam of her light where she had thought she had seen movement. It was nothing, a pile of dirty rags. She sighed and relaxed. But she noticed that the smell of decay was strongest in this area.

She stepped forward cautiously and prodded the crumpled heap with her foot. The heap reacted, a blackened chained ankle, fell into full view. Startled by the movement, Miryam jumped back, then turned and searched the grotto again.

She inched forward, reached down, and threw off the rest of the rags that had concealed the decaying body. The victim had chains on one arm and one leg on its left side. The chains were attached to a ring embedded in the wall and had allowed the victim to just reach the water, which probably prolonged its agonizing life. The cruelty of the act revolted her. She bent down to get a closer look. She couldn't see the face but the hair—something was eerily familiar about the blue-black tint of the hair. Some of it had been torn out by the roots. Bloody scraps on the floor led Miryam to believe the murderer had dragged his victim around by the hair.

She backtracked down the path and found clumps of hair scattered over the floor, long dark strands with that familiar hue. She didn't want to think what she was thinking.

Then she saw it: a silver comb clenched in the corpse's fist. It had been a gift from Miryam to her friend, Rijah. She could not contain her anger. "No!" Miryam cried. She bent over, gently touching the body on the shoulder.

As if in response to her cry, the head pivoted toward her. Sunken, pleading black eyes stared at her. "Oh, no, forgive me. Forgive me," Miryam repeated. She knelt and embraced the decomposing figure, rocking back and forth, asking for forgiveness. "What have I done to you?"

But she knew exactly what had happened. And once again Miryam's friendship had cost someone their life. Tariq had found out that Rijah had been feeding her information.

Miryam slackened her embrace and Rijah's corpse slid easily from her arms. This horrendous act had leached away any remaining feelings of compassion. Hatred that she had thought could not get any stronger blazed inside her. The heat of it sharpened her wits. She had failed Rijah, but she was determined not to fail again. She swore over Rijah's body that she would do whatever she could to save her brother, Ali. *And, if along the way, I can kill the savage who did this to Rijah, it will be a bonus,* thought Miryam, knowing Tariq was ultimately the responsible party.

Methodically, she examined the crime scene. Rijah had many broken bones, including fingers, a wrist, and her nose. Her killer had kept her alive for several days, playing with her, hurting her. The injuries were quite obvious to Miryam's trained eyes. Although Rijah's skin showed signs of decomposition, the still-sticky blood and body fluids on her clothes suggested that she had died less than 72 hours before, though the damp air in the cave had accelerated the decomposition process. Rijah's skin had many discolorations: bruises from a fist, bite marks, rope burns and a hand print around her neck—possibly a threat to strangle her, yet it was obvious she did not die from asphyxiation by the color of her nail beds and lips.

Miryam removed the rest of the rags and exposed Rijah's naked body. It was crisscrossed with wide cuts, as if a hatchet or some other broad-bladed instrument had been pulled across her abdomen and back. The appearance of a great deal of blood around the wounds told Miryam that she had been alive during this part of her interrogation.

"And history labels the Assyrians as cruel. Well, there's one thing Assyrians do know how to do very well and that is to extract revenge," Miryam said as she stepped back and surveyed all the death in the small grotto. Miryam thought, *this mountain breeds nothing but evil.*

She forced Rijah's fist open and extracted the silver comb and placed it in her own hair. Then she covered her friend with the rags lying about. One last time she looked at the corner where Rijah lay and then at the horses' skeletons. Miryam spoke to all the spirits in the grotto. "I must go, my friends. There are a few more waiting to take their place among you."

Chapter 29

The Find

Tariq was pleased. At last he had found his power. He smiled at al-Tubar. "Old friend, I have sent for Dr. Seven. Tell the guards at the entrance to bring him down as soon as he arrives."

"When did he arrive in Iraq?" asked al-Tubar.

"Would you deny me my little secrets?" Tariq answered wryly. He stared unblinkingly at his friend for a moment, and then a mask of congeniality covered his previously thoughtful face. He smiled warmly. "It doesn't matter now. Dr. Seven has been sequestered at another facility for the last four months, making preparations." Tariq patted the bombs then pointed at the MKs that had been adapted for biological attacks. "These will be taken to mobile rocket launchers along the border. Dr. Seven will supervise the transfer," he extended his arm to encompass the many stacks and containers around him.

"Sir," the colonel asked, "who exactly is this Dr. Seven?"

"The man who found him for me said his name was Basson, Dr. Basson or something like that. I believe he had some problems in South Africa. He is a man without the complications of loyalties and whose conscience can be successfully soothed with large amounts of money." Tariq patted al-Tubar's shoulder. "Not unlike you," he added.

"This is just the beginning," Tariq continued. "Dr. Seven

has spearheaded the building of my underground laboratories for production and supervised our equipment and supply acquisitions from France. He's here now to see things through to the final stages. I've not yet met him, but we've been in continuous contact through a mutual friend. You understand, this type of business is best done through a middleman. No trail for the prying eyes of the CIA or the Mossad."

Al-Tubar brought over a clipboard with several inventory sheets attached and the two busied themselves for over an hour, checking the labels on the many different containers.

When they had finished taking inventory, Tariq moved away to have a private conversation with the young sergeant.

Al-Tubar had always thought that he had known all of Tariq's secrets, but today he was finding out his friend had kept some very important information hidden. He would have to risk Tariq's displeasure and ask some questions if he wanted to elevate his bargaining position with his CIA contact. "You have another facility? This is good since we lost the farm. It will not be a problem for launching the bombs then?"

Tariq looked at al-Tubar. "It is not like you to concern yourself with details," he said fiddling with his mustache. "Curiosity is not part of your job description, old friend."

Tariq turned to the approaching guards. "So, where is my son?" he asked. No one answered. "Well? My son," he demanded.

"He went to explore a few of the tunnels in hopes of finding a passage large enough to transport these containers to the surface," one of the guards replied sheepishly. "An hour ago he radioed in that he found the passage Saddam had used, but it is blocked, because of a cave-in. He should have been back by now."

Tariq stood looking at his men, his face growing angrier every second.

"Form a search party," commanded al-Tubar, taking charge of the situation. "Make a thorough search." He turned to Tariq. "My men will find him, general."

"I want him by my side. There is much he can learn from this operation," Tariq said. He strolled around the ancient city with his hands behind his back, watching his men disappear into the many tunnels to begin the search. Then he placed a hand on his hatchet man's shoulder and they strolled together around the town center. "Huh... your men?"

Al-Tubar's eyes widened. "My general, they do not follow me. As I have always been your loyal servant, so are they." Perhaps for the first time in his life, al-Tubar felt he could not correctly read the thoughts of his childhood companion. His inner voice whispered, *be careful*. This was a new sensation for the ruthless hatchet man and he found the phenomenon disturbing. Have I done *something to arouse the general's suspicion?* He smiled at Tariq. "General, can these bombs," his hands swept over the stacked missiles, "be launched from mobile units? I was not informed of mobile launch sites. I ask only for purposes of security," he added cautiously.

"My old friend, there is much you do not know. I will give you an example. Listen carefully." His arm was still around al-Tubar, in a posture a father might take with his son. He squeezed al-Tubar's shoulder warmly. "You should never have taxed your limited mental capacity with complicated intrigue."

Colonel Abbas, known as Abu al-Tubar, the hatchet man, the most feared man in General Saeed's army, never heard or saw the young sergeant come up behind him. His brain recorded the shot to the back of his head as a stinging, blurred sensation. The hatchet man's only reaction was a feeble attempt to lift his left hand and swat away whatever had stung him behind his left ear. It was painless. Remotely, he wondered what was happening. In slow motion, his head turned toward his old friend and through the forming haze he heard Tariq's voice. "You sold me out to the Americans."

Then he heard, more than felt, a dull thud as his body hit the floor. His blubbery carcass rebounded several times after it hit. He rolled slightly from side to side from the momentum of the fall, like a child's toy that would not fall over. Eventually, the body came to a halt on its back, face up in front of Tariq.

Tariq bent over him and removed the hatchet from the dying man's belt and stuck it in his own. "A memento." He gestured toward the young man who had performed the execution. "Abbas, you haven't met my young friend."

The hatchet man heard everything but with some surprise found it impossible to speak or move. He blinked.

The sergeant stood over him, a satisfied grin on his face. "I am Rijah's brother, Ali. General Saeed told me how you abducted and murdered my sister. As her only living relative, the general allowed me the honor of dispensing justice. Your death was too gentle for your crime." He spat in al-Tubar's face.

Tubar's vision became distorted. An intense sensation of rage flooded over him like a tidal wave, and then there was nothing.

"Well done! Your first kill?" Tariq patted the sergeant on

the back and thought, *how easy it is to replace one hatchet man with another.* He placed his hand upon his new assassin's shoulder in an all too familiar fatherly gesture. "Ali, remove the body. Put it in one of those cubicles," he pointed to the alcoves in the side of the walls surrounding what he described as the town center.

The general turned as he heard soldiers running toward him. "They probably heard the gun shot," said Tariq. "Ali, get some of those men to help you move him." He pointed to the two approaching guards while he poked absentmindedly at al-Tubar's still jerking body with his foot. "Then secure the area."

Tariq thought he was very clever. *There was so much you did not know, my dead old friend. I have a second platoon of my elite guard from Mosul on their way with Dr. Seven. Even if you had told the Americans about this cave, they will find an empty nest by the time they arrive.* His eyes followed the path of blood on the floor marking the direction in which al-Tubar's body had been taken. An ironic smile lingered on his thick lips.

Two soldiers from the search party, accompanied by Ali, approached Tariq fearfully. "Sir," Ali said, "they fear the ceiling may collapse from the gunfire. These caves and tunnels are most unstable."

General Saeed noticed the dust in the air for the first time. "Yes, I was aware of that from the moment I arrived." he looked at the ceiling, "but as you see, your general is still here. But my son, Mohammad, is not. Report!"

In a shaky voice, the soldier spoke, "We cannot find your son anywhere, sir and... and... he doesn't answer his radio."

Chapter 30

A Gathering of Spirits

The storm outside the cave had been captured by the ravine and it wept and wailed, straining to escape its rocky prison. From their hiding place outside the cave entrance, Wayne's team felt the power of the storm increasing and they clung to whatever they could to retain their footing. Without their communication devices, the noise from the wind would have made conversation impossible. "I can't believe we're in another storm," Wayne said over his communicator.

"I don't mind the wind," Matt replied. "It's the damn sand. Personally, I may never go to the beach again."

"Then aren't you lucky? We're the first to get out of the storm," said Rich and he motioned for Matt to follow him. Rich inched forward along the cave wall, his back scraping against the rough rock surface. Matt, his revolver drawn, was a few feet behind him. Dirt and sand misted the air, creating an unpleasant but penetrable tan haze. Behind them they felt the pressure of the storm increasing. Strong air currents pulled at their bodies, threatening to suck them from the cave.

As they approached the alcove where the guards had taken refuge, Rich stopped. He extended a hair-thin wire from his computer so he could look and listen in on the guards. Through the computer's automatic simultaneous translator they heard the guards speaking. "This storm may keep our reinforcements from reaching us," said one. "Yeah, then what do we do?" replied another.

The soldier in charge grew irritated. "Shut up and be glad you're here and not at the borders when we start bombing the Israelis."

"Won't they be surprised." He laughed and the others joined in; glad indeed they were not at the border where the bloodiest action would be.

Matt and Rich heard the whole exchange. Rich smiled and glanced once again at his PI, or private investigator, as he'd nicknamed the pulse indicator. With hand signals he told Matt that there were still only four guards. All four were sitting in a circle, according to the little red heartbeats on his monitor that indicated their location.

He had already programmed in the physical statistics of the team. He had added Ghariba's EKG during the climb. She and the others could be located and identified anywhere within a mile of his PI device. Not only could he pinpoint someone's location, he could also identify each person by their heartbeat. Every person's heart rhythm and the sound of their heartbeat were unique and could be used to identify them as accurately as a fingerprint. Right now Rich was looking at the guards' readout on the side of the screen and with one tap of the screen he recorded their IDs to read 1bg, 2bg, 3bg, 4bg, to keep it simple. If, later, the PI signaled 3bg, Rich would know that he had come across one of the bad guys—bg—he'd tagged at the cave entrance. The device came in handy in espionage work when villains hid in the dark and wore disguises.

Rich slipped his PI back into one of the many pockets of his fishing vest and pulled out a metal box labeled Altoids. He removed several small waxy looking pellets from the box and began to roll them around in his hand. Then he extracted a small gray spongy ball from another pocket and pressed the warmed pellets into the ball's elastic surface. He inched to the edge of the opening of the alcove where the guards were stationed. He kneaded the ball a few more times for good measure, leaned over, rolled the ball silently into the alcove, and then started the timer on his watch. Rich gave Matt the signal to cut off his communicator and put in his earplugs and signaled the others at the entrance to insert their earplugs in case the sound traveled on the wind from the storm. Rich checked his watch and, at the last second, popped in his own earplugs.

One of the guards noticed the ball and picked it up. "Where did this come from?" he asked and, in the next instant, he collapsed to the ground, unconscious. The rest of the guards fell seconds later.

The silent, high-pitched melody the ball emitted lasted for one minute longer, then Rich signaled for Matt to follow him in. They bolted into the guards' station, pistols ready in the event the sound paralysis hadn't worked. Rich checked his watch and gave Matt the nod that it was safe to remove his earplugs. The guards lay unconscious on the floor, knocked out by Rich's sonic sleeper.

"OK doc, do your thing," Rich reminded Matt. "It lasts two minutes."

Matt pulled his kit from his pocket and, with the dexterity of an accomplished surgeon, injected each stunned man with enough drugs to keep them out for several hours. "No sense taking any chances. I gave each one enough for a nice long nap. The secret is to provide sufficient retrograde amnesia so they won't have a clue how they got here."

Rich collected the guards' weapons, dismantled the firing mechanisms, and stashed them in a crevice at the back of the alcove. "I really hate these things," he said as he threw the rifles carelessly in a corner. Hey, Matt," he called, suddenly serious, "come over here and take a look."

Matt walked over and stood next to Rich. Eight bodies were stacked against the wall in a side alcove. Matt checked each man for a pulse then shook his head. "Nothing. I'd guess they were farmers from the look of their clothes." He turned to leave, nudging Rich to follow him. "Come on, Rich, they're gone."

Red-faced, Rich said, "Someday, doc, we are going to have a serious discussion about how you respond so casually to seeing dead people."

Matt stopped and turned to Rich. "Inside I'm not so casual. It's just that outside, I've seen a lot of death."

"Yeah, you probably have seen a lot more than I have," Rich replied. "And I bet that surprises the hell out of you since you thought it would be the reverse with me in the CIA." He walked away and gave the all-clear signal by way of a vibration in everyone else's receiver. "Come join the party," Rich said. "These guys are a drag."

Now that they'd completed their first move, they were on a fast track. Matt had already stripped off his clothes and, standing naked in the alcove, pulled out his biohazard suit. The three-ply lightweight suit slipped on easily. The inner and outer linings were impenetrable to bacteria, viruses and most acids. The new fourth generation Kevlar sandwiched between the layers prevented needle punctures, cuts, tears, and even some bullets from breaching the containment.

Rich rummaged through his bag of tricks, pulling out several unusual objects from his pack. He ran back to the main tunnel, scattering them about as Qassem and Ghariba hurried by him and into the alcove. Qassem gave

Rich a strange look. "Americans," he said under his breath disdainfully.

Matt chuckled. "Qassem, it's not what it looks like." Qassem still didn't understand and Matt explained. "Rich makes all his surveillance devices environmentally friendly, which means to him that they have to look like they belong in the place where they were being used, in this case bat guano disguises his receivers around the tunnel." Qassem just shook his head and waved Matt off.

Wayne began stripping as he walked into the shelter and quickly suited up. The gloves and hood were not yet necessary and, like Matt's, remained folded neatly in a small pack hanging from the self-contained air-filtration system at his side.

Rich hurried back into the alcove and pulled out his laptop computer, the powerhouse for his multitude of gadgets. With an audible click, he snapped his PI in to his main computer for quick recharging. As Rich waited for his computer to come online, he pulled out several sticky hot-spot bombs. They were plum size and wrapped in aluminum foil; looked more like Christmas ornaments than the powerful bombs they were. Rich tossed four to Matt and another four to Wayne.

"Careful," Matt chided Rich as he and Wayne placed them in their backpacks.

Rich smiled. "Don't worry; they're safe enough to bounce around. At least until we place the timers or I say the magic word." Rich had pre-programmed the bombs so that they could be detonated either by voice command or coded electronic signal via remote control. The voice option was only as a last resort as it had to be given in person, within twenty yards of the bombs. The bombs would not detonate over a communicator.

Wayne motioned for everyone to huddle up around Rich. "Okay, do your thing. You're on, Blitz."

Qassem stared around, puzzled. "Who or what is this Blitz?"

"The short answer is a magician, Antonio Blitz." Wayne turned back to Rich. "What do we have?"

Rich interjected, prepared to give the long version. "You're not doing the old boy justice. The man was awesome. He could catch a bullet in mid air with his bare hand."

"Have you shot yourself lately?" Matt chimed in.

Rich smiled sheepishly. "I'll get it," he said with determination. "Now, to business. I detect no sound in the outer tunnel for seventy-five yards; that's my listening surveillance limit." He lifted his computer in a scanning motion. "No chemical or bio leaks detected within a hundred yards."

While he talked, he handed one-inch soft discs to each person. "These are your early warning systems. Each one is a particle sensor. You remove the backing and press it to your skin." Rich demonstrated, putting his on the underside of his exposed wrist. Everyone else did the same. He pointed to the center of the disk. "Listen up, this is muy importanta. Notice it is divided into two sections. If the yellow half turns orange, chems are in the air. If the blue half turns purple, you've just been exposed to a biological agent. The discs are very sensitive and detect low levels of contamination so you should have time to get away safely. Check them often and, if there are changes in the color, haul ass out of the area and call the professionals." He pointed at Matt and Wayne.

"What do you call these things?" Matt asked. He was looking forward to one of Rich's colorful answers.

"It's my version of a dirty mood ring. Oh, I almost forgot: is anyone color blind?" No one answered so he moved on to the next item. "Gather around and take a look at the interior of the mountain. It's a simple layout: tunnels arranged one on top of the other to a depth of five hundred feet. Give or take a few feet." They all moved closer as Rich pointed at the lavender computer screen. All of their faces now took on the ghostly purple glow from the computer.

Matt pointed at Richard's purple face. "Just your color, old chum."

The smile lines on Rich's face deepened. "Well, old chum," he came back, mocking Matt's British accent, "science has discovered that it's easier to read LCD screens if the read-out is in the red-blue wave band."

"Get on with it, Rich," Wayne urged.

"Listen carefully, children, you'll have to be quick studies. I'm going to do this only once and it's going to be fast." Rich pulled a laser-pen the size of a toothpick out of his pocket. "This is where we are and here's where we entered." Every section on the screen that he touched with the pen-like device pulsated and then grew larger, showing them the twists and turns of each route. A corner of the display held a read-out of the length of each individual route from cave entrance to a central grotto several levels below them. "On this level there seems to be one large main tunnel running clear through the mountain. We know Saeed's men have that under their control. Our territory, for the moment, is here," he pointed to several smaller tunnels. "These semi-passable tunnels run off at different angles from the main tunnel, where we are now, and extend down to the lower levels." Their eyes followed the pen as it moved along each route.

"Where is the general?" asked Qassem.

Rich shrugged, "I don't have him or the rest of his men on my scanner yet. But, if I was him, I'd head for that large centrally located grotto. Just like us."

"Rich, wrap it up," urged Wayne.

"The red lines show the pattern of the highest level, where we are now. Then yellow, blue and green indicate the tunnels that meander farther below ground." The screen now looked like a three-dimensional revolving Rubix cube. "All roads point down. I'm getting some variation in the signal, but they definitely converge at an enormous grotto one hundred and fifty feet below us, with several, smaller alcoves along each tunnel's route." He pointed out their location on the screen. "Most of these alcoves are of sufficient size to hide Hussein's stuff."

"By the way, what exactly does 'semi-passable' mean?" asked Matt.

"What Matt means is: how do we know which tunnels are large enough for a person to fit through?" Wayne corrected.

"All are clear except the lowest levels where there've been some recent cave-ins. It may be difficult to maneuver through some areas, but all appear to be passable." Rich emphasized the word passable for Matt.

Qassem was impressed with the technology. "How many levels are there?"

"Six. But only the tunnels in our search grid contain caves that the computer has identified as possible storage sites. For all we know he could have stuff stored in every one of these caves. Multiple sites means reconfiguring the locations of the hot spots."

"Your computer tells you all that?" Qassem asked. "How do you know the cave ins are recent?"

"I don't have time to explain the details, but it has to do

with temperature variations and density that my sensory beams identify," Rich replied.

Wayne took over. "Look, Saeed hasn't had time and doesn't have the technology to search the mountain thoroughly, the way we can. This," he held up his map, "gives us an advantage. They have superior force, but we have Rich's tech toys to monitor their movements. As long as our presence goes undetected, we can move around in here," Wayne waved his arms around to encompass the mountain, "like ghosts."

"So…" Matt smiled and joked, "you're saying we have the advantage?"

Rich corrected Matt, "You know how he uses the 'advantage' mission rule to boost our confidence." He was about to name each advantage their puny group had when Wayne frowned.

"We'll split up into three groups," Wayne said as he watched Rich out of the corner of his eye. "Each group will search a grid to increase our odds of finding the treasure. After we find it, we set the hot spots, get out fast, blow it with the remote, and wait for Rich's cavalry. Matt, you and Qassem pair up, he'll watch your back. You two have the smallest area to search. It's also the most direct route to our rendezvous site, here, if we don't find the weapons along the way in our individual grids." Wayne's finger stabbed at the large grotto in the center of the mountain that Rich had pointed out earlier. It really did seem like the most likely WMD storage site. "You'll still have to traverse about three miles of tunnels to get there, old boy." He slapped Matt on the back. "It shouldn't be a problem since you're an experienced caver."

"Hal, you're with me," said Wayne. "Rich takes this tunnel with the least number of alcoves to check and he'll set up shop at the rendezvous site ASAP." Wayne pointed to that spot on the computer screen. He turned to Rich, and smiled. "You're our eyes so keep the surveillance rolling. Rich, can you print out some maps?"

Rich was way ahead of him, already handing out small maps. "Just like a board meeting: everyone gets a copy of our agenda. Travel distances are in the upper right-hand corner and on the back is a cut-away layout of the overall tunnel systems we'll be searching. Everything is color-keyed to make it easier to understand. I'll continue to monitor any movement in the larger caves and tunnels, and let you know if hostile forces are in your area, so keep your communicators turned on."

"You can do that?" asked Qassem.

Rich smiled. He loved impressing people with his toys. "Yeah, if it has a heart, I can track 'em... if they're in range."

Qassem turned to Wayne. "What about my sister?"

"She stays here as a lookout," Wayne was quick to answer. He didn't want her anywhere near the action.

Rich immediately objected. "We don't need her here. I've got the tunnel near the entrance mined with my bat guano surveillance devices. I'll know the minute anybody enters or leaves the cave." He gave the others one of his stubborn looks and turned back to Wayne. "She's with me!"

Wayne was about to object when Hal stopped him with a squeeze of his hand on Wayne's shoulder, so he acquiesced to Rich's wishes.

"The ledge over the entrance where we entered will be our fall-back position," Wayne reminded them before they set out. "If for any reason any of us gets separated or is unable to meet at the designated rendezvous point, fall back and wait. Let's do it."

The three friends briefly glanced at each other and then turned away. There was no need for heroic rhetoric. They had discussed several scenarios long before they had reached this point and had agreed that the final resolution to operation Crescent Veil had to be the destruction of any and all biological and chemical weapons they might find, at any cost.

And, they had agreed that, if something went wrong with remote detonation, if they could not get to the weapons, they would each detonate their hot spots in tunnels that would seal off the mountain and prevent retrieval of the weapons by anyone else.

"In your packs," Rich continued, as cool as a man getting ready to spend the day at the beach, "is a tin with six wax pellets. Put your earplugs in before—and I emphasize before—you start warming them in your hands to heat-activate them. Then quickly throw them away from you and onto the ground. They activate at body temp and I've had them go off in my hand once or twice. One pellet takes out anyone within four feet of the pellet. The stunning effect lasts two minutes." He glanced at Matt and shrugged. "The usual drill."

Matt nodded his understanding as Qassem began to question the last part about the pellets going off in his hand but checked himself. Matt grinned at Qassem and muttered, "Rich is a like an American hot dog, you never know what you're getting."

Wayne glanced at Matt and said, "Ready, Huck Finn?"

Matt smiled as he and Qassem left the grotto first. They crept along, stooped over, trying to stay to the dark side of the tunnel and out of the lit areas. They froze when they heard two guards walking toward them. Rich was warning Matt of the soldiers' approach, when Matt whispered into his mike, "Shut up, Rich, I hear them."

Matt and Qassem ran the last few feet and ducked in behind a rocky outcrop and immediately found the entrance to their tunnel. They felt their way along without their lights for a few yards to avoid attracting the attention of the guards. As they walked, Matt laughed to himself. *I'll have to tell Rich he's behind the times; these maps should glow in the dark, like the Star Wars wallpaper in my son's room.*

"What are bee-gees?" Qassem whispered into his mike.

"Bad guys," laughed Matt. "You pick up how Rich's mind works after you're around him for awhile."

"Americans, huh: everything is a game." Qassem shook his head and frowned.

"Not this time, old boy. Not this time," Matt said under his breath.

The rest of the group inched out of the alcove. Rich scanned the main tunnel and reported that the two guards had gone back to join the other ten assembled at the far end.

The rest of the group scrambled along the unlit segment of the main tunnel and were almost to their branching off point when Rich cautioned as they ran, "A truck just pulled up out front and we have three uninvited guests coming up behind us."

Wayne chimed in, "Go! Go! Go!"

They were almost to the protection of the dark tunnel. They could see the black mouth of the passageway ahead, branching off on the right side of the main tunnel. Wayne and Rich jumped into the tunnel. Hal heard the scraping of boots on stone as the guard's feet came into view seconds after they rounded the corner. Ghariba stumbled and, in trying to maintain her balance almost tripped Hal, who was right behind her.

In one fluid motion, Hal's muscular arm picked the faltering girl up and threw her over his shoulder, knocking the wind out of her as he jumped in close behind Wayne and Rich.

Moving swiftly, deeper into the passageway following Rich and Wayne, Hal pulled a struggling Ghariba along behind him.

Then Rich seemed to materialize out of the darkness and pulled Ghariba from Hal's grasp. He held her to him and looked at Hal. He covered his communicator with one hand and whispered, "I'll take her from here."

Hal stared at Ghariba but said nothing.

Wayne, scouting the tunnel ahead, returned and said, "They'll find the sleeping guards soon and start hunting for us. This tunnel branches off twenty feet in."

As Wayne and Hal took the left passage and Ghariba and Rich the right, Rich told them that the soldiers in the main tunnel were sending out an alarm. They had found the sleeping guards.

One advantage down, thought Rich. He checked his monitor as he walked and whispered to everyone, "Eight, no, twelve soldiers searching the main tunnel."

Once they were a safe distance down the tunnel, Rich paused briefly and switched off his and Ghariba's communicators. He turned to her, flashing his light onto her angelic face. "I guess this is as good a time as any. Ghariba, you know I love you. But I know more about you than you think." Ghariba started to object but Rich put his hand up to stop her and said, "For God's sake, girl, I work for the CIA. What did you expect? We'll talk about this later but in the meantime, don't do anything I can't undo."

Again, she started to speak but Rich signaled that their communicators were back on. He grabbed Ghariba's hand and pulled her with him down the passage.

As they walked, Ghariba wondered how much and what Rich knew. This was the most important mission of her life. She reassured herself that she did indeed love Rich. She was also sure he'd never harm her. Nevertheless, she feared the consequence of failure more than anything. It was even stronger than the pain of losing Rich's love. In reality she had no decision; she was compelled to follow the plan set for her a long time ago. A chill of regret ran down her spine as she fell in behind Rich's comforting outline.

About ten minutes had gone by when Rich's voice came back through everyone's earpiece. "All-points bulletin: they have reinforcements, TNTC, heading through the main tunnel. Wayne, tell me when."

Matt and Qassem heard the message also. Qassem asked what TNTC meant and Matt obligingly explained, "It's an old scientific term: Too Numerous to Count!"

"What does he want from Wayne?" Qassem asked.

"Rich is waiting for Wayne to tell him to blow up the main tunnel above us."

Qassem did not blink when he said, "Let's keep moving then."

Tariq's face was mottled with vivid red blotches of anger. No one could find his son and now there were intruders in *his* mountain. He shouted orders and, in response, soldiers ran to obey. Everyone present had experienced Tariq's volatile personality and jumped when he spoke.

"General, I am Lieutenant Achmed. I have brought Dr. Seven with me, as you requested," said the lieutenant as he saluted.

The thin wiry doctor was entranced with the volume of stacks and crates around him, all labeled with the names of different chemical or biological agents. Clipboard in hand, he immediately began to check the crates against the inventory record that Tariq handed him. He patted each container as he made a check next to the corresponding item on his list. He came to the missiles already laden with virus. "General, may I suggest that we load six of these onto the truck waiting outside and move them to their launching sites?" It was the first time the doctor had acknowledged Tariq's authority.

Tariq looked at the man curiously and instantly disliked him. "Yes! My very thought. They have an appointment with the Israelis." He turned to Achmed, who was at his elbow. "See to the loading of these six missiles. I want them en route at once!"

"Let me just double-check to make sure the missiles will fly," said Dr. Seven as he inspected each bomb methodically.

From a tunnel beneath the town center, Miryam listened to Tariq's every word. Her despair rose when she heard the heavy groans of men laboring to maneuver the missiles up the ladder. *I am too late.* Then she turned at the sound of a scraping boot perhaps in the same passage as she. She stood very still and listened. There it was again. She would take an alternate route to the temple. She wondered how she could lure the general to the temple. She didn't think gems would tempt him, but then she realized she had something likely to be more precious to him than jewels.

The approaching footsteps of two men were still far off,

so she stayed listening, her ear against the borehole that opened to the chamber above her.

"Well, doctor, what do you think?" Tariq watched Dr. Seven's every move. "Your talents are required to help my children grow," he pointed to the receptacles holding the viral seed stock. Dr. Seven said nothing. He handed Tariq the clipboard with the completed inventory of the containers.

General Saeed rubbed his hairy hand over one of the stainless steel refrigerated containers that had ceased to function a long time ago. "You have been hidden from me for too long." He patted the container one more time, then signaled for his new hatchet man to begin breaking away the wooden supports on one of the crates. "Ali open this one," directed Tariq.

Everyone stood still, frozen with fear, as the inactive refrigeration container was removed from its crate. The general pointed to the container and signaled for two of his men to detach the concussion-proof outer shell. After it was removed, the inner container and consecutive inner layers of protection slipped out slowly and were lined up in a row on the floor. Including the wooden crates, the cooling receptacle and the concussion-proof shell, three seals were broken. Inside the last tube-like structure sat several large cigar-shaped titanium tubes covered in a cushioning mesh.

They were all afraid to breathe. Everyone gathered in the town center turned to listen. Tariq raised his arms above his head, like a preacher on Sunday morning singing Hallelujah. "This is my Holy Grail and the world will feel its power."

General Saeed only saw the power that the contents would give him; the death and destruction was incidental to making his vision a reality and certainly a far cry from the Holy Grail.

Tariq stooped down and, when the mesh had been partially rolled back, he slowly began to slide one of the tubes out of its rack. The smooth titanium cylinder was twelve inches in diameter and difficult to grasp. He gripped the container firmly with both hands and rose to a standing position, proudly extending his treasure for all to see.

This was a profound moment for him. The fact that he had actually found and had control of Hussein's WMD would be seen by his followers and investors as a sign of power. He had found what the world had been searching for since Saddam's arrest. He had accomplished something that even the Americans with all their technology had let slip though their fingers. He had control of the world's largest stockpile of WMDs in existence. His hand began to shake. The magnitude of the power he had available to him was overpowering.

The tube began to slip out of Tariq's hands and Dr. Seven jumped forward and grasped the cylinder, carefully replacing it in its original location. "The nunc tubes inside might be brittle," said Dr. Seven, indicating the cone shaped temperature resistant storage device. "We must be cautious. General, may I suggest that I take these with me?" He lifted one of the trays of tubes and handed them to a waiting soldier. "I am told this chamber may be unstable. This seed stock is a valuable commodity. I can take it to a safer location." He motioned for some of the soldiers to re-pack the rest of the cylinders. "Make them ready for travel."

Saeed was not accustomed to having any one tell him what to do. "One moment doctor," General Saeed circled the Doctor, a cat sizing up a flittering moth.

The diminutive Dr. Seven shrunk back as Tariq came

closer. Fingers shaking, the nervous man pushed his glasses further up on the bridge of his nose and stepped away from the virus containers.

"You've forgotten one very important point. I give the orders here, and I prefer to have the vials remain here." Tariq spoke through clenched teeth as he reached down to release the last seal and expose the rack of vials.

"I would not do that," the doctor's tone was anxious but insistent. "We don't know the condition of the nunc tubes. The original freezing apparatus stopped working a long time ago, so the contents have certainly thawed. While Hussein's scientists developed stabilizers to protect the virus from the effects of freeze-thaw, if the tubes inside have even a microscopic crack, everyone here could become infected." He motioned to the stacks of containers. "These should be returned to cold storage as soon as possible, for all our protection." Again the doctor gestured for the soldiers to remove the containers. "I've prepared facilities for that specific purpose."

Tariq stopped him. "You forget yourself, doctor," he said, gritting his teeth. "You get paid quite handsomely to follow my orders." The general's patience was at an end, he struggled to keep his voice and emotion in check. Pointing his finger at the doctor, he said in a cool voice, "But you are right; we should be cautious." He moved closer to the doctor and smiled down at him. Danger rippled through the air.

Dr. Seven looked at his feet, fearing to make eye contact with the general. For the first time, he noticed splashes of fresh blood on the stone floor around him. He felt acid fear rising in his throat. On thin rubbery legs, Dr. Seven stepped away from the containers holding the world's most deadly viruses.

"Let us see," Tariq was thinking out loud. "I must know for certain that the viruses are in fact inside these vessels." He paced in a circle, his hands folded behind his back. "I know how Hussein thinks." Then at last he yelled, "Clear the area. Dr. Seven, assemble the biohazard gear and bring it over here," Tariq pointed to the ground in front of him.

Within seconds the town center was empty except for Tariq, his new hatchet man Ali, and Dr. Seven. When the Doctor began to don a biohazard suit, Tariq stopped him. "Yes, you are much too anxious. This is the first time we have met, so your presumptuous behavior is forgiven."

Tariq wrenched the gear away from the doctor and began to put it on himself. "I demand unquestioning loyalty, and now you will show me where your allegiance lies. You will open one of the cylinders and together we will see if the virus is inside."

The doctor turned to run, but Ali stopped him, knocking him roughly to the ground. His head hit the stone with a crack and blood began to ooze from a small cut above his right eyebrow. "No!" he protested. His normally pasty complexion turned a sickly green. His fear erupted from his throat and he vomited. When the panic subsided he stood, removed a white linen handkerchief from his pants pocket and wiped his mouth. "We will all die," he said in a weak voice.

"Pull yourself together, doctor," said Tariq in a chillingly calm voice as he clamped his hood in place. Then he commanded, "Begin!"

Ali placed a cylinder at the cringing doctor's feet.

Resigned to his fate, Dr. Seven sat cross-legged on the cold stone floor. Drops of sweat formed on his face and his glasses fogged and slid down his thin nose. He took them off, cleaned them, and ran his soiled handkerchief across his wet brow. His right hand bumped the cylinder and it began to tilt over. White knuckled, he grabbed the teetering container. His first attempt to break the seal and release the locking device failed and the cylinder slid through his sweaty shaking fingers. Again and again he had to stop and dry his hands. Wet stains, the evidence of his fear, steadily grew larger under his armpits and down his back. Now the inner container opened, and General Saeed leaned forward over the doctor in anticipation. Like the child's toy, mahtrushka dolls, where each is slightly smaller than the other and stored inside one another, Dr. Seven began to remove the shields lining the interior. He looked at the three cylinders of decreasing size lined up alongside him. He inhaled deeply, realizing that holding his breath would not protect him. Once again, he wiped his hands on his pants and prepared to raise the lid to expose the nunc tubes holding the viruses. His hands were steady now, for he had come to grips with the inevitability of the situation. A simple flick of his thumb and he released the hinge, exposing a row of the polystyrene tubes.

Tariq hovered over Dr. Seven with the young Ali at his side, watching the doctor's every move. Seven's brow furrowed as he attempted to peer deep into the interior at the container's contents. "Hurry," demanded Tariq, "lift the tubes."

With his bare trembling hand, Dr. Seven reached into the cylinder. From the rack he pulled a polystyrene cylinder, the final layer of protection. He unscrewed the cap, stuck a finger inside, and felt the top of one of the Nunc tubes. Its conical shape was easily identified.

Dr. Seven grasped the top of one of the sealed tubes

with his thumb and index finger and agonizingly began to withdraw them from the container. At last it was fully exposed to the harsh lights in the town center and he held it out in front of him to see the virus solution inside. But the aged thick yellow tube obscured the contents. Gently, Dr. Seven held the tube, not wishing to exert too much pressure and risk cracking the seal in the cap. Unhappily, he remembered that Saddam's scientists bought and used a lot of hand-me-down, deficient equipment from the Russians' now supposedly defunct biological weapons program. He soon found out that his cautionary movements were unnecessary. As Dr. Seven adjusted his grip around the neck of the tube, the top of the tube broke off from its base and fell to the floor.

As if bitten by a rabid dog, Dr. Seven recoiled to his knees and dropped the remains of the tube shrieking.

Tariq bent over the rack of tubes and with a gloved hand withdrew the whole assembly. It contained eight tubes and all eight had broken seals. He carried the rack closer to the light and examined each tube. He called for the frightened doctor to come closer. It took Ali's vise-like grip on his arm to persuade Dr. Seven to obey.

"You stupid fool," reprimanded Tariq. "Look at the tubes! Look at them closely!" He held the rack of tubes in his left hand and rattled them in front of the doctor's face. Dr. Seven recoiled and Tariq grabbed the man's collar, forcing the tubes in his face.

The Doctor stared down into the tubes. "Empty!" He fell to his knees with joy and fumbled through the racks inspecting each tube. "They're all empty."

General Saeed took the doctor's arm and pulled him roughly to his feet. "You spineless idiot. Didn't you think this was too easy? The filled bombs were the bait, the decoy. I know him as I know myself: always a plan within a plan."

"General," asked Ali, "what are your orders?"

Saeed patted Ali affectionately on the arm. "Get Lieutenant Achmed down here." He looked at Dr. Seven sitting on the floor. "You will remain here to help examine the real virus stocks when we find them."

The lieutenant appeared from the upper level. "Is everything ready?" Tariq asked. "Have the missiles been loaded and secured?" Lieutenant Achmed nodded and Tariq turned to Ali. "You will have the honor of accompanying the missiles to their destinations. Lieutenant, go with him."

Shortly after, one of Tariq's men returned to report that the trucks were safely on their way. He also said that the intruders had not surfaced and they had doubled the guard on the upper level and secured every tunnel leading down to this level.

"And what else?" asked Tariq.

"There is only one way to this cave and that is through the narrow gorge where we entered. Besides us, only the Kurds know how to maneuver through the ravines and wadis," the soldier assured his commander. "We will find the Kurds and your son very soon."

"Do not fail me," Tariq warned. "No one," his voice rose as he repeated, "no one is allowed down to this level without my permission. Shoot any trespassers."

Four soldiers remained behind to protect the general, and he quickly put them to work. "Search these tunnels. The real storage containers have to be somewhere nearby, I can feel it." He growled as he made a tight fist with his hand. Pointing at each man individually, he rattled off their orders. "You search the cubicles above the town center. You take the tunnel leading off on the left. And you two men take the two tunnels on the right. Hurry!"

When he was satisfied that his orders were being obeyed, his voice softened and he turned to the man on the floor. "Come, come, Dr. Seven, stay close to me. These intruders are a minor distraction. My men are well trained and will quickly nullify this annoyance." General Saeed rubbed his hands together, pleased with himself.

One level below, Miryam listened and breathed a sigh of relief that she still had time to find the weapons before Tariq. There was nothing she could do right now about the bombs Tariq had removed. Miryam circled back to where she had left the young soldier. He was still lying tied up where she had left him and was just coming around when she bent over him. "What happened?" his voice, when he spoke, seemed very young. "Did my father send you?"

"Yes," she lied. "You are Mohammad, his son?"

"Yes."

"He sent me to find you and bring you to him." If the hostage came willingly, thought Miryam, it would make getting to the temple easier.

When Mohammad recovered, he rubbed the lump on his head. "Someone knocked me out." He scrambled unsteadily to his feet. "My father's not going to like that."

Miryam motioned for him to follow her. "Stay close. There are intruders in the cave, probably Kurds." She held the light low so he could negotiate the narrow passageway and not see her. The young man chattered and asked questions but this time Miryam did not answer. She hardened her heart to the youthful resonance of his voice. "Stay close, you wouldn't want to get lost down here without a light."

Then she simply walked away, knowing the frightened boy would have no other choice but to follow her.

With Miryam leading the way, they moved smoothly through the tunnels. They stopped to rest once and she gave the boy some water. He didn't speak during this rest time and gulped the water. Miryam glanced over at him and knew he posed no threat to her. When her injured hand smacked against a rock it sent a shooting pain through the hand and she jerked back. It had gone numb a long time ago, so this sudden sting was unexpected. She hoped it would not affect her ability to fight.

Just then a horrific explosion rocked the mountain. Loose rocks crumbled and tunnels collapsed as the mountain heaved, throwing everyone inside it to their knees and disabling the generator. The town center was plunged into darkness.

Chapter 31

Dead End

Wayne immediately called Rich. "What did you do?" he asked in a breathless, harsh whisper.

Rich replied quickly. "No! It wasn't me! Trust me. It must have been a huge bomb. Hold on, I'll switch to my monitors in the main tunnel above to see what's going on." He was off the air before the rest of the team on the same channel could say anything.

Wayne took inventory while he waited. "Is everyone out there OK?"

He waited anxiously for his team to check in. Matt came back, "We're both all right, but what the bloody hell is Rich thinking, detonating before giving any signal? He could have killed us all." Matt and Qassem brushed dust from their faces.

"It wasn't Rich. Whoever or whatever it was, we have to consider that the safety of the virus might now be compromised," said Wayne.

"These tunnels look very unstable. The whole bloody mountain may come down on us," replied Matt as he watched dust sifting down from the ceiling in the tunnel, fogging the air and giving them an uneasy feeling.

Wayne glanced at Hal's dust-covered face. "If the containers have ruptured," he said into his communicator, "you know it's already too late, Matt. All we can do is set off the hot spots and hope it limits the extent of the contamination. Your badges. Check them for exposure. Anything?"

Thankfully, they all reported zero color change: no biological or chemical exposures in their areas.

"News bulletin," Rich interrupted, "listen up, sports fans. I've got some really good news and some bad news." He didn't wait for them to make a choice. "I listened in on the soldiers talking in the main tunnel. It seems an avalanche has blocked the entire ravine and Saeed's reinforcements can't get to the cave."

"An avalanche? Damn, it felt like an explosion!" Matt said.

"What about the trucks with the missiles, Rich?" Wayne asked. "Did they get through before the avalanche?"

"That's the good news. The trucks blowing up are what caused the avalanche."

"How is that good news?" Wayne's tan brow furrowed, wondering how to warn any people in the area of a biological accident.

"The guards up at ground level are running around trying to get away from the heat. They're saying the whole ravine is an inferno. It almost sounds like a hot-spot. From the way they're describing the heat, those bios are toast. But that can't be, right? Has anyone been moonlighting?" Quickly, Rich rummaged in his bag to take inventory. "Wait a minute, I'm three hot spots short."

"Forget it," Wayne said. "What else did you find out?"

"FYI, the generator is out of action, so the bee gees inside the town center are in the dark, like us," said Rich, his tone left something unsaid.

"What else, Rich?" Matt asked.

"I only got bits and pieces of the general's orders to his men up top before he lost his connection, but the gist of it is, the stuff in the town center was a dummy, a decoy. I think the bombs were real but not the contents of the freezer." Rich took a breath. "He won't or can't move the plastic containers with the VX and mustard gas until he gets better control of the situation above. He might even be trapped on the lower level, like we are."

"That's good news," said Wayne dubiously. Then he asked, "We're trapped?"

"And FYI," added Rich, "the electromagnetic pulse I planted in the upper level near the cave entrance to take out their communications system, well, it went off prematurely. I didn't have time to shield my up-link. So ours is out also. We can't communicate with the outside world from in here but, of course, neither can General Saeed." After a short pause Rich added, "I suppose I could rig a signal to bounce off the lake when we move outside but..."

"Forget it, Rich," Wayne cut in. "Focus. Anyone find anything in their search grids?"

No one had.

"Forget about reinforcements. Forget about everyone and everything outside this mountain. We are in the here and now. We destroy the virus stock, anything Saddam might have left, goes." Wayne's voice was strong and compelling. "Rich, I want you to locate everyone in the cave that might be in a position to oppose us. I need to know numbers. How many are we up against on each of our levels? Matt, are you there?"

"Yes," Matt's voice came back in Wayne's earpiece immediately. "Where else would I be?"

"You and Qassem have the shortest route to the chamber located directly behind the rendezvous point. Do you see it on your map?"

"Yes."

"Get there ASAP and hold that position until the rest of us arrive. Hal and I will meet you there as soon as we can. Rich, I'll leave my line open so you can feed me info on the location of bee gees. How long before you'll be at the rendezvous point? I'm going to need all your magic tricks to pull this one off."

"It should take Ghariba and me about half an hour to reach that location," Rich replied.

"Be there," said Wayne.

After everyone had signed off, Rich called Wayne back on a secure line to tell him about his last communication before he lost his up-link. He'd been talking to the American ambassador, Arthur Jenkins. "He said we have a green light. He also said Iraq's president has retained control of the country. The attempted coup has been averted."

"Did you set up the contingency plan we discussed?" Wayne asked.

"If we can't do this from the inside of the mountain," Rich answered, "Jenkins will send in the diggers and seal the mountain from the outside. Magic time is 1:00 am."

Diggers was what the army had nicknamed its latest weapon, developed for fighting the Al-Qadea in Afghanistan. It was several bombs inside each other. The first bomb burrowed into the earth on impact, knocking debris out of the way when it exploded. This allowed the sequential bombs—which were equally mighty—to explode ever more deeply. The result in this instance would be incredibly deep penetration into what were previously thought to be impenetrable caves.

Wayne checked his watch. "Good," he said as he walked. "Now I have a few questions about this cave and what you remember about our last visit to Iraq."

In another part of the cave, Matt and Qassem were

moving toward the cavern behind the rendezvous site as quickly as they could. As they rushed downward, they came to a fresh cave-in that partially blocked the tunnel.

"You can't expect me to get through that small space," Qassem complained.

"You can make it," Matt said with confidence. "I've seen Hal get through smaller spaces. At least you don't have to do it underwater."

"Underwater! That would be impossible."

"If you say so," said Matt as he pulled Qassem's arm, grunting under the strain while helping him through. "Perhaps a diet would be in order, my large friend."

They laughed in the darkness as Qassem's body finally slid free through the narrow slit in the rubble. "I may seriously think about it if we get out of here." Once they were on the other side of the cave-in, the tunnel was larger and they could move more quickly. They expected to be at the chamber behind the rendezvous point at any moment.

For Matt, the death of his mother was still an open wound and he relished facing the man who had orchestrated her murder. Not even his close friends on the team knew how deep his hatred ran. He had no thoughts of exacting justice, for that was God's realm. His motivation was pure revenge.

Now the tunnel widened and the two men ran shoulder to shoulder. As they rounded a slight bend in the passage, they narrowly avoided crashing into a stone wall when the tunnel abruptly came to an end.

Matt signaled Rich, who immediately came on line.

Rich filled everyone in on his findings from his scan of the area. "I've confirmed that the people who were below ground when the trucks exploded are trapped here along with us, which narrows the odds."

"You always bring such good news," Matt quipped.

"It's not so bad," Rich said. "I see the six of us, General Saeed plus five other bee-gees and two more of his men off in a remote area. The last two must have become separated from the main group up near the cave entrance. They'll never find their way through the tunnels to the town center. Matt, you should be at the chamber behind the town center, according to my scan. Be careful: General Saeed and his soldiers have retreated back to the center after the explosion, and there's a door between you and them."

"How does it look?" Wayne asked.

Matt didn't hide his frustration. "We're not in the chamber. Rich, the tunnel you sent us through came to a dead end. Your maps are wrong, Blitz!"

"Impossible," was Rich's confident reply. "I have your exact location on my PI. Just walk up a slight incline about fifteen feet above you and it will open into a large chamber."

"There's no incline to walk up. The only way to go is back out the way we came and it will take us well over an hour to go around and catch up to you."

"What do you think?" Wayne handed Hal the map.

Hal studied the map, rubbing the paper and tracing the lines with his large rough fingers. Then he placed his hands on the stone walls of their tunnel. Finally, he nodded and spoke into his mike. "Sorry, Matt, I don't think you're going to like this."

Matt frowned. He and Qassem looked at each other. "What is it?" Matt asked.

"Do you see any water dripping nearby?"

Qassem answered, "Yes, it's dripping down the wall in front of us."

Not again, thought Matt.

Hal's voice was calm. "The path is behind that rock. It's an ancient drain for the lake above you."

"Wait a minute," Matt said, "did you say lake? Rich, you missed picking up a whole damn lake?"

"Not possible," exclaimed Rich as he began to explain temperature variations and the numerous variables involved.

"Later, Rich," Wayne interrupted. Something had sparked a memory and Wayne's voice lightened. "That's it! OK. Go ahead, Hal."

"You two are going to have to open that drain. There ought to be a lever nearby. There's not a lot of water in the lake—maybe three or four feet—so after the first surge, you should be all right. It's going to hit you hard, but the pressure should lessen fairly quickly. Find something to hang onto until the tunnel floods, then you'll be able to swim through up to the surface."

"Hal," Matt asked, "I thought we were draining the lake, so why would we have to swim?"

Rich answered for Hal. "Sorry, the blast collapsed the tunnel you're in about forty yards behind you. The only way out is up. The tunnel you're in will fill up, not run off."

"This just gets better and better," Matt said.

"OK," said Qassem, "We have no choice. We can only go forward. I have one small problem with this plan, my friends."

Matt turned to Qassem, wondering what would come next.

"I cannot swim." Qassem shrugged as if to say you should have known that.

Matt ran his fingers through his hair thinking, *this can't be happening.* With a weak smile of confidence, he turned to Qassem. "No problem. How long can you hold your breath?"

Qassem smiled. "This is a joke?" Matt didn't smile. "Well," said Qassem again shrugging, "we go up." Then he said loud enough for everyone to hear, "I found the lever. I'm pulling but it's not moving."

"Of course it's difficult, it's hasn't been used for thousands of years," said Matt, "let me help." He pushed in next to Qassem and added his strength. Together they leaned hard against the lever and soon a grating sound throbbed through the rock.

"Something's happening," said Matt.

The rest of the team strained to listen.

Wayne, Hal, Rich, and Ghariba felt a slight vibration travel up their feet and a quiver went through their bodies. "Are you guys still there? Come back, Matt," Rich called. Matt and Qassem were silent.

"It's the only way to get out of there, right?" Wayne asked.

"It's the only way," said Hal.

"They'll make it. We all know how obstinate Matt is," said Rich.

"Let's get going," said Wayne.

In their separate tunnels the three men and one woman resumed their arduous trek.

Soon Wayne and Hal found themselves in a very low passage and had to duck walk to get through.

Rich, feeling responsible for Matt and Qassem's predicament, had broken into a run. Ghariba placed a comforting hand on Rich's arm. "They'll make it through."

Rich came out of his momentary self-pity. "I'm sorry. You must be worried about your brother."

"He's a strong man, I'm sure they'll make it through the

water. Why do you think getting to the lake is so important to Wayne?"

"I don't know. Earlier he was talking about our inspection days. He was trying to remember something but I wasn't much help. Wayne's brain is like a filing cabinet. He pulls stuff out of a drawer whenever he needs it. His hunches have gotten the job done too many times for me to doubt him. We'll find out when we catch up to them. Let's keep going." Rich gave her a peck on the cheek.

The next thirty minutes felt like hours as Rich set a harrowing pace. The sweat poured down their faces and Ghariba had to stop several times for water and to catch her breath. Sections of the passageway they were in had collapsed after the explosion above them and they had to crawl and remove rock debris to get through. Ghariba suggested they try some of the side tunnels that branched off from the passageway, but after checking them out on his computer, Rich said they were either blocked or led away from the town center.

After a while, Rich checked in. "Wayne, it looks like it's going to take us a little longer than I thought. Parts of the tunnel are collapsed and Ghariba is tiring. It's slow going."

When Wayne answered, his tone was harsh. "We all have the same problem. Safety is not an option." Something had tickled at his memory all day. Then, when he was talking to Matt and Qassem, it had come to him. "I remember something from one of the documents I reviewed during our inspections in Iraq, a quirk of Saddam's. I'll explain later."

"Gotcha." Rich took whatever Wayne said on faith. He helped Ghariba through another crawl space. "We're moving too slowly, baby. We can't take the time to pick the safe route. If I go ahead, do you think you'll be all right? I'll mark my route with these glow markers." He pulled several small fluorescent sticks from his pocket. "Take this map. Watch your badge. Get out of here if there's the slightest color change. Promise?" he asked.

Ghariba did not hesitate, "Don't worry, I'll be fine," was her confident answer.

Reluctantly, Rich left Ghariba resting in the tunnel as he hurried ahead to meet his friends.

❧

Tariq stood tall among the frightened soldiers hovering around him in the town center. They had been unnerved by the explosion and the darkness.

"You," he said, pulling at the arm of the soldier closest to him, "give me your light. Where is the man that was with you?"

"Khali was killed by the cave-in," answered the soldier.

On the outside, Tariq was a beacon of confidence as he leaned unconcernedly against the well. On the inside he was smoldering, and his mind raced from scenario to scenario. "You there, try to make contact with the men on the upper level again," he pointed at another one of his men and then at the communication link.

"Yes, my general." The nervous soldier tried his small hand radio and satellite phone but, after fiddling around for a few minutes, he gave the general the bad news: there was no answer.

Tariq paced thoughtfully around the cavern, needing time to control his rage. He examined the route he had taken to reach the town center. The ladder was twisted and broken. The opening to the tunnel above was clogged with fallen rock. When he finally spoke his voice was steady, but anger saturated his words. “Understandable, the communication line was severed during the cave-in. I will not let years of planning be destroyed by those demonic Kurds.” He pointed up at the level above his head and, in an almost cheerful tone he said, “Our comrades above will soon reach us.”

“But the tunnel leading up is blocked,” said one of the soldiers apprehensively.

Tariq moved closer to the man and said, “I think we can safely assume the Kurds who dispatched the guards at the cave entrance are trapped or were killed somewhere. We will resume our search of the surrounding area while we wait for reinforcements.” His commanding voice left no doubt that he expected them to obey. “We do not cower in dark corners. Dr. Seven will stay with me while you three search as far into the tunnels as you can go. I’ll keep two torches and each of you will have one.” He unsnapped the cover on the leather case holding his sidearm, then grabbed an M-16 from the soldier nearest him. “I will hold this position for you to fall back to in case you run into any Kurds. Go!”

The soldiers looked at each other. To a man, the soldiers knew the Kurds were a dangerous lot and wandering around in the tunnels alone seemed foolhardy. With trepidation and what he hoped was a plausible reason to change the general’s mind, one of the soldiers approached Tariq. “General, we are entrusted with your safety. We cannot leave you.”

Tariq, however, would not tolerate dissension and emphasized his authority by pointing the M-16 at them. “Go at once or join Abu al-Tubar.”

The three soldiers quickly obeyed, disappearing down the side tunnels.

Tariq sat down on one of the dummy containers. "Doctor, what do you think this place was in ancient times?" The beam from Tariq's flashlight played on the domed ceiling. His mood seemed to lighten while he looked around thoughtfully, continuing to let his light skip around the grotto.

Dr. Seven found the sudden shifts in Tariq's mood and the accompanying darkness unsettling. "I don't know. It almost looks like a town was built around this well in the center." Seven pointed up at the ceiling. "It's like being inside a giant beehive, with those holes honeycombing the ceiling."

"Yes, I thought the same thing. This was the town center for some tribe." Tariq started to walk around, kicking angrily in the dirt. He moved closer to the doctor. "What do you say, Dr. Seven, shall we do some exploring while we wait?" It was not a question, but an order. Tariq left the M-16 propped against the well and drew his Berretta. He pointed it at the doctor and, with the beam from his flashlight, motioned for the man to walk ahead of him into a tunnel off the town center.

The unarmed Doctor obeyed.

"The tunnel over here looks very interesting. My men searched it earlier, but I have a theory that I would like to explore." Tariq smiled in the semi-darkness. "An appropriate term to use under the circumstances, wouldn't you agree, Dr. Seven? Ha. Ha." His laugh was hollow.

The doctor had the unsettling suspicion that he was being led into a trap, but he did not know how to avoid it.

Tariq didn't wait for an answer. "It is an interesting name you have chosen for yourself. I remember very well your enthusiastic explanation of why you took this name. It is an amusing story. Perhaps you can retell it for me." Distrust dripped from his words.

Dr. Seven wouldn't have believed he had any sweat left in his body after his earlier experience, but he was again sweating. He stalled for time, wondering what direction General Saeed's distorted mind was now taking.

"May I have some water? You've heard the story before, general. It would be boring to hear it again." He walked ahead, directed by the beam of the general's light and the Berretta at his back.

Chapter 32

Homecoming

Miryam and Mohammed emerged into the temple from a partially collapsed passage at the back of the underground lake. The were both coughing and covered in dust. After the explosion, they'd had to scramble through numerous collapsing tunnels and the safety of the temple was a welcome sight.

"What is this place?" asked Mohammed.

Miryam shined the beam of her light at the domed ceiling and the light show began. Shimmering waves of pinks and blues danced between the waters of the underground lake and the calcite that covered everything else. "A temple," answered Miryam.

As he straightened, rubbing his aching back, Mohammed's eyes widened with wonder.

For Miryam, it was a satisfying and comfortable feeling to be back at last, physically, instead of just in her dreams. Without looking, she reached back to the ledge that held the flint. With one stroke of the familiar instrument, she lit the thick residue of oil that still clung to the bottom of the trough that circled the temple area. The flame sputtered and then caught. The boy watched in awe as the flames grew in strength and raced ahead of them, lighting their way as they walked around the perimeter of the chamber. The eerie glow filled the chamber and Mohammed, still fascinated but cautious, followed closely behind Miryam along the narrow path that surrounded the lake and led to the broader area cluttered with statues.

Once they reached the shoreline, Mohammed wandered further from Miryam's protection and closer to the idols. His hand reached out to the calcite encrusted statue of Ishtar. He climbed up and rubbed away years of dust and dirt. "She is beautiful," he said. "These are Assyrian."

"The Assyrian empire was the most advanced society of its time. This was a temple and it is where the seeds of that civilization took root."

Now, in the bright light of the temple, Mohammed could see Miryam clearly for the first time. "You are injured," he said, indicating the cuts on her shoulder and right forearm, and the dried blood at her throat. "Were you hurt in one of the cave-ins?"

"What?" snapped Miryam, her mind in another place and time. She turned and glared at the boy and he cringed. She thought quickly. "Yes. One of the tunnels collapsed." *I must keep him calm and compliant.* Her right hand rested lightly at her waist where she could feel the end of her concealed laser wire. "Your father is a very... powerful man." She had wanted to say "evil," but stopped herself in time.

"Yes, he is, and he wants me to be like him, but I..." he stopped. Mohammed looked to Miryam and something about her encouraged him to continue. "If I tell you a secret," he said, "do you promise not to tell him?" Miryam promised, and he continued. "I want to study the history of my country and show the rest of the world the real Iraq." He became excited and spoke faster, his fervor carrying him along. "I want to help my people build a decent future without all the death and pain they have endured under

Saddam's sword." He continued to talk but Miryam did not hear him. "Did you know..." his voice trailed off.

The absence of Mohammed's voice pulled Miryam back to the present. She smiled at Mohammed and noticed that he was staring at her curiously. She was standing beneath the statue of Ishtar, absentmindedly rubbing a skull she had picked up from a pile of crumbling bones lying at the foot of the idol. It was, of course, Ninyas' skull and Miryam immediately had recognized it and the bones of Queen Semiramis scattered all around her. She was not alarmed, but merely curious to see where her own bones would soon rest. She had lit the torch in the holder at the statue's base and the glow of the torch's beam exposed her full face.

"I've never seen any of the women in my father's army wear their hair in all braids like you. It almost looks like a helmet," said Mohammed. Not wanting to offend her, he added, "Kind of cool."

He noticed the necklace of doves around her neck and the corroded green bronze brooch attached to her tattered blouse and thought it was strange dress for someone in his father's army. He moved closer and his eyes went from Miryam to the statue of Ishtar and then back to Miryam. The firelight shining on the faces of both Ishtar and Miryam defined and accentuated their similar Assyrian features. In a sudden flood of recognition, he said, "Hey, you look exactly like her." He pointed up to Ishtar. As he stepped closer to get a better look at the statue, something crunched under his feet. He quickly jumped back and a horrified look replaced the wonder that only moments ago had filled his youthful face. He pointed at the temple floor. "Are those someone's bones?" Mohammed's eyes fixed on Miryam when he realized that her hand was resting on a skull.

"Yes. This was a young prince named Ninyas. The other skeleton is that of the prince's mother, Semiramis, she was the Queen of Assyria."

Mohammed backed away.

Miryam strolled to the edge of the lake. Without looking, she bent down and picked up a ruby ring perched on a boulder. She put it on her finger. It fit perfectly. She walked toward Mohammed. "I have no intention of hurting you. It is your father that must pay for not learning the lessons of history," she said while she picked up an ancient sword and twirled it in her hand.

The boy retreated further, frightened and confused. His eyes locked on the woman with the sword and he could not look away. It took all of his courage to speak and, when he did, his voice faltered. "You aren't one of my father's soldiers?" The question did not need an answer. Again he mustered his courage. "How do you know all this? What are you talking about?"

"Entire populations have been annihilated by the same type of biological warfare your father wants to wage on this world. He would deliberately inflict these insidious plagues on innocents. Do you know how agonizing their deaths would be?" Miryam's voice burned with hatred and the faster she talked the more her words took on an unfamiliar accent. She placed her hands to her ears to block crying that only she could hear. "We had to put hundreds to the sword in a feeble attempt to save a few. Oh, the stench from the burning bodies!" Her voice swelled as her thoughts became random. "Their blood soaked the earth, Hazael..." Finally, she heard her words echoing around her and lowered her voice. "Whole cultures will be lost and the future will be altered..." Her voice trailed away, but she continued to walk slowly toward Mohammed and he continued to back away.

Mohammed stopped and stood waiting for her. Her face looked so troubled that he was no longer frightened. His heart filled with compassion. Like any child, his face showed his thoughts. Tears welled up in his eyes and trickled down his young face.

Miryam stared at his shining tears and then her eyes went to a lock of hair, black, that fell onto Mohammed's forehead. Memories flooded through her. She reached out and ran her fingers through his hair. Then she wiped away the boy's tears with her fingers. "If only Ninyas had had a small measure of your compassion." She turned her back to him, and spoke. "Your father has been consumed by the same greed and desire for power that obsessed Ninyas. In his quest for wealth and glory, he destroyed Assyria, just as your father now threatens to destroy Iraq and other nations." She circled him as she spoke.

"I'm sorry. I pity..." Mohammed saw the ancient sword turning over and over in her hand and he cringed.

The hand that carried the sword tightened and whirled around to bring the point to bear against the center of the boy's chest. "You pity me! Do not pity me. I am fulfilling my destiny. Your father will never leave this mountain alive."

Alarmed, the boy tried to step away, but a giant stalagmite blocked his retreat. Miryam walked around him and forced his arms behind his back so she could bind them. "This rock will do," she said. He winced but did not cry out as his arms were dragged across the dolomite fossils. Blood welled up from numerous cuts and the red fluid ran down his arms, staining the rock formation, ending in small drops drizzling from his fingertips. A small bloody pool formed at the base of the stalagmite where he stood.

When Miryam had finished tying him, she stepped out from behind the stone and noticed the blood and inspected his cuts. "You are brave. You did not cry out when the rock tore your flesh. The wounds are not deep and will stop bleeding on their own. I do not intend to harm you, but the sight of your blood may be an added incentive for your father."

Mohammed looked into his jailer's eyes. "You don't know my father well, do you?"

It was not what she had expected. She checked his bonds to make sure they were tight, then faced the boy.

"I hate my father," the boy blurted out, "and you're just as cruel." Emotions held at bay for years erupted. "My entire life I've fought with myself, knowing my feelings were wrong. I have tried very hard to live up to his brutal doctrine, but whatever I do is not enough. Failure to meet his standards is always severely punished. If you don't believe me, look at my back. It has my father's signature all over it."

"Calm yourself. This will be over soon."

His cheeks flushed with anger. "He beats my stepmother all the time," the boy cried out. "She lives in fear, sometimes taking the brunt of his unpredictable temper just to save me. Do you know what she says when she prays every day? She asks that I survive until I can find a way to escape him." The boy trembled with frustration. "My father knows I hate him and he will not hesitate to sacrifice me, so forget any ransom." His face contorted. "Do you really think you could hurt me more than he already has?" He stiffened and stared at Miryam through tear-filled eyes. Then he stuck out his chin defiantly.

Startled, Miryam could not hold back her comfort. She

untied the boy and placed his stricken face upon her shoulder and held him.

"When you leave, can I go with you?" the boy pleaded. "Please, please, take me with you. I'm afraid one day I will kill him."

"Is it so bad that you're willing to commit patricide?" asked Miryam.

He nodded. "I know it is wrong."

She almost wept as she told him, "No. You cannot go where I am going."

With a stricken face he confessed, "I can only despise him. My hate for him and his cruelty is all we have between us."

She hesitated a moment, then lifted his face to hers. "There is someone coming to this temple who will help you." She knew that she could not use this boy as bait. He had been used enough for one lifetime. Once he had quieted, she took his face in her hands and smiled to reassure him. There was something familiar in his gold-flecked eyes and the line of his chin. Something *very* familiar. But now was not the time to think about how this piece of the puzzle fit. She took his hand in hers. "I want you to stay out of the way when the fighting starts. There is an alcove behind that pile of fallen rocks near the entrance to this temple. I will hide you there and, when no one is looking, I want you to get out of here."

Gently, Miryam tended to his cuts. She wanted to say, *Mohammed you are one of the innocents. You will not have to carry the burden of your father's death. I will carry it for you.* But in the end she simply said, "This is a place of death and you have a lot more living to do."

They stood holding each other for a while—still and silent like the statues around them, two lost souls comforting each other—until they were stirred by what started as a low rumble. They turned from each other and looked down at their feet where the vibrations had started. The lake quaked and water splashed over its edge. They watched, astonished, as a whirlpool slowly formed at the center of the lake. As it grew progressively larger, the water picked up speed. The level of the lake began to drop and then the draining slowed. Next, most unexpectedly, two sputtering heads popped out from where the center of the vortex had been.

Miryam took Mohammed's hand and they ran to their hiding place. He started to speak but she signaled for him to be silent as two men rose from the center of the lake.

❧

After a turbulent swim against the rushing water, Matt broke through to the surface first, dragging a sputtering Qassem by the arm. The moment Matt wiped the mud and water away, his eyes locked onto a bizarre structure immediately in front of them.

Coughing in an attempt to clear his lungs, a mud smeared Qassem managed to ask, "What is it?"

At first Matt did not respond. But then, still wiping mud from his eyes said, "Let me get a good look."

Qassem reached out to grab onto the metal object and pull himself up. "Stop," Matt shouted, "you know, you can stand up here." Surprisingly, Qassem did not argue, but pulled his hand back as if he had touched a hot stove, and pushed his feet down, searching for the bottom.

"I think it's some kind of freezer," Matt exclaimed as he examined the stainless steel object with meticulous attention, peering into every convoluted crevice. "Wayne's hunch was right on target." He motioned for Qassem to stay back and Matt circled the unit a second time, fingering its workings. Finally, his shoulders lowered and he relaxed, exhaling with a gush. Feeling confident and a little cocky he turned to Qassem, "I guess we're the first to the party. This is it, my friend, Saddam's virus seed stock."

"Is it safe?" Qassem had been eager to find the weapons but now, in close proximity to so much death, he cringed.

Matt did not notice that Qassem was not only standing, but he was retreating to the edge of the lake. The storage device and its contents consumed all of Matt's attention and he did not even hear Qassem's question. *Fascinating, the freezer is still functioning. It must somehow run on—or be regenerated—by the circulation of the water of the lake. Wait until Rich sees this: he's going to love taking it apart.*

Qassem again tried to get Matt's attention. "My friend," he asked from the edge of the lake, "shouldn't you put your hood and gloves on?"

Matt sloshed though the water and thick mud to join Qassem at the shore. "I think it's OK, but..." He glanced at the small disk still stuck to the inside of his wrist. The colors had not changed. "I don't see any booby traps, but we'll let Rich give us the all-clear before we play around with it. Our badges are clear. There's nothing to fear," Matt reassured Qassem. "As long as the freezer unit continues to function, and the water hasn't screwed up these badges."

Qassem's smile was weak. "My friend, you have been too much with the Americans. You've picked up their strange sense of humor. You forget I have seen, firsthand, the devastating results of the contents of that," and he pointed at the freezer in the middle of the lake.

❧

Wayne and Hal were startled when Rich appeared out of nowhere in front of them. He was his usual exuberant self. "Isn't this cool? It's got secret passages and listening holes all over the place."

They sat on the steps and guzzled water and splashed their sweaty faces.

"Hal and I hit a cave-in back a ways, but your map gave us an alternate route here," Wayne said.

"Yeah, Ghariba and I ran into similar problems."

Wayne noticed her absence for the first time. "Where is she?"

"Oh, she's all right. It was tough going for her, so I came ahead and marked the trail. She won't have any problem finding us. I ran into two bee gees, but they were nothing to worry about. They're resting peacefully in the passage back there, wrapped in duct tape." Rich pointed to the tunnel he had emerged from.

"It's a good thing you came along. They'd have had us," said Wayne. "Anything from Matt and Qassem?"

"Not a peep. Their communicators aren't receiving. They don't show up on my PI either. It might be because their body temperatures have decreased. They're all wet. So I've broadened the temperature range."

Wayne forced his concern for Matt to the bottom of his list. "We've been following these spiral stairs down to what looks like a large grotto or the town center the general talked about. According to your map, it should be about fifty yards ahead," he pointed the beam of his light down the steps. "Damn, I can't see very far ahead because of the bend in the stairs. We only have one bee gee left out there on our level, right? Plus, General Saeed and this Dr. Seven, that makes only three we have to worry about. Rich, can you locate them?

Wayne and Hal watched as Rich checked his PI read-out.

"Talk to me, Blitz," Wayne urged as they stood and started walking down the steps.

Rich frowned in concentration. After several thoughtful seconds he said, "The general and his companion are closing in on our rendezvous point."

"Three, like I said, right?" Wayne asked.

"On this level?" Wayne scowled and Rich refocused, "Yes and not um... exactly. Remember the two guys I thought were isolated in a remote part of the tunnel? They're back. And they're right below us, in the same place Matt and Qassem ought to be."

"How do you know it's the same two?" asked Hal.

"I tagged them, look." He turned his monitor so Hal could see. First, Rich pointed to the signals denoting the location of each team member, as well as the soldiers, Dr. Seven and the general. When he was finished, the 3-D image on the screen clearly showed two more red hearts beating at the bottom of the list on the side of the computer screen. At the side of each of the hearts were a number and a letter. "See, 11bg and 15bg. The PI recognized them as soon as they showed up on my scan. I moved them to the bottom of my list, thinking they were too far away from us to get into the action, but somehow they got back here fast." Rich's fingers were flying across the keyboard. "I'm widening the parameters to search for smaller tunnels. I think we might have a few interconnecting crawlways behind these walls that we could use."

"Later. Rich, any other surprises? I don't want unexpected company dropping in?" Wayne stood and pointed up.

"No. But, I didn't notice this until now, the heart rate is significantly slower for bee gee number fifteen. This bad guy could be a bad girl. Women aren't uncommon in the Iraqi army."

"Yeah, but I hate to shoot them." Wayne was not joking.

Matt and Qassem rested on the lake shore, their heads hanging, taking in long drinks of air and relaxing their tense and tired muscles. Qassem sputtered and shook like a cat dunked in water for its first swimming lesson.

Matt looked around at the flames that illuminated the chamber and it finally struck him. "Damn, someone got here before us." He quietly slid his sidearm from its holster.

Qassem smiled grimly. "I don't care which team got here first, I'm glad to be breathing air instead of water. I will not forget that you saved my life." The soggy Kurd stiffened at the sight of the revolver in Matt's hand. Without hesitation, he smacked a dry clip into his AK-47.

"Let's make sure we didn't crash someone else's party," whispered Matt cautiously.

Quickly and, quietly, they picked up their packs and slung them over their shoulders. With his automatic, Matt pointed to a large mound of boulders that once had been part of the ceiling. They began to retreat to the protection of the boulders, covering each other's backs. Everything was quiet with the exception of the low steady hum of the freezer unit. Silent alarms went off in both their heads. Now that they had taken stock of their surroundings, they realized that the scene was too peaceful and the light was from a fire pit circling the lake, not modern illumination.

Matt whispered, "Could it be your men?"

Qassem shook his head.

Matt decided to apprise the rest of the team of the situation, but discovered his communication gear was missing, probably lost during his swim. Matt tapped his ear, signaling Qassem to check for his device. Qassem signaled back with some of the hand gestures he'd been teaching Matt and explained that his communication apparatus was also missing.

Matt didn't like surprises, whether they were birthday parties or villains popping out unexpectedly. A closer inspection of the area was in order.

They slid their packs off and left them behind the boulders. Then, crouching low, they separated, taking opposite routes to circle and search the temple.

Miryam watched Matt and Qassem from the security of her hiding place. She wished she could greet Matt, her old friend and colleague, but she knew there were others, dangerous men like Tariq, close by. Concealment was her best option. Miryam pressed the boy farther in behind her to protect him, squeezing deep into the crevice, to become part of the darkness. Qassem walked close to their hiding place. He paused for a moment to listen and then passed on without noticing them.

After circling the temple, the two men returned to the boulders. "Nothing," said Qassem.

"How can that be? The fire," Matt indicated the smoky flames in the trough. "And look at this." He went over to one of the stalagmites and dipped his fingers in the red puddle at the base of the formation and rubbed it between his fingertips. "It doesn't take a genius to know this blood is fresh. It's not even had time to clot."

Qassem agreed. Something strange was going on, but he was fairly certain they were alone. Beyond that, he didn't know what to think about this strange place. He lowered his rifle. "Perhaps one of the general's men was hurt by falling rocks during the explosion and came in here. They couldn't see the freezer when the level of the lake was higher, so they left."

Matt couldn't relax, but he reluctantly agreed with Qassem's assessment. "You're probably right. What you say is logical." He craned his head around to study his surroundings. "I saw something like this in Syria on one of my digs. Ancient tribes, nomads, used places like this as both home and temple."

"That's probably true. However, when you live in Iraq and are a Kurd, these caves are not archeological sites but safe havens for the hunted. We mountain people have run into many places like this, with similar ancient writing on the walls." His fingers pointed to the cuneiform script carved into the stone at the base of one of the statues. "But I've never seen anything this elaborate."

"The statues are covered with gold and look," Matt paused, reaching behind the statue, then holding up his hands: they were filled with glittering gems. "I think these are real." He groped around again at the back of the statue. "There are more hidden under the base of the statue." He discarded them. "Interesting, but not why we're here."

Qassem was not interested in the gems and started back toward the lake. "Watch yourself." His brow furrowed as he stared at the freezer unit. "Matt, you..."

"Something just occurred to me..." Matt interrupted.

Qassem persisted. "Matt, I think you better come over here."

Matt walked closer to the lake and Qassem.

The water had continued its slow seeping and the level had dropped considerably since they had emerged. It had been hip deep when they had entered the temple, now it was only as high as their ankles.

Matt started to walk into the lake, but Qassem grabbed his arm and stopped him. They stood still and listened. The low purr of the freezer unit was conspicuously absent.

"Is this bad?" Qassem asked.

"What do you think? Of course it's bad," replied Matt sarcastically. "And there's something else. Did you notice an exit from this place when we reconnoitered? I've been looking around and I don't see any way for your wounded soldier theory to work without an exit." They looked around. "Check that mood thing Rich gave you," said Matt as he checked his own wrist, thankful he hadn't lost the detector. "I'm clear."

Qassem followed suit. "Clear." He raised his rifle and released the safety. "So, the freezer has stopped working and we are not alone. Always the unexpected when I work with Americans."

❧

Tariq had also heard the rumbling when the lake began to drain. He pinpointed the location as somewhere on the other side of a wall in what appeared to be a dead-end tunnel. "Look around for some lever or mechanism to open this," Tariq pounded on the stone wall to indicate what he was talking about and yelled at Dr. Seven to assist him.

The frightened little man didn't understand. "I don't know what to look for."

Tariq propped his rifle in a corner and shoved the pistol in his belt, then pushed Dr. Seven against the walls. "Check the walls," he said, demonstrating and indicating that Seven should follow his example.

"You think this tunnel opens up to a secret chamber, like King Tut's tomb?"

"Yes, you imbecile, that's what I've been trying to tell you. Even you should be able to recognize a well-traveled footpath when you see it. Look at your feet, man," Tariq said, pointing his torch down at the stone floor. "Do you see how smooth and worn the rock floor is and that the path stops at this wall? It leads to something or somewhere special. Many feet have taken this path. I'm sure Saddam figured out the secrets of this place. What could be a more appropriate hiding place for the viruses than a tomb?"

Dr. Seven smiled and rubbed his hands together, his fears temporarily relieved. "This is exciting. A tomb, you say?"

Tariq's hands felt along the left wall adjacent to where he thought a secret door might be. Inch by inch, he searched.

Dr. Seven followed Tariq's example and inspected the wall on the right side. The inspection was a difficult process in the shallow light of the lantern and one flashlight. But only a few minutes had passed when Tariq's experienced fingers recognized man-made carvings in the stone. He focused the beam of his light on the carvings and rubbed the dust from the chiseled writings. "Look at this," he said.

Dr. Seven came up behind him. "Can you read it?"

"No," replied Tariq angrily.

Dr. Seven continued to peer over Tariq's shoulder, excited and interested in the find.

"You are beginning to irritate me, little man. Move back and give me some room. There has to be some connection between these writings and opening the wall."

Not wanting to test the general's patience, Dr. Seven sat down, resting his back against the immovable wall. He was wriggling around, trying to get more comfortable on the hard rock, when his hand brushed up against more symbols. His situation was so tenuous, did he dare speak? In a shaky voice he called, "There's more of that writing over here."

Tariq abandoned the inscription he had been studying and went to where Dr. Seven sat, tossing him out of the way. "These symbols... see, they look like birds." He puzzled over them a while, speaking more to himself than the doctor. "They're indented, as if your fingertips..." Tariq placed a finger into each of the four indentations, one at a time, pressing down on each bird inscription. Nothing happened.

Dr. Seven smirked, careful not to let the general see.

Tariq repeated the same procedure again and again, hitting each individual symbol in different sequence, without any result. In a fit of anger, he cursed and kicked the wall. Frustrated, he pounded violently on the four symbols simultaneously and a lever glided out from the wall to the right of the tomb entrance.

The two men stepped back in awe. Tariq took the lever firmly in his hands and pulled down. The entire wall began to slide open effortlessly.

Inside the temple, Matt and Qassem reacted instantly to the groaning sound of the door opening. They sprinted back to their defensive position on the far side of the lake and ducked for cover behind some massive boulders. From this position they had an excellent view of the whole temple. Matt extracted his hot spots and ran back to the defunct freezer and slapped all four down low on the back of the freezer and out of sight.

Matt had returned and ducked behind the boulders just as they saw a beam of light break the darkness in an alcove that they had thought was a dead end.

They looked at each other curiously. "Remember," Matt whispered, "Rich has the remote detonator. So, if this isn't him, we hold this position until he gets here."

Qassem nodded agreement, as General Saeed and Dr. Seven stepped into view.

"The creature has finally crawled out of his hole," smirked Qassem, his voice seething with hatred. "General Tariq Saeed, the butcher. I don't know the other man."

❧

When Wayne, Rich, and Hal got to the bottom of the stairs, they rushed into the town center. They paused by the crumbling stone well in the center and again checked their map for the passage that led to the lake. It was difficult to see beyond their circle of light. Hal nudged Wayne, signaling caution. Rich glanced at his PI and motioned for the others to look at the monitor. No one talked. They put in their earplugs and Rich began to warm a couple of pellets between his palms. Then he patted his chest to get the attention of the others and placed his hand flat against the front of his chest. In the dim light they could see he had three fingers extended. Hal and Wayne nodded that they understood and Rich began the silent countdown by curling in one finger at a time: three fingers, two fingers, one finger.

Rich's hand hung loosely at his side. As he curled in the last finger, he let the ball roll unnoticed from his hand. It landed a few feet in front of the soldier waiting in the darkness, rifle raised, to ambush them. A few seconds passed before the soldier fell unconscious to the ground. They heard the thud in the darkness.

Rich gave the all-clear and said, "Let's get him tied up." He pulled out a roll of duct tape and began to bind the soldier. "I know it's old fashioned but we don't have any of Matt's sleeping potions for this guy."

"Why did you wait so long to give the all clear?" asked Wayne. "I thought it knocked them out quickly."

Rich checked the luminous dial of his watch while Hal pulled the bound man out of the way. Rich finished explaining. "I keep telling you, science is not exact. I place the pellets in the nerf ball to make sure they stay warm. They might not go off if they get too cool on the stone floor, so I gave them a little extra time to activate. It's cooler down here than at the entrance. I have to allow for..."

Wayne interrupted. "Forget I asked. Let's get going." Wayne, Rich and Hal jogged toward the passageway that led to the lake.

Chapter 33

Treachery has Many Faces

Matt stared in amazement as the two figures walked into the light.

Tariq crept cautiously into the temple but, like everyone who entered the temple for the first time, he was immediately distracted by his surroundings.

From her hiding place, Miryam watched and listened, studying every aspect of the man she had waited centuries to kill.

"Doctor, do you see these idols?" Laying his pistol down, Tariq rubbed his hands over one of the cold, lifeless statues. "This is gold!"

From behind another idol, Dr. Seven extracted the gems. Like so many other unfortunate men before him, he found them tantalizing. He extended hands and said, "Look."

Tariq rushed over and bent down to fondle the gems. "Worth millions. These will more than make up for what I lost at the farm. I wonder if this is one of Saddam's hidden reserves."

Miryam was so absorbed watching Tariq that she didn't have a chance to stop Mohammed as he pushed past her. "They are not for you, Father," he yelled.

Tariq's eyes never left the gems, "I am happy you're here, my son. I have been worried about you."

Mohammed continued to walk toward his father and

with a boy's naive enthusiasm said, "Build a hospital or do something decent for the people."

"A hospital? What foolishness is this?" Tariq paused, then said sarcastically, "As always you disappoint me."

"There are people here who will stop you this time," challenged Mohammed. Too late, he realized he had alerted his father and compromised Miryam.

A wolfish grin crossed Tariq's face as he rose and faced his son. "What do you know about the intruders that I do not?" He retrieved his pistol; the clicking metallic sound as he released the safety echoed through the temple. He walked past Mohammed to search the place where his son had been hiding.

After his initial passionate outburst, Mohammed recovered his composure and walked up to his father. "There is no one else." He knew his new friend's life depended on his ability to trick his father.

Tariq looked at his son. "You know what the consequences are if you are lying to me." He swiveled around to Mohammed and put a hand on his shoulder.

His father's grip was vice-like. Mohammed winced in pain, but he did not cry out.

Then, Tariq saw the cut on the boy's arm and backhanded him viciously. As Mohammed fell to his knees Tariq said, "Stupid child." He waved his pistol around as he talked. "Not only do you get lost and humiliate me in front of my men, but I have to take men from their important duties to search for you. And you are so clumsy you injure yourself. I expected more of you. But, no, you continue to disappoint me." He continued to mock him. "Worst of all, you forget all you have been taught and insult me with your pathetic lies. Where are they?" He quickly glanced around the temple. As he prepared to hit Mohammed in the face with the grip of his pistol, Miryam stepped into the light.

"Stop!" The three-foot sword rested lightly in her hand, the rusted tip pointing at Tariq.

Shoving Mohammed aside, Tariq turned and quickly raised his pistol to shoot the intruder.

With surprising swiftness, Mohammed kicked at the gun with all his might, sending his father's pistol skittering across the stone floor and into the mud at the edge of the lake.

Tariq twisted around and gave his son a murderous look, and then laughed. "Well, I guess you *have* learned something."

Miryam quickly moved in and cut off Tariq's route to the weapon. "I have waited a long time to meet you, general."

Tariq called to Dr. Seven to help him. "We are two against a woman with only a sword. Doctor, go around her on the right and I will take her on the left." To his fury, the doctor did not respond.

"Try and kill me or get out of my way," Miryam said to the doctor. He backed further away. She turned her attention to Tariq, "Ultimately, evil must fight its own battles."

Tariq looked to his son with a pleading gesture and open hands, asking for his help. "Mohammed? Please."

The boy had never heard his father use the word "please." He swallowed hard, his frozen heart thawing a little. Then he remembered how frightening Miryam had looked when she had told him that his father would never leave this mountain alive. Tariq's miserable plea tugged at the naïve boy. He raised a hand and reached out to his father.

It was all Tariq needed. Swift as a snake, he pulled a knife from his boot and grabbed the boy, mercilessly twisting

Mohammed's arm behind him. Using his son as a shield, Tariq faced Miryam. The blade of the army knife flared at his son's throat. "I will do it!" the general yelled callously. Tariq waited for the measure of his words to be absorbed and then, with an insane smile, he taunted Miryam, "I see you have a fondness for the child."

Miryam stopped her forward progress, appalled. "He is your son," she cried out. "Only a child."

Matt and Qassem watched from the other side of the lake. It took listening to Miryam's voice to convince Matt that this was indeed the same Miryam Stollar he once knew as a friend and now looked forward to killing.

"We must blow up the freezer," Qassem whispered. "You said if it thaws and the tubes leak then the virus could spread. I will not let it infect my people or fall into the hands of that maniac."

"We still have to wait for the others," Matt whispered. "Those hot spots won't ignite without the electronic signal or the code from Rich, even if they take a direct hit from a bullet." They moved further apart so Tariq and Miryam would be clear targets for either of them. In the meantime, they would watch and wait.

"You are supposed to be dead, doctor," Tariq said. "You've been a thorn in my side for years with your spying. I thought your Mossad would have killed the notorious Dove by now. And how did you escape the captain?" Tariq's eyes went to the knife strapped to Miryam's leg. "I see... the captain met his match," he chuckled. "Drop the sword and remove the knife and throw them into the mud." He twisted Mohammed's arm tighter. "Do it!" The boy screamed with pain.

Miryam's brow raised, but she remained silent as she complied with Tariq's request.

In his hiding place, Matt's jaw constricted as he gritted his teeth. His hand tightened around the grip of his gun when Tariq identified Miryam as the Dove and the provider of the virus that killed his mother. He raised his pistol and brought Miryam in his sights. Never in his life had he wanted to kill someone as much as he did at this moment. Without realizing it, his finger tightened on the trigger. He glanced at Qassem who shook his head. Reluctantly, Matt slowly released the pressure on the trigger of his pistol and watched as Miryam took a menacing step toward Tariq.

Tariq countered and tightened his grip on his son. "I warn you, doctor. Don't test me!" Tariq's eyes never left Miryam and her eyes never left his.

While still staring at Miryam, the general said, "Come right in, gentlemen."

Without turning, she knew who approached: she had felt his presence drawing nearer for some time. She had heard the footsteps of Wayne and the others in the corridor approaching the temple's entrance long before Tariq. The ears of the huntress were as sharp as ever.

Seeing the unexpected group gathered in the temple, Wayne, Hal, and Rich had stopped in the shadows. At Tariq's invitation to enter, they fanned out as they walked into the light.

"Stop! Move a little closer together," Tariq ordered, motioning for Miryam to move over with the others. He dragged his son in front of him—his human shield—with the knife still at his son's throat. Tariq's back was to the rock wall and the others had their backs to the lake. Only a few yards separated them.

Tariq thought of retrieving his pistol from the lake, but it was too risky. His son had surprised him once and he didn't want any more surprises. He had to keep the boy under control and would have to rely on the soft hearts of his enemies. "You still don't know if I would kill my own son, do you?"

For a brief moment, Wayne and Miryam came together. Then Wayne stepped away and held Miryam at arm's length looking at her. Her appearance bewildered him.

"What do we have here, a member of the Mossad and a CIA spy?" Tariq said. "How interesting. Perhaps this invasion into peaceful Iraq is a plot perpetrated by the Zionists and the Americans to destroy the Arab world? That would incite other Muslim's to join me. Your bodies will be proof of the conspiracy."

Wayne, Hal and Rich noticed a small trickle of blood running down the boy's neck where his father had nicked him with the knife. Tariq's tension was obviously increasing and the boy was in real danger. Wayne hoped Matt and Qassem were hidden nearby. He weighed his options. They outnumbered Tariq, but Wayne wasn't sure whose side the general's companion, Dr. Seven, was on.

"Let's see what the maniac has to say," Wayne said. "We have time." He glanced at his watch. It was 11:18 p.m. If all went well, the cavalry would be here in a few hours.

"Drop your weapons. That is the first thing this maniac wants. And thank you, Dr. Swift, I like the title. Remember that before you make any rash decisions. I still have the boy. You wouldn't want the life of a child on your hands, would you? Drop the weapons now! Dr. Seven collect them," ordered Tariq.

Dr. Seven moved from Hal to Rich collecting their weapons. When he picked up Wayne's pistol, Wayne whispered, "What the hell are you doing?"

Elliot—alias Dr. Seven—whispered back, "My job."

Tariq looked curiously at Rich and asked, "What is that in your pocket?"

"Here?" Rich asked, pointing to his breast pocket and pulling out his Altoid tin with the sonic pellets. "Peppermints," he said. He held the tin up for Tariq to see, then said sarcastically, "Do you want one?" He started to step forward and open the tin.

"Stay where you are ordered," Tariq said. As Elliot stacked the weapons behind Tariq, he slipped a pistol into the waistband of his pants. He had also deliberately left Rich's bag of tricks behind.

"Pick up a rifle, Dr. Seven, and guard our prisoners," commanded Tariq.

"Sorry, I don't like guns and I don't know how to use them."

"You're pathetic," the general scoffed.

Elliot pointed to the object in the center of the empty lake. "What's that?" he asked.

For the first time, Tariq and the others noticed the stainless steel device in the middle of the lake.

Rich smiled and nudged Hal in the ribs, as if to say: that's it.

"Could this be what we are all seeking, Mr. Lee?" Tariq said. "You see, I know you all. Sorry, your side loses."

At the sound of footsteps from the entrance to the temple, everyone turned to look.

"My reinforcements have arrived!" Tariq laughed.

Rich sneaked a look at his PI and, under his breath and in a tone of disbelief, said, "No!"

There was Ghariba, a rifle in one hand and a pistol in the other, jogging effortlessly into the temple. She went straight to Tariq and stood at his side, two guns raised, ready to defend him.

Tariq promptly delivered a crushing blow with the butt of his knife to the back of his son's neck. The boy crumbled to the ground. Then, taking the rifle from Ghariba's outstretched hand, Tariq primed the weapon in one smooth, practiced motion and leveled it at the center of Wayne's chest.

Wayne stopped Rich from going to Ghariba, but he could not stop Rich's mouth. "What the hell is this, Ghariba? You can't seriously be in with this crazy?"

Ghariba's chin rose in defiance and she stood her ground without speaking.

Tariq answered for her. "You have no idea what a remarkable woman Ghariba is. She and I have planned this day for many years. Our bond is unbreakable. She has many talents you are unaware of. And I suppose, Mr. Lee," Tariq's eyebrows peaked, "we have also shared some of her more pleasurable talents."

It troubled Ghariba to see the pain on Richard's face. She tried to stop Tariq. "There's no reason..." she said. "Let's get on with it."

"I disagree, my love. I think they should all know you are the real mastermind here. May I introduce the Dove? She was educated in the United States, under the name of the girl she replaced. While in America, she became absorbed with the possibilities that biological weapons offered our besieged country." He looked over at Rich. "The CIA didn't uncover that information, did they? You must agree she is a most skillful terrorist."

"Stop," pleaded Ghariba.

"No, No. There's no going back, Ghariba. Your 'boyfriend,' over there," he motioned toward Rich with his rifle, "still thinks you love him. He must know it was part of your job to get close to him. And he was useful. Isn't that right, my love?" Through clenched teeth Tariq glared at Ghariba, demanding her to answer.

"Correct." This short, cold answer was all Ghariba could manage. The best part of her heart broke away as she looked into Rich's stricken eyes.

Tariq finished with the coup de grace. "She designed the delivery devices used on the plane and in the airports. In fact, she is so dedicated that she insisted on planting some of the devices personally. The BA flight from Australia was her work."

They were all shocked. Wayne was the first to speak, "Ghariba let me be the first to apologize for underestimating your capacity for treachery. I had no idea you were that intelligent or that insane."

Wayne's words enraged Ghariba. Her voice sounded constricted and strained when she said, "It was precisely that arrogance all you Americans display that motivated me. You have always looked down on me."

Wayne knew anger was often accompanied by careless actions and he continued goading Ghariba. "I still don't think you're smart enough to insert a suicide gene. It's a complicated process to alter the genome of a virus so that it will self-destruct after one cycle. Or was that an accident?"

Miryam turned to Wayne and said, "I'm sorry. That was my doing. My government would not support my work. So I obtained cell lines for most of the agents used as weapons: the hemorrhagics, smallpox, and Ebola. Wayne, I've been experimenting with the production of aerosol vaccines for mass immunization. A few years ago, I decided to find a way to inactivate all the strains of bacteria and viruses used for biological weapons. I thought if I could find a way to make them self-destruct genetically during their initial replication cycle and then neutralize the virulence factors, I'd be able to use them in an aerosol form for mass immunization if there was an attack."

She paused and took a deep breath. She hated herself for her contribution to all of those deaths. "Months ago, someone broke into my lab and stole some of the virus I'd been working on. Too late, I found out General Saeed was behind it. My informant, a friend..." she turned from Wayne and glared at Tariq. Visions of Rijah's broken, tortured body nauseated her. The muscles in Miryam's jaw tightened as she took several steps toward Tariq. "I promise you, you will suffer as she suffered. And death will be just the beginning of your torment!" Her words echoed around them, sending icy chills through everyone.

The cruelty and ferocity in Miryam's voice surprised Wayne. He reached out to take her arm but she pushed him away and spoke to him as if from a great distance. "Do not interfere." She moved closer to Tariq so that only he could hear her. "My revenge has been a long time flowering but your suffering, general, will be worth the wait."

Miryam continued, louder, so that everyone could hear. "Men like you without souls, who go beyond the conventional boundaries of war are filthy murderers, not soldiers. Death is not a person to you, only a number. Do you think your thirst for power justifies your crimes against humanity because you tie them up in a deceiving package of rhetoric and religion?" Miryam edged even nearer to Tariq.

Tariq's hollow laugh was false bravado. "Your threats are meaningless. I have the power, crazy woman."

Wayne's wily smile lit his face when he added sarcastically, "I wouldn't count on that." He had no idea what was going on outside, but he wanted to give Tariq something to worry about.

"You should thank me, Miryam," Ghariba said. "When you went to the board crying for funding to update Israel's defenses against biological weapons, I was at your laboratory taking what I needed to prove you right. Of course, I didn't know you'd altered the virus. I was hoping to eliminate many more of our enemies. But the world got the message just the same."

Rich held out a pleading hand to Ghariba. "But why?"

"Power! Why should we live at the whim of the United States and Israel? When I was young, in Saddam's Iraq, I met all of you. With your superior attitudes, you proved that his propaganda was indeed true. You entered our country like a father holding a blanket to comfort his needy children, but chains were hidden in the folds of the blanket. Your humanitarian efforts were merely ploys so you could take control of the people and rape the land. Oil is power and you tried to take it. Now we have a weapon that makes our little country as formidable as the United States." Snarling, Ghariba added, "Maybe even greater."

"No. You're wrong," Rich spoke in a low, controlled voice. "Greatness isn't measured by your capability for death. I am sorry you think that." He hesitated, then turned and added in a soft but firm voice, "I will stop you, Ghariba." From his tone and the look on his face, everyone knew it was a promise, a statement, a fact.

"Death has always been my companion. Think carefully before you invite it to you. You have no idea what or who I am. Our time has ended." Ghariba raised her rifle and aimed it at Rich.

Across the lake, Matt and Qassem searched for a clear

shot at Tariq and Ghariba and cursed under their breath that their friends blocked their targets.

"Excellent!" Tariq applauded. "But I see that you have lost your necklace, Ghariba." He pointed to Miryam. "Come here, you have something that belongs to my Dove." Miryam walked closer and he continued. "You played your part perfectly, doctor. Even if you escape, you can never return to Israel. To the world, you are the Dove, a terrorist." His phony smile vanished and his volatile personality surfaced. His face darkened as he screamed, "Take off the necklace!"

Matt listened. He knew Wayne was waiting for an opening in Tariq's defenses to make his move. Ghariba's death would give Wayne that chance. Infuriated by the casual way Ghariba had spoken of his mother's agonizing death, hate welled up inside him. He needed an avenue to release his pent-up emotions and Ghariba certainly qualified as that target. Matt maneuvered to bring Ghariba into his sights and slowly increased the pressure on the trigger.

Miryam fiddled with the clasp on the necklace as she moved closer to Tariq. Now they stood only a few feet apart. Mohammed, on the ground, separated them. She glanced around the temple. She caught a glimpse of movement across the lake. *Yes, Matt and the Kurd. I'd almost forgotten they were here.* She was certain, knowing Matt, that he would take Ghariba out for her. Miryam was positioning to attack Tariq and shifted slightly so her body blocked everyone else's view of him. He was her responsibility just like Ninyas had been. She wouldn't let anyone get in her way.

Tariq liked Miryam close, it suited his plan. "Watch the rest of them, Ghariba." He snarled at Miryam, drops of saliva stuck to his mustache, "I've something for you. Rijah especially enjoyed it." In a flash of movement, he dropped his rifle and pulled the hatchet from his belt, raising it high above Miryam.

Miryam saw the hatchet and heard Mohammed moan in the same instant. The dazed boy rose to his knees, rubbing his bruised neck. If the boy stood up, he would be directly in the path of the descending hatchet. As Miryam instinctively reached to push Mohammed back down, she was knocked off her feet. Crashing into Mohammed, they both rolled safely away.

It was Ghariba who had lunged in front of Miryam and Mohammed and who took the full force of the hatchet in the middle of her chest. The sound of the deadly instrument penetrating flesh and crushing bone was horrendous.

Suddenly there was movement everywhere. The instant Matt's shot exploded into the rock wall where Ghariba had been standing, Elliot pulled the pistol from the waist of his trousers and raced to join Wayne and Hal as they rolled behind one of the idols.

Tariq grabbed his rifle and got off a couple of rounds in Wayne's direction as he also scrambled for cover.

Matt and Qassem returned Tariq's gunfire simultaneously, pinning him down behind a rockslide near the entrance to the temple.

"Where the hell have you been?" Wayne said to Elliot as he rolled in behind him.

A few shots crumbled the corner of the statue where Wayne, Hal, and Elliot huddled and they moved closer together. "Are you forgetting about your boss? I thought you were going to save this stuff for him," asked Hal sarcastically.

"That man," Elliot pointed in Tariq's direction, "is a lunatic." He waved his gun around as he talked. "Fry it all. Can you imagine him with this stuff? And believe me, there are plenty of madmen out there. Don't forget, I'm from D.C."

During the confusion, Miryam extracted Mohammed and pulled him back to the alcove where they had hidden earlier. As she pushed him to the back of the crevice she said in a firm voice, "This time, stay where I put you."

"I will," replied a subdued Mohammed.

Rich made a dash to Ghariba during the shooting spree and picked her up as gently as possible, carrying her behind the nearest group of rocks for protection. Her limp body seemed so light in his arms. As he placed her on the cold rock floor she stirred. He was astonished but happy to find out she was still alive. The hatchet however protruded from her chest and he had to bend over it to kiss her. Her breathing was ragged. She tried to speak, but frothy red foam seeped from her nose and mouth. Rich leaned closer, his ear almost touching her lips. "You were the best part of my life," her words came in irregular whispered breaths. "Forgive me. Pull it out."

Ghariba whimpered weakly as Rich pulled the ugly weapon from her chest and tossed it aside. He cradled her in his arms. He had one burning question and he needed to know the answer before she died, "You loved this lunatic?"

"No," she responded. "The boy..." her voice faltered. Desperately, she had to find a way to communicate. With the last of her strength, she raised her right hand in front of Richard's face and let her hand speak for her. After repeating the message several times, she was spent. She attempted to reach up and touch Rich's face with her trembling hand, but her strength was gone and her hand fell back to the dirt floor with a dull thud. She managed a weak smile and locked onto Rich's eyes with her own.

Her beautiful amber eyes—now filled with so much pain and regret—slowly dimmed. She strained to hang onto Rich's gaze, but lost the battle. As her eyes turned flat and dull, Rich held her to him for a last good-bye, then relaxed his embrace and just stared at her beautiful face. He had no tears. He pulled away from Ghariba when the sound of intensifying gunfire aroused and angered him. "You haven't a chance scum bag," he yelled to Tariq. "There are six angry men here who are willing to die rather than let you ever leave this cave alive!"

Wayne had never heard such venom from Rich, whose motto was usually, "let's take 'em alive."

Tariq's agility astounded them all. They watched as he danced from boulder to boulder to gain a better position. Occasionally he got off a few rounds, forcing everyone to take cover.

Wayne's team was not heavily armed: their weapons were their brains. They had not expected a firefight. And because of the mountainous route to the cave, even Rich had been forced to leave his weapons with the Kurds.

Elliot returned fire a few times, until Hal took the pistol. "Let me do that."

"I'm not doing so badly," Elliot said.

"Didn't you notice? You keep missing him," said a smiling Hal as he checked the weapon.

Wayne saw Miryam pull the boy away and was glad they were both safe. He was happy and relieved that her name had been cleared. "Matt! Qassem!" he called across the mud-filled lake. "Glad you made it. Can you see the general?"

"No," Matt's voice came across the muddy lake loud

and clear. "I think he's on your left. It's hard to tell, he's in the shadows and the echo..." he hesitated, then added, "If you're taking a vote, it's all right with me if he stays and gets toasted with the biologics." Qassem gave Matt a silent and very American thumbs-up signal in agreement.

Tariq was pleased that they didn't have his correct location. But he had to think. He needed the freezer and its contents undamaged and he needed to regain control. He edged closer to the temple entrance.

Rich crawled over to Wayne and the others. He showed no emotion, but his blood-soaked clothes were evidence of Ghariba's violent death. He did not make eye contact with anyone. "Let's finish this and get the hell out of here." He dug around in his pocket for the tin. "I've got pellets to put Tariq to sleep. Then we can tie him up and I'll set up for remote detonation. That should give us enough time to get out of here." Rich worked as he talked. "But the general stays."

Wayne called over to Matt and Qassem, "Do you have your earplugs?"

"No. Everything got washed away except the hot spots and they're in place." Matt knew Tariq wouldn't know what hot spots were so he was free to tell Wayne the bombs were on the freezer.

Quickly, Wayne asked Rich, "Maximum safe distance allowable if we remote detonate while someone is still inside the cave?"

"In a contained space like this cave..." Rich's mind was calculating while he talked, "we'd have to be at least five hundred yards from the blast or we'd feel the heat. This place will be like the inside of an oven. The mountain is solid rock, so it'll hold the heat and travel through the tunnels and consume everything in its path. If Matt and Qassem get knocked out along with the general, then we'll have to carry them and we'll never make it to a safe distance. A vortex of heat will hit us long before the flames. Our blood will sizzle like popcorn in a microwave."

Shots ricocheted off the ceiling and they ducked down. "Suggestions?" Wayne asked. "There has to be another way. Hal, can you find us a quicker way out? Think, guys! There are always options."

"You always did get the Star Trek quotes wrong. Spock said, 'Possibilities, there are always possibilities,'" said Rich.

They all smiled. "Someone start coming up with other pos-si-bil-it-ies," Wayne said.

"The tunnels we came through are already weakened. The detonation will collapse them for sure. Our best bet may be to go down deeper in the mountain before going back up and out," Hal offered as he pressed his hands against the walls of the temple and 'listened' to the rocks. "I can't see it all clearly. It would be a long shot. Rich, you would have to detonate while we're still in the mountain."

"We find Miryam and the boy and get them out of here too," Wayne was emphatic. "We need to get Matt and Qassem over here. At least they have weapons. What do you have left in that thing, Hal?" He pointed to Hal's weapon.

"Half a clip," said Hal.

Tariq had managed to work his way almost to the entrance. He decided that if he could find the rest of his guards, he could come back with the firepower he needed to secure possession of the freezer. He would have to chance leaving Wayne and the others alone with the freezer for now. He was about to slip from the shadows and out of the temple when he heard a familiar voice whispering in the darkness. It was Mohammed.

"I won't leave you," said Mohammed. Tariq easily recognized his son's voice.

"Oh, yes, you will. No more arguments. Now get ready to slip out when I tell you," Miryam insisted.

Distracted by her squabble with Mohammed, Tariq's shadowy shape slipped silently to within inches of Miryam. It was not until the cold barrel of his gun pressed against her ear that she knew the shadow was flesh and blood, not one of her ghosts. She cringed as Tariq's fetid hot breath poured into her ear. "That's the problem with children today: always arguing with their elders. Now, if either of you makes a sound, the doctor is dead."

Tariq, Miryam, and Mohammed stood crushed together in the tight fissure listening to Wayne give orders.

"Matt, you and Qassem make a run across the lake when Hal starts firing. Do it now!"

They burst from their hiding place shooting just as Hal let loose in the direction he'd last seen Tariq. Most of the bullets ricocheted off the domed ceiling and chunks of limestone rained down. They exploded on impact when they hit the rock floor. As Matt passed the freezer, he glanced at the hot spots on the rear surface without breaking his stride. He wanted to make sure they had remained attached to the freezer. Seconds later, he and Qassem slid in behind one of the statues near the rest of their group.

Everyone stopped talking as they waited for the limestone dust to settle.

"Did anyone notice that no one returned fire?" Wayne asked. Perhaps the crazy General has slipped away?"

Tariq's voice rang out loud and clear. "Sorry to disappoint you." He stepped out from between the rocks, herding Miryam and Mohammed in front of him.

Wayne and his team walked out to face Tariq. "I think you've already tried this human shield thing. We know he's your son and you won't harm him. Give it up, general," Wayne said.

"The maniac has no imagination," an angry Rich added. "No self-respecting pervert uses the same ploy twice. I say we rush him and let the chips fall." Rich stepped toward Tariq with murder in his eyes.

Not wanting the situation to escalate, Wayne put up his hand. "Rich, back off."

"Yes, we've been in this situation before, but that was when I was a reasonable man." Tariq's tone changed dramatically. "Drop all your weapons," he commanded.

No one moved or surrendered their weapons.

In unexpected, fluid, and professional movements Tariq pushed Mohammed aside, pulled Miryam tight to his chest, and shot Elliot.

Stunned, they cried out in anger.

Hal had no time to take aim at Tariq before he ducked behind Miryam. Hal stooped to check Elliot.

"My next shot will kill." He paused as an actor would, for the assembled group to feel the full effect of his words. "Who will it be?" Tariq's words were confident and menacing. If it were not for the gun pointing from person to person, he would have sounded like a magician looking for someone in the audience to assist him with his next magic trick.

"You won't get out of here with the bioweapons," Wayne managed to say. He needed time to think.

"Is there a volunteer? Someone willing to take a bullet

to save the rest? One of you definitely has to die this time," said Tariq.

"Someone already did," Rich said, his tone cold. He looked over at Ghariba's body.

"She was a soldier. She once told me, a soldier's purpose was to die." Pausing Tariq smiled and shrugged. "So, she fulfilled her purpose. You are all soldiers, correct?"

They did not drop their weapons. Qassem grew impatient with this standoff, he believed the only way to deal with the general was with a bullet. If he had to shoot the woman and then the villainous Saeed, so be it. If the team would not take action, he would.

His fingers and hands moved with subtle gestures. For a few seconds no one moved or spoke and a strained unnatural silence prevailed. Matt and Rich picked up Qassem's message and, as Rich asked Tariq to give them a minute to see about Elliot, Qassem and Matt opened fire, while Hal supported their action.

Hal and Matt's firing was a diversion. Qassem's was not. His first shot hit Miryam and she stumbled against her captor.

"Mohammed, run," yelled Miryam.

Frantic, the boy obeyed and disappeared through the entrance to the temple and into the darkness. Tariq had Miryam in a choke hold, forcing her to move with him as he weaved, seeking shelter.

Tariq fired rapidly at the dome ceiling, shattering the fragile stalactites hanging precariously above them. Huge columns of calcite exploded when they hit the floor. An impenetrable cloud of dust blanked the entire area. Miryam and Tariq, an unholy couple, stumbled and staggered to the middle of the drained lake and the freezer.

Qassem's first shot had grazed Miryam's calf, but it did not prevent her from keeping up with Tariq. In fact, she went willingly. Another ricocheting bullet glanced off her right shoulder and streaks of blood peppered her blouse.

Tariq took a shot in the shoulder, but it didn't faze him.

"Miryam's hit," roared Wayne and he got up to follow her, but Hal's strong hand caught him and dragged him to safety behind one of the statues.

"No!" Miryam yelled as Tariq positioned himself to take a shot at Wayne. With all of her strength, she elbowed Tariq in the middle of his sternum as another shot grazed her right ear. Her sudden attack knocked the wind out of him, and his shot went wide. Tariq nearly crushed her neck as he tightened his hold on her. "Die now or later," he grunted.

Miryam could barely breathe as he bent her back. He punched her in the head with the butt of his weapon and a rainbow of lights flashed across her vision. "Later," she responded in a hoarse whisper.

As he pulled them both down, she stopped fighting him and relaxed into Tariq's movements. They crawled through the mud on their bellies, staying as low as possible to avoid ricocheting bullets and falling rubble. They reached their destination and crawled in behind the freezer. Miryam noticed the blood on Tariq's shirt and was glad someone had hit their mark.

"He's behind the freezer," Qassem yelled, as he continued to fire.

Wayne's voice rose above the chaos. "Cease fire! Don't hit the freezer! These are armor piercing bullets." Everyone stopped and dropped down behind the statues of the idols. Chunks of limestone torn loose by ricocheting bullets continued to pour down, even after the shooting had stopped. Two things were obvious after the exchange. First, the gunfire had threatened the integrity of the dome. It looked like it might come down any minute. Second, they had given Miryam a chance to escape, yet she had not taken advantage of the opportunity.

The combatants in the temple were white with limestone dust. The idols of the temple had lost their glitter and were covered in powdery dust streaked with the oily smoke of the fire pit. The dust made everyone look more like ghosts from the past rather than warriors of the twenty-first century. An injured Elliot clamped one hand tightly over the wound in his side as he inched closer to Hal and Wayne.

"Glad to see you're still with us. Can you walk?" asked Wayne.

"Better than he can shoot," answered a gutsy Elliot, pointing to Tariq.

Wayne patted Elliot on the back. "Miryam, are you all right?" he called.

Tariq answered for her. "She's still alive. For now." He signaled for her to say something.

"Wayne, get out of here," she said.

The vicious slap Miryam received for her comment echoed around the temple.

Miryam's head snapped back from Tariq's open hand and she caught sight of the hot spots attached to the bottom of the freezer. She inched her body into a position to hide them from Tariq's view.

"Hal, can you help Elliot and Qassem get out of here?" Wayne asked.

Hal grimly nodded yes.

"Good," said Wayne. "Don't stop. Lay a trail that the rest of us can follow. We'll be close behind. Leave your earplugs with Matt."

Hal nodded and handed his earplugs to Matt and his weapon to Wayne. "Only a couple of rounds left," he said.

Qassem and Rich looked at Ghariba's limp body. There was no sign of sorrow or grief on Qassem's face. As Qassem handed Rich his rifle, he answered Rich's unasked question. "She is not my sister. My real sister was in college in the United States. Tariq murdered her and this woman took the real Ghariba's identity."

"How can you be sure?" Rich asked. "You said it was thirty years since you'd seen each other."

"I had a sample of her hair sent for DNA testing. I had just received the results before we left for the mountain. I told you before, we Kurds are not an ignorant people. She is no one, a qizilbash, a redhead, possibly from Turkey, one of thousands who were lost—or should I say misplaced—by Hussein. I am sorry, my friend. I think even she did not know who she was."

"I know who she was," Rich said solemnly.

And that was all Rich could hold on to: what she had been to him. "Take the boy with you if you find him along the way," Rich called to Hal. Then with hand signals so Tariq didn't hear, he let everyone know that they had to be out of the mountain by one o'clock. He did not wait for Hal's response, he trusted him to do his best, but it was going to be tight. If anyone could find a way around the cave-ins and pass undetected by the general's soldiers to reach the surface, it would be Hal.

Hal slung Elliot over his shoulder and, using the statues as cover, he swiftly disappeared into the darkness at the entrance to the temple.

Before he left, Qassem spoke sternly to Wayne. "Do not forget your oath."

"Don't threaten me, Qassem. Just get the hell out of here and let us do our job," said Wayne.

"I like you, American, but my men and I will be near in case you cannot finish this." Qassem vanished from the temple.

"Gentlemen, I'm sorry some of your friends have chosen to desert you. My men above will take care of them," Tariq called.

"I don't care what's happening above, you will never leave here alive," yelled Matt.

Wayne placed a hand on his friend's arm to quiet him.

"We'll see who leaves this place alive. May I have your attention?" Tariq challenged. It was a command, not a question.

From behind their protective barriers, Wayne, Rich, and Matt looked to the center of the lake.

Tariq stood up, pulling Miryam with him. The hood of the biohazard suit that he still wore was pulled up and secured. With gloved hands, he opened the door of the freezer. The stainless steel lid now screened his movements, but even from a distance Wayne could see Miryam's expression of terror. Slowly, Tariq extracted one of the nunc tubes from its container and held it high above his head for all to see, twirling it in the air.

"Stand up so I can see you and your friends, Dr. Swift," he commanded. "No sudden movements, this tube is old and brittle." Tariq stared at the yellowish liquid in the tube as the thawing virus swirled and danced, coming to life with the movement of his fingers.

Matt winked at Rich and shifted slightly to screen Rich's hands from Tariq's line of vision. It gave Rich the opportunity to remove several pellets from his Altoid box. He held them tightly in his hand, hoping that even though his heart had gone cold with Ghariba's death, he still had some body heat left to activate them.

Tariq was impatient. He screamed for them to obey.

Matt, Wayne and Rich had already inconspicuously inserted their earplugs as they walked out to face Tariq.

It infuriated Tariq to see them calmly smiling back at him.

Rich flicked the pellets in his hand as far as the shallow movement permitted. This time he did not have the nerf ball to keep them warm and active, it was in his bag of tricks and out of reach.

The pellets rolled from his hand along the stone floor, one coming to rest at the edge of the lake, several others rolled into the cool lake mud. *So far, not so good,* thought Rich. Tariq and Miryam were within the pellet's range, but would the mud or the stone floor cool the pellets off before they had a chance to activate?

Tariq was talking but Wayne, Matt and Rich didn't hear anything he said. They waited for Tariq and Miryam to pass out—nothing happened.

Mentally, Rich counted: forty seconds, fifty seconds, precious time was passing. Rich shrugged, signaling to Wayne that he didn't know what had happened. Just as Wayne was about to remove his earplugs, Miryam toppled over into the mud, followed by Tariq, who collapsed on top of her. Rich had Matt and Wayne wait another ten seconds before giving the all-clear signal, and they removed their earplugs.

Wayne wanted to rush to Miryam, but Matt grabbed his arm and jerked him back. He pointed to the circle on Wayne's detector. The liquid-like substance that swirled within the disk had a slight purplish tinge.

"Everyone check your discs," yelled Wayne urgently.

Only Wayne's had begun to change color.

Wayne pulled up his hood and closed his bio suit. "What's going on with these things?" he said to Rich. "Make it quick: we only have a few minutes before they come around."

"The short and not sweet answer is that you were the closest to them, sort of down wind, I suspect," Rich explained. "Matt and I aren't in danger and I doubt you got enough to matter for right now." Rich checked all the disks again. Matt and he were still clear.

"Matt, take off your suit," Wayne demanded.

"What? Are you crazy?"

"You two get the hell out of here, fast. Follow Hal's trail. I'm going to get Miryam. I'll bring her out in your suit so she won't contaminate anyone."

"This is insane. You know she's infected. She's dead already." Matt's voice had a hard edge to it.

"You've one minute to decide before they wake up," Rich said.

"Don't argue. I'm going to get her with or without your suit. And I'm going to detonate those hot spots whether you're clear or not." Wayne's voice was steady and determined. They'd heard that voice before and knew it was useless to argue.

Matt slipped out of his suit and handed it to Wayne. "Once again my underwear seems to be my cave garb. Not exactly James Bond," Matt smiled.

Rich briefly explained how the detonator could be activated and handed it to Wayne, who set off toward Miryam, carrying Matt's suit. "See you later," he said over his shoulder with that wily smile set on his face.

Matt and Rich jogged out into the town center and quickly found the trail Hal had left for them. They sprinted down tunnel after tunnel. "Do you think Wayne can make it out in time?" Matt asked as they ran.

Rich checked the luminous dial of his watch and stated the facts. "If he can detonate the hot spots remotely, he might have a chance. If we can get out of here in the next fifty-four minutes and confirm the destruction of the biologicals, we could call off the air strike. That might buy him some more time."

"We both know he wouldn't want us to give him that option," said a resolute Matt.

"Yeah, he told me not to change the schedule. He wants to make sure the diggers seal up the mountain." Rich's voice faltered. "With that scenario, there's no way he'll make it."

In the darkness of the tunnels, neither man could see the other's expression. If they had, they would have seen that they had already begun to grieve for their friend. They would do what Wayne always did: whatever it took to get the job done. Even if it meant an air strike while Wayne was still inside. They jogged on in silence.

Back in the temple, the first thing Wayne did was tie up Tariq with a roll of duct tape Rich had given him. He quickly checked Miryam's wounds, and saw that they were superficial, but still a perfect place for the virus to attack.

Tariq began to come around. Wayne hurriedly added his four hot spots to those around the bottom of the freezer, then attached the remote detonator. As Rich had explained, eight hot spots were overkill, but they'd wanted to be sure.

Now he could give Miryam his undivided attention. She moaned weakly as he picked her up and began to dress her in Matt's biohazard suit. Her movements were sluggish as she rubbed her head. Wayne tried to comfort her. "Sorry. Being stunned can leave you with a nasty headache." He continued to help her into the biohazard suit and wished he could physically touch her, but that was impossible.

Miryam's mind cleared and, as the temple came into focus, her first thought was of Wayne. She looked deeply into his eyes. "Wayne, why are you here?" She looked around for Tariq.

The old, fragile nunc tube had crumbled in Tariq's gloved hand and been swallowed by the mud in the lake. It was probably the reason exposure had been minimal.

Tariq groaned an objection, but it took little effort for Wayne to uncurl his fingers so he could read the label still adhering to a fragment of the tube. Small drops of thawed virus oozed out from between Tariq's gloved fingers. Careful not to come in direct contact with the viscous liquid, Wayne shifted Tariq's hand so he could clearly see the label. Miryam's treatment depended on identifying the virus. When he read the label, Wayne gasped. "Ebola." It was one of the deadliest viruses know to man. "Why did it have to be Ebola?" Wayne muttered. There was no cure or treatment. Wayne knew the invisible Ebola was in the air all around. Now that it had been aroused from its long sleep, it would immediately begin hunting a host to start its replication cycle.

Miryam looked at the broken nunc tube laying only inches from her. She forced her eyes to focus and read the label. She looked up at Wayne and weakly tried to push him away. "Are you crazy? There's no cure for Ebola. What do you think you're doing?"

"I'm getting you out of here!" He insisted. "They'll be a decon team waiting to hose us down when we get outside."

"And then what?" Miryam asked, but Wayne had no response. Her mind was returning faster than her body. Her arms and legs still slept and kept her from physically objecting to Wayne's actions. Gradually, her limbs began to tingle as the nerve activity increased through her body.

Miryam placed a hand over Wayne's. "Wait. Please listen to me. I'm supposed to die here. I belong here." Wayne refused to listen to her. Miryam did not resist him. His sincerity and love prevented her.

Tariq awoke and began to thrash around. "Don't struggle, general." Wayne's voice was hard and unforgiving. He had no pity for this tyrant. "It will be over soon. But not before you have had an opportunity to think." Wayne ripped off Tariq's protective helmet. "It's a pity that you won't suffer the agonizing death you wanted to inflict on others, but I'll settle for you thinking about it just before you become a small pile of ashes."

Tariq saw the broken tube lying next to him. He panicked. "I must have medical treatment immediately! I will pay you. Whatever you want, I will pay!"

Wayne laughed. "What is it with your kind? You never get it. Money doesn't mean anything. Money can't fix this!"

"You're a doctor. You took an oath. You *must* help me." Tears glazed Tariq's insane eyes.

Miryam's strength had returned fully. "Doctors aren't gods. We all die. Some of us die many times before we find our peace. This is your dying day."

Wayne bent down and offered Miryam his gloved hand to help her stand. Although she didn't need his help, she took his hand in hers and for a brief time imagined she could feel him through the glove. They came facemask to facemask. Wayne smiled. "We have to make a run for it. Ready?"

"You know we probably won't make it and, if we do, I'll die anyway," said Miryam.

Wayne nodded that he understood. He squeezed her hand tighter. "But not with this scum. And we'll be together." They looked at Tariq one last time and ran from the temple.

Wayne followed the glowing marks Hal had left to guide them. They stumbled and knocked their heads and bumped their knees a few times, but the Kevlar reinforced suits protected them from injury. They were making good time.

Miryam tried to explain her dreams and how she had arrived at the mountain, but Wayne seemed unable—even resistant—to believing her story. They were within inches of each other, but their words sounded hollow and distant through the communication devices built into their hoods. Deep in her heart Miryam knew that Wayne's inability to accept what she was saying as truth came not from a communicator problem, but something much deeper. Over two thousand years separated them now and nothing on earth could close that chasm.

"How far do you think we've traveled?" Wayne asked after about half an hour. "It must be at least five hundred yards." He pulled Miryam to him. "Here we go. I'm going to detonate, hang onto me when the shock wave hits us."

They held each other tightly as Wayne depressed the trigger, trembling and clinging ever tighter to each other as they waited, their apprehensions intensifying. The seconds ticked by and the stillness of the dark tunnel remained undisturbed.

Five seconds passed, then ten and still nothing happened. A low rumble sounded and quickly dissipated. "What was that?" asked Wayne.

Miryam knew explosive devices as well as Wayne and said, "Something's wrong."

Wayne agreed. "The explosion should have shaken this entire mountain."

"Tariq," was all Miryam said.

Wayne checked his watch. "He must have gotten loose and done something to the detonator." It was 12:36 a.m. He would have to go back. He could do it faster without Miryam. He had to get back to the temple, then he'd have to reattach the hot spots and detonate them by voice command. He glanced at his watch again: 12:37 a.m. There was no way he was getting out, there simply wasn't enough time.

He looked at Miryam. Her face was dimly lit by the small green light inside her hood. Wayne's voice was hoarse with emotion. "I have to go back. You continue on. Follow the markings and I'll catch up with you later."

Tears filled their eyes. They knew this was their last goodbye. In an all too familiar gesture, Wayne ran the back of his hand gently down Miryam's facemask. He imagined how her warm skin would feel against his. "I wish I could touch you." Wayne began to take off his gloves but Miryam stopped him.

"No. I don't want you to risk becoming infected."

Wayne wished he could kiss her. "We both know what's going to happen."

"No!" Miryam was adamant.

"It would take a miracle for us to survive this."

"It's a miracle we found each other again," said Miryam softly. "I believe..." She could not finish.

Wayne squeezed her hand and nodded. The pain of saying their last goodbye made it almost impossible to part. Abruptly, Wayne pulled away and ran back toward the temple.

Back in the temple, Tariq raved like a madman. He cursed and rolled around in the mud until he had loosened his bonds and freed himself. The first thing he did was to remove the detonator. He tore at his biohazard suit as if it was poison. Then he had an idea. Running from the temple, he retrieved two grenades that had been left in one of his men's packs by the well in the town center. He pulled the pins, dropped them at the entrance to the temple, and ran for cover in the temple. He paid scant attention to the explosion and the rocks that fell as a large part of the domed ceiling collapsed. Instead, he ran to where the gems lay scattered near the statues of the idols and began to stuff his pockets with the jewels. "I'll need these."

He had always thought himself invulnerable, but as the realization of his exposure to the lethal virus seeped into his mind, rational thought slipped away. He had never experienced true fear, the kind of real terror he was experiencing now. He rubbed his body as if to detach the irrational fear that clung to him. His eyes darted everywhere without focusing on anything.

Tariq ran to the temple exit and saw that rocks blocked the tunnel. He jumped up and down like a child. "Yes, that's good, very good. With the entrance blocked they cannot take my treasure. Now I am safe. I can just wait for my men to dig me out."

Tariq rocked back and forth as he sat with his back against the freezer. His wild eyes darted around the temple until he saw the empty nunc tube lying in the mud of the lake. He picked it up, brushing off the mud, looking at it curiously, forgetting his previous exposure. "Perhaps it was a decoy like the others and I'm not infected at all. They just wanted me to think I was." He jumped up and looked into the open freezer, picking up one of the racks of nunc tubes and holding it up to the firelight. He checked each tube in the rack. "Such tiny amounts. Surely such small amounts cannot be as lethal as they would like me to believe." He gently replaced the tubes in the freezer and closed the lid, replacing the clamps he had removed earlier. It was a senseless gesture, but it seemed necessary. He sat down next to the freezer, resting his sweating face against the cool stainless steel and repeated again and again, "My men will be here soon, my men..."

He closed his eyes and dozed until a small noise brought him fully awake again. He listened, staying perfectly still. Rocks and dirt were being shifted near the temple entrance. He relaxed at the sound of booted feet. Anticipating his rescue, he jumped to his feet and called out, "Abu al-Tubar, old friend." He hesitated then remembered, "Oh, no, you are dead." His voice trailed off then reignited, "My son and my army are here to rescue me." He ran toward the entrance, calling, "I'm in here! I'm in here!" No one responded. *Caution,* whispered the unseen voices in his mind. He backed away, retreating to hide behind his treasure, the freezer. Again, he heard the faint scrapping sounds of someone digging.

Wayne had reached the temple entrance and was devastated to find what Tariq had done. He grabbed a flashlight that was lying on the cave floor and surveyed the damage. He heard Tariq's muffled voice from somewhere inside the temple and thought, *good, at least he and the bios are still in there.* The entrance was completely blocked. He walked around the pile of rocks, shining the light on different areas, then checked his watch. It was getting late and before he died he wanted to know for certain that the freezer had been destroyed. Maybe he could squeeze through and set off the hot spots with a verbal command. He was thankful Miryam was out of this and at a safe distance.

Wayne laid his rifle and pack at the foot of the pile of rocks that blocked the tunnel to the temple. He climbed up to the top of the pile and began to remove rocks. When he had formed a channel wide enough for his body to fit through, he climbed back down to retrieve the rifle Matt had given him as well as Rich's spare detonator. He was shocked to find that they were gone. Even worse: his entire pack was missing. Then, without warning the precarious opening he had made collapsed, bringing down even more rock than what had been there before he started. Dejected, Wayne sat at the bottom of the pile of rocks. A familiar voice filled his ears with words he did not want to hear.

"Do not be alarmed. I will finish this for both of us," Miryam's words sounded ragged through the communicator like she was running. "One sacrifice is enough to appease the gods and they have chosen me. There isn't much time so listen: We both know there is no medical treatment for this plague that is already growing inside me. It would go against everything I have fought for to bring this infection into the world above. What I do now allows me to die with honor and purpose." Miryam paused thinking, *it would be so easy to die in his arms.* Queen Semiramis intervened in her mind and whispered, *this is not his time.*

Speechless, Wayne hung on Miryam's every word. He panicked and his fear for her was renewed. He couldn't let her go. "No! Miryam, No!"

Miryam ignored Wayne's plea. She loosened the seals and stepped out of the biohazard suit, but left on her communicator and earpiece. With a small penlight she searched the walls of the secret passage. The symbols for the number fifteen were easy to find if you knew where to look. She had placed them there, thousands of years ago, for just this purpose.

She slipped into the secret passage, closed the door and crept into the temple. Her toe hit something metallic. "Huh." She wondered why she hadn't seen it earlier and stooped to pick up the golden band that had fallen from her head when Ninyas had tried to kill her by pushing her off the steps above. Reverently, she put her crown in its proper place upon her head. As the circle of doves touched her brow, Wayne and what he meant to her were pushed into an inaccessible part of her mind. Now she was prepared to focus on another man; one who also meant a great deal to her, though he was a man whose very presence rekindled memories of hate and betrayal. With the hate ignited, and in an almost inaudible blistering whisper, she hissed: "General, I am coming."

Tariq was on the ground by one of the statues, gems in gleaming piles around him. He slowly raised his head and opened his eyes. He was stunned by her mystical appearance. "How did you get in here?" He stared around, fearing others were with her. "You are alone?" he asked in a conspiratorial voice as his bloodshot eyes darted about wildly.

"No one else is here. It will be only the two of us, just as I promised." Miryam's voice was calm and eerily gentle.

"We can come to some agreement. I could be a valuable friend." A sick smile was fixed on his face as he walked menacingly toward her. "What do you want? I will give it to you. Anything," he added. His old coat of confidence and swagger attempted to return.

"Very well, I'll tell you what I want," she smiled assertively and began to circle him, "your heart in my hand." She reached out to him and opened her hand, palm up. Long graceful fingers beckoned him to grant her wish.

Wayne listened to Miryam and Tariq's conversation through his headset. It was eerie, like listening to a bad soap opera that was being inadvertently transmitted through his communicator. It was Miryam's voice, but something in her tone sounded as if she were a puppet under someone else's control. The soft lilting voice he'd heard moments ago was now hard and the words were spoken with an accent he didn't recognize. He was confused. How had she managed to get inside the temple with Tariq? *There must be another way in.* He searched the town center feverishly in a futile attempt to find another entrance. Frustrated and sobbing, he gave up his search and ran to the debris blocking the temple entrance, frantically tearing away the rocks. He had to be with Miryam. He would not accept this ending.

Inside the temple, Miryam prepared for battle. Her eyes never left Tariq. She smiled and watched the way he walked toward her, waiting for any hint of aggression. Her smile was enigmatic and merciless, like nothing Tariq had ever seen.

He paused. She looked so ordinary, but she moved with strength. For the first time in his hideous life, he understood what it meant to have his blood run cold. He shivered while he watched her pick up the ancient sword she had relinquished earlier. Without any outward signs of pain, she forced what was obviously a badly injured left hand around the hilt of the sword, then used a rag to bind it into position.

Miryam felt his eyes on her and smelled his fear. The black braids of her hair fell loose about her shoulders, strands hugging her sweating face. She watched her enemy. Beads of sweat and panic trickled down Tariq's face. He was like a cornered beast: finished and with the end at hand. She cautioned herself to remember that a dying beast could be dangerous. "Are you ready?" she taunted.

Her words broke the spell that had bound him. "'Judge not lest ye be judged.' Is that not one of your Jewish God's commandments? Are you to be my judge?" He reached into his boot and withdrew a ten-inch serrated army knife.

They began to circle, each matching the other's movements.

"I am your judge and have found you guilty of inhumanity. There is nothing else to say except, perhaps, something from another time." She paused then said, "Let the dying begin." Miryam smiled, then spun and twisted, her sword cutting intricate patterns in the empty air. She came to rest in a guarded stance, sword held high above her head in the way warriors of old would advance on an opponent.

The stillness lasted but a few heartbeats. With a flash of movement, Miryam darted forward and kissed Tariq's cheek with a flick of her blade. Blood trickled from the jagged wound and ran down his face to mingle with his sweat.

Tariq cried out in pain, and Miryam chided him, "You sound like a woman. Not even Rijah would have made such a sound when your butcher tortured her."

Like street fighters, they sparred back and forth, but Tariq lacked the skill to mount a suitable attack. His blade, while dangerous, was shorter than Miryam's and she played with him mercilessly. At one point he tried to punch out at her with his free hand as his knife thrust fell on the empty space where she had been. His reward was a broken finger as she grabbed and twisted it while he tried to spin away. "Ha! You are no soldier. You are less than a man." She enjoyed taunting him. It fed her flagging energy, instilling her with new vigor.

Tariq's breathing became ragged and his khaki shirt was stained with blood from numerous superficial cuts and stinking infected mud from the bottom of the lake. Tariq was visibly struggling to regain some of his former dignity.

Miryam sidestepped around him. "I've seen your kind before," she hissed. "They have all died in the most inventive ways. Ancient Assyrians were masters at destroying their enemies."

Confused, he backed away. Suddenly he saw an image of warriors taking their enemies and sticking a post through their bodies and letting them hang there until they were dead. He wondered if somehow she had planted that image in him to distract him. He fought off another attack, slashing at her injured hand, trying to force her to give ground.

Miryam smiled that disarming smile again. "Yes, that was one way a man could die, but there are hundreds. And not one of them involves infecting our enemies with deadly diseases. Perhaps we were not as barbaric as history would have the world believe?"

They moved in and out between the golden idols as they verbally played their mind games, all the while slashing at each other, looking for weakness.

Tariq cried out, enraged, and charged. Miryam brushed him aside with little effort. Slipping in the sludge of the lake floor, Tariq fell and came to a crashing halt, headfirst in the freezer. He lay motionless for several seconds. A large gash had opened on his forehead. Miryam approached cautiously. As she got closer, she saw a widening patch of blood on his shirt collar.

She stood over him thinking, *this was too quick, you deserved worse.* Now the time was right to set the charges and bury the past and present in the mountain. She kicked him out of her way and he rolled over, lifeless. She removed the cloth that held her sword in her injured hand and laid her weapon on top of the freezer, then ran back to the passage where she had left the pack and rifle she had stolen from Wayne while he worked on the collapsed entrance to the temple.

"Miryam, answer me!" Wayne called out. "You still have your communicator on." He had heard the fighting and the silence that followed was horrifying.

She hesitated to answer. Goodbyes had been said, there was nothing more. But the torture in his voice was compelling. As she returned to the temple, she removed the back-up detonator and secured it to the freezer. "Wayne," she called out, "I am safe, you are not. I'm attaching the detonator to the bombs."

He pleaded with her, but she closed her mind to his appeals and removed her communicator, placing it on the freezer knowing he would still be able to hear her. She leaned out and grabbed Tariq's flaccid arm to check the time on his watch: 12:55 a.m.

Tariq growled and erupted, plunging his knife up to the hilt in Miryam's exposed right side. She grabbed him and held him in a bear hug close to her so that he could not free his arms and remove his knife and again attack her. Still in an embrace, they fell over and rolled through the mud on the floor of the lake. Their blood mingled with the mire, smearing red and purple Picasso-like strokes across the lake bed.

Wayne yelled, "Miryam, Miryam!"

Tariq wrestled against Miryam's embrace. She held on as long as she could, but her wound was deep and her blood loss great. Tariq broke free and Miryam struggled to her feet after him, the knife still buried deep in her. She collapsed onto the freezer.

Tariq's head wound slowed his movements and made both his mind and vision fuzzy. Moving like a blind man, one arm extended, he stumbled around, actually passing near the secret passage.

Miryam stumbled toward him. She couldn't take the chance that he would find the detonator or the way out of the temple. She knew she must kill one last time. Waves of darkness passed over her and she fought against them. Falling to her knees, she wrenched the laser wire from her belt and activated it. When she was within range, she lashed out at Tariq. He howled with anger. Miryam pulled him to her like a fish on a line, tightening the laser. Once taut, it cut a burning path through his lower abdomen. Tariq's cries echoed his anguish.

He fell and, in a last desperate effort, reached out for the freezer to try to remove the detonator. His body smoked and sizzled as Miryam held onto her end of the laser wire, trying to prevent him from reaching the detonator.

Pain washed over Miryam in tidal waves, but she held fast to the wire with all her fading strength. *Just a few seconds more and it is over.* She knew she had few words left and she was aware that Wayne had heard the struggle.

The laser changed tunes, slowing and grinding as it hit Tariq's ribs and then his spinal column. He was dead, but the smoking laser continued its journey through his body.

Miryam's voice wavered. "Listen, Wayne: I will not speak to you again. Go to the well, now."

Wayne's body was strangely compelled to obey. He didn't want to abandon her, but he couldn't resist her command as he stumbled toward the well. Panting, he collapsed on the ground and called to her, "Miryam?" No answer. His despair was complete. He sensed Miryam was already gone. He began to sob. Any vestige of will to live was decimated by his despair. Then he heard Miryam yell, "Jump!" Without consciously making the decision to jump, Wayne found himself falling, falling, headlong down the dark well. He bounced off the sides and hit hard as the well curved and slowed his descent. His suit provided some protection from cuts, but he still was taking a beating. He tried to stop himself, but couldn't get a hold of the slimy rock and he slid deeper and deeper into the mountain.

From the blur of blackness racing by him, Wayne heard Miryam shout with the last of her strength. It was Rich's voice command to detonate: "Beatles!"

Chapter 34

Escape

Hal easily found a passage and a fast way out by going down two levels, following a branch of the underground river that had fed the well and the lake but had dried up when the dam outside was built and the water diverted. He was first through to the outside and he pulled Elliot out into the night air behind him.

They fell to the ground, gratefully filling their lungs with fresh air. It wasn't long before Qassem surfaced guiding a bewildered Mohammed. Everyone was happy to see Rich and Matt come out about ten minutes later. Dust from their clothes clouded the air around them as they joyfully embraced one another. They had escaped and they were grateful. No one asked about Wayne.

They had come out of the mountain on the opposite side to where they had all entered. They were above the dam and the reservoir.

Rich was the first to speak. "It feels like I've been in that mountain for years." He checked his watch, "We better move further away from the mountain."

"That might be a problem," said Matt as he and Rich inched their way to the front of the group.

They were packed together on a small ledge and there was nowhere else to go. The sheer rock wall would be impossible to descend without climbing gear.

Qassem pointed down. "If someone could get to that shack by the dam, maybe there's a rope inside that the rest of us could use to get down?" Qassem laughed and tried to say, "Blitz," but it came out all wrong.

Matt smiled at Rich who said, "Time for Blitz to make another appearance." And with that he activated his suit, jumped over the ledge and down to the edge of the lake twenty feet below them. This time he didn't hit a rock wall, but landed in the lake.

Rich retrieved a rope from the shack, successfully jumped back onto the ledge and handed the rope to Qassem. Rich then jumped back down to hold the rope taut. This time no one made fun of his landing.

Matt was the last to shimmy down the rope. As he and Rich ran shoulder to shoulder along the top of the dam, Rich was rubbing his sore elbows. Matt couldn't resist saying, "I guess you don't have to worry about flying in that thing, just the landing, eh? By the way, does it come in a pinstripe?" asked Matt tugging on Rich's slowly deflating suit.

Once they were on the other side of the dam, the exhausted men trudged up to a small ridge and collapsed. The sky was a normal midnight blue, the air thankfully cool and clear. The clouds were gone and the crescent moon shone brightly above them.

"The storm is over," said Matt meaning more than just the Sharqi.

Rich's computer sang out: "It's a hard day's night." He opened it to receive the incoming message.

"Blitz, this is Starblaster."

"Who's Starblaster?" Qassem asked.

"Arthur Jenkins, the American ambassador to Iraq. Starblaster was his call sign when he was a Navy fighter pilot," explained Rich.

Arthur's voice came back again. "Do I have a green light? Over."

Matt jerked upright, "What time is it?"

Rich checked his watch and reluctantly said, "It's time."

"Wayne..." Matt's words fell on their bruised emotions, battering them like the bombs would batter the mountain.

No one spoke. Rich hit a few keys on the computer and picked up his scanner. They moved in, surrounding Rich. The eerie light from his computer glowed on their faces. They watched in cautious anticipation, hardly daring to hope. Perhaps Blitz had a magic trick left that would find Wayne and transport him safely out of the mountain.

"He may be too deep in the mountain for me to pick up with the PI, but if he still has his ring, I can use the chip inside it to find him." Rich hesitated and then called excitedly. "I've got him!" They all pressed in closer to the scanner. Rich's smile evaporated as he fixed Wayne's signal. "He's still in the town center. The signal is not moving. Maybe he's already dead. I don't know. The signal is stationary."

"If the hot spots went off, shouldn't we have felt something?" Matt asked.

"Yes, and we didn't. Something must have gone terribly wrong in there," replied Rich.

They looked at each other and nodded agreement. It had to be done and it was best to get it over with quickly. Rich finally answered the annoying beep of his communicator. "Starblaster, it was real nice of you to come yourself, over."

"I'd like to take care of this one personally before I run out of fuel. So, I repeat: do I have a green light? Over."

Rich looked from one face to another before responding, "Let's do it. Green light, diggers go." He closed his computer and sat back with the others to watch the fireworks. In the distance they heard sporadic gunfire and helicopters.

"It's my men cleaning up the remnants of General Saeed's army," said Qassem. Later, Qassem would be astounded to find out his men were fighting alongside the new Iraqi army that had come to help the Kurds. The Iraqi president and the Kurds had forged an unexpected alliance that day.

They stared up at the night sky as three F-26 fighter jets streaked across their line of vision, escorting a Class VI stealth bomber en route to delivering the first round of diggers. It wasn't long before the earth began to tremble and deep rumbles convulsed the mountain. For an instant, this didn't make sense because they had not seen the streaks from the bombs being released from the stealth aircraft.

Simultaneously they all realized what had caused the explosion. Qassem was the first to yell, "He did it! Wayne did it!"

They celebrated, yelling and slapping each other on the back.

"I knew the old boy was incapable of failure," Matt said as tears filled his eyes.

Seconds later, a cool stream of white smoke exploded from the fighters as they let loose with their missiles. Behind them raced the shadows of the diggers. Consecutive explosions rocked the earth and nearly knocked them off their feet. They stared at the mountain. After a slight delay, a stream of dirt and dust flew, like a volcanic eruption, from the hole they had crawled from minutes earlier.

It was like the grand finale of the fireworks display on the Fourth of July as explosion after explosion tore at the interior of the mountain. Shockwaves rumbled under their feet and snaked through their bodies. At first, in slow motion, parts of the mountain collapsed. Then the convulsing increased and became one deafening, long-lasting quake that tore the mountain apart. The cliffs they had traversed a short time ago disappeared as the mountain fell in upon itself. The lake behind the dam trembled but, fortunately, the dam held.

As the implosion settled, they relaxed. Like a man with an upset stomach, low internal rumbles were the only complaints coming from the mountain. It didn't need to be said that nothing inside the mountain could have survived. Wayne had incinerated the virus stocks in the mountain and the diggers had neatly closed every tunnel. And, if the heat inside from the hot spots hadn't kill Wayne, the explosion and collapsing rock from the diggers most certainly would have.

Elliot was the first to break their silence. "It's over. Finally we can say all of Saddam's weapons of mass destruction have been destroyed."

Matt looked at Rich as he squatted down. "Tell him," Rich said.

Matt's voice was steady and firm now. "Elliot, do you remember when Saddam threw out the UNSCOM inspectors?" He did not answer and Matt continued, "It was December of 1998." He drew in a deep breath before going on. "Do you really think that, during all those years, he would have prepared only this one storage facility?"

Chapter 35

The Remains of the Mountain

Richard, Matt, and Hal remained in Iraq to help with the clean up. Ambassador Jenkins' influence with Iraq's president had enabled them to stay. Everyone in the group said they accepted Wayne's death, even though, hoping for a miracle, they hung around the remains of the mountain another five days. Wayne's last wishes had been to see the destruction of the weapons and they were going to make absolutely sure nothing toxic escaped.

On that fifth day of the clean-up work, Matt and Hal sat talking to some construction workers sent to check the structure of the dam and the nearby power plant. They had made an exciting discovery. Hal listened with special interest and learned that a network of tunnels leading to an ancient mass grave on the other side of the reservoir had been uncovered. That night, while everyone else slept, Hal did what they had become accustomed to him doing every night: he roamed the mountains like a restless spirit. Some time after midnight, he came to the archeological site the workmen had mentioned.

He was a boy again, following a path that magically appeared to light up before him. He moved along, losing track of time. Eventually, he came to a solid wall. He could not read the symbols carved into the smooth surface. Exhausted, he fell into a deep sleep at the base of the wall, tossing and turning, tormented by his dreams. Unlike his times in New Mexico, these dreams were more like nightmares in which bodies piled as high as a two-story building were being set on fire. He jerked awake and then froze in terror. Something heavy lay across his legs. He pushed it away, stood, and backed up to the stone wall. He heard a moan. At his feet lay a muddy, battered Wayne. With inexplicable joy, Hal knelt and gathered him in his huge arms like a baby and carried him back through the tunnels and up to the surface.

It was a miracle. Even the stoic Qassem was overjoyed.

The medics found that Wayne had second degree burns on about five percent of his body, a few broken ribs and minor cuts and abrasions almost everywhere else. He was dangerously dehydrated and his bio-suit had melted to parts of him. After a few days of fluids and wound care, it was clear that Wayne's body was healing.

What no one had anticipated was how detached Wayne was, in spite of this triumph over Saeed. No matter how much his friends worked to bring him out of it, Wayne remained distant.

Wayne was released from the hospital ten days after Hal found him. Accompanied by Hal, he returned to New Mexico, a much different man. As Matt and Rich said goodbye at the airport, they wondered if Wayne would ever be at peace with Miryam's death or his own survival.

Epilogue

"Look, doc, I've been coming here for three months and we still aren't getting anywhere." Wayne's exasperation was evident, but he continued in a lower, more controlled tone, "I want you to do it. I can't say I believe in all this. But if it works, it might just be the breakthrough you keep saying we are looking for."

Wayne stopped pacing and sat down on the psychiatrist's couch. He was well past worrying about being the stereotypical crazy stretched out on his shrink's couch. He was actually comfortable on that couch. Yet it was more than that. Both that couch and Dr. Koates gave him a sense of security.

"As I explained before, not everyone can be hypnotized and regressed."

Dr. Koates leaned forward in her chair and placed a hand on Wayne's shoulder. "I am a traditional psychiatrist. I do, on occasion, use hypnosis and regression therapy. I see it as a way to help my clients connect with the origins of unpleasant thoughts and emotions that are a barrier to their recovery. But, I still think you will recover without hypnosis, even if it takes longer than you'd like."

When he spoke, Wayne's voice was strained. "Driving down to see you twice a week is not letting me get on with my life. I'm a biocriminologist. My work demands concentration and accuracy. These days, my mind wanders all over the place and I get antsy. I can't focus on one thing for more than a few minutes before I have to get up and walk. What do you think my day is like, doc, without any form or connection to anything? I can't sleep and yet that's all I want to do. I can't stand it."

"I thought you were sleeping better?"

"Yes, a little better, but it's more like three or four hours at a clip. I'm not taking the drugs you prescribed because they make it even harder to focus. I can't function if I'm in a stupor."

"Then you're still not dreaming or you can't remember dreaming?" asked Dr. Koates.

Wayne shook his head.

"This is unusual. Dreaming is a natural outlet for the mind. You are still holding something back. Perhaps something that happened in the mountain before Miryam died?"

Wayne had always detested psychiatrists, but he liked this one. He looked into her deep brown eyes. The sincerity they expressed was amazing. She was warm but professional, letting him find his own solutions with her gentle guidance. "I've told you everything," Wayne said. "I just want to get rid of this feeling of... it's hard to describe."

"Failure, abandonment..." The tone was gentle, but the doctor's words hit home like a jolt of electricity.

Wayne got up and began to pace again, then abruptly returned to the couch. "That's what I like about you, doc. You don't pull any punches."

Dr. Koates noticed he did not disagree with her comment. She knew Wayne set high standards for himself and that he perceived Miryam's death as his failure. "All right, Wayne, I think we've covered everything you consciously remember." She went over to the bay window that looked down on the street and closed the blinds. "You must be ready to hear what your mind has blocked out. Our minds put up these barriers as an act of self-preservation. Taking them down can be destructive if you're not prepared to face what's on the other side."

Wayne started to say that he was ready to be hypnotized when Dr. Koates interrupted him. "Let me describe the process so you'll know exactly what to expect. There are several different layers of consciousness. One layer is the conscious mind, which we use every day for reasoning, analytical thinking and decision-making. The next level, or layer, is the subconscious or storeroom of the mind. This is the place we will explore during hypnosis. Some psychiatrists feel there is a third level that deals with the memories of alter egos or past lives experienced but consciously not remembered. The jury is still out about this third level. How does it sound so far?"

"Let's do it," Wayne said, but his tense body posture and tapping foot said he wasn't sure. "How will you be able to tell if I'm really hypnotized or only dreaming?"

"When you dream and sleep, your brainwave patterns are in the delta state. When you're awake, your brain emits beta waves. People who are really hypnotized or put into a trance, pass through a contemplative alpha stage and into the theta stage, which is not sleep, but true hypnosis. I will connect you to an EEG and monitor your brainwaves to know where we are physiologically. Where your mind will go is what remains unexplored and unexplained." Dr. Koates gave Wayne some time to absorb the information she had just given him then asked, "Are you ready? I'll tape the entire session and we'll listen to it together later."

"Whatever it takes, doc, I'm ready. I want to do this." He laid back stiffly on the couch his hands at his side, trying to find comfort in her words.

Dr. Koates went to the door and told her associate to hold all calls until further notice. "Wayne, you don't have to lie down if you're more comfortable sitting up. I know this is brain surgery, but there's no operating table. Remember, don't be disappointed if there are no revelations this first time. This is a process, a therapy."

Dr. Koates was surprised at how easily Wayne slipped into the theta stage. Her monitors verified he was physiologically stable and ready for the next step. His personality had told her he would resist letting anyone take control, but he was accepting her instructions. She took him back to the beginning of his most recent adventure. The first real challenge was when he relived the death of his friend's mother. He released a torrent of emotions around this event and his body's physical response nearly broke the hypnosis, but after taking him to the safe house and reassuring him, she was able to continue. The passion that this man possessed and repressed was impressive.

Wayne then began to talk about his meeting with the president. She stopped this, recognizing it as a diversion that even the subconscious could take to keep an underlying issue hidden. Gently, she coaxed him forward to Iraq, when the group was under attack as they tried to blow up the trucks holding the first set of biological weapons.

"The fighting is intensifying. We're caught in crossfire," yelled Wayne.

"You are not in any danger. You can see these events but you are safe." She checked the monitor and watched as his heart rate returned to normal. She realized he'd gone through a lot more than even their discussions had revealed.

"Wayne, I want you to clear your mind and relax for a moment," Dr. Koates saw his breathing slow and the muscles in his face relax. Fortunately, she did not need to take him back to the safe house and in a few moments she was able to continue. "I want you to go to the time just before you saw Miryam in the mountain."

"I'm with Hal and we're running down one of the dark tunnels. I smelled her perfume." He breathed deeply, as though consuming the scent.

How interesting. I've never heard of a patient experiencing sensory stimulation while hypnotized. "Wayne, go back to the first time you see Miryam and can touch her." She was puzzled. Wayne was not the type of man to see ghosts, but she was sure he did see something. She also believed him incapable of perpetuating a hoax while under hypnosis, besides, he had no motivation to do so.

She glanced at the EEG monitor and confirmed no change in the theta wave cycle. Such a change would have indicated a conscious effort to fabricate responses to her questions. But that didn't happen: the EEG remained constant.

"We're in some kind of an ancient temple. General Saeed is there, too." Wayne held his arms out in mid air. "I'm holding her. It's been so long. She feels wonderful in my arms; her scent is all around me."

Dr. Koates sniffed the air. Amazed she said, "Nina." She recognized the scent immediately. It was one of her favorite perfumes, but she never wore perfume to the office. The scent grew stronger, filling the room. Dr. Koates got up and walked around her office intrigued. "Wayne, I want you to tell me, word for word, everything you and Miryam said to each other and what she said to the others."

Wayne bolted up right and yelled, "No! Miryam, no, don't!"

The doctor calmed him and he explained that Miryam

was in the temple, fighting General Saeed. Dr. Koates knelt down on the floor next to Wayne. She couldn't believe what she was hearing. She'd heard similar stories from colleagues but had never given them any credence. She checked the EEG as it bounced back and forth between the theta and delta. "Wayne, stop and sleep without dreaming for a moment." He was sweating and his hands twitched. She went to the tape recorder and put in a new tape. When he was calm she said, "Continue."

"Miryam, answer me," Wayne's voice sounded desperate.

"I am safe." It was a female voice that was speaking. Dr. Koates jerked round and searched the room then stared at Wayne. The woman's voice spoke again, "But you are not. Leave now. I am attaching the detonator to the bombs. I will not speak to you again."

Dr. Koates turned her back to Wayne and listened intently as the voice said, "Go to the well. Jump!"

Wayne tossed and turned, as if resisting some unseen force. "Wayne," the doctor said, "who are you with? What's happening?"

"I don't know who it is, but there are strong hands, many of them, pulling me, dragging me."

She could see he was trying to resist.

"They forced me into the well and I'm falling. Miryam! No, I can't leave you again!"

A different, softer voice, intensely feminine, said, "Dream, darling, dream."

Wayne visibly began to relax. His breathing slowed and he appeared to be resting comfortably. Dr. Koates was up and pacing the office, thinking. She reached over Wayne for a tissue to wipe her own brow.

She let him rest there a while and then suggested,

"Wayne, I want you to go back to an earlier time with Miryam, and I want you to stay there for a little while. Go to a happier memory, before the cave, maybe your time together in Iraq. Can you do that for me?"

"Yes, doctor. I am already there."

"Are you comfortable? Can you see Miryam?"

"Yes. She is more beautiful than I remembered."

Dr. Koates was amazed at how easily Wayne moved between experiences. "Are you at that secret beach in Iraq that you told me about?"

"No. Yes." Wayne's brow furrowed in concentration. "We're not on the beach, but I think we're in Iraq."

"What are you doing?"

"We're riding. The white mane of my horse is flying up in my face as we gallop across a lush green pasture." He smiled. "Now we're stopping by a waterway. I'm holding Miryam's hand." His hand reached out into the empty air. His fingers rubbed together, "Her skin is so warm. It's wonderful," Wayne flushed.

The doctor's brow furrowed as she leaned closer to her patient. This was not one of the romantic interludes Wayne had told her about. Then she smiled and asked, "What is your name?"

"Hazael. She calls me Hazael."

ENDNOTES

1. Kramer's *Cradle of Civilization*
2. Contenau, Georges *Every Day Life in Ancient Assyria*

Author's Note:

Like reality television, *Crescent Veil* captures the realities of the history of biological weapons threats and portrays them in the safe environment of fiction in a genre you could call "Reality Fiction."

The following events portrayed in the book are fact, *not* fiction:

- Dr. Wouter Basson, aka Dr. Death used biological weapons to assassinate and kill during the Apartheid regime in South Africa. Africa *did* have a biological weapons program and we knew it.
- Smallpox brought to the new world by early settlers decimated the Native American Indians in the numbers specified in *Crescent Veil*.
- In 1763 Sir Geoffrey Amherst did use smallpox on Native Americans as a military tactical weapon.
- UNSCOM (United Nations Special Commission) is now called UNMOVIC (United Nations Monitoring Verification and Inspection Commission).
- Dr. Taha, aka Dr. Germ sat across the table from inspectors and freely admitted that they had a program of weapons of mass destruction and it was not for defense or agricultural (production of pesticides is often a mask for developing WMD) but strictly offensive.

- The American government has refused to destroy its stockpile of smallpox — a stockpile that, if it got in the wrong hands (anthrax letters), or wrong pocket, could herald the return of one of our worst nightmares.

Our interest in writing and publishing ***Crescent Veil*** is based on our belief that "little finger-sized" vials of lyophilized (does not require freezing) agents may still be out there and will *never* be found. The inspectors search for weapons of mass destruction was based on *large capacity* manufacturing and bulk storage, as described in the book, which the Iraqis could have destroyed. But, many people involved in BW defense have told us they have been really annoyed that no one made the point that little-finger-sized vials are all that is needed to grow up thousands of gallons of the really bad stuff. It is a fact that weapons of mass destruction were there. And small vials could now, like the scientist involved in their development, be anywhere.

Is there more to the current, and evolving, reality of biological weapons in the "new world" of terrorism warfare? Absolutely. And, unlike *Crescent Veil,* we don't know how that will turn out.

ABOUT THE AUTHORS

Judith Sanders, RN, BSN

Judith Sanders was a nurse for fifteen years and became interested in the history of biological warfare while working as a civilian nurse at USAMRIID (United States Army Research Institute for Infectious Disease) at Fort Detrick in Frederick, Maryland. At USAMRIID she immunized scientists and soldiers who worked in the "hot suites," studying a variety of agents such as anthrax, botulism, and smallpox to name just a few. Judith combined her fascination with the history of Assyria — the present day Iraq — with her nursing experiences to write *Crescent Veil*.

Frank J. Malinoski, MD, PhD

Dr. Frank Malinoski has been a physician and virologist for over twenty years. His career began in military medicine and biological weapons (BW) defense research at USAMRIID where he was elected to inspect illegal offensive BW programs in the former Soviet Union and Iraq. He has consulted for Richard Preston's *Cobra Event* and *The Demon in the Freezer*. He has authenticated descriptions of biological weapons in *Crescent Veil*. Outside of his passion to prevent illegal research of biological weapons, Dr. Malinoski has been in pharmaceutical medicine, developing medicines and vaccines to prevent infectious diseases that burden our lives and the lives of our children every day.

Made in the USA